THE HOUSE WITCH

WITCH

Volume 3

THE HOUSE WITCH

WITCH

Volume 3

DELEMHACH

Podium

To Kraken and Pina, who offer me ample inspiration and are key figures in making our house a home.

To Kate at Podium for scouting me and giving me this opportunity to make a longtime dream come true.

And to Nicole at Podium, who is wildly patient with me as I muddle my way through this new adventure and work to improve and grow as a writer.

Cover design by Podium Publishing

ISBN: 978-1-0394-2128-8

Published in 2023 by Podium Publishing, ULC
www.podiumaudio.com

Podium

THE HOUSE WITCH

WITCH

Volume 3

CHAPTER 1
DEVIL IN THE DETAILS

M*any years ago …*
Aidan Helmer sat in a bustling tavern, his black eyes boring into his pale hand as his thoughts churned over how his current situation came to be.

His son … his eight-year-old *child* … had magically blasted him from the Isle of Quildon two nights before. Aidan had crashed into the icy springtime sea and felt as though a thousand knives were shredding him down to the bone. His magic could only warm him so much when he was surrounded by the antithesis element to his own magic.

When he had broken the surface of the Alcide Sea's waters, he noted that he was already aglow, his magical essence flickering as he burned more and more power to stave off the cold. He swam, and swam, until at long last … a fishing vessel picked him up. Bringing him onto its slick deck, the fisherman turned out to be a loathsome human neighbor. Mr. Corway …

"Ah, Mr. Helmer! I'll take you to the mainland first. I have to make it to the market, you see, but don't worry, my wife is waiting for me and can see about getting you a hot meal! Why were you swimming at this time of year? Could catch your death! Or is this one of them funny witch things?"

The lug of a man had prattled on, and on … but eventually Aidan was able to get back onto shore, and now the time had come to reorganize his plans.

Finlay had finally discovered his power.

Lightning had struck down on the earth … was the boy a fire witch like his father? Or was he deficient like his mother?

Aidan gave a dark chuckle. If Fin were a fire witch, perhaps he could be forgiven after a … *robust* lesson or two. Odds were that the boy would have to sleep for weeks after what he had just performed, so there was no hurry to return. Kate would be fretting over her son, and Aidan knew he'd have to bring more food to her if he wanted a hot meal made.

It didn't seem worth it … Not yet, anyway.

If only he had a way of keeping tabs on the little whelp. It'd save him some time and energy if he could know whether Fin was worth keeping alive and merely doling out proper discipline, or if he needed to show the boy what a pure fire witch could do against a weak mutated witch …

Shaking his head, Aidan brought his thoughts back to the present.

He would return later, but now was the perfect excuse to pursue his true purpose with all his might, free of his wife and son dragging him down.

He'd gather the few pure elemental witches he had recruited in his effort to overthrow the current Coven of Wittica, and from there … Should he travel to Austice? It was far … Though Sorlia had proven more or less pointless, and Xava was too near the isle where the core members of the coven resided …

A figure took a seat across from Aidan, forcing his black eyes upward to glare at whoever had made the mistake of seeking his company uninvited.

However, *who* sat across from him made him go still.

Straightening slowly, Aidan fixed them with a level stare.

"So, to what do I owe this … unexpected visit?"

Present day …

Norman sat at the council room table with his hands lightly clasped; his crown was making his head ache, but he knew better than to forgo formalities at such a time.

Aidan Helmer sat a few chairs down on his left wearing a long velour plum-colored coat that looked thin and breezy. Otherwise, he wore a black tunic and matching trousers. While his clothes were casual, however, his dark eyes surveying the nobility around him with a small, insolent smile were not.

"His Majesty King Matthias will be taking Lord Phillip Piereva back into custody and will place him under arrest at his family estate for a total of five years," Aidan explained while leaning back comfortably in his chair.

"That is obscenely lenient. Insultingly so," Earl Laurent snapped darkly. "Earl Phillip Piereva violated not only Daxarian laws, but Troivackian ones as well. Are you saying King Matthias is forgiving this malicious movement? How suspicious."

Aidan turned a charming smile to the man. "Lord Piereva has long been hotheaded. I am given to understand that one of his many crimes was even harassing my own son. Five years of his political power being stripped is more than fair in Troivack's harsh environment."

"That's right, your son was one of his targeted people while under our roof. I'm surprised you are not more personally offended by this," Mage Lee called out; he was not at all surprised to see a look of disgust mar the fire witch's features when he realized who had addressed him.

"Well, you see, *Mage,* I have complete confidence that my son, even as a deficient witch, can still best a mere human. I am not worried for his well-being." Before anyone could chastise his snide tone, Aidan turned back to the king. "This is the only punishment His Majesty King Matthias has offered, especially in light of our own discovery."

"What discovery?" Norman asked coldly, his shoulders stiffening.

Aidan smiled handsomely. "Why, we actually learned that Lord Phillip Piereva's younger brother, Charles Piereva, has been making frequent trips here to Daxaria and selling information. We are presuming this has been conducted between a member of nobility who is close to you, Your Majesty."

A weighty silence settled over the room.

"I have had no contact with Lord Charles Piereva," Norman informed the fire witch in even tones.

"That I believe. However, whether or not he had contact with say … his *sister,* Lady Annika Jenoure, or another member of your court who would have relayed the information, is another matter entirely."

The entire council room burst out in worried whispers, save for the king and the members of his inner council.

"Lady Jenoure has been in mourning for her late husband the past year, and she has not once hosted her brother here in the castle or in her estate.

Of this I am certain. Mr. Helmer, you have yet to offer any proof of this accusation of one of my noble citizens."

"I believe that in light of her husband passing, however, the closest male kin is responsible for the lady. Meaning Lord Phillip Piereva—who she refused to obey and return to her homeland," Aidan mused aloud while ignoring the king's demand for evidence.

"When Lady Jenoure married Viscount Jenoure, she became a Daxarian citizen. She holds no responsibility to her former home, or its laws pertaining to inheritance and ownership," Norman interjected coolly. "Once again I ask of you, what evidence do you have that Lord Charles Piereva delivered treasonous information to anyone in my court?"

Aidan waved to one of the Troivackian knights who had escorted him to the meeting, and the burly man proceeded to hand two notebooks with several loose pages to the fire witch.

"I have here documentation of suspicious deposits into Lord Charles's personal vaults shortly after he would go on trips he claimed were for business. Oddly enough, despite inheriting very little, and more than one merchant ship of his sinking, his finances seemed to flourish during his trips—trips that he made alone and in disguise. All rather indicative of someone making illegal profits, wouldn't you say?"

"That is all speculative, Mr. Helmer. It in no way ties Lady Jenoure to your claims, yet you drag her name into this." Norman tilted his head, unamused. "Show us his travel logs. Where did he stay? Who saw him? Where did they see him? You have shown no certain answers to any of these important questions."

Aidan's smile grew, and with it, Norman's hate for the man.

"Well, that isn't for Your Majesty to judge. Our king will determine the degree of guiltiness Lord Charles Piereva is due. We were being quite ambivalent in opening the case to include Lady Jenoure, as her defense and testimony could lessen the sentence bestowed upon Lady Janelle Piereva and his daughter. As you know, it is Troivackian custom that we suspect not just the culprit of treason but their entire family."

"What has happened to Lord Charles Piereva and his family?" Lord Fuks asked while eyeing Aidan Helmer cautiously.

"Ah, it is unfortunate, but the traitor and his kin are being held as prisoners aboard His Majesty King Matthias's ship a week's sail away. Our benevolent king did so in order to swiftly meet with Lady Jenoure and clear up the misunderstanding." There was a strange glimmer in the fire witch's eyes that sent chills down everyone's spines. "A pity, really, that you refuse her involvement. As I mentioned, Lord Charles Piereva's wife and young daughter could face equally grave consequences by association …"

"Is this the Troivackian king's way of threatening Lady Jenoure for not returning to Troivack?" Captain Antonio queried sharply.

"Not at all; we are only asking her to think of her family as we try to negotiate the punishment for *both* of her brothers. Her presence could be the difference between life and death for Lady Janelle and her daughter." Aidan resumed his charismatic grin, and it made Norman's stomach roil.

"Until better proof of her involvement is provided, King Matthias has no legal rights to summon Lady Jenoure. Evidence that Lord Charles Piereva and his family are not involved in treason in my court can be submitted through an ambassador or documents delivered by yourself," Mr. Howard, King Norman's assistant, pointed out in his usual distant tone.

"King Matthias may not have any legal recourse in summoning the viscountess; however, without her in-person testimony and subsequent questioning by our king, Charles's wife and young daughter will be slaughtered alongside the Piereva men without a second thought." The fire witch informed the assistant of this without a hint of emotion behind his horrifying words.

"Aside from the asinine punishment for Lord Phillip Piereva's actions of bringing hostile forces to our shores or Lady Jenoure's presence, what else could persuade your king to release Lord Charles and his family," Norman asked calmly, sensing the fire witch's carefully laid bait.

"Well … if it is to be an ambassador to deliver the written evidence, then I could recommend my own son in her place. He is well educated after all, and being one of the Daxarian citizens harassed by Lord Piereva, as well as being close with myself, he would make the ideal ambassador. He even could deliver Lady Jenoure's *written* response to the situation."

The room grew still as several nobles shifted awkwardly under the revised proposal.

Norman raised an eyebrow and leaned back in his chair.

So that was what he was after.

Either they surrendered Lady Jenoure … or Finlay Ashowan.

"If we agree to let an ambassador go with you to prove Charles Piereva has not committed any treason, are you also willing to negotiate Lord Phillip Piereva's execution?"

Aidan smiled. "I'm sure your willingness to send one of our requested parties will go a long way in favor of that objective, yes."

Norman's stare darkened as silence settled among the members of nobility who shared glances with one another, clearly confused about why there was any hesitation in risking the life of a mere peasant cook.

At long last, the king spoke. "I see. We will confer again when we all have had a chance to process this proposal. For now, I suggest we take a break to … discuss."

Rising from his seat, his handsome smile making him all the more loathsome, Aidan Helmer bowed to the room before he and the two Troivackian knights who had joined him in the meeting took their leave.

While everyone immediately burst out in discussion amongst themselves the moment the fire witch had left the room and closed the door behind himself, Norman was instead trading stony glances with Captain Antonio, then Lord Fuks, Mage Lee, and at long last, Mr. Howard.

Things had just gotten far more complicated.

CHAPTER 2
GREAT BALLS OF FIRE

Fin hammered the pork cutlet with added vigor as he tried to keep his mind off stressful topics.

Topics such as how he no longer could see Annika easily because he was back at work, and she was banned from the castle until after the war.

Or how the broom he had magicked to drag his father from the room was nothing but a pile of ash outside his kitchen door.

Or how his mother was in hiding because her former husband was in the same city and might do her bodily harm.

Or how his aides had forgotten once again that, yes, salt is necessary when making bread, and, no, it was not fine to leave bits of eggshell in the batter being made for a savory pastry.

"It just adds a bit of extra crunch!" Sir Andrews complained as he continued hunting through the dough for the tiny fragments of shell.

"We could always just start over again," Sir Lewis added hopefully as he, too, perused his own bowl of batter.

"You lot have wasted more ingredients than have been consumed. You will pick every bit of shell out of your bowls, or I will have you scrubbing the window from the outside," Fin replied without looking up. "Sir Taylor is already weeding the garden, and even Hannah is pulling carrots out. Peter is the only one of any of you to show any improvement."

The aide being praised blushed at the compliment as he worked his dough in a bowl at the opposite end of the table from where Fin stood.

Sir Andrews groaned. "You're too strict! Heather is sick again because of you!"

"It isn't your business to worry about Heather's delicate constitution," Fin snapped and finally looked up only to see that both the knights and Peter had their eyes fixed on the doorway.

Fin turned around, but with a twisting in his gut, he already sensed who had arrived.

"Good day, everyone." Aidan Helmer strode into the kitchen, his hands clasped behind his back as he nodded to the knights who were sitting cross-legged on the floor and to Peter who was nearest to him until the aide took a step back to stand closer to Fin.

The way Aidan carried himself and looked at them all made it very clear that he believed himself to be above them, even though the knights on the floor technically were titled whereas he was not.

His dark eyes swept over to the cook. "I was hoping to have a word with your superior in private."

Fin felt like vomiting.

"We are in the middle of preparing lunch. There is no time for an idle chat, Mr. Helmer, good day." Fin resumed tendering the cutlets and pretended not to notice the awkward pause that filled the room.

"I will wait here then," Aidan replied casually as he looked around at the surroundings. After giving a very obvious appraisal, the fire witch's attention shifted back to his son, who stiffened in response.

"You are in the way, Mr. Helmer." A low rumble behind Aidan made him turn back around. He hadn't realized there was someone else who had entered the—

Sir Taylor glowered at Aidan threateningly. He was a hulking mass covered in sweat and dirt, and he was standing two inches from the long slanted nose that was identical to Fin's. Somehow, Sir Taylor seemed even bigger than usual …

"There is plenty of room around me." Aidan's disdain dripped from his mouth as he beheld the threatening man before him and didn't bat an eye. "Are you the gardener? You should be more mindful of your place. You—"

"YOU!"

A shriek pierced the air, and for once, Aidan jumped back in surprise. What unholy creature had bellowed so crazily?

Sir Taylor grinned darkly and stepped aside to reveal a red-faced Hannah, who was clutching two bunches of carrots at her side and was shaking head to toe in obvious rage.

"Get out," she seethed. The size of her ominous aura far exceeded her small frame, and even Aidan had to wonder if the woman was a witch of some kind.

"Young lady, it is not appropriate for you to speak to your betters—"

"THE DAY A MAN LIKE YOU IS BETTER THAN ANYTHING OTHER THAN BIRD SHIT IS THE DAY I—"

Aidan turned his back on Hannah and strode over to Fin who was watching the entire scene with mild amusement.

"You dare let an employee speak to me like that?" Aidan shook his head. "I thought you were above such childish antics. I see you still have much to learn."

"And I thought I made it quite clear when I blew you off an island that you should stay away from me." Fin's eyes were beginning to glow, and a set of paring knives that had been peeling vegetables suddenly stopped their work and turned their points toward the fire witch.

Aidan's gaze narrowed, and any former arrogance in his face was replaced with hardness.

"You hate me. That much is clear, but I can at least say you've grown into a stronger person thanks to your time with me as a child. You are not the sniveling lump I feared you may become."

A bunch of carrots was suddenly slammed down on the table beside Aidan's hand, making him flinch.

Hannah had caught him off guard for the second time that day, and her wide blue eyes stared crazily up at him, only adding to the effect.

"I will shove each of these up every hole you possess and then carve new ones just to be sure I don't waste food if you don't get the *fuck* out of this kitchen."

The room rose by several degrees in temperature, as Aidan slowly rounded on the maid. Fin could sense the magic swelling up in the man as the fire witch and Hannah glared at each other.

"I will see you flogged for your insolence." Aidan towered over her, and yet as much as he tried, he could not get her to back down. Even when beads of sweat began to roll down her cheek, her small chin remained pointed up stubbornly.

"You aren't the first Troivackian to come in here trying to punish us. Though you *did* speak down to the eldest son of a baron just now and failed to bow to three knights." Fin gestured casually at Sirs Lewis and Andrews who waved with wide smiles on their faces at the fire witch, while Sir Taylor stood with his legs braced and arms crossed, his brow still frowning.

The witch didn't bow as manners dictated he should. Aidan's fury was palpable, but sure enough, he headed back to the entrance, and just before he slammed the door behind him shouted over his shoulder:

"We will have a private discussion soon, Finlay. Whether you like it or not. I promise, you will regret today, and you will be far more receptive to me in the very near future."

"Sir Harris, please rise," Norman called out over the sea of council members, his voice silencing the murmurs that were fluttering up and down the table.

The auburn-haired knight seated beside Captain Antonio glanced to his superior hesitantly, his face pale as more than a dozen eyes of nobility swiveled to him.

Antonio gave Sir Harris a nod of encouragement that he returned, albeit far more nervously as his pulse fluttered in his throat.

Once the knight had risen, he inclined himself toward Norman, and when he straightened, he noted the quizzical looks on the men around the table that made sweat trickle down his spine.

"Sir Harris, we are gathered here today to discuss whether or not you meet the legal requirements to inherit your father's dukedom of house Iones. Given that he has formally acknowledged you as his child, we will forgo all discussion of whether or not you are in fact related. Does anyone wish to object to this claim?" Mr. Howard called out to the council, his dignified tone nearing that of boredom. When no one raised a hand or voiced their objection, the king once again began to address them.

"According to your father's will, in order to inherit his lands, fortune, titles, and duties, you were required to spend five years in military service. Captain Antonio"—Norman's gaze shifted to the military leader, who bowed his head from his seat in response—"has Sir Harris served in our ranks for at least five years?"

Captain Antonio bowed his head again. "Yes, Your Majesty. He has served our military for the past *six* years."

Norman nodded his thanks and turned to Mr. Howard, who jotted down the confirmation, before the king's attention returned to Sir Harris whose hands had curled into loose fists at his side.

"Sir Harris, the other stipulation of this will is that you are required to have served under a dukedom for at least a year to become literate, and to understand the workings of a ducal house."

At this a few men began to whisper to each other.

"There's no way Duke Iones would've permitted that ..."

"Does the duchess know about this?"

"Thank God it'd be going to a Daxarian son and not Lady Marigold's future husband ..."

"I have here a signed and sealed letter of reference from His Grace, Duke Rubeus Cowan, confirming I served his household for a year and three months." Sir Harris grabbed the rolled parchment before him and with fumbling steps managed to make his way around the table to the king's assistant, who he then proceeded to hand the missive to.

Unfurling the message and reading through, quickly, Mr. Howard then handed the letter to the king, who in turn nodded along to its contents.

"Lords, this letter does indeed confirm that Sir Harris was educated under Duke Cowan, and he has issued a glowing review on this knight's behalf. We will submit this as official documentation as it bears Duke Cowan's one and only family seal. Both on the wax and at the bottom of this letter. Those of you who wish to see this proof for yourselves may make inquiries with Mr. Howard here after the meeting."

The men all nodded their heads in understanding.

"At this time, do we have any objections to proceeding with the paperwork for Sir Oscar Harris to henceforth become Lord Oscar Harris? Following this potential approval, each member will cast their vote regarding whether or not you will then officially inherit the Iones dukedom," Mr. Howard called out, all while scribbling away on the paperwork before him.

While the men in the room all varied in political opinions and outlook, when it came to the question of whether or not they would prefer a seasoned knight to inherit the dukedom, or their Zinferan guest who had irritated nearly everyone in the castle as skillfully as his betrothed, Lady Marigold Iones, had in her short life ...

There was the rare occurrence of a united opinion.

"Excellent. Sir Harris, we will ask that in light of our current negotiations with Zinfera, you refrain from announcing your upcoming ennoblement. An official ceremony will take place in two days' time. The council will discuss if there are any points of contention that may disrupt these proceedings before then, but given the straightforward nature of the will, and the necessary documentation and proof we have received, there is low chances of any adversity." Norman nodded to Sir Harris, a warm glint in his eye.

The knight let out a breath of relief as he even managed to give a small smile while bowing to his king.

"Thank you, Your Majesty, and to you lords," he addressed the council, his nervousness making many of the kinder men grin to themselves, while the more conservative nobility stared with an air of reluctance.

"Do you have anything you wish to say to us before we dismiss you back to your post?" the king asked while silently noting the council members he knew could take exception to the young knight based on his illegitimate birth.

"Yes, Your Majesty." Sir Harris's face suddenly lit up with a far more relaxed smile, which in turn made Captain Antonio's eyebrows lower in concern. "Thank you for your time, and for your support. While I know the circumstances of my birth are not looked upon favorably ... I will make sure to step forward using my worldly experiences and upbringing when taking command of the Iones knights for the upcoming war."

The reminder of what Sir Harris could bring to the war effort was an effective point, one that made Captain Antonio smile proudly ... that is, until the knight stayed true to his nature and once again opened his big mouth.

"Also, sorry about giving you all food poisoning. If it is any consolation, once made a duke, I vow to never try cooking again!"

Sir Harris bowed quickly, oblivious to the haunted expressions that consumed many of the noblemen's expressions.

Once straightened, the knight began to stride with a bounce in his step toward the door, only to add further insult to injury by exiting saying, "Oh, and don't worry, the Royal Cook has thoroughly impressed upon me that I have to wash off the manure thoroughly after pulling the vegetables from the garden!"

With a final exuberant wave, Sir Harris took his leave.

Captain Antonio was already leaning his forehead into his hand, while many of the nobility began to second-guess their earlier confidence in the young man ...

CHAPTER 3
SHELLING OUT TROUBLE

Kraken pondered his witch's father after observing his second intrusion of the kitchen and eventually concluded one important fact.

The fire witch didn't smell right.

It was a most unnatural scent … almost as though he had been in contact with something or someone … *else.*

Kraken blinked thoughtfully.

I need to go train the kittens, but … what can I do if my witch needs me?

The other humans around Fin were all speaking heatedly, but they didn't interest the young fluffy black feline. No, all Kraken cared about was that strange smell …

Tilting his head to study Fin a little more closely, the familiar speculated how stressed, and weary, his witch appeared … Apparently his new female mate could only do so much to soothe his worries.

Sauntering free of the potato sacks he had casually lain behind, Kraken made his way over to the redhead and immediately began nuzzling his shins.

Sure enough, the loving pets and scratches came, making the kitten begin to salivate in pleasure.

The humans continued their conversation, and it provided excellent background noise while Kraken began to drift into a pleasant slumber.

"—I've never seen *that* cat before."

Kraken cracked open an eye.

There was another cat?

Glancing over to the open garden door, Kraken's body tensed. Tipper sat, his tail swishing slowly as his great yellow eyes watched him.

Fin looked down at Kraken and immediately frowned. It was unlike the arrogant kitten to react to another cat.

"Friend of yours?" the witch asked, noting that his familiar didn't dare move his attention away from the new arrival.

"*It's Sylvia's mate …*" Kraken replied, sounding incredibly strained, but before Fin could ask about the elusive Sylvia, his familiar had bolted out of his arms and out the kitchen through the open window as fast as he could.

When the group turned to look back at the new cat, they found that he, too, had already left.

"I sometimes think that little beast has an entire secret life we know nothing about," Sir Lewis observed while wearing a small frown.

Fin shook his head and let out a sigh.

"As I was saying, Hannah, while I appreciate you standing up for me, you really can't make such … graphic threats to Aidan."

"You have to admit, it was a little bit funny …" Sir Andrews started then trailed off when Fin shot him a warning look.

"That man is prideful. He will seek revenge. Hannah, I'm going to talk to Ruby about perhaps having you go stay and help with my mother who is currently in hiding. I'll try not to give Ruby the details about what happened so she doesn't get angry with you," Fin explained as he reached for the pork cutlet on the table then plunked it in the bowl of flour, bread-crumbs, and herbs.

While he waited for the initial storm of Hannah's reaction to being disciplined, the redhead was surprised when instead the petite blond woman smiled.

"Oh, that sounds like a splendid idea! I think I'll go pack my things." As she moved to skip away, Fin caught her by the back of her dress and gently pulled her back until they stood face-to-face again.

"Why aren't you fighting me on this?"

Hannah stared innocently and batted her long eyelashes up at him. "I am merely being the dutiful servant to my maste—"

"I think you just explained to my father a minute ago that you aren't a dutiful servant to anyone," Fin pointed out, clearly unimpressed with her attempt at deceit as he resumed breading the cutlets.

"Well, not for that troll with dung for eyes! But for you! My goodness, the Gods couldn't have given me a better specimen of witch to order me around."

"She's scaring me," Sir Andrews whispered to Sir Taylor, who nodded silently in agreement.

"Hannah, are you sick? Dying?" Peter asked with genuine concern on his face.

The blonde had done her best to keep her angelic façade going for as long as possible, but finally her shoulders slumped, and she let out a long sigh.

"It's supposed to be a secret, but … I overheard the captain and your mum talking about where she was going to hide while I was delivering snacks for her trip."

Fin glanced perplexed around at the aides, but no one else seemed to know what she was going to say.

"Your mother is staying with Lady Jenoure at her estate in Austice."

The pork that had been in Fin's hand fell into the bowl in a heap, and his eyes grew wide.

"How … Why … How?"

"You asked how already," Hannah pointed out cheekily with a wink.

Fin braced his hands on the table and stared earnestly at the young woman.

"Good Gods, woman, he's been through enough!" Peter blurted desperately.

"Alright, alright! Apparently the viscountess had requested to be kept informed about the proceedings surrounding her brother's trial, but I think it's just to check up on yo—"

Fin stopped her with a look, so she cleared her throat and continued.

"Anyway, during their chat the captain mentioned that Mrs. Ashowan was going to be in hiding when she divorced Troivack's chief of military, and I guess Lady Jenoure offered to have her stay with her. Given that her keep is difficult to find and well protected from what the rumors say, it made the most sense." Hannah finished her retelling with a small shrug before smiling deviously and adding on, "And I won't say no to getting to go and see how that drama plays out."

"You're evil." Sir Andrews shuddered.

Fin appeared catatonic, as his aides discussed the new discovery.

"I wonder how they'll get along … I mean, does your mother know you're betrothed yet?" Hannah asked, her eyes glittering with interest.

"You're betrothed?!" Sir Andrews exclaimed, stunned.

"Congratulations!" Sir Lewis and Peter cheered, grinning.

"Well done, Ashowan." Sir Taylor nodded, with a broad smile of his own.

"We'll have to have a proper celebration once Sir Harris returns from his meeting regarding his dukedom!" Peter added jovially before clapping Fin on the shoulder.

It was then the group realized that the redheaded witch had yet to speak, and he was still staring off into the unknown.

"I'm sure they're getting along fine— I was just teasing!" Hannah remarked, a hint of nervousness entering her tone as she then looked around and realized that all magical cookery had ceased.

"The last ..." Fin's voice was hoarse. "The last time those two spoke ... was a disaster ... and now they are staying ... under the same roof? Oh Gods. No wonder Annika said she had to leave last night." Fin's hands snapped to his face as his panic fully set in.

"How often has she been staying overnight at your cottage?" Hannah asked with renewed delight.

"And here I thought you'd be the prudish type until marriage ..." Sir Andrews muttered to both Sirs Lewis and Taylor who immediately nodded their agreement.

"Well, not all women look like Lady Jenoure," Hannah reminded them, though the men wisely held their tongues on commenting on how desirable the cook's future wife was.

Fin dropped his elbows to the table, his face still covered with his hands as he tried not to assume the absolute worst scenarios happening between Annika and his mother.

Peter gingerly reached out and patted Fin on the shoulder before they all shifted awkwardly and began to resume their duties.

"Poor bastard," Sir Andrews whispered to Sir Lewis who quietly agreed before they once again began hunting for the eggshells in their batter, and this time they decided not to complain quite as much as before ... the poor cook could only take so much in a day.

Katelyn Ashowan sat uncomfortably in Annika's solar, clutching her cup of tea, grateful to have something to do with her hands. The sun was setting, and the viscountess sat across from her with a tray of fruits and cheese between them. The noblewoman looked every bit as ill at ease as Kate felt, and she kept glancing out the window longingly.

"You said you saw Fin last night?" Kate asked, her voice strained.

"I did, yes. He seemed stressed. I suppose his father tried to talk with him."

Kate waited for a brief moment before lifting her teacup to her lips and taking a sip.

"We anticipated as much. His Majesty hopes that Aidan will let something slip when they meet …" Kate slowly lowered her teacup to the table in front of her before leaning back into her seat. "Thank you again for allowing me to stay here while my ex-husband is in Daxaria. I don't like infringing on the goodwill of others."

Annika's smile was pained. "It's quite alright. While I can't be open about my relationship with—"

The flash of irritation on Kate's face made Annika hesitate, but with a quick gulp she continued.

"With … Fin … I still want to help however I can."

Kate nodded, but it was clear she was already wanting to end the discussion as quickly as possible. Thus far since her arrival, the pair had managed to avoid running into each other, but Clara, Annika's handmaiden, had oh so kindly arranged for a small meal to be shared between them.

Letting out a long sigh, Annika dropped her forehead to her fingertips before fixing Kate with a weary defeated expression.

"I … I don't like us acting so strained around each other. I deeply regret announcing the betrothal that day in the queen's chamber. I should have let Fin be the one to tell you; truly, I am sorry." Annika bowed her head slightly, and she heard Kate shift uncomfortably at being treated as more important than a viscountess.

"Please don't bow to me. This is already … far too awkward."

Annika lifted her head with a weak smile. "I can maneuver many different types of scenarios with many different types of people, but I have not once ever had to be in a close-knit family. I'm at a loss."

Kate frowned. "I thought I heard you had family back in Troivack."

"My mother died shortly after giving birth to me, and my father was more interested in his boys. My brother Phillip murdered his twin, John, and my other brother, Charles, is … well … he just wanted to stay on their good side …" Annika didn't need to mention that Charles had been left with next to nothing when her brother Phillip became earl, and so he was supported by his baby sister for being her ears in the Troivackian courts.

"Family is important to Fin. That much is obvious." The viscountess's smile turned a little more confident as she straightened in her seat and leaned back.

"It is … though other than with each other, Fin and I don't have much experience being a family either. I'm not sure we can even call us close-knit, so perhaps you can relax a little. My concerns are the class differences between the two of you and … well … your overnight … visits."

Annika decided to reconsider her original urge to fling herself through the window right then and there.

With her cheeks deepening in color, she managed to force out a reply.

"I … understand … but … I'm sure things will be fine."

Just then a loud knock on the door broke the tension, forcing Annika to jump up from her seat.

"Come in!" she cried out gratefully, already feeling as though she could hug the newcomers within an inch of their lives.

Clara and Captain Antonio stepped into the room. The military leader looked incredibly grim, while Clara curtsied dutifully to her mistress.

"Lady Jenoure," he greeted with a bow. "I do not mean to impose so suddenly on you, but I need to speak with Mrs. Ashowan immediately. Also, a messenger from His Majesty is down in your entrance with a formal missive for you."

All at once Annika's face turned stony, but dutifully and with flawless composure, she bid a brief polite farewell to both the captain and Kate and took her leave with Clara silently following in her wake.

"Antonio, what is it? You look … angry," Kate observed worriedly while reaching out to grasp the captain's hands.

"Yes, lass, I am furious. Please sit. I need to explain to you what Mr. Helmer is trying to do now."

Seating herself hastily, the healer's heart began to pound against her chest in an all too familiar wave of fear.

"He is trying to bargain for Finlay to join him aboard his ship as an ambassador, and he's making a hell of an argument for it."

Katelyn's face paled, and for a moment she didn't even bother breathing, then a slew of expletives left her mouth that left the captain in shock, until he noticed that she was already beginning to cry.

"Godsdamnit, Fin was right … he knew it … he knew Aidan wouldn't just leave him be."

"It'll be alright, Kate. While the council is leaning strongly toward Finlay going, his acting as an ambassador would protect him legally. If we instead forced Lady Jenoure, she would be far more susceptible to—"

"What's this about Lady Jenoure?" Kate frowned, before a greater alarm started growing on her face. "Why is Aidan dragging her into this?!"

"King Matthias has imprisoned Lady Jenoure's other brother and his young family, claiming that he was leaking Troivackian secrets to her. It seems as though the Troivackian king is trying to wipe out the entire family in one fell swoop. Most likely the king is eyeing the family's hefty coffers to help fund the war. Or he truly was displeased that Lady Jenoure refused to marry the suitor they had sent for her from Troivack, and this is her punishment for not obeying."

"W-Wait, then … why would she be required to go as an ambassador?"

Antonio paused. There was a desperation in Kate's face that seemed odd … then again the two women had probably formed a bond already since the viscountess had graciously offered to hide his affianced.

With a sigh, the captain decided to try and briefly explain the complexities surrounding the recent developments.

"The viscountess is suspected of being a part of this alleged information leak. She is also the only remaining family member who is not imprisoned. The Troivackian king insists she go to him to submit a testimony and defense for Charles Piereva, and he is attempting to force her to obey by holding her sister-in-law and niece hostage. If King Matthias gets Annika on Troivackian waters, however … things could go south incredibly quickly. For one, he could force her to wed someone aboard his ship and then not only seize the Piereva assets, but house Jenoure's as well. However, if we do not acquiesce, that would mean the immediate death of her innocent family members."

Kate clutched her skirts tightly as she listened, her ire deepening at the new information surrounding Annika. For several moments she was unable to say a word, as she realized just how villainous her ex-husband's intentions were.

Swallowing with great difficulty, Kate at long last managed to speak.

"I need … I need time to absorb this information. Do you mind if I have a few moments to think by myself?"

Antonio smiled sadly and kissed her forehead. "Of course. I need to head back to the castle immediately, but I wanted to keep you updated and came as soon as our meetings concluded. I doubt Fin would want you knowing, but both of you seem to underestimate each other."

Kate tried to smile but couldn't, and so with another small shoulder squeeze, Antonio left his fiancée alone with her thoughts.

As soon as the door had closed, and the only sounds surrounding her were the peaceful lull of waves from the open window, Kate began to tremble. Anger, fear, and helplessness rose within her, choking her voice as she realized the magnitude of what was transpiring.

Aidan knows Fin would never let a defenseless woman sacrifice herself in order to save people ... He's backed us into a corner, and he's going to make my boy leave with him. Then ... Fin will be powerless ... and alone ... and I can't do a damn thing.

Kate dropped her face to her hands as the absolute horror of the situation overwhelmed her.

Fin had been right about everything ...

Aidan was coming for him, and he intended to use any dirty plot or web of politics he could to get what he wanted.

Kate broke down into sobs and couldn't stop her tears as an innate sense of foreboding overtook her mind.

CHAPTER 4
TRUTHFULLY TERRIFIED

Annika approached the council room, her expression stony and her heart thirsting for blood. Aidan Helmer and his desperation to see himself murdered was at the forefront of her mind. Effectively, this made the viscountess forget to be nervous over the nature of the message she had received from the king.

It had come as a great surprise to Annika when she found out that the messenger Captain Antonio had been speaking about was in fact Mage Lee. The elder had informed her of Charles's abduction that had come to light during the council meeting with Aidan Helmer, and then he cryptically insisted she go to see the king.

The guards in front of the council room shared looks of uncertainty as they beheld the fearsome ire in the dark eyes of the normally composed viscountess, but they quickly granted her entry without a word.

Despite her blinding fury, Annika was shocked when she stepped into the room and saw that Fin already stood before the king, the tired worry lines in his face making her go still for a moment.

"Ah, Viscountess Jenoure. Thank you for coming so quickly. I have just informed Mr. Ashowan of the situation," Norman said after Annika had recovered from her surprise and had given the appropriate curtsy.

"The ... The situation?" Annika asked slowly, unsure of what exactly was transpiring.

"Yes, I'm not sure if Mage Lee informed you but ... the other ambassador suggested to argue against the charges against your brother Lord Charles Piereva was Finlay Ashowan. Aidan Helmer's son," Norman explained with a sharp gleam in his eyes.

Annika risked a small glimpse at Finlay, though he did not do so in return.

"Is it possible that the Troivack's chief of military is pursuing Mr. Ashowan here as a vendetta given the well-known bad blood they share?"

Norman nodded slowly. "Ah, of course you have heard the details of their past. I'm sure Katelyn Ashowan apprised you of some of what has transpired here in your absence."

Annika didn't even dare to blink, and she fought the urge to look yet again at Fin. She was beginning to grow fearful that their relationship may be revealed in the fallout of Aidan Helmer's meddling ... She prayed Fin could sense this possibility and knew to proceed with whatever he said about her with caution.

"It is more than likely my father is hoping to seek revenge from me; however, why the King of Troivack would allow Aidan's interference in his negotiations with regard to your family is still unclear," Fin explained, keeping his gaze fixed on the king.

Norman found it odd that Fin didn't spare the viscountess even a glance ... most men had trouble taking their eyes off her ...

"Your Majesty, do you want me to return to Troivack?" Annika could feel Fin's eyes snap to her profile.

Norman sighed and leaned against the council room table while shaking his head.

"Well ... that is why I have called you both here. The way I see it, there are three options. Either you, Lady Jenoure, agree to go and most likely are forced into marriage that the king inflicts. Or you, Mr. Ashowan, agree to go and risk your father ignoring the legalities that would be protecting you as an official ambassador, or the third. We outright refuse to send either of you, and Lord Phillip Piereva returns home to bear his horrifically light sentence, and Lord Charles Piereva and his family are put to death for treason."

The air was heavy, and for a brief moment, no one spoke.

Annika began to step forward, already deciding she had enough tricks and information up her sleeve that she may as well take the risk, when Fin's steely gaze stopped her as he then subtly blocked her from the king.

However, before he could speak, Annika still beat him to it.

"I'll go. I may be able to negotiate with the king for a different type of deal on Charles's behalf given my connection to Troivack," she announced confidently.

Norman considered the possibility, but he was forced to stop and try to quell the obvious anger and disagreement he noticed on Fin's face, as the redhead clearly gritted his teeth together.

"Mr. Ashowan, Lady Jenoure is perfectly capable of handling herself in these kinds of scenarios. She survived Troivack until her marriage to Hank Jenoure, and she knows her family's activities best in this matter. I recognize it seems callous of me, but—"

"Over my dead body." Fin's words were frostier than any Winter Solstice morning.

Annika stiffened over his emotion. One wrong word, and they could reveal their secret and bring upon themselves yet another problem …

She needed to caution him quickly.

"Mr. Ashowan, I understand you do not know me very well, but I do believe that if I go the situation will not be as dire as—" she began with a forced authoritative calm, only for him to interrupt her.

"We are not betting on the Troivackian king—who is about to wage war on us, behaving fairly toward a woman he is angry with. We can simply imprison Aidan here and now and prolong discussions with the king to buy us time."

As the air rang with the witch's words Norman stood straighter, his expression growing wary in light of Fin's emotions besting him during the discussion.

"If we do that, there is no chance that Charles's family will be left alive," Annika explained softly.

Fin turned his head to face Annika behind him, but stopped himself, already sensing that if he were to look at her, it would be obvious to the king precisely why he was beginning to unravel.

There was a beat of silence before Norman crossed his arms and spoke. "Mr. Ashowan, I'm aware you know some of Viscountess Jenoure's efforts in the past; however, I do believe she may hold more insight with regard to—"

Fortunately for both Finlay and Annika, a soft knock at the door interrupted them.

"Your Majesty, Royal Mage Lee wishes to speak with Mr. Ashowan, if possible," one of the guards called through the door.

Norman shook his head, the burden of the discussion making him more exhausted by the minute.

"Very well, I need to discuss this further with Lady Jenoure alone regardless. Once your conversation is finished, please wait outside the door for me to call for you."

Fin didn't immediately leave, as he stared at the king with such intensity that for a moment it seemed as though he were going to begin shouting.

Behind Finlay's back, where the king could not see, Annika gently pressed her fingertips to his back. Softly pleading with him ...

Upon feeling her touch, Fin managed to blink, allowing her subtle comfort to pull him out of the dark whirl of emotions and panic that were dragging him into their depths. Once he'd regained a respectable amount of his control, he allowed himself to release a long steadying breath before bowing and taking his leave.

Annika didn't dare look at him and instead directed her attention to the king, her stomach churning over Fin's reaction. Norman turned to her, his gaze calculated as the door gently closed with the witch on the other side of it.

"You will have to forgive Mr. Ashowan; he has a protective nature. I'm sure he didn't mean to insult your capabilities. In truth, I wasn't certain how much you had revealed to him when you reported that he had helped you in the past."

Annika bobbed her head subserviently. "It is alright. I'm given to understand this is a sensitive time with his father being a part of this. I do wonder, though ..."

Norman waited expectantly.

"It is possible Mr. Helmer convinced King Matthias that Finlay is a suitable alternative to myself because he is a house witch? Especially if word had reached the king about how the cook was able to suppress Baron Gauva's men when he attempted to attack the queen."

Norman nodded. "This entire thing is strange ... they've managed to pinpoint two great allies of mine ... and I'm beginning to suspect that when I interrogate that man named Red we apprehended before Mr. Helmer's arrival, I should be asking questions about traitors amongst the nobility."

Annika agreed wholeheartedly. When she had been looking amongst the various ships and their arrival and departure logs, there were a few belonging to nobility that she had not been able to access ...

"If Mr. Ashowan insists on going on that ship, please don't accept immediately," she suddenly requested, her wide eyes leaping to Norman's face.

The monarch raised an eyebrow, it was unlike the lady to show so much worry …

"Then are you absolutely certain you should be the one to argue for your brother's innocence?"

Annika opened her mouth to give an immediate reply, only the look on Fin's face snapped into her mind's eye and she hesitated … so instead, she looked to her king and told him something that wasn't at all what he had been expecting to hear.

"You need to tell the king. About … the two of you," Lee whispered urgently in the shadowy corridor. The intensity of the statement, however, did little to ease the stiff expression on the redhead's face.

"Why is that?"

"Do you not think it strange that Mr. Helmer is going after Lady Jenoure as well as yourself? His Majesty needs to know everything if he is to make the wisest decision regarding—"

"Her Majesty the queen knows. If she believed it to be relevant, do you really suppose she wouldn't mention it to him?" Fin's voice, while quiet, had a deadly edge to it.

Mage Lee balked immediately. "The *queen* knows?!"

"It would seem so. Though it is strange that not only Aidan, but the Troivackian king agreed that I would be an acceptable representative … Even if I am a witch that wouldn't be enough to … to cause …" Fin trailed off, a sudden frown settling over his brow.

Turning around sharply, the house witch strode back down the corridor back to the council room door, leaving Lee to drop his forehead to his hand.

"Son of a witch," he muttered while slowly beginning to follow Fin.

"I need to speak with His Majesty immediately," the redhead informed the two guards with a note of urgency.

The two men shared a quizzical look over the abrupt shift in the cook's attitude, when the chamber door opened, and Annika stepped out looking somewhat pale.

"Good evening to you, Mr. Ashowan." Without raising her gaze to him, the viscountess began to turn away from him, only to have Fin gently cup her cheek and turn her face back to him, startling her thoroughly.

The guards exchanged nervous glances, and one began to clear his throat.

"We need to go back in there," Fin whispered quietly. "Together. I think we need to … I think we need to … talk. I have a suspicion." Mage Lee halted a few feet away and his jaw dropped when he noticed the very obvious affectionate touch the cook was giving Lady Jenoure.

"Oh for the love of— You know we can all see you, right?!"

Annika's eyes grew round and hesitant, and she completely ignored the mage's presence when she answered her fiancé. "Are you sure we need to right now?"

Fin let out a small sigh and smiled with a mixture of resignation and sadness. "Yes."

Slowly closing her eyes, the lady let out a breath of her own before she pressed her cheek into his palm, then turned and kissed it. There was a squeak from one of the guards behind her that could be heard as Annika straightened her shoulders and faced the two armed men, who both had their jaws wide enough to catch an entire fleet of flies.

"We need to go back in," she announced, her cool composure intact and her gaze unwavering.

Fin's heart was in his throat, and his palms were already drenched in sweat, but if he was right … then it was better if the king knew. He glanced at Annika worriedly; he wished they had a chance to discuss it beforehand, but … She was trusting him …

The guards tried to maintain a professional attitude, but not even Mage Lee was able to do so as he threw his hands in the air. "Your grand realization was that I was right? You're going to go tell him?"

Fin shot the elder a flat expression before entering the council room with Annika at his side.

Norman was looking at one of the maps fanned out on the council room table, but when he realized that both the viscountess and cook had returned, he immediately straightened.

"Lady Jenoure, I thought we were finished for this evening," he observed curiously.

Annika glanced at Fin, and her controlled equanimity momentarily flickered in her eyes when she saw how obviously terrified he was. Hastily, she took a fortifying breath and clasped her hands demurely in front of her skirts. Resuming her self-assured façade, she faced the king.

Fin looked as though he were about to fight the entire Troivackian army single-handedly. His face was ashen, and he was breathing a little too quickly. "Your Majesty, there is something else Aidan might be aiming to accomplish and … it is better for you to be aware of the details of it …"

Norman frowned in concern. What could it possibly be that had the cook so distressed?

"Your Majesty … it is possible that Aidan is trying to remove me from the castle using Lady Jenoure as bait because … he is aware of something that he shouldn't be …" Fin swallowed with great difficulty.

"Mr. Ashowan, please speak plainly. It has been a long day, and there is no need to dance around important matters with this war." The king stepped toward the pair slowly.

"Your Majesty, Viscountess Jenoure and I are … are …" For a moment Fin thought he would vomit before getting the words out, but he knew there was no other choice. "We are betrothed."

The silence that followed the announcement made Fin's chest ache. Annika stood beside him, her face serene, but he could feel the rigidness in the air around her. The two then waited for the king to react to the secret they both had been hiding, both terrified beyond measure.

CHAPTER 5
POINTS OF A CROWN

The king's face was unreadable as he looked at Fin for a long time without saying a word, then he turned his head to stare at Lady Jenoure. No one could say exactly how much time had passed, but the redhead could feel sweat building along his brow as he waited.

"It is odd, Viscountess, that you believe yourself to be betrothed. Last I checked, it is *my* seal that officiates an engagement for a member of my court." Despite his light tone, there was a coldness in the king's voice that the couple had seldom heard before.

After a tenuous breath, Fin risked speaking. "I only meant that I had asked and she said ye—"

"You will remain *silent*, Mr. Ashowan, until I get to you, am I clear?" The faint boom in Norman's voice made the cook flinch. He dropped his gaze to the floor, his cheeks burning as he gave a single nod.

"Lady Jenoure, I had been wondering what was the cause of your recent out-of-character behavior, and I suppose I have my answer. Now I want nothing but the truth from you."

Annika lowered her eyes and bowed her head obediently.

"Have you disclosed any secrets I have entrusted to you on behalf of the kingdom of Daxaria to Mr. Ashowan without my authorization?" Norman's intense gaze was fixed on the viscountess.

"No, I have not."

"Is your relationship the reason you were so adamant against getting married?" There was a warning note in the king's tone that made Fin have to fight against speaking up.

"I never intended to get married to one of the suitors; Mr. Ashowan had nothing to do with that," Annika answered while once again managing to sound calm.

Norman stared at her for several moments and felt the tiniest bit of his anger ebb away.

"How long has this … *relationship*, existed?"

"A few weeks." Annika's unflappable even tone, Norman had to admit, was impressive.

"I see." Looking back and forth between the couple, the king took another step closer to them, his eyes still hard. "The two of you have betrayed my trust in your actions. You have acted duplicitously, and immaturely, and I do not sanction this absurd union in any way."

The pair remained quiet.

"Who else is aware of this … ? I am guessing Mrs. Ashowan given that she is currently residing at your estate, Lady Jenoure," Norman surmised scathingly.

"She does. She is not in support of it," Fin admitted.

"I said you were to remain quiet," the king snapped before turning back to Annika whose eyes remained downcast. "Who else?"

"My household staff."

Norman's slightly dulled anger flared with renewed life. "Do you mean to tell me … Oh Gods. That was why, Mr. Ashowan, you stayed with Lady Jenoure when I gave you a week to rest, and that was when she sent her personal knights to save you from Madam Mathilda's."

Both Annika and Fin silently nodded.

"Yes, Your Majesty," the viscountess confirmed without lifting her gaze.

"Mr. Ashowan, if no royal secrets were shared, how is it Lady Jenoure knew you were in need of aid that night?" Norman demanded, moving toward Fin.

"I followed Mr. Ashowan, Your Majesty. He never told me what you asked of him." Annika cut in swiftly.

The king froze and turned his attention back to her. "Why did you follow him?"

For the first time ever, the monarch witnessed the forever controlled, manipulative viscountess blush.

"I was ... jealous ... and worried ... when he hadn't returned that night for dinner, and ... I saw him speaking to a prostitute."

The reply threw Norman further off balance than he ever thought possible. It sounded like something Ainsley would've done when they first started courting ...

The thought of his wife managed to pull the king back to the strange reality unfolding before him.

"Does Her Majesty the queen know about this?"

Surely Ainsley wouldn't condone or keep this matter a secret from me ...

Norman's heart thudded against his chest when he noticed how rigid Annika had gone.

"Do you mean to tell me ... my *wife*, your ruler, was aware of this?" The king's voice had risen substantially, but Annika still didn't reply. Turning his chin sharply toward the door, he then called out, "Guards!"

The door opened, the poor infantrymen startled by the sight of their king's fearsome expression.

"Send for Her Majesty this instant."

The guards shut the door hastily after a quick bow, both overly eager to distance themselves from whatever drama was taking place.

Turning back toward the couple, Norman fixed Finlay under his murderous stare.

"Now, I will address you, Mr. Ashowan."

The witch straightened his spine with great difficulty.

"Did you ask me for time away so that you could spend a scandalous week with the viscountess?"

"No ... actually we weren't speaking to each other at the time due to an argument." Fin cleared his throat and felt even the tips of his ears deepen in color.

For some reason unbeknownst to himself, Norman couldn't help but ask before thinking.

"What was this argument about?"

"Er ... it was about how Lady Jenoure ... wouldn't ... communicate with me. I was also worried because her brother had just grabbed her arm, and—"

"I get the idea," Norman cut him off firmly. It was strange hearing Finlay sound like ... well, like a man in a normal relationship. The king looked back to Annika.

Perhaps it was more one-sided and she was merely going along with it because she could be the one in control?

"Lady Jenoure, how did this relationship transpire?"

Annika visibly squirmed in discomfort, and Norman couldn't help but become even more intrigued.

"I used to spend a great deal of time in the kitchen as it was a source of information, but Mr. Ashowan banned anyone who wasn't an aide from entering. So I ... tried to persuade him."

The king frowned. "So this has been going on since Mr. Ashowan first arrived?"

"No ... not ... not exactly ... Mr. Ashowan ... kicked me out repeatedly."

Norman blinked and then nearly snorted, but he caught himself in the nick of time.

This should not be funny! Any other pairing of nobility and peasant would be different, but these two ...

"How is it your attitude changed?" The king turned to Fin, who he realized was staring at Annika with a smile that couldn't be suppressed.

"I thought she was a manipulative bratty noble who just wanted something from me, but then ... I overheard noblewomen speaking ill of her and watched how she handled it with grace. I realized I had fun bickering with her, and she even brought me my familiar—"

"*You're the one responsible for bringing that demon furball into my castle?*" Norman suddenly exploded at Annika who nearly jumped out of her skin.

"S-Sire? Her M-Majesty the queen has arrived," the guard outside called out nervously.

The interruption proved a blessed respite for the couple to gather their wits back.

Norman barely registered the announcement, however, as he stared wildly at the viscountess who had unconsciously moved a little closer to Fin.

When Ainsley entered the room, her cheeks a little flushed from her walk, and saw Fin and Annika facing Norman, she immediately regretted not bringing down Lina with her as well. At least there wouldn't be as much shouting with the baby in the room ...

"My dear, please take a seat. It would seem we have much to discuss," Norman addressed his wife while still glowering at the viscountess.

Ainsley winced at his tone. It was clear as day he was livid.

Slowly taking her time to seat herself, Ainsley neatly folded her hands atop the table and waited. When the king still didn't speak after several long moments, and both Finlay and Annika appeared too petrified to move, she decided to get the ball rolling.

"It would seem that … you have been made aware of Lady Jenoure's plans to marry the cook," the queen began lightly.

"Yes, and you knew about their relationship and hid it from me." Norman rounded on his wife. The murderous aura around him dimmed greatly, however, when he noticed the tinges of red in her cheeks from the exertion of the short trip from their chambers to the council room. While she had started going for small walks up and down the corridor at Mrs. Ashowan's request, she had a great deal more to do before becoming fully recovered.

"I only found out the day before Lina was born. Since then I've been a little bit busy," she explained, raising an eyebrow toward her husband.

"Why didn't you tell me *before* Troivack's chief of military arrived?" Norman walked around the table so that he stood across from his wife's spot at the table.

"It wasn't my place to tell you. That was up to the viscountess and Mr. Ashowan."

"Ainsley, this affects everything now!"

"Now it does, yes. Which is when I am guessing these two came to you and told you."

Norman let out a long breath, clearly still angry about being deceived, when he turned to look at Annika and Fin and noticed that he was holding her hand.

"Good Gods, not here. Not right now." The king's voice rasped as he tried to remain in control.

Fin visibly struggled with releasing Annika's hand as he gave it one final squeeze and very slowly moved away from her.

With his eyes closed, the king shook his head and gave a long-suffering sigh before speaking.

"Ashowan, tell me exactly what you are theorizing your father is trying to do."

"I think he knows something is between the viscountess and me, and he is trying to remove me from the castle—most likely to attack. If we remove Annika, they will delay the war long enough to seize her funds here in Daxaria. It could even give us months of time to stop the war from starting, but we would lose her, and her family members as a result. Then there is the other possibility that Aidan did not announce … and that would be to oust our relationship and have us both removed from the castle as a result. Which, again, would lead to the loss of her family, though the Troivackians would not be able to get their hands on Lady Jenoure or the wealth she has built."

Norman's frown began to ease as he realized what this meant. "Your father thinks you are a threat in this war."

"Yes," Fin responded firmly.

The king then turned to face the viscountess. "And you, Matthias wants killed or at the very least removed from court just to be safe."

The room fell silent as the multiple implications of the new theory settled over everyone.

"Mr. Ashowan, I have been wondering this for quite some time, but … is it possible for you to identify say … an entire city, or country … as your home?" Ainsley interrupted suddenly, leaning forward toward Fin with an interested glint in her eyes.

"I … I … don't believe so, Your Majesty. If I do not feel that, without a doubt, a place is my home, my abilities will not work. Even if I have an inkling of hesitancy. My magic can't be tricked. At this point, I'm only confident that I could protect the castle and its grounds." The witch added the last sentence at the end with more confidence, though there was a wariness in his gaze only Annika noticed.

"What about Austice? Do you not feel at home in the city?" Norman asked, a desperate note in his voice.

Fin swallowed with difficulty.

It was happening again.

People thinking his magic was the answer to everything … putting responsibility on him when he had warned them time and time again …

The cook turned his saddened blue eyes to the king, and in that moment, Norman knew exactly what he had done. He remembered yet again why Finlay had been so adamant about hiding his abilities.

Because of moments like this.

"No. My home is where I am safe, and where I can be comfortable. In Austice I can be pickpocketed, murdered, and the people haven't a clue who I am. It is not my home. It is just a place that happens to have my home within it."

"You can be murdered or robbed anywhere. Even in your own—" Ainsley began, but Norman shot her a soft gaze and shook his head.

"What is it your father is worried about you doing, then?" the king asked more quietly.

"Perhaps protecting the castle is enough of a threat for him to want to intervene. Though I can't say for certain." Fin bowed in apology, the pained expression on his face not completely gone.

Annika once again moved closer to him, and while Norman stiffened as a result, there was a sharpness in her features that made him allow the show of affection.

"Well, if that's the case, then how is it we stop him from revealing this secret— Also, how is it he even found out about you two?" Ainsley asked, frowning.

"I told Your Majesty everyone on my side who knew of us, but I think Mr. Ashowan has his own list," Annika admitted slowly.

Fin hesitated and debated whether or not to report Mage Lee's awareness of his relationship …

"My aides and Lord Ryu know."

"Lord Ryu knows?!" Norman exclaimed, completely stunned.

"Er … yes … he is one of the people who encouraged—"

Norman held up his hand to stop the redhead from saying more and dropped his forehead into his other palm.

"Also, Mage Lee knows."

The king's head shot back up in an instant as incredulous outrage filled his entire face.

"GUARDS! PLEASE SUMMON MAGE LEE IMMEDIATELY!"

A beat later the door opened a crack. "Your Majesty he … er … he is here. He's been waiting outside."

"I bet he has," the king growled as the door then swung open and the old git hobbled in while leaning dramatically on his staff.

The door swung shut behind him, and immediately Norman rounded on him.

"Your Majesty! Before you say a word, I tried to talk him out of it and told him to report to you—"

"Lee, I was unaware you had grown to be such good friends with the house witch."

"We're not friends," both the mage and the witch blurted out immediately in unison.

A frightening smile climbed up the king's face when he looked back at Finlay. "Well, you must be close friends, for Mage Lee to harbor such a dear secret to you."

"He found out by accident. He kept trying to get me to marry Clara—"

Norman's flat expression silenced Fin immediately.

"Alright, Mr. Ashowan. We now know everything. So we will need to determine who is the spy—if there is one at all, and we will also need to figure out what we are doing about sending an ambassador to negotiate without it coming to light that you and Lady Jenoure are involved."

Turning to the mage, Norman slowly began to roll up the sleeves of his tunic. "Lee, I need you to summon Mr. Howard, Captain Antonio, and Lord Fuks. We need an emergency plan."

Norman then gestured to the table before turning a steely gaze to Fin and Annika.

"You two, sit. I need to decide whether or not to get you married and by some miracle make it acceptable, or kill you both myself." Shifting then to Ainsley, Norman was momentarily distracted by the odd expression on his wife's face.

"What is it?"

Ainsley smiled at Annika, who grew so immensely uncomfortable she blushed deeply enough for the color to match Fin's hair.

The queen's devilish grin only broadened before she turned to her husband. "I think they make quite a charming couple, don't you, my dear?"

CHAPTER 6
FAMILY SUPPORT

Mr. Howard, Lord Fuks, and Captain Antonio glanced at one another, confused, before silently musing about why in the world Viscountess Jenoure and the queen had been invited for a meeting. Meanwhile, Fin looked terrified, the king murderous, and Mage Lee ... well ... he looked as though someone had taken his staff and was using it to herd sheep.

"Your Majesty, is there a reason we have been summoned at this hour of the night?" Lord Fuks asked without his usual bravado. The elder was clearly aware of the underlying tension in the room.

Norman didn't even bat an eye as he rested his elbows on the council table and peered blindly ahead of himself over his clasped hands. "There is indeed. Mr. Ashowan, I would like you to announce your *news.*"

All eyes shifted to the redheaded cook, who suddenly wished he was anywhere in the whole of Daxaria than right there.

Clearing his throat, and sensing Annika holding her breath at his side, he lifted his gaze to the men. "Lady Jenoure and I are betrothed to be wed."

The moment of silence that followed was deafening.

The first to explode was of course Mr. Howard.

"Mr. Ashowan, while you might think yourself capable of taking over for the court jester's empty position, I can assure you Lady Jenoure does not find such sarcasm funny! Furthermore, you should be reprimanded for—"

"Mr. Ashowan was not making a joke." Annika's serious yet eerily calm gaze rested on Mr. Howard, whose mouth was already beginning to form the rest of his tirade. When he could not continue on as he planned, the assistant settled for allowing his jaw to remain open.

Mage Lee had his forehead in his hand, unable to lift his gaze, Captain Antonio looked strangely proud, and the queen looked as though she were trying not to laugh.

There was yet another beat of quiet before Lord Fuks decided to break it.

"Mr. Ashowan, I must confess your … romantic objectives are impressively ambitious. However … this union is not … feasible … is it?"

Fin felt his cheeks flush with heat; meanwhile, Annika's intense stare moved to the elder.

"It is entirely feasible, Lord Fuks. Is it not true that the topic of Mr. Ashowan being knighted in the near future was recently addressed?" Annika volunteered patiently.

The earl straightened in his seat, a glint of interest in his eyes as he met Annika's gaze without so much as a blink.

"It was indeed, Viscountess. However, there is still a significant difference between yourself and a knight."

At this, Captain Antonio cleared his throat, and all eyes but the king's swiveled over to the military man.

"While I am somewhat … surprised by this announcement," Antonio began slowly, "a baron's son is not considered a poor match for a viscountess."

As everyone in attendance fell into stunned silence, Ainsley couldn't help but grin at the captain.

"Gods … Captain, did you know about this?!" Mr. Howard burst out of his chair onto his feet, his palms slamming against the table.

The king's stony expression turned to Antonio, his entire body rigid. "You will answer the question immediately."

Antonio shook his head sincerely. "Please trust me when I say I knew nothing of it, Your Majesty. I am merely stating facts. This union … Lady Jenoure may be correct in believing it to not be entirely far-fetched."

"How attainable it is is the secondary issue at hand." Norman's voice boomed. "Mr. Ashowan, would you care to share how this information now impacts the current situation with Mr. Helmer?"

Swallowing with great difficulty, Fin slowly recounted the new potential motives of both Aidan Helmer and the Troivackian king; the more he explained, the more thoughtful the group became, until Ainsley spoke up.

"While you were correct about Aidan Helmer's trick about arriving earlier than what he led us to believe, Mr. Ashowan, it may not be the case that you are right about how much he knows. The problem is, we need to find out if there are any spies, and if so, who are they?" the queen pointed out seriously.

"We need to question everyone who knows about the two of you," the king declared while leaning an elbow on the table and staring pointedly at the couple.

"We can probably shorten the list quite a bit by thinking logically about who had the means and the opportunity to communicate with Mr. Helmer, or any other Troivackian diplomats," Mr. Howard sniffed while plucking small crumbs of sleep from the corner of his eyes.

"We shall begin deducing this by reviewing the schedule of their visits, as well as any noteworthy exchanges that others may have seen or heard of in the castle during the timeline of Mr. Ashowan and Lady Jenoure's *brief* courtship." Norman nodded and slowly covered his mouth as his hazel eyes at long last dropped to the table instead of looking at his subjects.

Lord Fuks leaned forward then, the mad energy around him suddenly surging as his attention shifted to Fin, which made a twist of dread rise in the pit of the witch's stomach.

"So … are you going to tell us how you did it? How you wooed Lady Jenoure?" The old man smiled with pure demented joy.

"Lord Fuks!" the queen gasped, though she was already beginning to laugh. Fin had turned the color of a tomato, and Annika looked so alarmed that she couldn't mask her expression quick enough.

"I must admit … I, too, want to know how in the name of the Gods the two of you formed an attachment. Even if we have far more pressing issues to deal with," Mr. Howard looked up from his notes, his own curiosity palpable.

"Yes, Mr. Ashowan, how did you get the noblewoman known as one of the most beautiful in Daxaria, when you're so … you?" Mage Lee spoke flatly, as he addressed the redhead through half-lidded eyes.

Fin looked to the ceiling and then turned to face the mage while his hands gripped each other under the table.

"I annoyed her until she decided she wanted to annoy me back for the rest of my life," he mumbled after an awkward moment of silence and avoiding eye contact with those around him.

Fin's atypical bashfulness succeeded in making Ainsley burst out into a series of snorts.

"That *does* make a lot of sense." Mr. Howard nodded idly.

At this, Annika finally spoke up, her eyebrow raised interestedly. "I've heard rumors that you know *exactly* the type of charm Fin possesses … apparently there is something to those stories."

While Ainsley was beginning to laugh to the point of tears, even the captain was beginning to join in at that point, as the assistant turned scarlet and stood up indignantly.

"*I have never had feelings for the cook!*"

"Yet you understood how I could fall in love with him so easily." Annika smiled prettily, and Fin wondered for a moment if Mr. Howard were going to attempt to flip the long heavy table under his flexed palms.

"That's enough. From all of you. Once we learn who this spy is, we will decide what will have to be done about the Piereva family. For now, no one is to share this new information, and we are to carry on as though nothing has happened. Understood?" When Norman spoke, the weariness in his voice drew every eye to him. It was clear that, while the man was incapable of hanging on to his anger for very long when his wife was in such good humor at his side, it did not mean he was able to set down the weight of responsibility as easily.

"You all are dismissed. Mr. Ashowan and Lady Jenoure, provide the captain with the list of people who are aware of your relationship this evening. Antonio, you are to commence the interviews before dawn, and I expect answers before the final meeting of Mr. Helmer's stay."

Everyone eventually quieted down and stood. They bowed to their king and queen and dutifully filed out of the room leaving the monarchs alone.

As Ainsley wiped the residual tears from her enjoyment from her cheeks she turned to her husband and reached out to clasp his hand.

"Norman, you know Annika and the cook … make a strange amount of sense together. Captain Antonio looking to marry Katelyn Ashowan and naming Fin as his heir would also make the union an entirely reasonable match. It would just have to be conducted carefully. When it comes to Mr. Helmer trying to muscle them out of the court or onto his ship … We'll try to find another way around it."

The king let out a long breath as he rested his elbows on the table and rubbed his eyes, and all at once the queen was reminded of the young man she had met and fallen in love with. The way he had stressed about becoming king and stayed up countless nights to study … always with his tunic sleeves pushed up, and his hair unkempt …

"I don't like that there was such duplicity from Finlay and Annika. The ones closest to me lying and hiding details that affect the entirety of the land … I feel betrayed. Even by you, Ainsley. You did not trust in me enough …"

"I'm sorry, Norman. I truly believed it was best coming from them."

Giving his head a shake at her words, the king continued muddling his way through his thoughts. "I see the two of them together and it is … strange. There's a power about them that is intimidating, and it makes me uneasy with everything happening, because between the two of them I think I could understand why someone would think their presence could be the difference of a win or loss in a war."

Ainsley reached out and gently touched Norman's hand, brushing her thumb against the back of his warm knuckles.

"There is something rather striking about them, I agree, but they aren't the only important factors in this war, love. You having faith in the hearts of your vassals, even if they aren't always forthcoming, is also important. Honestly, you and your council seem to have a great deal of fun together. I am glad you have found your own friends." Ainsley added on her observation at the end while perking up significantly.

Norman turned at long last and gazed into his wife's adoring eyes, finally letting out a long sigh.

"I think Mr. Howard might try to stab Finlay one of these days …"

"It's fine. Mr. Ashowan will just wave a flagon of wine at the man and he'll be spared until their next spat."

With a slow nod, Norman shifted his seat closer to Ainsley. "I wish there was a simple answer to this issue with the Piereva family. I know toward the end of our meeting just now there was a great deal of jesting; however, I think we all know that things are more than a little ominous."

Ainsley immediately grew serious. Reaching out to cup her husband's cheek, she managed to smile serenely. "We'll investigate the people that know about them and finish off with Madam Mathilda's interrogations … and who knows? By the end of all that, we might find a simple solution to this whole dilemma."

Norman couldn't help but light up under his wife's touch, even if she was suggesting a painfully optimistic outlook. So instead of bringing up his sincere doubts, he leaned forward and kissed her. When they pulled apart, a strange expression suddenly crossed his face, and Ainsley immediately grew curious.

"Is something wrong?" she asked while dropping her hand to his shoulder.

Norman's eyes darted to the table beneath his elbow, his brow ever so slightly furrowed as he hastily dipped into a new thought. "I just might … have come up with a solution to at least one of our problems, but … it isn't ideal …"

Fin rubbed the back of his neck and stared off into the night in front of his cottage. Annika had left the castle through a secret entrance of sorts that she would not disclose to her fiancé after giving the captain her list of people. Fin had requested he give his own list over a cup of tea, and so Antonio and he had headed out, both not saying a word until they reached the redhead's threshold.

"Captain, I …" Fin trailed off and let out a long breath. "Thank you for your support in front of His Majesty. You have been … far too generous with me than you need to be."

Antonio gave a small smile and gestured toward the door of the cottage.

The pair entered, and immediately Fin saw to getting the fire and candles lit, and the kettle set to boil. The cozy scene welcomed the two men into its embrace, and they sat down by the hearth while the witch magicked the room to keep their discussion from reaching any curious ears around them.

Once settled, Antonio leaned his forearms on the table and fixed his lone blue eye on Fin, his mood somewhat somber. "It was reckless, Fin. Going after a woman of Lady Jenoure's status."

"I swear I never meant to use you to earn my place beside her. We were already together when I found out about—"

Antonio held up a hand and silenced him. "I know. You are not that kind of man to take advantage of your mother's new husband. If you don't mind my saying so, your political savvy and ambition is embarrassingly poor."

Fin said nothing; he knew that, while insulting, it was true.

"Your mother has told me a great deal about the life you led before your time here in the castle. She loves you dearly, and as you know, I lost my own wife and son during childbirth. In my mind, the two of you are the Gods' way of lessening the pain, if only a little. That I have the love of another wonderful woman and a stepson who is a good man … I want to embrace this gift of goodness. I never know how long I will live."

DELEMHACH

Antonio smiled as Fin shifted awkwardly over his heartfelt words. "You are a grown man, I do not wish to make you uncomfortable around me. I only want you to know, if you need my support, my name, my protection, you have it. You have been the one protecting people for many years, and it doesn't hurt to have family at your back when embarking on such a noble endeavor."

Fin couldn't quite manage to look the captain in the eye over his benevolent encouragement.

"Sirs Taylor, Andrews, and Lewis have all come to me and informed me that they wish to remain under your command even when their time of punishment has come to a close. It seems on top of family, you have yourself some loyal friends. These are powerful things in our lives if we are lucky ... but I shouldn't have to tell you, house witch. I merely mean to remind you that, together, all is not lost."

Fin straightened and met the captain's gaze head-on, feeling entirely undeserving of the man's kindness, and at the same time ... grateful that his mother was going to have a husband who was one of the best men he had ever met.

The captain was right.

Having good friends and family helped fight back against the darkness and uncertainty that the near future brought forward; Fin only hoped that it was enough to save it from swallowing them all whole.

CHAPTER 7
A LADY'S LAMENT

W hy can't she see him again?"
      "Because apparently that woman, Mrs. Ashowan? Is his *mother!*"
    "Oh, Gods ... wait, why does Mr. Wit have a different last name than
his own mother?"

    "Perhaps he is a bastard?"

    The maids who had convened to discuss their mistress's bad mood in
the Jenoure keep shot Raymond scathing looks at his suggestion regarding
Mr. Wit's bloodline.

    "He isn't a bastard." Clara entered the kitchen with a sigh. She had just
delivered a cup of coffee to the viscountess who was having a great deal
of trouble getting out of bed that morning. Whether or not it was because
she was hoping to avoid a certain guest was debatable ...

    "The viscountess is acting in everyone's best interest keeping her ...
Mr. Wit's ... identity a secret. Or have you already forgotten that there is
the much bigger issue of a spy amongst us?"

    The staff looked properly chastened as they each swiftly recalled the
fact that they had spent most of the morning being questioned by the
king's knights. Lady Jenoure, meanwhile, had remained fast asleep well
into the day and had only stirred past the luncheon hour when Clara had
gone in with the coffee.

"Raymond, I came in here to inquire what you will be making our guest, Mrs. Ashowan, for lunch." The maid moved her icy blue eyes to the burly cook who was in the process of shifting his great weight back and forth on each foot.

"I was thinking of preparing some sandwiches," he muttered, when he suddenly lifted his gaze. "Wait! Mrs. Ashowan ... isn't that the last name of the castle cook?! Is Mr. Wit actually that cook that everyone is—"

"That makes so much sense!" one of the younger maids burst out as she spun around to continue gossiping with the cook.

Clara closed her eyes and sighed. In all fairness, it was rather surprising they hadn't figured it out sooner ...

"Raymond, Mrs. Ashowan will have her luncheon in the solar. I will let you know shortly if Lady Jenoure will be eating with us."

The maid then swept out of the kitchen and headed back toward the front entrance where a knight was awaiting Lady Jenoure with an official summons from the king.

The viscountess had finally managed to prepare herself for another long day despite her painfully slow efforts at waking up. Lady Jenoure had returned late the previous night from the castle with only a brief explanation regarding the interrogations that would be beginning in a matter of hours in light of there being a suspected spy.

Clara had just stepped foot in the entranceway when Annika came barreling down the stairs, her hair not yet adorned with any of the customary finery for a meeting with the king, her purple skirts with fine gold embroidery hiked up in her hands.

"My lady! What is the matter—" the knight who had come as a messenger asked while placing his hand on the hilt of his sword.

"No time, get in the carriage! Go! Go! Go! Clara, hurry!" the viscountess gasped as she sprinted past the knight, showcasing impressive agility for a noblewoman.

Both the knight and Clara stared at each other for a brief moment before turning to stare at the top of the stairs where no one appeared, further deepening both their suspicions and concerns.

By the time the knight had mounted his steed at the front of Lady Jenoure's carriage horses, he was shaking his head wondering if the woman was ill.

Clara stared at her mistress who had plastered herself against the wall of the carriage and fixed her eyes out over the water. Sweat beaded on her forehead as she tried to quiet her breathing.

"What ... happened?" Clara asked, openly bewildered.

"Fin's mother," Annika whispered quietly as though the healer was standing right outside their carriage.

"What about her? I know the woman isn't necessarily fond of you just yet, but did she threaten you or—"

"She was waiting for me outside of my chamber and wanted to talk ... then ... she wanted ..." Annika let out a small breath of relief when the carriage jolted into movement.

"What did she want? I'm at the edge of my seat."

"She wanted to ... *hug*."

Clara stared at Annika and waited for further explanation.

When none was forthcoming, Clara burst out hysterically laughing. A worsening habit of hers since Annika's relationship with the cook first started.

"She hugs everyone, yes. I thought you would've known this about her nature."

Annika gradually relaxed into the seat of the carriage and dabbed at the sweat on her brow using the back of her sleeve.

"I knew her to be an affectionate woman, but ... I thought she wouldn't *demand* it of a person! Good grief ... Fin was bashful just brushing my skin for months and—" The viscountess abruptly stopped talking when she noticed the amused smile on her maid's face. "One day you are going to fall in love and I am going to find great joy in tormenting you," Annika declared through slitted eyes.

"Hopefully by then you and Mr. Ashowan will have wed, and you'll be too busy to pay me much mind."

Annika's expression indicated that the entire world could be on fire and she would make sure that Clara would experience the same treatment she was being given.

"I understand you are not ... a *warm* person," Clara began, a smile already working its way up her face. "But did you physically run away from the woman who is set to be your in-law when she wanted to hug you?"

"A maid walked by fortunately, and I said that she was summoning me for the impatient knight in the entryway. Even so, I'm sure I've left yet another negative impression."

Clara continued laughing as Annika resumed staring out the window, her eyes lost in thought as the carriage pulled her toward the castle.

"It's a good thing Mr. Ashowan has been away from the estate lately," Clara announced suddenly while staring at the viscountess closely.

Annika's gaze cut back to her maid and frowned. "Don't worry, I'll manage this. I've overcome everything in my life thus far."

Clara's lips pursed as she stopped herself from saying a great deal many opposing thoughts. Instead, after a moment of silence, the maid settled on a single barb.

"I still can't believe you hiked up your skirts in front of his mother and literally bolted. That's the fastest I've seen you move since that night with the prostitutes—"

"Clara, shut up." With a sigh, Annika closed her eyes and did her best to ignore her maid's snickers on the opposite end of the carriage. The viscountess could already tell that despite the late start to her day, it was going to be a long one.

"Mr. Ashowan, my boy! Just the fellow I was hoping to see!" Lord Fuks called out, nearly making Fin jolt from his daze. The redhead had just walked Hannah to the barracks to have her interview with the captain, when the earl appeared at the castle's west entrance.

The witch turned around to face Lord Fuks, revealing the dark bags under his eyes and making the elderly man tsk from atop the stairs before he descended them with a small spring in his step and made his way over to Fin.

"I trust you have already completed the preparations for dinner this evening?" Lord Fuks clasped his hand on Fin's shoulder, a mischievous smile on his face.

The cook blinked slowly down at the man. It was obvious that he hadn't slept properly, and while standing under the hot summer sun, he was in danger of keeling over at any moment.

"I have … It will be a feast of cold meats, fresh bread, and fruits. It is too warm for there to be a hot dish."

The earl had already begun ushering Fin back into the cool shelter of the castle while noting the dark clouds that were beginning to roll in from the east, indicating a storm was coming.

"Wonderful, sounds delicious … now, do you remember how you owe me a debt of servitude from when you insolently laughed at my name?" Fin stopped in his tracks and faced the man with obvious mortification.

"It seems you do, how splendid. I'd hate to have to call Physician Durand and Mr. Howard here as eyewitnesses of our first meeting." The lord reached up and idly brushed off some flour from the cook's tunic.

"What … is it you want, Lord Fuks?" Fin asked slowly.

"Well, you see … I have a great many questions regarding you and your betrothed. It is the type of story I normally would like to hear while sharing a good bottle of whiskey, but ah … thanks to yourself I can no longer drink more than a glass."

"Lord Fuks … you want me to … tell you about my future wife and my relationship and … have a drink for my punishment?"

"I said *I* would also have *a* drink. Even Physician Durand says having one very rarely should be perfectly fine. *You*, on the other hand, are quite entertaining while drinking, and I think you being responsible for the rest of the whiskey will be just the ticket to perking up these dismally stressful times." As he spoke, Lord Fuks grabbed Fin by the arm and began pulling him farther down the castle corridor. "Mr. Helmer is visiting Lord Piereva today, so we don't have to worry about running into his nasty arse."

Fin finally had the presence of mind to stop being literally dragged along; he stood still and faced the elder who was looking a little too delighted with himself.

"Lord Fuks, I have work that needs to be completed, and we are trying to find out … important information. I do not think drinking before it is even the dinner hour and discussing my relationship is what we should be—"

"I could always bring up to the king how rude you were the first day we met. Of course, I don't think he is particularly fond of you after last night …"

Fin sighed and rubbed the back of his neck wearily. The old bastard was too cunning for his own good, and he really was in enough trouble with the king as it were …

"If I can at least see that dinner is delivered, I—"

"You already said the dinner is ready! You had to finish early because your aides are being questioned. Now, I will have a bottle sent to them to enjoy as well to make up for your absence. How's that sound, hm? Onward, Mr. Ashowan!"

Lord Fuks with his wispy white hair in his glaringly bright red tunic waved his finger in the air and continued marching toward the north end of the castle. Fin sluggishly began to wonder if the earl was the spy and was leveraging him for information …

If not, Lord Fuks was perhaps crazier than the witch initially realized.

Annika's face bore its usual mask of indifference as she left the new baby princess's chamber with Physician Durand at her side.

"Her Majesty seems to be recovering well," the viscountess announced as a pair of noblewomen passed her and immediately began whispering behind their hands to each other.

"She is indeed. It is Mrs. Ashowan we have to thank for her still being here with us," Physician Durand admitted with a smile. "I hope you are faring well with these new dilemmas surrounding your brothers, Lady Jenoure."

"Thank you for your thoughtfulness." Annika bowed her head to the man as they walked away from the nursery and neared the staircase where they would undoubtedly have to part. The smell of wet earth had filled the castle thanks to the storm that had broken out during dinner, which ended up barring the viscountess from returning to her estate. Instead, after meeting with the king to discuss the results of his interrogation of her keep's staff, she had filled her time with catching up with Ainsley. A great blessing indeed.

Once at the stairwell, both Physician Durand and Annika began to bid their farewell to each other, when a sudden commotion rang out in the corridor.

Turning around swiftly, both the physician and Annika were stunned to see none other than Fin being hauled out of the council room by Mr. Howard and the captain.

Annika straightened her shoulders in alarm when she started to make out the things he was saying …

"Of course Mage Lee can't unlock a door I lock! It's … It's *my* door!" The redhead's speech was heavily slurred as the king's assistant and captain tried to manage the cook down the hall toward the servants' stairwell.

Physician Durand stepped forward, blocking Annika from view.

"Gentlemen, Lady Jenoure is here, perhaps we save her having to bear witness to such an indelicate sight."

"What? Why is she still here?!" Mr. Howard hissed conspiratorially to Antonio.

With a frown, Annika stepped out from behind the physician and gave both the members of the inner council a steely glare.

"What in the world is going on here?"

Fin's head rolled forward, his blue eyes blearily landing on the viscountess. "It's you—!"

Mr. Howard slapped his hand over Fin's mouth in an instant while Captain Antonio had the decency to look apologetic.

"Forgive us, Lady Jenoure, His Majesty just finished having Mr. Ashowan undergo … a different type of questioning. With regard to … to …" The captain glanced at Physician Durand briefly before continuing. "Mr. Ashowan's future career."

"He's drunk!" Annika snapped angrily. "Why in the world was his inebriation necessary?"

"Aye … well … Lord Fuks suggested it, and then, well …"

"ARGH!" Mr. Howard suddenly snapped his hand back from Fin's mouth. "This newt with cobwebs instead of brains just bit me!"

"Didyouknow everyone thinks you're beautiful?" Fin asked Annika with a teasing, drunken grin. "They're not wrong, but I think you are—"

Both the captain and Mr. Howard managed to slap their hands over the witch's mouth at the exact same time, then immediately bowed while forcing Fin to do the same.

"Pardon us, Viscountess. We will be off now!" Captain Antonio bobbed his head before quickly ushering Fin around Annika, though he seemed to stumble a great deal in the process.

As they continued forcing Fin farther down the corridor toward the servants' stairwell around the corner, Lady Jenoure stared after the three men with clenched fists. She was fighting the urge to demand just what the hell they thought they were doing to her betrothed …

"WHERE'S KRAKEN?! HE'S SO SOFT! HAVE YOU EVER PET HIM?" The very excitable remark made by the cook echoed back up the corridor to Annika who winced and suppressed a groan.

Why must he be so terrible at hiding his nonsense? Why are they even making him drink at a time like this?!

As she turned back around, Physician Durand wore an amused smile though his eyes were remorseful.

"I apologize you had to witness such a scene. Be sure to take good care of yourself, and … avoid unnecessary risks, Viscountess." The man bowed again, and with another reassuring smile he took his leave and began descending the stairs.

With a small huff, Annika turned back and stared off after Fin for another moment.

Occasionally she could hear the odd shout, or … singing?

Gods. Was he drunkenly singing?

Closing her eyes, and taking a deep steadying breath, Annika's heart skipped a beat when she slowly raised a hand to her abdomen.

Man that I love … man of my dreams … father of my unborn child … we better convince the king to let us get married soon …

CHAPTER 8
BOILING OVER

GodsdamnitGodsdamnitGodsdamnitGods*damnit!*" Annika muttered under her breath in a steady stream as she stepped into her carriage and slammed the door behind her before the footman could do so.

"Are you cursing because of the meeting with the king, or because of your meeting with Physician Durand?" Clara asked casually as though she hadn't been sweating the entire day trying to maneuver the queen out of the nursery so that the viscountess could have a private word with the physician.

Annika didn't answer as she shoved her elbow on the carriage windowsill, then dropped her forehead to her hand.

"The physician."

"Congratulations," Clara replied, her tone light and uncompromising.

"Son of a mage, I was drinking the contraceptive tea like you told me to, how in the world did this happen?" Annika snapped accusatively to her maid who responded by lifting an amused eyebrow.

"It generally does work, but the two of you spent a great deal of time in your chamber. Plus, I seem to recall a night you were out of your chambers before I gave you those tea leaves ... In fact"—Clara frowned for a moment as she counted on her fingers, and a slow devilish smile crept across her cheeks—"given your current condition, your new bundle of joy must be a result of the masquerade."

The stricken look on Annika's face lasted for several moments, before it crumbled into mortification.

"Gods … *DAMNIT!*"

"Come now, you always love a challenge. Just think of this surprise as a political hurdle to overcome." Clara waved her hand while leaning back into her seat comfortably.

"Even *I'm* beginning to think I'm biting off more than I can chew …" Annika sighed wearily.

Turning to stare at the passing scenery, the viscountess's mind flitted back to when she had first noticed feeling somewhat off …

Fin had proposed and she had felt dizzy …

Then she had burst out in tears after the redhead had left, a sight that had had Clara blinking in astonishment. The maid had then tactfully asked, "What in the world is wrong with you? Are you pregnant?"

Of course right after becoming betrothed, Annika had then gone to see the queen and been faced with Katelyn Ashowan.

One touch from that woman and she would know for certain before I do …

When the healer had handed her the baby princess, Annika's heart had been in her throat as she thanked the Gods that she had worn gloves.

Then her dresses had felt snug in certain areas … and her cycle hadn't started.

All small changes, but luckily, Fin wasn't around enough to notice them. She had just been hit with the waves of exhaustion in the previous two days … and at long last Clara had demanded she see a physician.

Annika mentally berated herself soundly for an extra breath or two before allowing her mind to return to the present day, albeit without her usual mental quickness as fatigue pulled at every fiber of her being. Despite sleeping in, she still felt as though she'd been run over by a stampede of horses.

"So how are you going to tell Mr. Ashowan?"

"Gods … it's too early to do that."

Clara's eyes cast down to Annika's breasts and rose back to her mistress's annoyed gaze.

"Mr. Ashowan is not an idiot, my lady. Though did you ask Physician Durand about the weight gain? Even if it was from the masquerade, you've thickened at least two or three inches—"

The deadly glare Annika gave the maid stopped her from finishing her sentence. With a sigh, Clara tried a different tactic.

"My lady, I'm not trying to poke fun at you, but you do seem to be changing quite quickly."

Annika continued to scowl for a moment as the carriage jostled around them before she turned back to the window.

After a few moments of tense silence, she finally spoke.

"I brought it up. I have been eating more and that could just be because of having Fin cook for me so often, but the physician did say ... for my first pregnancy it was a bit strange. He then said that for some women ... if there was more than one babe—"

"*Twins?!*" Clara's normally calm exterior was suddenly nowhere to be found as her blue eyes widened and she leaned forward earnestly.

Startled by the maid's loud response, Annika ended up shushing her hastily.

"It isn't a guarantee, only a possibility ... It could just be how much I'm eating," the viscountess declared confidently, though her eyes flickered with doubts.

Clara's jaw remained dropped, until she finally managed to mutter, "Gods, who knew Ashowan would be such a one-shot wonder ..."

"Stop looking at me like that. Just make fun of me for indulging too much like you have been and let's not discuss this unless absolutely necessary."

Annika turned back to her carriage window yet again and did her best to push thoughts of pregnancy and scandal as far from her mind as possible.

She was beginning to succeed while thinking about the meeting with the king, when Clara suddenly burst out laughing.

Turning her head, Annika stared at the maid glumly.

"Pardon me, my lady, it's just ... Gods ... can you imagine how much of a family hug Katelyn Ashowan almost got this morning?!"

"Clara, I think you should walk the rest of the way back to the keep."

Fin awoke in the middle of the night to the forced hushed voices of his mother and Captain Antonio. His head was pounding, his mouth felt dry … He couldn't remember how he even got to his cottage. Wasn't his mother supposed to be at Annika's estate?

"—get him drunk!"

"It honestly helped the king forgive him a little bit; it was not as bad as you think."

"Why is this job turning my son into an alcoholic?!"

"Hardly an alcoholic. Besides, he didn't blast anyone off the grounds this time!"

"I'll blast *you* off these grounds if you—"

Fin vomited into the water pitcher beside his bed before he could hear the rest of his mother's threat to the captain.

The door to the room opened and light poured in, making Fin let out a long groan.

What he was unable to see at that moment was Kate's exasperated expression as she gestured to her pained son and faced off with the captain.

"I'm sorry, lass." Antonio cleared his throat and averted his gaze from the very obviously hungover cook.

"Because he was *demanded* to drink yesterday, I will fix him up with minimal suffering. I want you to wait here, I'm not through with you!" Kate snapped before entering Fin's room and slamming the door behind herself.

Antonio did his best to ignore the terrible noises that were omitted from behind the door, but after an hour had passed, he began to wonder if he'd ever be able to look Finlay in the eyes again.

"There. He should be able to recover enough to work in a few hours," Kate announced while exiting the room and storming over to the captain who was doing his best to pretend that the scent of sick wasn't churning his own stomach.

"Now, what does the king want to do about Finlay and Annika's betrothal?"

"Well, between you and me … the king thinks if Fin heroically agrees to magically protect the castle and go as an ambassador on the ship to save Charles Piereva's family, we could use it as grounds for ennoblement. Though there would also be required lessons …" Antonio watched his betrothed and noted the guarded moves she made. She was angry, yes … but beneath all of that she was scared.

Kate frowned. "What sort of lessons?"

"A good amount of etiquette and what is deemed courtly behavior."

"I see."

"Fin will be fine. Lady Jenoure has even volunteered to schedule a meeting with Mr. Helmer to try and discover how much he knows … but she does not want Finlay finding out about it. She thinks he'll try to stop her from doing so."

Kate's lips pursed as she vividly recalled how only that morning the woman her son intended to marry had literally bolted from her when she had tried to mend the rift between them.

"Is the viscountess capable of handling someone like Aidan?" she asked, the tension in her voice noticeable.

"I don't know, but it's not a bad idea. It was strange that he happened to fixate on both her and Finlay … we want to figure out how much he knows, and I doubt he will expect the viscountess to want to speak to him herself."

Katelyn crossed her arms over her chest and began to chew her bottom lip, but after a brief second of thought, she straightened her shoulders and met the captain's eye boldly.

"I want to be there."

"Where?" Antonio asked perplexed.

"In the meeting with Aidan and Lady Jenoure," Kate announced boldly.

"I don't think that'd be wise," Antonio started slowly.

"My future daughter-in-law is going to be in a room alone with my ex-husband. She needs someone on her side, and … I can make sure he gets rattled." There was a fire in her eyes that made Antonio hesitate before trying to argue with her.

"It would have to be cleared by the king, but Kate, I don't want you agitating your former husband. He could try to hurt you."

"I'm tired of being scared of Aidan!" the healer burst out vehemently, her hands falling to her sides and balling into fists.

"I know, lass. This isn't the way to—"

"No! This is *not* about me overcoming my fear, I just don't want it used as an excuse to hide. There is no need for me to still be cowering from my ex-husband … I spent nine years doing just that, and it's high time I should be able to act without fearing his reaction."

Antonio stared at Kate for several moments, his head cocked to the side as he watched her flushed face and rapid breaths. He had seen enough men caught up in the heat of their emotions to know that given a few extra minutes, there would be a slight dip in their intensity, and it was then that a message would be better heard.

Sure enough, Kate's breathing mellowed after a few quiet moments, and the color in her cheeks lessened, and so, he spoke quietly.

"Lass, I respect what you're trying to do, but we need to first confirm with His Majesty and Lady Jenoure before we can allow such a thing."

Kate's jaw screwed itself shut.

Antonio knew that expression as well.

Defiance.

With a long sigh, he resigned himself to a lengthy night of talking with his betrothed, and he cursed Aidan Helmer for the millionth time since learning his name.

Kate sat in the solar, her legs and arms both crossed as she waited for the viscountess to join her.

She had not slept a wink, yet the Lady Jenoure was apparently able to sleep soundly despite the calamity surrounding her betrothed.

The icy maid named Clara entered the solar, her porcelain face as serene as ever.

"I apologize for the wait, Mrs. Ashowan. Lady Jenoure has been stressed as of late. She will join you as soon as possible."

Kate felt her teeth set themselves on edge as the rest of her body grew rigid.

"I recognize that the viscountess is being incredibly generous to a lowly physician such as myself by hosting me as a guest. However, what I wish to discuss is important."

Clara didn't bat an eye as she curtsied in response and took her leave.

Meanwhile, Annika dragged herself from her bed with great difficulty and cursed Finlay in several colorful ways despite knowing she, too, bore responsibility for the situation.

"Mrs. Ashowan seems quite annoyed, I suggest you try to hurry," Clara informed her mistress as she entered the room in a blur.

The maid was forced to halt, however, when she noticed that her normally spritely and lithe mistress was blearily evaluating her clothing options with her hair wildly unkempt.

"Going … as fast … as I can," Annika mumbled with half-lidded eyes before she selected a burgundy dress with more layered skirts.

Resisting the urge to again tell the viscountess to hurry up, Clara aided her in donning the gown. Though when it came to lacing her up, Annika let out a small "oomph."

"Truly, you are growing remarkably quickly. If Mr. Ashowan sees you anytime soon without your gowns on, he will notice." Clara dropped her hand to the undeniable growth in Annika's abdomen that had appeared over the past week. Her normally flat and toned middle had suddenly swollen by her hips, and it was taking on a very telling shape.

"The physician predicts I will give birth at the beginning of next spring, so I'm sure this is just my carelessness in my food consumption."

"Or twins," Clara reminded helpfully.

Annika suddenly felt like weeping.

Sensing the shift in mood of her mistress, Clara changed the topic. "What is your plan for today?"

"I need to find out what Mrs. Ashowan wants, then I have the meeting with Aidan Helmer. After all the in-law meetings … have a nap. Perhaps eat some fruit …"

"Fruit?" Clara asked, bewildered.

"Yes. Peaches specifically. If you find me a bushel of peaches, I will give you a raise," Annika explained before straightening her skirts to hide her physique and fixing her maid with a blunt stare.

"Gods, does pregnancy make everyone this mad?" Clara asked with obvious dread.

Immediately, Annika felt moisture well up in her eyes, and it made her want to murder someone as a result.

"I am still myself! I can still do everything I could before, it's just I've … I've been compromised!" The damned tears were already spilling over from her eyes—though she hated every single one of them. "I'm just so tired!"

Clara watched as though her mistress were being gutted before her, the disgust and fear clear on her face. "This is going to be a very long seven and a half months."

Annika dabbed the tears with the back of her sleeves before facing her maid with obviously forced gusto.

"Can you tell my state if you didn't know?"

Clara sighed. "No. I can't. I must say, you are not making motherhood seem very agreeable"

"Gods, I wasn't even sure I wanted children; what in the world am I doing?! We've only been together a few weeks!" Annika burst into fresh sobs that sent her maid's eyes rolling until she sported a spectacular view of the back of her skull.

"A veeeery long seven and a half months," Clara muttered with a sigh before reaching out and patting the normally formidable viscountess on the back with the feeble hope of calming her down.

CHAPTER 9
HOT UNDER THE COLLAR

A nnika sat with a pleasant smile on her face as Clara handed her a plate laden with fruit and cheese; the viscountess tried to ignore the irritated calculating stare from her soon-to-be mother-in-law.

"I apologize again for the wait, Mrs. Ashowan, it must be from the stress of everything lately that has me so tired."

"I had to go heal Fin last night," the healer announced glibly.

Annika's eyes shot up to Kate's face, the fear and worry potent. "What happened? Is he alright? I saw him being carried out of the castle, but thought that—"

"You *knew* that they had gotten him too drunk to walk in order to be questioned yesterday?" The sharp note in Kate's voice was not lost on either Clara or Annika, and immediately the viscountess's demeanor changed.

Setting down the plate, and staring steadily into the healer's eyes, Annika's expression turned stony.

"Mrs. Ashowan, I knew nothing of the king's plan or motives. I only crossed paths with Fin on my way out from the castle. I already bent the captain's ear about it yesterday."

"Antonio saw you?!" Kate's exasperated tone followed by a huff made Annika raise an eyebrow and lean back in her seat, appraising the woman before her.

"Mrs. Ashowan, did you sleep at all last night?" The viscountess's gaze roamed over the healer's face.

"No! Unlike some people I have trouble sleeping when my loved ones are going through—" Kate stopped herself from finishing her sentence and closed her eyes wearily. "I'm sorry, my lady."

"Mrs. Ashowan, I can't imagine the stress you are feeling right now. I know you are fearful for your son, and that you do not have the kindest opinion of myself; however … there is no need for any animosity. If you doubt the depth of my feelings for your son, I'd be happy to have a lengthier discussion when I am not pressed for time." Annika waved to Clara over her shoulder and stood, while adjusting her voluminous burgundy skirts.

"That was actually what I wanted to discuss with you today, Viscountess," Kate interrupted, looking sheepish. "I would like to be a part of the meeting today that you have with my former husband."

Annika hesitated and raised an eyebrow. "Mrs. Ashowan, I do not believe now is the time to enact a personal revenge. This meeting is—"

"I know why it is taking place, and I agree with the logic that you will have better luck catching Aidan off guard simply by being a human woman, and him not knowing you personally; however … you do not know that man."

"Mrs. Ashowan"—Annika stood as Clara opened the solar room door, signifying their departure—"I've known many men like Aidan Helmer. I am sorry, but my answer is no."

"Then at the very least, would it be possible for you to take me to the castle with you? I would like to check up on Fin," Kate said, her disappointment abundantly clear.

Annika hesitated for a moment, a move that didn't help the healer's agitated spirit in the least.

"Of course, are you prepared to leave right now?"

Once safely stowed in the carriage, the two women contented themselves to look out the window as they began to pull away from the estate; Clara remained on the steps, her objective of finding a bushel of peaches for her mistress set.

When the carriage turned onto the main road in Austice leading up to the castle, Kate turned to the viscountess.

"You mentioned before that you were married once."

Annika slowly turned back to the healer, a sad smile on her face. "I was, yes. Hank Jenoure ... he was a good man."

"When was it that he passed?" Kate asked, a more sympathetic feeling worming its way into her heart at the lady's obvious tenderness for her former spouse.

"More than a year ago now ... sometimes it feels like it's been a decade since then, and then some days I walk into his old study and expect him to be staring at the painting of his favorite place." Annika's gaze shifted from Kate as her first husband's face flashed in her mind's eye.

"Where was his favorite place?"

"His estate in the countryside in Sorlia. His first wife, Mael, had the land as a part of her dowry when they married."

Kate looked puzzled then. "How many estates do you own, if I might ask?"

"I own one in each city, but most of the tenants I'm responsible for are outside of Xava and Sorlia. I own a handful of ships as well, but Hank never liked them ... he preferred to sink his funds into livestock and farming. I've shifted some of my investments into a few vineyards and fishing boats in Rollom, but—" Annika suddenly stopped her explanation when she saw Kate's face grow pale. "Are you feeling alright?"

"Gods, the rumors are true, aren't they? You're quite ..." The healer didn't finish her thought as she shook her head in wonder. "How in the world did you take to my son?"

Annika smiled and laughed a little. "We've been getting that question quite a bit lately I suppose if I were to try and have it make sense, I'd say ... he is strong where I'm weakest, and vice versa. Yet we both have felt ... alone in our own ways."

Kate smiled then as well while folding her hands in her lap, her thumb nervously stroked the back of her other hand.

"Fin struggles with hiding his opinion if he disagrees with someone ... and he struggles with tact ... Given your political power, I take it you are quite adept in these areas."

Annika's smile dimmed a little, but she gave a single shoulder shrug without committing to an answer. Instead she replied with, "One lesson Hank taught me is that what matters most is being honest with those dear to me. Fin brings out my honest side quite easily."

Kate nodded thoughtfully and resumed her quiet, though it was clear she had a lot on her mind.

"Mrs. Ashowan, I have to ask ... you seemed perfectly fine with me when we first met, but ever since learning about my relationship with your son things have been ... awkward," Annika explained haltingly. She knew it was a gamble to try and broach the subject, but she was growing tired of the tension between them.

The healer let out a long breath, and her shoulders slouched forward slightly as a result.

"I've expressed the brunt of my reasons. I didn't like the significant disadvantage of your class differences and thought that such an obstacle would prove too devastating—especially to Fin." Kate's hands gripped together a little more tightly in her lap before she continued. "You seem like a very put-together lady. I admit, I find it hard to understand you at times as your thinking as a noble is different than mine ... but I will put it behind me eventually. With regard to the ... *nightly* visits, I'm sure you've taken precautions to ensure that the road before you two doesn't become even more difficult."

Annika wondered if debating suicide every time she talked to her future mother-in-law was going to be the norm ... She already regretted volunteering to have her in the estate ...

"Would you look at that, the baker is selling fresh bread!" Annika pointed out the window and hoped Kate would take the bait.

"Of course they do, they're a bakery— Viscountess, are you feeling alright?"

Kate observed the sheen of sweat by Annika's hairline and raised an eyebrow. For once the day wasn't brutally warm, and a pleasant cool sea breeze was drifting in through the carriage window. Extending her hand, the healer went to feel Annika's brow, only to have the lady then plaster herself out of reach against the carriage wall.

"Goodness, I don't bite." Kate couldn't hide how startled she was. "I understand I haven't been the most accepting of you, but surely you don't think I will do you any harm ..."

"No, no, I just ... wouldn't want your hand to get my sweat all over it." Annika waved off her future mother-in-law's concern and once again tried to change the subject. "As you know, we all handle stress differently."

"I suppose so ..."

Annika forced a smile on her face and turned back to the window, hoping to hide the flush in her cheeks. So far, her day had not been going well at all ...

~~~~~~~

Tapping her finger impatiently against her arm, the viscountess waited for Aidan Helmer to join her in the council room. She hadn't had a chance to eat that morning, and her hunger was somehow beginning to make her feel queasy …

At long last, the door opened, and in strode the man who sired her betrothed, with his cream tunic sleeves rolled up and a black vest hanging open.

"I apologize, Viscountess, for keeping you waiting." Troivack's chief of military bowed before striding over to the chair across from her and seating himself.

"Quite alright, I'm just enjoying being free to leave my estate." Annika sighed and made her stare vacant. She needed him to believe she was an idiot through and through, to help make her seem as harmless as possible.

"Yes, I heard you were asked to leave the castle in light of Earl Piereva's actions. Is your arm healed?" Aidan asked kindly.

Kindly …

He's going to play it that way, is he? Annika smiled at the man despite wanting to slap the friendly expression from his face.

"It's feeling much better now, thanks! It really is too bad Phillip had to be such a baby." Annika rolled her eyes in a most undignified manner before turning back to Aidan and blushing prettily. "Not that I don't love him, you know … My brother. He just likes to boss me around too much."

Aidan nodded sympathetically and smiled encouragingly. "Of course. Now, the Daxarian king has arranged this meeting for us because you wanted to speak with me?"

"Yes, I … I'm worried about what's happening back home … Charles has been arrested?"

"Yes, he has been. Didn't His Majesty tell you that we are more than happy to escort you to King Matthias to defend your brother?" There was a predatory glimmer in Aidan's eyes that had Annika's stomach churn unpleasantly.

"I … I did hear, but … I'm worried King Matthias may be mad at me." Annika cast her eyes down shyly like a child.

A long moment of silence stretched between them as Aidan studied her closely.

"You seem quite different from what I've heard about you, Lady Jenoure."

Annika let her doe-eyed expression fly up unguarded to Aidan, and she tilted her head over her right shoulder. "What have you heard?"

"I've heard that you are a quiet, mature, composed lady of the court."

"Oh!" Annika laughed freely. "I'm friends with the queen, so I try to be on my best behavior ... I hope it doesn't sound like I'm boasting! You seem nicer than what I've heard, too, and— Oops," Annika squeaked and covered her mouth.

Gods, if Fin saw me like this he'd be laughing at me, the lady couldn't help but think to herself.

"S-Sorry, Mr. Helmer, I didn't mean to say you're mean; I think people are just scared because of the war ..." Annika batted her eyes and gave an unsure smile up at the man who she could see was beginning to relax his shoulders.

"Oh, no, I can be quite cruel when I need to be, but there is no need to be so now. Though I must tell you, Lady Jenoure, His Majesty King Matthias would be far less upset with you if you were to obey his summons. He may even forget all about Lord Charles Piereva's ... discrepancies ... if you do so." Aidan's smile reminded Annika of a snake, weaving its way closer to its prey.

"But I ... I don't want to get married and go back home like he wants me to! Here I can do whatever I want ... besides, I didn't like Lord Miller, the last Troivackian he wanted me to marry. He just wanted to talk about books and helping people all the time ..." It didn't take long for Annika to bring theatrical tears to her eyes to sell her performance.

"Shh, it's alright, my lady. I understand that expectations aren't always easy to follow. Truthfully, we are trying to find out who is the spy here in Daxaria. I wondered if it was you."

Annika sniffled then took on a desperate pleading look. "Of course I'm not! I just want my brother back safe, and I don't want to go back to Troivack and not be able to buy what I want, or, or, or ..." She trailed off as she allowed more tears to fall.

Gods, why do I have to cry so much lately? First the brat I'm carrying makes me a human fountain this morning, and now I have to convince this vile being that I'm useless ...

"It is quite alright, Viscountess." Despite his words and tone being kind, Annika could sense Aidan's displeasure over her tears.

Good. Be uncomfortable, you cretin.

"Well, I am sorry I wasn't of more help to you, Viscountess, but until you or my son agree to come with us, I don't know that King Matthias will be able to look fondly upon Lord Charles or his family."

"T-There has to be something I can do without having to see the king! He's so scary!" Annika trembled, while shrinking in her seat and covering her mouth.

She could sense Aidan's perverse pleasure in seeing her cower and wished she could snap his neck then and there without risking losing her family members.

"Nothing, I don't think … then again, perhaps you can convince my son to join me on my ship for a little while. A pretty face like yours has ways of moving men's hearts." Slowly standing, Aidan plucked up Annika's hand, brushed a kiss against her knuckles, and clearly relished how she stiffened with her teary doe eyes that regarded him with helplessness.

Then he bowed and took his leave, perfectly pleased with how that meeting had gone.

Strolling leisurely through the castle corridors, Aidan began to hum to himself as a small smile worked its way up his face.

That is, until he saw a figure standing before his chamber door. A figure he knew all too intimately.

Katelyn Ashowan stood glaring as he approached, her stance braced, her arms crossed, and in one hand dangled … a frying pan?

CHAPTER 10
HELLMAKER HELMER

"Whatever brings you to see me ... Is it Mrs. Helmer, or is it Ashowan now?" Aidan asked Katelyn with a pleasant smile on his face. The healer noticeably twitched when he stuffed his hands in his pockets and strode closer to her.

Gods, he even walks like Finlay ... Kate's anger and hatred for her former spouse immediately tripled.

"It's been Ashowan since the day I was free of you," she replied as coolly as possible.

"Oh, then a day or two? Seeing as the divorce was only finalized when I returned."

The healer didn't bother responding, knowing he was only seeking to enrage her.

"Is there a reason you are waiting outside of my chamber door?" Aidan asked in a bored tone.

"Yes. I came to tell you to abandon whatever awful plot you have against our son. Stay away from him. He has a life of his own entirely separate from you and has earned as much," Kate bit out with her grip on the frying pan tightening.

Aidan cocked his head to the side. "The boy has been without a father—"

"He is not a boy. He is a grown man. He needs nothing from you," Kate informed him curtly.

"Hm, well, in that case, if I am not expected to give him any familial preference … I suppose I'll have to be a bit more aggressive in my approach." The fire witch's black eyes somehow burned darker. "Say … has Fin been in touch with that old friend of yours? You know. Sky."

Kate felt her insides quake. Rage mixed with pain but worse, most sickeningly of all … fear. Irrational sickening fear.

"Fin's business is not yours. A-Apparently I'm not m-making that clear." Kate hated that she stammered and felt her cheeks blush brightly over the fault of her speech.

"Hm, well that answers that question. How interesting … Tell me, when did you come to the castle? You seem to have a good relationship with the Daxarian king for him to personally handle your request for the dissolution of our marriage." Aidan smiled coldly.

Taking the opportunity to gain back some of her fortitude, Kate gave a small "Ha" before adding on, "Still bothered about that are you?"

The temperature around the fire witch increased, and a small spark cracked between them, making Kate jump and brandish the pan.

"It isn't nice to be surprised, is it?" Aidan asked softly, a hint of cruel pleasure in his voice.

"It isn't nice to be blasted off an island either, I b-bet." Kate stuttered again, but at least her words had the desired effect of removing all the fire witch's friendly façade.

Aidan took another step closer to his ex-wife, his hands coming out of his pockets, and moving to his hips. Kate didn't budge; her heart was pounding so recklessly that it became difficult to breathe.

"Enjoyed seeing that, did you? Didn't even send out a boat to see if I were dead or alive."

"I was too busy trying to ensure our son didn't die," the healer replied coldly.

"I thought I wasn't to consider him my son anymore. Make up your mind—not that I care much either way … he always was a bit of a disappointment."

"You wanted him to have powers, to be stronger, and the moment he was, you were outmatched," Kate reminded him despite the color in her cheeks remaining high.

"You think I'm scared of him? I don't even consider him a witch. He is powerless the minute he steps off the grounds of what is his home," Aidan scoffed.

"Yet— Wait. How is it you happen to know so much about his power?" Kate's brow furrowed, and Aidan's smile grew.

"I have friends in high places."

Aidan began to step even closer to his ex-wife, when the stones of the castle suddenly reverberated. The smell of lightning filled the air, and the former couple turned to see their son standing twenty feet away with his hands in his pockets, his shoulders hunched, and his blue eyes aglow.

Aidan faced Fin, his eyes widening with cold interest.

"Ah, how fortunate of you to come. Mrs. … Ashowan, was it? We were just having a small discussion. What brings you here, Royal Cook?"

Fin strode forward, but as he moved, tapestries shivered, and the stones beneath their feet rumbled.

"Are you by chance threatening a diplomat?" Aidan asked while chuckling.

The redhead continued to move forward, despite recognizing the intense heat that was beginning to rise around them.

"Cook, if you take violent actions against me, I will have to—"

"Mrs. Ashowan, you seem to have my frying pan. I need it back." Fin addressed his mother, his voice hoarse as he ignored Troivack's chief of military.

"Ahh, yes … a frying pan must be quite dear to a mere servant." Aidan chortled to himself, but he stilled when Fin turned his electrifying blue eyes to him.

"Mr. Helmer." The cook didn't even bow his head before he grasped his mother's forearm and guided her away from the fire witch who continued grinning.

"I hope you're ready for that chat, Finlay. Viscountess Jenoure should help motivate you to be a bit more respectful in the near future."

Fin slowly turned around and once again stepped closer to Aidan.

"You will not win here. Even if it kills me, you will lose any war you start with me in my home." Fin's voice echoed with power, and despite the fire witch's confident jeer, there was a hesitancy in his eyes.

"Your emotional reaction is very telling," the fire witch observed, his tone frustratingly light and pleasant.

The castle trembled around them, and Fin's eyes began to glow even brighter, as Aidan suddenly discovered there was less oxygen available to him. He gasped and subsequently raised the temperature in the area even further.

Kate let out a yelp and released the pan in her hand; the iron had flared to a searing temperature and burned her.

"Do you think you will not be punished for this?" Aidan gasped, his attempt at looking cavalier barely successful.

"That's what I want to ask you." Fin's eyes began to fill with lightning as his hand drew out from his pocket and fisted at his side.

"ASHOWAN!"

Fin hesitated, but after a moment he glanced over his shoulder to see Captain Antonio and Mr. Howard making their way toward them.

"The queen would like to inform you of the menu she has planned for this evening," the captain announced, his blue eye steely.

"Ashowan? Not even addressing you properly … you two must be friends," Aidan observed suddenly, a delighted smile lighting his face. "Good. I'm glad my son has at least enough ambition to curry favor with the captain of Daxaria's military. Good day, gentlemen." He bobbed his head briefly before turning toward his chamber, his charcoal eyes only briefly flitting to Kate. In the moment they locked gazes, however, a keen sense of dread filled the healer.

Once the chamber door was closed, Fin dropped his angered stare to his mother. His frying pan flew into his hand, and he began striding away past the captain and assistant.

"Ashowan, we need to have a word with you and your mother, if you could please follow us," Mr. Howard announced, making Fin halt in his tracks. The assistant's shoulders were tense despite his calm voice, indicating that he was more than a little intimidated by the rumbles of power he had felt before.

Giving a single nod, Fin waited for the others to catch up to him before he continued walking. All the while he seemed unable to look anywhere but directly in front of himself.

The group moved back to the second floor and entered the council room, where Annika sat, across from the king, looking incredibly grim.

"You were right, Viscountess. Mrs. Ashowan was waiting for Mr. Helmer by his chamber," Mr. Howard announced disapprovingly.

Kate shot a frown at Annika, but she was immediately distracted by the king's equally somber gaze.

"That was unwise, Mrs. Ashowan. Though I must ask, Fin, why was the castle shaking?" The monarch's expression clearly indicated that, despite inquiring, he had already theorized what had happened.

"I went to retrieve my mother. Hannah said she had loaned her my frying pan, and when it comes to Hannah, it means there is a chance for violence," the redhead explained, his voice flat as he failed to move his gaze from Annika. At a glimpse he could tell she was deep in thought, but he did his best not to show his concern in his face. "The castle shook because I was being a mediator to two former spouses."

Deciding not to delve too much into what Fin had just informed them all, the king moved on to other matters.

"We have some good news today I'm glad to say ... Lady Jenoure believes that Mr. Helmer has no inkling about your relationship. So that is one potential catastrophe off our plates. However, before we delve into more details, Mrs. Ashowan, I am ordering you to stay away from Mr. Helmer. He is not only dangerous, but he might also learn more than he should if too many of us talk with him. Our strength in this war is that, at this point, we hopefully have more information than Troivack does regarding their numbers and methods."

Fin could tell his mother was displeased, but she said nothing when she bobbed her head in understanding.

"Good. Now, everyone else please leave the room. I must talk with these two." Norman gestured toward Fin and Annika.

After everyone had bowed and exited, the witch slowly rounded the table to join Annika's side, his brow furrowed as he continued silently worrying.

Norman took his time before speaking, clearly dreading what he had to say. "Lady Jenoure believes that she has dissuaded Mr. Helmer from suspecting her being the spy. That means he is looking elsewhere, which could end up being beneficial to protecting the viscountess if we act carefully. But I think it is time we begin to prepare for the worst-case scenarios we have previously discussed—just in case."

"I've already said I will go. Now that they don't think I'm a spy, there is a greater chance I won't be killed, and if I'm forced to wed I can find legal loopholes after the fact with your help, Your Majesty," Annika interjected firmly while bowing her head to the king.

Fin's blood ran cold as he turned and stared appalled at Annika.

"If Fin and I wed before I go on board the ship, once I return to Troivack, I can reveal the fact and use my connections to find a way to flee back to Daxaria without them having any legal recourse … though it will most likely make me a target for more assassination attempts. The tricky part would be convincing the king to hold off forcing a marriage on me until later—"

"You are not leaving. I'll go."

Annika finally met Fin's eyes, and he could see the depth of her strength when she said, "Fin, your father most likely intends to kill you. You will be powerless to stop him. If I go, I can play dumb for a little while longer and buy us time. I have allies there. You have no one."

"No. You are not going, and that's final." The cook's voice was growing hoarse, and Annika's stare flashed in anger.

"This is not for you to just unanimously decide, Fin."

"While I agree with Lady Jenoure that it is not your decision to make, Mr. Ashowan, I concur that it should be you who goes with Mr. Helmer if either of you do," Norman announced quietly, drawing the couple's attention. The king had never seen a more murderous expression on the viscountess.

"While Mr. Helmer clearly wants you to join him on the ship, it isn't clear whether or not he truly intends to kill you. Furthermore … if you were to hint that you, Mr. Ashowan, were in fact the spy with allies in Troivack …"

"No!" Annika stood up, her palms pressed flat against the table, her face worryingly pale. "I will not let you force him to sacrifice himself!"

"If I do this …" Fin started slowly.

"You are not doing anything! We already discussed how it was obvious that Fin being out of the way is integral to Aidan's plans," Annika burst out, yet she couldn't meet his gaze.

Fin continued his initial question as though she hadn't said a word. "If I do this, will you consent to letting us marry?"

The king raised an eyebrow, then proceeded to smile sadly. "I would, yes. However, Mr. Ashowan, while I may have suggested this, it is entirely within your right to reject the offer. The reason I believe you should be the one to make this venture is that the Troivackian king's notoriety for killing traitors and those who disobey him makes it almost a certainty he will cut down anyone of Piereva blood. The Troivackian king has no grudge against you. Additionally, Lady Jenoure's informants during this war will be more important than ever, and to lose them would weaken us far too much to ignore. I am deeply sorry, Mr. Ashowan. I make this request knowing it isn't fair to you, but only with the greater good in mind."

"Will you let us marry *before* I leave?" Fin's direct, somber stare cut through Norman brutally. He knew logically there were laws and practices that would protect the house witch while amongst enemies, and yet … even he had a bad feeling about it.

"I will. The council will be presented with a list of your heroic deeds and future commitments to magically protecting the castle during the war, and that should be enough to persuade the nobility to accept you once we reveal the two of you are wedded."

"HE IS *NOT* GOING!" Annika boomed one final time before she turned and stormed from the chamber, her lack of courtesy to her king a strong indication of how upset she was.

After she fled, Fin addressed the king quietly.

"We need to move quickly, Your Majesty, and negotiate terms with Mr. Helmer. Otherwise, Annika will do something clever and drastic, but put herself in danger."

The king nodded knowingly; the redhead was entirely correct.

"Normally I wouldn't even suggest such a plan, Mr. Ashowan … but it is not just Charles who is in jeopardy now. Annika's sister-in-law and infant niece are now in danger as well … and you are the safest person to send."

"I understand, Your Majesty." Standing stiffly, Fin turned and walked toward the council room door to have a guard summon Mr. Helmer and Mr. Howard to draft the terms of exchange.

With his hand on the handle, Fin hesitated and turned around once more.

"I'm going to do my best to return, but if I don't … please protect Annika and my mother, Your Majesty."

Norman bowed his head and rose while placing his hand over his heart. "I, Norman Reyes, vow to protect and ensure a good life to your loved ones should you not return home, Mr. Finlay Ashowan. Rest assured, though, I will do everything in my power so that I never have to carry through on this promise."

Satisfied, Fin swallowed down a hard lump in his throat, then opened the door. "Guards, please summon Troivack's chief of military and Mr. Howard immediately. It is on behalf of His Majesty."

Norman stared at Fin's back and felt a swell of respect and sorrow for the man fill his chest. Despite knowing he had his own plans to ensure as little harm as possible would befall Fin, it didn't minimize the guilt he felt over causing him such distress.

I wish it hadn't come to this. I'm sorry, Lady Jenoure … but you fell in love with a good and honorable man.

CHAPTER 11
LIGHT IN THE DARKNESS

Katelyn Ashowan, Lord Fuks, Mage Lee, Lady Jenoure, and the captain all sat in silence in Fin's cottage for a long time.

Annika was frowning deeply, her eyes lost in thought, while silently wringing her hands.

"If only we had more time to figure this all out ... Or if only we knew the Zinferans would be here in time for us to be able to act confidently in this whole situation without worrying about numbers ..." Antonio lamented gravely.

"It could be that Troivack needs more time as well and won't risk endangering Fin while he's aboard the ship ... I understand His Majesty's reasoning that King Matthias has no reason to be hostile toward Fin as opposed to Lady Jenoure," Lord Fuks mused carefully.

"It could also be useful if Mr. Ashowan is able to learn anything while on the boat. I'll say this for that witch: he has the strangest luck in getting out of trouble," Mage Lee added while shooting Annika a reassuring stare.

"I'm sure His Majesty will try to take every precaution to ensure he is returned in one piece ... Though ... does anyone else get the feeling that the king became very invested in Mr. Ashowan becoming the ambassador rather suddenly?" Lord Fuks asked abruptly.

His words made Annika pause, though she had to remind herself that no one present knew anything about her valuable work as the king's spy.

"How has this war not already grown more hostile? Thousands of Troivackians were found illegally living in the kingdom with violent intent," Kate's voice rasped, making Antonio reach under the table and hold her hand.

"We are only reporting the unit of men under Lord Piereva's orders. Therefore, we maintain some element of surprise, and we can delay the physical fighting beginning so that our Zinferan aid might arrive in time to bolster our forces," Lord Fuks began in an oddly composed manner while addressing his present company. "We know that some of the Troivackian units will fail to contact their superiors, and Matthias will grow suspicious, but ... if he doesn't know exactly how many men remain hidden, that is to our advantage. Instead, for now, we lay the blame on Lord Piereva, and take this extra time to prepare," the earl concluded.

"I suppose there is nothing we can do but put our trust in His Majesty, and Mr. Ashowan ..." Mage Lee acquiesced with a halfhearted sigh.

"We will wait to see what comes of the meeting where the legalities are drawn," Lord Fuks agreed. "My bet, though, is that perhaps our king has a trick up his own sleeve. At least I'd like to hope so."

The group then fell once again into quiet as they all speculated how much their lives were going to change over the coming days ...

Fin sat across from his father, whose pleased expression was barely concealed as he sat with his arms folded, Mr. Howard on his right and the king seated at the head of the table.

"Mr. Helmer, Mr. Ashowan will be with you on your ship for no more than a week. During that time, I expect a prompt report on the negotiations pertaining to Lord Charles Piereva and his family. Once it is proven they have not partaken in any treason, we expect proof of their well-being."

Aidan bowed his head gracefully in agreement.

"Our Royal Cook will be treated amicably, and it is expected that he will return unharmed and alive. Every day of the journey, he will write a letter that is to be sent, before, during, and after the meeting regarding Charles Piereva. Do I make myself clear?" Norman's steely gaze bore into the fire witch, but the man didn't notice as his attention had already moved to his son, whose deadened stare bore no emotion.

"Yes, yes. I'm sure Finlay's educational background as well as his filial alignment with myself will help matters run smoothly."

"Your ship is not to leave Daxarian waters. The Troivackian king is only permitted to cross our borders for a day to dissolve these issues. Following that time, Mr. Ashowan will be returned here promptly."

"Goodness, Your Majesty, you must think my son to be in grave danger in my care."

Norman didn't respond and instead waited for the fire witch to sign the contracts Mr. Howard laid before him.

"Now, despite the council not being present, I would like to know how this change of events affects your punishment toward Earl Phillip Piereva."

Aidan gave the slightest of shrugs before giving a very chilling answer, "I'll put him to death myself after lunch. Bury him in a pauper's grave or burn him to ash. He is no longer of any consequence to Troivack and he leaves no widow or children."

"You have no remorse for the loss of one of Troivack's courtiers?" the king asked curiously.

"I think our next great concern should be the safety of Lord Charles Piereva. Don't you? Now, I must return to my ship to send word to His Majesty about these changes. Finlay, I will see you the day after tomorrow. That should be enough time for you to find replacements for your position in the kitchens."

The cook didn't give any indication he had heard his father's farewell, and he continued to stay catatonic until the door latched behind the fire witch and Mr. Howard, who escorted him from the chamber, casting the occasional irritated glance at him. There was a moment of silence between the monarch and his loyal subject laden with meaning to the point where words would have felt burdensome.

"Well, Mr. Ashowan ... would you like to ... bathe before your wedding?" Norman's voice was quiet, but kind.

At long last, Fin dropped his chin to his chest, then raised it again with a sad smile on his face.

"What, you don't think every noblewoman wants a sweaty groom who smells like turned meat?"

The king chuckled. "Tonight, Mr. Ashowan, you will bathe while being served by my personal stewards who will keep the marriage a secret, and you will spend the night in Lady Jenoure's old chamber together."

"With all due respect, Your Majesty ..." Fin began slowly, a funny blush beginning to spread across his face. "Could I perhaps have a chamber that is not between yours and the princess's nursery?"

Norman couldn't stop his laughter then, while the redhead grinned sheepishly.

"Fair enough ... I imagine if Eric catches wind he might take it upon himself to visit ..."

"Oh Gods." Fin covered his face while Norman proceeded to laugh even harder.

After a few minutes the two men eventually settled down to an amicable quiet.

"Lady Jenoure is going to be furious with you," the king noted a little more somberly.

"I know ... After hearing all the precautions, it seems a bit more likely that I will come out of there alive, but Your Majesty ... are you still not going to tell me what your backup plan is?"

"Sorry, Fin, only the queen and I can know at this time, but rest assured, I'd never have taken this gamble with your life if I wasn't fairly confident about the safety nets in place. While aboard, keep your ears out for where they intend to attack first. Austice is a military city and we have the high ground, so it isn't a wise decision on their part. Xava makes the most sense, but even that isn't easy to access given its relatively small harbor."

The redhead nodded in agreement, then with a sigh, he stood and bowed to his king.

"If Your Majesty could tell me where I might find that washtub, I will first go inform my aides of the change of plans and send word to Viscountess Jenoure's estate to have them prepare a few items."

"Of course, I will communicate with my stewards to prepare you a bath in one of the east wing chambers. Unless of course you'd like Ruby to assist you?"

Fin's immediate wince and rejuvenation of color in his face set King Norman off laughing yet again, the former darkness of the day gradually beginning to shift back toward the light ... if only for a brief interlude of time.

Phillip Piereva sat in his cell, eyes fixated on the dark stone floor.

His king would not abandon him like this ... After he had supplied Matthias with men, funds, and even his military expertise in preparation for the war that was to break out soon ...

No, all he had to do was sit and wait to be freed.

Once he was released, he would check on the hidden men, and he would also find his traitorous sister.

How he could kill her discreetly was the next matter ... then again, once the war broke out, there'd be no reason to have to be subtle about it.

"Lord Phillip Piereva, Mr. Aidan Helmer, Troivack's chief of military, is here to inform you of your sentence that was agreed upon as a representative of King Matthias, and by King Norman himself," an imperial voice rang out.

Phillip's mood blackened, as his eyes rose and he beheld the fire witch. When he slowly rose from his cot, his chains jangling around his ankles as he moved, he noticed then how uncanny the similarities were between Troivack's chief of military, and the Royal Cook ...

"Good day, Lord Phillip." Aidan greeted him with a small eyebrow raise.

The earl prowled over to the bars, his lips nearly curling into a sneer.

Observing this with an unimpressed tilt of his head, Aidan turned toward the guards and the king's assistant, Mr. Howard, who, even in such circumstances, was buried in paperwork. The man looked incredibly stressed, his hair sticking up in strange angles and dark bags under his eyes ... whatever could be so important when they were there to execute a member of nobility?

"Might I have a moment alone with Lord Piereva before informing him of what has happened?" Aidan asked over his shoulder, his eyes not leaving the earl's face.

"No, you may not; I'm a busy man, Mr. Helmer," Mr. Howard barked while barely glancing up from his book.

Due to the assistant's absorption with his work, he failed to notice Aidan's sinister glance in his direction.

"Very well then," Aidan leaned forward and dropped his voice to a whisper so that only he and Phillip might hear. "You should have been more careful, Piereva. If you hadn't been so insolent to me, I might have fought harder against this sentencing."

Phillip frowned as he opened his mouth to object, but the fire witch had stepped back and idly put his hands into his pockets while beginning to speak.

"I, Aidan Helmer, Troivack's chief of military, delegate for King Matthias Devark the Sixth, have agreed to sentence Earl Phillip Piereva to death. He has been found guilty on accounts of assault and harassment of Daxaria's nobility as well as common civilians. He is also found guilty of the more serious crime of illegally smuggling soldiers onto Daxaria's shores with the intent of waging battle on the kingdom's civilians and crown."

"HOLD ON A MOMENT!" Philip roared, incensed at what the fire witch was recanting in a rather casual tone.

"Would if I could, Earl Piereva, but the king's assistant did just inform me he was a busy man. So without further ado, I will be your executioner." Aidan Helmer held up his hand, and a burst of flames roared in his palm, making both the guards and Mr. Howard leap back in alarm.

"Mr. Helmer, you could have warned us!" Mr. Howard spluttered, his face pale from the shock.

"Ah, did that startle you? I merely meant to try and carry out this meeting as expediently as possible for you. I suggest you leave if you are uncomfortable with this method of execution." Aidan's black eyes glinted in satisfaction at everyone's fearful reaction.

"NOW SEE HERE, THIS MAN WAS A PART OF THE—" Lord Philip began to shout while pointing at the fire witch, the earl's eyes wide and wild as he registered that he was about to be burned alive.

He never got to finish whatever it was he was intending to say, however, as Aidan proceeded to shoot a stream of flames at the man, silencing him as he leapt back.

Mr. Howard darted out of the room, his stomach roiling as Lord Phillip Piereva's shouts of agony echoed around the Lendenhoff Holding ... The guards weren't far behind him, though duty dictated they remain close by.

As the assistant stumbled away from the scene frantically, his mind filled with horrified panic, one thought managed to press its way through with great clarity.

While I may not be Finlay Ashowan's biggest fan ... I sincerely hope he returns unscathed from his time with that monster ...

Mr. Howard then suddenly stopped himself from taking another step; he took a steadying breath before glancing at the paperwork in his arms that he had been furiously making his way through moments before.

It was paperwork that was to make the Royal Cook an official noble ...

Clutching the book tightly, a steely resolve settled in the assistant as he glanced back over his shoulder toward the cell in which Lord

Piereva was dying a most painful death; Mr. Howard decided then and there that despite Finlay Ashowan being annoying, troublesome, and at times, an arse …

He was proud to be the one helping ennoble the house witch who had grown up to be good and honorable, despite his father being Aidan Helmer.

CHAPTER 12
PEACHES AND WHISKEY

Annika strolled out of Fin's cottage wearing a cloak and being blocked from view by the three men surrounding her. Kate Ashowan had stayed behind, saying she needed time to herself while earning a sad, worried gaze from her betrothed. All words of comfort that had been offered had seemed to fall upon deaf ears.

By the time the viscountess had returned to the castle, the men strategically peeled off from her one by one as they moved in the most natural way possible, while she also removed her cloak.

Annika had just arrived in the castle courtyard and was on her way toward the staircase to further argue against the king's decision on sending Fin with Aidan instead of herself, when she discovered Clara standing under an archway on the opposite end directing Hannah as well as ... A maid from her own estate?

"Ah, Lady Jenoure. You are to stay the night at the castle under Her Majesty the queen's orders. If you could please go to your old chamber, there is a bath drawn and waiting for you. Your brother was executed not even an hour ago, and she would like you to be nearby."

Annika hid the frown she almost made immediately and forced her calm composure yet again.

Her brother's passing meant surprisingly little to her, but … something was strange …

Following her maid up the stairs to her old chamber, hundreds of questions and worries burned through the viscountess's mind. When Annika eventually made it to her former room and opened the door, she saw that the window had been covered so tightly that the evening sun had been completely blocked out, and a golden fire was the only source of light. Then her eyes fell upon Ainsley, wearing a loose-fitting pale green dress, sitting on the bed wearing a broad smile. A most inviting bath sat waiting in front of the hearth, and all at once, her previous volume of questions and concerns doubled.

"What in the world—"

"I have got to give it to your cook, he seems quite determined to marry you." Ainsley nodded to Clara who had just closed the door behind herself.

Annika's stomach dropped. "What? Your Majesty, you can't honestly expect me to get married so suddenly—"

"Viscountess, everything will be alright," the queen began soothingly. "I promise it will all turn out. Now, is it truly impossible to enjoy your second wedding? I know it may not have been how you envisioned it … I'm sure you planned something massive and elegant—"

"Gods, not at all. I just wanted it small and private," Annika blurted out before realizing that Ainsley was smiling a little too smugly.

"Does his mother know?" The dread in the lady's voice was blatantly apparent.

Clara couldn't resist letting out a small snort that had the queen raising a skeptical eyebrow.

"I believe Captain Antonio will be telling her in another hour after you two have bathed … I understand she must be quite distraught right now at the idea of Fin leaving with Mr. Helmer."

"This news won't help that," Annika bemoaned, dropping her forehead to her hand.

Ainsley chuckled then and stood, crossing over to her friend; placing her hands on the lady's shoulders, she tried again to placate her worries. "Very rarely in life do things happen the way we imagined them. Are you having second thoughts on marrying him?"

"She better not," Clara muttered under her breath as she drizzled one of Annika's favorite oils into the bath.

The viscountess shot her maid a withering stare, but fortunately the queen was focused too intently on her friend's reply to think anything of it.

"I want to marry him, but … not like this. I don't want to marry him because he might die if we wait." Annika sighed. "I know timing-wise this is most likely better in the long run—"

"Why would you say that?" Ainsley raised a quizzical eyebrow.

Clara straightened a little too abruptly with a cough behind her mistress, and Annika immediately wished she could shove the maid right into the tub.

"The war," the viscountess lied easily, when suddenly a scent caught her nose that had her turning swiftly toward her annoyingly bold servant. Ainsley shook her head to herself and moved her attention toward the women unpacking the items from the Jenoure estate.

"Clara, did you happen to get your hands on what I—"

The maid reached into a basket that was set down by the tub and produced the heavenly peach Annika had been craving with every ounce of her being.

Grabbing the fruit and biting into it without thinking about present company, she sighed.

Gods, this is even better than moonshine. The viscountess continued to eat the fruit down to its pit as she slowly moved back over to the bed with Ainsley who conferred with the maids on how Annika's hair could be arranged while they rummaged around one of the trunks they had brought up.

"I take it you haven't eaten today yet?" Ainsley asked laughingly when she watched as Clara wordlessly handed her mistress another peach that she tore into desperately.

"… No, I have not. Wait, what dress am I wearing? Is the one I have on not good enough for a small ceremony?"

"Your betrothed had a specific dress he requested you wear … apparently this made an impression on him at some point." Ainsley moved over to the small trunk that had been brought to the room and lifted out a bright teal silk gown …

It had been the dress Annika had worn on Beltane, when she and Fin went on the walk through the rose maze. Immediately she smiled and started tearing up at the memory of when her relationship with the redheaded cook had first really begun to change.

Fortunately, the room was darkened save for the lit fireplace, and Clara hastily moved in front of Annika, blocking the unseemly sight of her mistress becoming emotional from the queen. The maid covered for this quick move by beginning to untie the front laces of the viscountess's dress.

"Get it together, my lady," Clara muttered hastily before turning back to the queen. "We will bathe her now, Your Majesty."

"Very well. Annika, I will return to lead you to the ceremony; let me know if you need anything else."

Once the door was shut, Annika let out a long breath and wiped an errant tear aside while the maid Hannah turned around with her hands on her hips.

"Right, I've never helped with this sort of thing, but I've scrubbed potatoes until they've glowed. So shall we give it a try?" The petite blonde gestured to the tub in a brisk manner, stunning both Annika and Clara for a moment.

"It's alright, Hannah … er … I honestly do most of the washing myself. Combing out my hair can be quite arduous, though, so perhaps maybe just tend to that today."

The blonde nodded in understanding. "Sounds good. Aside from my own hair, I've only really brushed boys' hair. I have a younger brother you see … well, I suppose I have brushed a horse's mane at one point …"

Clara, to her benefit, wasn't showing any signs of needing to laugh, but Annika wasn't sure how long the woman could last at that rate. For some reason the normally icy maid had grown to be quite the chuckle bucket in recent days …

With a small smile to Hannah, Annika stood and began stripping off the layers of her dress. While she stepped into the tub, Clara and Hannah turned their backs to allow her to get situated in private. Once eased into the water, the viscountess felt the warmth soothe some of the stress and aches from her body.

Her mind started filling with hazy contentment over the simple fact that she was about to marry a man she loved, surrounded by people who genuinely cared for them.

Perhaps it wasn't how she'd wanted it to happen … and she still worried for her brother's family and Fin's safety in the near future, but … Perhaps just for that night … for their wedding … she could just let herself be happy.

While leaning against the cold fireplace of the chamber he had been permitted to use to prepare for his wedding, Fin watched as Sirs Andrews and Lewis worked to fill the bathtub alongside Peter, who seemed even more quiet than before.

"You know you lot don't have to do this. I could magic the water up here and save you all the hassle ..."

Sir Andrews straightened, bucket in hand as he stared at the wall ahead of himself, his expression flat. "I ... completely forgot about that."

The house witch grinned.

"I didn't forget. I just thought it'd be a good excuse to try and have a brief stag party for you," Sir Taylor said as he appeared with the final bucket needed for the tub in one hand, a clean towel over his shoulder, and a bottle of whiskey in his other hand.

Turning with his smile still intact, Fin straightened away from the fireplace while eyeing the bottle.

"Are you all finished with your duties for the day then?" the Royal Cook asked while Sir Taylor uncorked the bottle and passed it to him expectantly.

"We are. Hannah had suggested to the queen that we all might be able to attend your wedding, and Her Majesty was kind enough to agree," Sir Lewis explained while Fin took a gulp of the liquor before passing the bottle to him.

"Gods ... Hannah really made that request directly to the queen?" Sir Andrews shook his head in awe.

"She isn't the same woman she was in the spring, is she?" Sir Taylor grinned.

Fin eyed the large burly knight thoughtfully then, as he reflected on the very first day he had arrived at the castle. "In nearly two seasons you've gone from making her tremble in fear from you all, to her scaring half of the knights should they even look at her inappropriately." Sir Taylor nodded, a brief look of guilt running across his face as he was reminded of his past behavior. "Yes ... I s'pose ... I'd never really known what it meant ... to be good to a woman. Or how it was to be powerless an' terrified ..."

Fin frowned suddenly at the end of the knight's musings. "When were you scared and powerless?"

"Gods, ever since Sir Taylor saw lightning in your eyes that one day we all attacked you ... you know ... the reason why we're all working under you now," Sir Lewis said with a small frown and nod of confirmation to his friends.

"We thought his eggs were getting a bit scrambled if you know what I mean." Sir Andrews tapped his temple. "He kept saying how he could tell you were a frightening bastar—person. Said there was something about you to be scared about. Though Peter wasn't too bad himself at terrifying us …"

Peter blushed scarlet as he then awkwardly accepted the whiskey bottle and took a quick drink that made him cough.

Blinking and feeling a mite uncomfortable himself at learning someone had been terrified of him, Fin shifted awkwardly.

"You weren't in the wrong for showing us our place, cook," Sir Taylor added on firmly when he noted the witch's reaction. "It's what a leader does."

"Well spoken, Sir Taylor."

Everyone's eyes moved up to see none other than Jiho Ryu entering the chamber carrying goblets.

Fin once again broke into a smile at Jiho's arrival. The house witch strode over to the Zinferan and began handing out the cups to everyone. "I wondered if you'd already be on the way to Rollom to welcome the military when they arrive."

"Ah, I was going to, but well … Lord Nam volunteered to try and win favor amongst the courtiers, so he has taken on the task. This has of course come up, as Sir Harris's ennobling is being disputed now thanks to the former Duchess Iones. Though even with the interference, at most his ennobling will be postponed a matter of a couple of days. I've listened to the details of Sir Harris's inheritance, and it is incredibly hard to refute. Meanwhile, it is best for me to stay here while the title and land transfers that make me a baron take place."

"Congratulations again by the way." Fin toasted his friend with the cup that Sir Taylor had just added more whiskey to before addressing the other topic Jiho had mentioned. "Is Sir Harris taking the interference well? I know he and the former duke's family are not on favorable terms."

Wincing slightly at the question, Jiho opened his mouth to respond, when the chamber door opened yet again, revealing the very knight they were discussing.

Sir Harris wore a sunny smile as he stepped into the room.

"Getting crowded in here, eh? Oh! Whiskey! Is that the bottle Lord Fuks sent to us? Pass it over, he only ever buys good quality stuff …"

"Harris," Fin said slowly as the knights hastily abided in getting the man a drink. "How are you doing?"

Draining his cup in a single mouthful, Sir Harris took his time swallowing and answering. "I'll be alright once I get to rub my ennoblement and inheritance in that crone's face. As for Lady Marigold, I'll settle for telling her how I'll turn her old chamber into my nude painting room."

Fin snorted while taking a drink from his cup, and very nearly had the burning liquor come out his nose.

"A … nude … painting room?" Peter couldn't help but ask with a humorous smile.

"Yes, you see, once I am magnificently wealthy, I plan on having every angle of myself painted. Nude. Holding a sword, on a bearskin rug. I will commission four large paintings to hang on each of her old chamber walls."

The men all laughed as they proceeded to once again refill everyone's cups; only Finlay pulled his away. "I better not be drunk when I get married, or I'm pretty sure I'll be spending our first night together in the shrubbery."

Several nods of understanding were passed as Sir Taylor lifted his cup to the air.

"A toast."

Everyone followed suit.

"To the witch who has tormented, taught, an' terrified us all … May your wife do the same to you," Sir Taylor finished, earning more guffaws from everyone before Jiho carried it on.

"To my first friend who gave me honesty and loyalty, may your wife give the same to you."

"Boring!" Sir Harris blurted, then added, "To my cook, who made me realize I could have everything. May your wife be everything to you!"

"That was oddly poetic," Peter noted with a quiet laugh.

"Well, if you're going to compliment someone you should do it in a special way … in fact I've been crafting some odes for Hannah—"

"To the house witch!" Sir Andrews interrupted loudly while shooting a disapproving glance at Sir Harris.

"To our friend!" Peter added with a smile.

"To Finlay Ashowan, who made us better, and stronger men, may your wife do the same to you." Sir Lewis was the last to speak, but he nodded to the redhead wearing a smile that could've split his face in two.

With a final raising of the cups, the men cheered, and together they celebrated not only Fin's marriage, but their bond that made every gain and loss they experienced a shared moment, for better or worse.

CHAPTER 13
NEUTRALIZING NORMAN

The day following King Norman learning about Fin and Annika's betrothal …

Staring off into the distance, his clothes rumpled and his expression cold, the king listened to the messenger as he gave his report regarding the members of Lady Jenoure's household.

"In conclusion, none of them are likely to be the spy," the monarch surmised in a dark tone, which startled the poor knight greatly. The king had never been seen in such a bad mood …

"Y-Yes, sire. Shall I start questioning the kitchen aides?"

"Yes, but I would like you to do so under Captain Antonio's supervision."

"I will request his presence, Your Majesty." The knight bowed and exited hastily; he was not enjoying the new side of his king.

Once the door had quietly latched shut, Norman rested his elbows on his council room table. He was hungry, but knowing that the very man who was causing him grief would have to prepare the meal somehow put him off the idea. Even so, he knew he wouldn't be able to make it through the day with so little sleep, and he was gradually working through his anger enough to summon a servant to fetch him his morning meal, when a small knock on the door interrupted him.

"Enter," Norman barked without much thought, but he found he immediately regretted his tone when Eric hesitantly opened the door, a frown on his face at the unfamiliar tone from his father.

"Sorry … Father … I just …"

Norman schooled his expression quickly and stood up. "Don't ever apologize for wanting to talk to me, come in. Is everything alright?"

Eric looked a little more certain of himself but still closed the door as quietly as possible behind himself, as though nervous to agitate his father.

"Yes, but … Mom wanted me to ask if you've eaten yet."

Norman sighed inwardly. Ainsley knew him all too well …

And that was just the way he liked it.

"I was just about to send for some food, would you like to join me?"

The boy nodded excitedly, his eyes alight with joy. "I was going to go see Fin because it's been a few days, but this is even better! What if we invite him to eat with us?"

Norman struggled to keep his expression neutral. "Mr. Ashowan will unfortunately be quite busy today for a few more hours, so I think it'd be best if we didn't interfere with his work."

Despite keeping his emotions in check, the prince immediately grew wary of his father yet again.

"Is Fin okay?" the boy asked while hoisting himself up into a chair on his father's left.

"He is fine … he …" Norman suddenly eyed his son curiously. "Eric, do you happen to know that Mr. Ashowan is interested in a lady friend?"

His son broke out in giggles that brought an unconscious smile to the king's face.

"Yes! He won't talk about it, but I know he has liked a girl for a loooong time." The boy sighed and shook his head as though he were forty years older than his current age.

Norman slowly sat back down, his interest piqued. "Did he ever tell you who it was?"

"No. He would always turn bright red when I asked him! Like a tomato!" The prince burst out laughing again, and for some reason, the king felt a small part of his stress lessen.

"I see … you really like Mr. Ashowan, don't you?"

"Of course! He's my friend!" Eric announced seriously. "He took care of Lina and Mom, and Kraken stayed with me when I was scared."

" … Yes. Kraken …" Norman's improving mood swiftly deteriorated in the blink of an eye at the mention of the large fluffy kitten. "Were you scared when I told you that Mr. Ashowan is a witch?"

The prince shook his blond curls. "No. Fin helps people, he doesn't hurt them."

The king stilled as that piece of insight sunk in.

It was true … Fin never hurt people. The only times he was a threat was when he was trying to protect those weaker than himself … He was a good person.

A good person, who gave everything he could, had found someone incredible who loved him back. Norman's agitation was reduced greatly yet again, and reaching out to ruffle his son's hair, he decided he needed to see Finlay once more, but this time he would be a little more receptive.

"Go tell the guards that we want some breakfast."

Eric laughed. "Daaad, it's lunchtime!"

Chuckling to himself, the king gestured for his son to get on with his request while leaning back in his chair. Closing his eyes briefly, the monarch wondered if his wife knew what effect Eric would have on him surrounding the matter of her best friend's fiancé … and subsequently if that had been her plan all along …

The father and son had finished their meal peacefully, and it wasn't long after Eric had gone to resume his studies, when yet another knock rang out.

"Yes?"

Lord Fuks entered wearing a strangely mischievous smile.

"Your Majesty, I have summoned the cook for you to question as you requested."

Norman blinked and gave the lord a flat expression. "That was nearly two hours ago. I've already finished speaking with Lady Jenoure. What in the world have you been doing?"

"Well, you see, sire, Mr. Ashowan during our first meeting seemed to find my name … humorous."

Norman groaned outwardly. "Oh Gods, Richard, you know I told you to just punish people like a normal earl. Why in the world do you keep—"

"It's one of the few things that always brings me joy," Lord Fuks explained with a bright smile. "Besides, I chose this punishment with Your Majesty solely in mind."

"What did you ask him to do? Shave his cat? That would definitely improve my mood …" the king half muttered to himself.

"No, no. Nothing quite that insane. Mr. Ashowan, His Majesty is ready to see you!" Lord Fuks called out in a strange singsong tone …

Norman was just beginning to rise from his seat, when Fin literally stumbled through the door holding a bottle of …

"Oh good Gods. Is that absinthe?" the king demanded while leveling Lord Fuks with a disapproving gaze.

"He got tired of my whiskey, a fact I am still trying not to be offended about." The earl sniffed a little as Fin bowed and nearly fell over.

"How in the world is getting the cook drunk helpful to me?" Norman asked as the redhead then managed to sidle over to one of the chairs and plunk himself down gracelessly.

"He's damn funny when he isn't thinking about what he should say." Lord Fuks grinned and slowly joined Fin and the king at the table. "Mr. Howard will be joining us shortly with the list of questions Your Majesty has compiled. We've also added a few of our own."

Eyeing Fin warily, Norman gradually moved back into his own seat.

Fin, on the other hand, appeared to be having trouble keeping his eyes open.

"Mr. Ashowan, are you aware of where you are?" the monarch asked tiredly.

"I'm … here … with Your Majesty," the witch slurred heavily.

"Yes. Are you capable of answering my questions?"

"I've answered … the first two … haven't I?" The cheeky smile on Fin's face had Norman closing his eyes as he silently begged the Gods for patience.

"Mr. Ashowan, I understand your current state isn't your fault; however, this is indeed a serious meeting. So please do your best to—"

"I'm serious! I promise!" the cook interrupted while slapping his hand over his heart in an effort to look more somber.

"… Good. I would like to first ask before the rest of the council arrives, why in the world does your cat only attack *my* ankles?"

Fin blinked and struggled to focus his gaze on the king. "He bites you?"

"Yes! Not enough to draw blood— But it is horribly annoying. He springs out from under my bed at the worst moments, has pooped in my shoes, stolen bites from my meals, paws at the door to my chambers at all hours of the day, and—"

Lord Fuks let out the smallest of snorts but quickly regained his composure after the deadly look the king shot him.

"Furthermore, on more than one occasion he has seated himself on my crown's pillow as though waiting for me to place it on his own damn head! The viscountess told me you have developed an ability to talk to him, so can you please demand why he is insistent on being such a nuisance?!" Norman pounded his fist on the table, startling Fin into sitting up straighter.

"Erm … I can call and ask him?" Fin offered while clearly at a loss at what else to say.

"Please do!" Norman snapped aggressively.

Fin closed his eyes, and was quiet for a moment, but when his eyes did open again, he nodded.

"He shooould get here in an hour or less …"

Norman grunted, but as if on cue Captain Antonio, Mage Lee, and Mr. Howard entered the council room.

After everyone had bowed, and stepped forward, Mr. Howard suddenly hesitated and narrowed his gaze when he stared at Fin.

"Why is the cook drunk?"

"Lord Fuks thought it'd humor me. It does not," Norman announced while giving the earl another disgruntled glance that didn't seem to bother the elder in the slightest.

"Am *I* allowed to drink then?" the assistant grumbled while plunking the book and inkpot in his hands down rather forcefully.

"Captain, I will listen to what you have found regarding Mr. Ashowan's aides after this meeting. Now, I need to discuss with all of you, what in the world we are going to do with our cook." The king ignored Mr. Howard's comment and fixed them all with a cool expression.

"Well, once Kate and I are married, I can name him my heir. Perhaps we move forward my ennobling and giving me the title of baron? While I don't think the other courtiers will take exception before the war, they may comment on the speed with which it transpires," Antonio began patiently.

"I'm aware, Captain; however, I want to hear more from Mr. Ashowan on what his plan was before you fortunately took a liking to his mother."

Norman turned to the cook who he then realized had slumped over in a dead sleep.

The captain kicked the redhead under the table.

"Bay leaves!" Fin burst out as he jolted awake.

Norman rubbed his temples slowly as a small headache began to build.

"Mr. Ashowan, how did you and the viscountess plan on making your relationship acceptable?" Mr. Howard repeated the king's question, sensing that the monarch was already on his last nerve.

"Aaa ... nnika said I'd get knighted before the war ... an' then ... I'd do ... good stuff. Good things, and ... and, yeah."

There was a thick silence that followed the poor explanation.

"Mr. Ashowan, did you seduce the viscountess hoping to elevate your position and wealth?" the king eventually managed.

"Nooo! She ... she kept ... bothering me. Then *she* kissed *me*! I said no ... but then ... aides and Jiho were saying, right, you know?"

The captain let out a long sigh. He had a hunch this was not one of Lord Fuks's better ideas.

"I will take that as a no." The king stared at Fin who smiled pleasantly back at him with fluttering eyelids.

"How did you propose?" Mage Lee suddenly burst out.

It was Mr. Howard's turn to groan. Everyone knew the old man was strangely obsessed with weddings.

"I asked her, an' then ... and then you showed up!" Fin pointed and laughed at Lee.

Everyone turned to the mage who was quick to hold his hands up defensively. "I went to ask Fin to come back after the food poisoning event."

A collective shudder passed through the group at the painful memory of the event.

Before anyone could stop him, the mage continued his original line of questioning.

"What do you mean you 'asked her'? Did you get down on one knee? Did you give her flowers? Cook her the best meal of your life?"

"No"—Fin shook his head dramatically—"I just said we were ... we were being stupid and should get married."

The tiniest laugh of astonishment that followed his explanation was from none other than the king.

"The viscountess agreed to marry you with that proposal? Gods, she must be quite fond of you," Mr. Howard announced in disbelief.

"It surprised me, too ... she bought me tunics!" Fin explained helplessly.

"So you're saying that the most beautiful woman on the continent wore you down so that you could start courting and decided to marry you after you just outright asked her? Gods, I knew the maids found you attractive, but that is ridiculous!" Mr. Howard's sickened expression made Norman press his lips together to contain a laugh.

"Mr. Ashowan," Once the king had regained his composure, he decided to try and move on to his next question. "Is there anything specific your father has said to you that makes you think he is aware of your relationship?"

Fin's expressive face fell flat as his gaze moved to the council room table, his mind clearly trying to fumble its way through coherent thoughts. "He asked if I was married … an' said that I'd wanna talk to him soon … which he said after talking with Ani-*hic*-ka …"

The men's jovial moods shifted immediately as the cook was suddenly reminded of the weight on his shoulders.

"I really … dunno for sure … but … I wanted to consider the possibility 'cause … 'cause … I can't mess up with her. I jus' wanted to cook. I like cooking. I didn't know how thingsss would … work out. She's the … the uh … the planner, but with my … father … I don't want it getting … messed up. I have to protect her … so *I'm* going on the ship … an *I'm* going to haffta be noble and not cook …" Fin was trying his hardest to make coherent sentences, and it was very obvious to everyone present.

Norman straightened in his seat, an idea brewing in his mind.

"Mr. Ashowan, I had once asked you to view Austice as your home … and you announced that it was not possible. If you are made a viscount alongside Lady Jenoure, you would be given duties to perform as a noble … You would be responsible for your estates and tenants, but you would also bear responsibility to your kingdom …"

"That's right," Lord Fuks jumped in, a glint in his eyes. "We all have duties to perform as nobles in service of the public. Yours could be, say … protecting Daxaria."

Fin slumped back in his chair, his entire body slanted a little too far to the left as his eyes became lost in thought for a while.

"So you're sssaying … protectin' the entire country would be … my … responsibility?"

"Yes," both Lord Fuks and the king said in unison.

"The problem … with … that … isss-us- is I might die really, *reaaally* quickly."

Everyone was stunned into silence at the casual declaration.

"Why in the world would you die?" Antonio demanded gruffly.

"Well … when someone iss intensely afraid … or hurt … I can sense it. I can … even see some images to know where … they are. If I was to protect ... everrryone? Especially during a war where no one feels 'at home' an' I can't refill my power ... I'd use up my magic too quickly, and die. Though it isssn't a bad idea ... if I die while casting a shield it'd become a curse, and protect ... the kingdom for ... forever."

"You dying while using up your magic makes a curse?!" Mr. Howard exploded in great alarm.

"Yeah ... though it can be unpredictable, which is ... why it'd only be an ... an okay option." Fin slurred and shrugged his shoulder before uncorking the absinthe and taking another quick sip.

"Gods, the more I learn about witches, the more I understand why people are scared of them," Mr. Howard breathed while glancing at the king nervously.

Norman said nothing for a moment, but he began to stroke his beard pensively.

"I feel like the ability to hold a war that has as little bloodshed as possible is within our grasp ... we just have to find insurance on Finlay returning from the ship ..."

CHAPTER 14
WEDDING A WITCH

Fin was finishing drying himself off from his bath when the door to the guest chamber opened, forcing him to hastily cover himself with the towel in his hand.

"Pardon the intrusion," Mr. Howard said, entering with two stewards behind him. One carried a small trunk, the other carried a razor and a dark red velvet box.

"What is this about?" Fin demanded immediately while shifting away from the men self-consciously.

"Well, as much as I'm sure you don't care about getting married in trousers and a tunic covered in flour and other questionable liquids, I think Viscountess Jenoure is already settling when it comes to you, so let's not remind her of the fact, hm?" The assistant cast the redhead a bored expression without showing any reaction to his bare chest before waving to the steward with the razor in his hand.

"Now, let's fix up that face of yours. His Majesty's stewards managed to find a tailor in Austice who had a tunic already made that should fit you. Of course you are being ennobled before the ceremony as well so we also have a cape that—"

"I'm getting ennobled before the wedding?" Fin blinked in astonishment.

The assistant let out a huff. "Of course. Can you imagine the shame if the magistrate reading the rites had to say the phrase, 'Do you, Royal Cook, take Viscountess Jenoure of Daxaria to be your lawfully wedded wife?'"

Fin stilled.

The reality of the day suddenly sunk in as the king's assistant continued watching him glibly.

"I'm … getting ennobled … and married …" All color had drained from Fin's face, and sensing the potential danger of this, Mr. Howard sprang into action.

"Yes, and good Gods, man, keep it together. You have no idea how remarkably lucky you are. If you ruin this now—"

"I'll still have you, won't I?" Fin asked faintly before cracking a smile.

"Seeing as you are calm enough to make such tasteless jests, I take it you are feeling just fine," the assistant snapped while ignoring the steward's interested glances behind his back.

"So where is the ceremony happening?"

"The center of the rose garden is being vacated as we speak. It made the most sense given that our king and queen often go there for their intimate dinners. No one will suspect anything amiss. We will sneak you and your mother in the long way from around the back of the castle to avoid any unwanted attention. We are taking a great risk by simply going through with this wedding and not running it by any council members, but once again, His Majesty seems to have some other motive in all this."

Fin nodded, but then noticed the razor nearing his throat and immediately stopped moving.

"It's a pity I can't have Eric attend," Fin said, attempting to change the subject to take his mind off even more stressful happenings that would come at a later time.

"We've discussed this, and an eight-year-old doesn't know when to stop talking. By the way, have you thanked Lord Ryu yet? Remember, if he hadn't come up with such an elegant solution after the dukedom title was taken from Lord Nam, your betrothed would most likely be marrying *him* tonight."

Fin fought the urge to smile as the blade moved closer to his mouth.

"If I'm honest, I'm surprised my ennobling is happening so quickly; Sir Harris has been attending meetings day and night … He just told us about the duchess making things difficult as well …"

"Yes, well, he didn't seduce a viscountess and isn't about to go aboard an enemy ship as an ambassador." Mr. Howard eyed the steward and gestured to the man that he needed to move the razor closer to Fin's ear. "His illegitimate birth doesn't help matters, but one way or another, he'll become a duke. Most likely while you're away in fact."

Fin smiled appreciatively at the steward, whom he recognized as one of the main servants who would come to the kitchen to fetch food for the king.

"You'll have your hands full with a noble like him."

"Don't remind me," Mr. Howard murmured while rubbing his eyes. "Don't go thinking you're going to be any better … Honestly … you as a knight would have been chaotic enough, but then somehow you convinced Lady Annika Jenoure to adore you …"

"I told you before, *she* made the first advance on *me*. I just somehow wound up here."

"Like anyone believes that," Mr. Howard sniped while crossing his arms and sidling over to a vacant chair beside Fin.

"It's true, though. Whenever she is involved, things just go her way."

"Did she kidnap her own brother then?" Mr. Howard asked with only a hint of genuine skepticism.

"No, she didn't." Fin fell quiet as the steward began to finish off his work, wiping away the remaining suds and then patting a strange oil on Fin's face.

As he stood, Fin was stunned to see the tunic and vest in the other steward's hands.

The tunic was made of a fine black material, its collar and cuffs embroidered with gold thread. The vest was made of a similar quality material with gold buttons and had edging to match.

"This is … this is far too—"

"Dressing up is not for you, you arrogant arse. It's for your betrothed," Mr. Howard snapped yet again. "Now get on with it! We haven't got all night!"

"We do if you want to join us for our honeymoon." Fin shot the assistant another devilish smile that just about had the man go apoplectic.

Ah, yes. Nothing settled wedding jitters like teasing the snobbish Mr. Howard …

Annika tried not to let her nerves get the better of her when she stood amongst the rose maze that no longer bloomed.

The teal dress had not fit her new figure, though fortunately Clara had managed to block most of the changes from Hannah who seemed all too happy to try hunting down a new dress in Austice with only a little more than an hour until needing it.

"I don't think I've ever seen you nervous," Clara whispered to her mistress, whose blank expression was not at all indicative of her feelings.

"You do know that I'm about to get married for a second time and then have a wedding night where my husband will of course notice some … differences," Annika replied quietly.

"Make sure he has a healthy dose of moonshine beforehand, and he'll just assume there's two of you."

The viscountess was about to bite back in her retort, when Mage Lee appeared from around the corner.

"Everything is ready, my lady. I must say, a spectacular choice for the dress." The elderly man was visibly beside himself.

Annika managed to restrain herself from letting her anxiousness snap at his imposing enthusiasm and instead smiled. "Thank you, Mage Lee."

"Ah, I went to the Royal Botanist and had him prepare this for you." The mage brandished a very large bouquet of flowers at the viscountess who blinked in astonishment at the arrangement of white fragrant blooms.

"That's perfect, thank you." Annika bowed her head dutifully while accepting the beautiful arrangement.

When the elder had disappeared back to the center of the maze, Clara turned to her mistress.

"Well, that'll help cover your cleavage."

Annika rounded on the woman, prepared to issue a rather uncouth chiding, when the maid hastily grabbed the viscountess's arm and tugged her along.

"Come now, have you ever heard of a bride who curses like a sailor?"

The lady opened her mouth, ready to prove that she could be that very bride, when her eyes rested on the sight before her.

The king was seated with his wife under the pergola near the center that had two torches burning bright from their pillars.

Katelyn Ashowan, the kitchen aides, the knights, Captain Antonio, Lord Jiho Ryu, Lord Fuks, Mr. Howard, Mage Lee, and … was that Kraken wearing a red ribbon around his neck? They were all seated on the garden chairs, but the brick pathway lay open to Annika, and at its end stood Finlay.

Annika's breath was stolen from her body when she laid eyes on him.

He looked … noble.

Clad in black head to toe, with only gold edging and buttons on his vest, he wore a cloak clasped with a gold chain. His hair was clean and swept to the side, and for once it didn't have a dusting of flour … His bright blue eyes rested on her, and his cheeks flushed bright with color.

Fin couldn't stop his heart from skipping a beat when he beheld the pale blue gown with its silvery thread in the faint torchlight around the garden.

Annika's hair was unbound, and her jewelry every bit as sparse and tasteful as usual, but the look in her eyes when she saw him … that was what made Fin struggle to stay still.

Fireflies began to drift into the air, lighting the garden even more and illuminating the flowers in bloom around the fountains and benches.

There was music suddenly … Annika glanced around in confusion, but when she caught a glimpse of the crystal atop of Mage Lee's staff lit up, she assumed some kind of particular magic was happening that she didn't understand.

The mage also happened to already be in tears.

Annika bit down on her tongue then and slowly moved toward Fin, whose face then split into a brilliantly warm smile.

Without a hope in the world of stopping herself, she smiled just as brightly back at him.

She hadn't even realized that Clara had released her arm back by the entrance of the maze, and that she was moving on her own.

Once she stood before Fin, he offered her his arm, his blue eyes alight with emotion.

Resting her hand on his arm, Annika took the last few steps and faced the king and queen.

Ainsley was smiling so exuberantly that there was even a hint of tears in her eyes.

The royals' crowns gleamed in the firelight, and as the king stood, he moved the thick velvet mantel over his shoulder and placed his hand on the hilt of the ceremonial sword that hung at his side.

"Mr. Finlay Ashowan of Quildon, please kneel."

Giving Annika's hand a brief squeeze, Fin released her, lowered his knee to the ground, and bowed his head before his king.

"On this day, I, King Norman Reyes, dub thee Sir Finlay Ashowan, the first ever hearth knight to serve the kingdom of Daxaria, and its people. You will carry out your sacred duties with your home and Goddess close to heart, without greed or selfishness. Do you agree to these responsibilities?" The monarch's blade grazed Fin's shoulders and back.

"I do."

Norman sheathed his sword, and Ainsley was the next to stand, holding an ornate golden bowl. Dipping her thumb in the small pool of oil, Ainsley bent down and touched her thumb to Fin's forehead, mouth, and chest.

"The oil of peppermint is the oil representing protection of the Goddess. Your thoughts, words, and heart will all work to serve this higher calling from the Goddess and your king."

Fin said nothing but waited as the queen slowly went and seated herself.

"Sir Finlay Ashowan, you are now to be ennobled under the name Baron Wittica. Your duties are to maintain the balance in your coven and protect your kingdom of Daxaria, your home."

Fin's spine stiffened. He hadn't heard about his official title …

"You will see to the righteous treatment and innovative development of witches and humans working in harmony together to better the kingdom you serve. Do you accept your new title?"

"I do."

Norman nodded regally. "Please rise, Baron Finlay Ashowan Wittica."

There was polite applause as Fin slowly rose and bowed. The king nodded to him briefly before turning and gracefully returning to his seat.

"Now, shall we carry on with the event that truly brings us all here today?" the monarch called out, making everyone burst out in loud clapping cheers and whistles.

"Won't someone hear this commotion in the castle?" Annika murmured to Fin worriedly as he gently took her hand and placed it back on his arm.

"I set a soundproof shield around us. No one else can enter or hear a thing," he explained briefly as Mr. Howard suddenly pulled himself from the audience and mounted the steps to stand before the viscountess and baron.

When Finlay frowned in confusion, the assistant visibly twitched.

"His … Majesty … decided to *permit* me the … the honor of reciting the marriage rites to avoid a magistrate spreading the news."

"Try not to cry during the ceremony!" Lord Fuks called out gleefully, making the assistant tighten his grip on the scroll in his hands. Both Annika and Fin were willing to bet money that he was envisioning clubbing the old earl to death with it.

"Shall we get on with it then?" the assistant managed with a defeated sigh once he clearly decided imagining violence just then was not in his best interest.

When he finally looked upon the couple, Annika smiled beautifully at him, and that seemed to take some of the bluster from the man.

"Do you, Baron Finlay Ashowan Wittica, Knight of the Hearth, vow to take Viscountess Annika Jenoure as your lawfully wedded wife? To honor and cherish, to protect and care for through sun and storms for as long as you both shall live?"

Fin glanced at Annika who was beginning to look more than a little emotional.

"I do."

"Do you Viscountess Annika Jenoure take Baron Finlay Ashowan Wittica, Knight of the Hearth, as your lawfully wedded husband? To honor and cherish, to protect and care for through sun and storms for as long as you both shall live?"

"I do." Annika's grip tightened on Fin's sleeve, and his face felt like it'd be sore for days from his smile.

"We have taken it upon ourselves to prepare rings for the two of you to exchange as a symbol of your commitment to each other." Mr. Howard nodded to Captain Antonio who stood and stepped forward, handing the rings to the assistant before giving Fin a warm smile and an encouraging nod.

Fin easily slid the band onto Annika's finger, and he could tell that it would need to be resized for her … He felt a stab of guilt given that he had not prepared anything for the ceremony …

Annika managed to slip the gold band over his own finger, and Fin suddenly grew incredibly self-conscious of how sweaty his palms were.

"With this marriage, there is a joining of two noble houses, as such …" The assistant couldn't help but let out a small agitated huff. "Baron Ashowan will henceforth become Viscount Finlay Ashowan Wittica Jenoure, Knight of the Hearth."

Fin blinked.

He had been knighted, ennobled twice, and married in less than an hour … even he was moderately taken aback.

"By the power of Their Majesties King Norman and Queen Ainsley Reyes bestowed upon me, I now pronounce you: husband and wife. May your marriage be blessed by the Goddess and Green Man. You may kiss the bride."

Fin turned to Annika, whose entire smile made her appear to have a golden glow about her.

In fact ... there seemed to be a golden glow around himself as well ... but the house witch didn't have a chance to give it a second thought, before Annika grabbed him by the front of his tunic and brought his mouth to hers, kissing him soundly.

As the small crowd of people clapped and cheered, Mr. Howard leaned over to Norman and Ainsley so that only they might hear his words.

"I'm beginning to suspect the cook wasn't lying about the lady making the first move."

Ainsley burst out laughing before reaching over and grasping her husband's hand.

Katelyn Ashowan wept tears of joy that could only be outmatched by Mage Lee who had decided to become a human fountain all on his own.

The kitchen aides were the loudest of the ones cheering, while even Clara let out an impressive shrill whistle.

Everyone laughed and celebrated well into the night, all aware that a different kind of magic was present amongst them. Yet without a word needing to be spared to try and acknowledge it, there wasn't a doubt in anyone's mind that it would be an event that would go down in history for centuries to come.

CHAPTER 15
SUSPICIOUS BEHAVIOR

W ell, you did it."
Fin turned to grin at Jiho, though it was hard to tear his eyes away from Annika, who was in the process of laughing with the queen as the rest of the wedding party were in the midst of dancing and celebrating. The redhead had come over to join his friend after getting his ribs cracked by Hannah and the knights who were liberal with their congratulatory hugs and back slaps. Jiho and Fin sat farther back from the group, sipping wine and sharing an amicable silence, until the Zinferan noble had fixed his old friend with a studious gaze.

"How you managed to convince the king to not only ennoble you but to make you a viscount is beyond me," Jiho announced while shaking his head and sipping from his glass thoughtfully.

"Everyone keeps thinking I've been incredibly persuasive as of late … but honestly, it's just pure dumb luck." Fin shrugged and tilted his head as he watched Annika glance over at him and smile. He raised his wineglass to his new wife in a silent salute.

Jiho eyed his friend, a sudden sober mood settling in his mind. "Do you really think you'll board the ship, meet the king, free her family, and return in one piece?"

Fin's smile froze, then drifted further away until his sincere, weary feelings shone through.

"No. No, I don't. If I'm honest … I just think I'll be lucky to come back alive …"

"I wouldn't be so certain about your fate … your king is a surprising man. He could have some other trick up his sleeve." Jiho's gaze roved over to the monarch who was speaking with Katelyn Ashowan.

"He might, but it depends how determined my father is to burn me to a crisp," Fin explained, his tone turning somewhat bleak.

"I did not create a rift between a Zinferan noble and myself just for you to die pitifully like this." The Zinferan's annoyed tone drew Fin's gaze back to him.

"Pitifully? Jiho, I was knighted and ennobled twice in one night. I got to marry the most beautiful woman on the continent, who also happens to love me. What part of this makes you feel sorry for me?"

Jiho managed a brief laugh before it once again faded to a more serious expression.

"Meeting your end because of a man you bested as a child is the part I'm thinking of …" The Zinferan's dark eyes moved over to the aides and the viscountess's maid who were all still enjoying the music and free alcohol.

"Are you honestly upset to no longer be on friendly terms with Lord Nam?" Fin asked in hopes of holding on to the jovial atmosphere.

"One thing you are going to have to learn very quickly if you do survive on that ship is that half of being successful in politics is getting along with some of the most atrocious people. You're in for a rough few years in my estimation." Jiho swirled the ruby liquid in his cup before taking a healthy drink.

"I'll just have to learn to shut up more often I guess … luckily Annika is the smart one."

"Lucky for you, *very* unfortunate for her." Both men laughed to themselves before settling back into an easy quiet once more. It was a few moments later that Jiho spoke again, his expression far more somber than before.

"Did your king discover who the spy was?"

"How did you know about there being a spy?" Fin turned to face the Zinferan with a frown.

"My dear friend, even I was questioned. Anyone who knew about the two of you had to be, remember?" Jiho reminded with a raised eyebrow.

"Right ... sorry about that. No, His Majesty hasn't told me about what he's learned ... but everyone is here aside from people at Annika's estate, so perhaps there wasn't a spy at all."

The Zinferan noble didn't say anything in response to Fin's speculation, but there was something in his eyes that indicated he disagreed with the notion.

"How did your mother take the news of your hasty wedding?"

Fin smiled somewhat sadly then. "Asked me over and over if I was certain I wanted to go through with it. Then said that I better come back alive and not leave my bride a widow again. After that she cried a good deal. It's amazing that she isn't still sobbing ..."

"That sounds like Kate ..." Jiho looked at his friend, a playful glint in his eyes. "Then again, if you die and leave the viscountess a widow I might have a proper chance with her ..."

A thorny vine from the hedge behind them shot out and jabbed the Zinferan brutally.

"I was making a jest!" he cried out, clutching the back of his head defensively.

"The king will take care of Annika if anything happens to me, but ... if things don't work out with the captain and my mother ... would you be able to check in on her?" Fin's stare was direct and more than a little mournful.

The Zinferan nodded gravely. "You have my word."

"Well, I best go see why my wife hasn't had a proper glass of moonshine; odds are high that she doesn't want to make a bad impression in front of my mother."

"I have heard from Hannah that the two of them are having ... trouble bonding."

"When have you been spending time with Hannah?" Fin asked with renewed interest as he stood up to rejoin the party.

Jiho gave a single shoulder shrug. "Unlike some people, I can keep a secret."

Fin cursed the man out with a laugh before he turned and strode over to his bride who had just turned her beautiful smile to him, making him a little weak at the knees.

Fin grimly clutched his head the morning after his wedding. Why Annika had insisted that he keep drinking moonshine to compete with Jiho he hadn't a clue.

All he knew was his wedding night was incredibly hazy in his memory, a fact that he thought Annika would've been upset about, but she had been awake before he had been, fully dressed and glowing with happiness.

"We can't really leave this room without raising suspicion, so perhaps we could discuss what will happen once you return? Where our primary residence will be after the war, a new wardrobe for you, if you want anything changed in the estates …" Annika rattled off items to discuss while sitting at the small table near the empty fireplace.

Fin looked up at his wife and smiled deviously despite the pain in his temples. "I'd prefer to discuss more immediate plans for the day. Why are you all the way over there?"

"Well, I will have a lot to organize while you are away. I'd prefer hearing your opinion as much as possible. Besides, aren't you in a bit of pain after last night?" Annika gave him a sympathetic smile in hopes of dissuading him from his obvious objective of getting her back out of her dress.

Instead of him acquiescing to her like the viscountess had hoped, the redhead swiftly climbed out of the bed, crossed the room, and picked his wife up.

As Annika spluttered and squirmed in astonishment, Fin proceeded to drop her back on the bed and placed his hands on his hips authoritatively as she hastily fixed her dress and sat up.

"Fin, I know we just got married, but we don't have to—"

"Maybe it's because this was your second wedding that you seem to forget how these things are supposed to go, but it was my first, and I don't intend on letting you forget that until tomorrow morning at the earliest."

Annika's jaw clamped shut as Fin slowly leaned down to kiss her to prove he meant what he said, when a knock on the door interrupted him.

Letting out an annoyed grunt, Fin began looking for his trousers while Annika leapt out of the bed and opened the door a small crack.

With a quick sigh that sounded oddly as though she were relieved, the viscountess found herself staring at Mr. Howard, who looked more than a little embarrassed to be there.

"I need to speak with …" Mr. Howard cleared his throat and looked up and down the corridor before dropping his voice. "I need to speak with the cook. It should be fine for him to be the one to come out."

Annika quickly closed the door and retreated out of view as Fin strode over and wrenched it open. It was clear he was not pleased to be bothered so soon after forming his own plans for the day.

Beaming his wife one final smile, he stepped outside into the corridor and quietly closed the door behind himself.

"Don't look at me like that; you've been given plenty of time this morning." Mr. Howard scowled as the two men began to walk away from the room.

"What is it you want?" Fin asked while keeping his voice low and reaching out with his magic to soundproof the doors they passed in case there were any curious ears that could overhear.

"You have to go to the kitchen and make arrangements for your time away. His Majesty says we must be careful that no one, especially your father, learns of what happened last night."

Fin's shoulders slumped forward as he dropped his chin to his chest.

"Yes, yes, no rest for the wicked, I'm afraid. We will let you and … *her* share the room again tonight, but you will need to leave early tomorrow morning with Mr. Helmer."

"Fantastic," Fin replied wearily.

"So … what are you making us for lunch?"

Fin shot Mr. Howard a flat sardonic stare.

The assistant held up his hands in defeat. "Sorry, sorry … What are you making for lunch, my lord?"

"You're awfully casual about the whole situation. Need I remind you my wife's family is being threatened," Fin pointed out as the duo began descending the servants' stairwell.

"I'm less worried about her family and more about you. Why in the world does even the Troivackian king want you going to negotiate? If it is because they think you are a threat, they will either try to imprison you or kill you outright." Mr. Howard shook his head with a puzzled sigh.

"I knew you cared about me." Fin pressed his hand to his chest and smiled at the assistant who gave him a stern look in return.

Mr. Howard stopped and turned to face the cook, his face once again serious. "There is much to be uncertain and wary of, Lord Ashowan. However, until we know more, this is the safest means of proceeding. We've done our best to protect you legally and otherwise for this endeavor. Just remember, if you fail to save Lord Charles Piereva and his family? It is not your fault. Don't do anything foolish that will get you killed in turn."

Fin wanted to make another flippant comment or jest, but the truth was he already worried about the possibility of returning home and having to tell his wife her only remaining family members had been executed. So all he could do was send a silent prayer to the Goddess for his brother-in-law and his family, gird himself for the very long day ahead of him, and try not to worry about what he could not control.

Norman's cold stare only worsened the bitter silence in the room as he regarded the three bowed heads before him.

Captain Antonio's blue eye was hardened, his arms crossed and his legs braced as he stood next to the king and regarded the three people in front of him.

"You realize the type of man you have betrayed?" the monarch asked quietly.

"Yes."

Two out of three people answered him.

"I will not tell him before he has to leave, but I hope you know how disappointed he will be. He counts you as his friends. Except for you, of course, Karter Dawson," the king remarked without even bothering to look at the Troivackian knight.

One of the other two responsible for the information leak began silently crying.

"Mr. Ashowan will be in charge of deciding your fates when he returns. Regardless of what intentions you might or might not have had, you have betrayed the confidence of your superior. We will hear your full statements once Mr. Ashowan is back with us, and until then you will be isolated in the cells below the castle. I will instruct Ruby to find suitable replacements while you are absent."

The crying one trembled, while Karter Dawson kept his head bowed, and the third individual nodded while swallowing with great difficulty before trying to speak.

"I can only speak for Sir Dawson and myself, Your Majesty, but we … are truly sorry. I swear I did not say the name of the woman Mr. Ashowan was interested in."

"That is enough for now. Unless there is any useful information you have for His Majesty," Captain Antonio growled menacingly.

The three fell silent yet again.

"Captain, please escort them to the cells. Baron Gauva has already been moved, correct?"

"Yes, sire."

With a wave of his hand, Norman dismissed the trio from his sights as he leaned back in his chair and closed his eyes briefly. When he opened them again, he sat staring at the table in front of him, his finger gently tapping its surface as he mulled over the new discovery. The smiling faces of the aides and knights as they cheered for the cook the night before flashed in his mind. Norman remembered how Fin had spoken and jested with them …

I am sorry, Finlay … Even good people make mistakes.

After a few silent moments, a knock echoed out.

"Your Majesty! I have lunch prepared for you," one of the king's stewards called out before opening the door and bringing forward the platter filled with two different kinds of cooled salads and chilled meats with cheese.

Norman waited as his steward set up the meal and filled his goblet with water before bowing and heading back to the door.

"Oh, and, sire, Mr. Ashowan was wondering when his aides Heather and Peter might be returning. He said something about them needing to learn about oil fires?"

Norman's stomach twisted as he turned to face his steward.

"Please tell Mr. Ashowan that I had to reassign their duties today due to the castle being short-staffed."

"Yes, Your Majesty."

Idly picking up his fork, Norman went to dig into the salad, only to find that his hand was lowering on its own accord. His chest aching, the king closed his eyes with a small disappointed breath. He suddenly wasn't feeling particularly hungry at the moment …

CHAPTER 16
FAREWELLS

Fin stared out at the cloudy early morning sky blankly before turning toward his wife sleeping peacefully. His first day married he had spent an annoying amount of time working. Then when he had gotten back to the room, he had been more than a little disappointed to see that Annika had fallen fast asleep, and rousing her was incredibly difficult. At first he had been upset that on his final night she couldn't be bothered to stay awake; however, when he had touched her cheek he was shocked to discover she was burning hot.

She was sick. Which may have been why she had been acting oddly the morning after their wedding ... she most likely was trying not to let on she was unwell. Perhaps she had even felt unwell during the wedding. It certainly would explain why she hadn't accepted any of the drinks offered to her ...

With a long sigh, Fin clambered out of bed and began dressing. It was going to be time to see his father, but first he wished to speak with his mother regarding healing Annika's fever and then the king regarding another small concern of his.

Standing upright, the cook looked at his sleeping wife once more, then turned and quietly left the room.

Making his way down to his cottage, the humidity and smell of rain made Fin smile grimly.

"At least this weather will piss off Aidan …" he mused to himself.

As the cottage came into sight, Fin was pleased to see two armed knights standing guard. The king had allowed Katelyn to stay in the cottage the night before the redhead was set to leave, but even so they did not want to take any risks. Even with Aidan not being on castle grounds …

After giving the two knights a brief nod, Fin walked into the cottage as the first drops of rain began to fall. He was surprised to see his mother already up and seated at the table with her hands wrapped around a cup of tea that had very clearly gone cold. After a brief look at her face, it was apparent Kate hadn't slept well for a few days … A pang of guilt ran through Fin as he turned and closed the door.

"Morning, Mum," he greeted quietly as he joined her at the table.

"Morning." Her eyes met her son's and searched his face for several long moments. "Are you ready?"

"Almost. Annika is running a fever, and I haven't been able to wake her up since last night," he explained as his thumb unconsciously began to stroke the golden ring around his finger.

Katelyn frowned. "That is worrying. I will go check on her once Antonio confirms it is safe for me to go."

"Thanks … I hope … I know you two apparently aren't getting along the greatest, but—"

"It's in the past. She's your wife now, and I will treat her well." Katelyn tried to smile reassuringly, but the corners of her mouth didn't seem to want to obey.

"Mum, please … don't hesitate to ask the people here for help. I know you had only come here to temporarily treat the queen, and wound up getting pulled into everything, but … everyone here … well, they've obviously fallen in love with you …"

Katelyn reached out and clasped her son's hands in her own. Tears welling up in her eyes, she stared lovingly into her son's face, making a firm lump rise in Fin's throat.

"You … are the greatest part of me. I am proud of you, my sweet boy, and I love you more—" Kate's voice broke off as Fin moved his hands to hold hers instead, tears filling and spilling from his own eyes.

"I love you more, than absolutely anyone, or anything. This world … this world did not deserve you," Kate managed to finish before dropping her forehead to their joined hands and allowing the grief to fill her.

Kissing his mother's hands, Fin continued to cry quietly as his heart ached with the love for his mother. The pain he knew he was causing her tore him apart … and he hated that there was nothing he could say or do to make it better.

An hour later, Fin stood in the council room before the king, Captain Antonio, Mr. Howard, Mage Lee, and Lord Fuks. They all wore grim expressions as they regarded the house witch with varying looks of sympathy and regret.

"Your Majesty." Fin bowed. "I heard that Mr. Helmer is on the way from his ship to retrieve me."

"You heard correctly. Are you prepared to depart?" Norman asked while folding his hands loosely over the table.

"Just about … I wanted to talk with Your Majesty about Peter and Heather before I left."

Everyone seated at the table shifted uncomfortably.

"Your Majesty, I'm sure you were trying to be considerate of me by not telling me you found out they were the spies. However, when they didn't return from being questioned, it was relatively easy to guess."

The king gave an apologetic nod of his chin. "Forgive me, Lord Ashowan. I wanted to spare you having to discover their betrayal before facing Mr. Helmer."

"Thank you for your thoughtfulness, sire. However … can I ask that they not be punished too severely?"

Norman's eyebrows shot up. "Were you aware of their actions?"

"I did wonder why Heather was sick so often … and so when we began investigating I did suspect her. Peter, I … I did not foresee … I still do not believe he did so maliciously," Fin managed to say, though it was clear on his face that it still pained him greatly to think about.

Norman let out a long sigh before sharing a brief look with Captain Antonio.

"Heather was a paramour of Lord Piereva before he was arrested. She swears that she only admitted that you went to the ball, but more so because he threatened her when she refused to answer him properly. I think the guilt has been wearing away on her constitution …"

Fin nodded, though he was incredibly surprised that meek little Heather had the gumption to bed Lord Piereva …

"Peter's case is even more troubling … He has formed a relationship with a Troivackian knight visiting here by the name of Sir Karter Dawson. Apparently, Peter relayed that you were seeing a woman you were in love with. Karter alleges that he did share this information, but nothing more. Apparently he has had to have been isolated from the other Troivackian knights because they've taken to beating him in the cells for his betrayal of them. I'm given to understand Karter and Peter are still in a relationship and that this knight is looking to … avoid taking part in any hostile actions toward Daxaria as a result."

Fin nodded. "It sounds to me like the most they shared was gossip. Lady Jenoure's name was never mentioned."

"Ashowan," Mr. Howard called out suddenly.

Fin looked to the assistant expectantly.

"No, not you. You called the viscountess Lady Jenoure. Her name is Lady Ashowan now. Though both your official titles when conducting noble business would be Viscount and Viscountess Jenoure as it is still a noble house …"

Fin stared dumbly at the man before managing to give a faint smile.

"Just want to make sure you get it right after the amount of paperwork it took to—" Mr. Howard's complaint was silenced by the looks of chastisement every other member of the inner council wore.

"Right, well … I'll remember to refer to my wife properly from now on … Speaking of, I would like to go check on her one final time before saying farewell if that is alright, Your Majesty."

"Very well, but I recommend you hurry. We have to smuggle the viscountess out of here and bring her back in a carriage to make it look as though she is coming to thank you for going to save her family members."

Fin bowed. "Your Majesty, thank you for going through all these lengths for us."

"These lengths are not just for you, Lord Ashowan. They are also for the innocent lives we are aiming to save … so … Rise."

Fin did so, his chest tightening as he stared at the look of pride in the king's eyes.

"Hold your head up, Lord Ashowan. You are my comrade, and my friend, and soon the world will know how much you have done for your kingdom and home."

Fin managed a half-morose smile before he inclined his head in thanks, suddenly too overcome with emotion to speak the gratitude he felt in that moment for his monarch.

~~~~~~~~~~~

When Fin opened the chamber door of the room he had shared with Annika since their wedding, he was momentarily stunned by what he saw.

His wife was fully dressed in a long purple gown that appeared a little too loose on her, with a white cloak clasped around her shoulders, and she was doubled over what looked to be the chamber pot that had been moved to the table.

"Gods!" Fin rushed into the room, not caring that he slammed the door behind himself as he reached Annika just in time for her to vomit.

Gathering up his wife's silky black hair in his hand, he proceeded to rub her back as she emptied the contents of her stomach. When it seemed as though she had finished, Fin went over to a pitcher of water that sat at the bedside gathering condensation in the heat and poured her a goblet of water.

Once she had rinsed her mouth and successfully swallowed some water, Fin watched as she slowly seated herself. Her complexion was still sickly, but her eyes looked clear, which was a good sign.

"Why didn't you tell me you were unwell?" Fin moved over to her and rested his palm against her forehead, only to discover she was still incredibly fevered.

"I didn't want to worry you before you left," Annika lied as she used the back of her sleeve to dab her forehead.

"I told my mother to come heal you so she should be here any—"

Annika jumped to her feet hastily, showing a great deal more energy than she had moments before.

"I … I can see her after we see you off. We don't have time for that. I need to sneak out and—"

Fin stood, then reached out and wrapped his wife up in his arms.

"It's okay. My mother promised me she'd be nice to you from now on, so don't be afraid of her, alright?"

I'm not afraid of her. I'm afraid of what she'll find out, you handsome idiot. Despite her panic, Annika sunk into Fin's embrace. She knew it would be the last time they would be able to hold each other for a while …

"I really am fine, love. I will see your mother after you leave, I promise. We can't risk Mr. Helmer learning anything." Annika's gentle insistence succeeded in making Fin release her before planting a kiss on her forehead.

"Don't overdo it. You need to take care of yourself so that when I get back we can have a proper night together."

Annika laughed. Her coloring had improved greatly already, but the warmth of her body really was strange ... Fin knew she had put on weight and knew it was his own fault for always baking desserts for her, but perhaps it was the weight gain that had stressed her body too much.

"Alright. I will do my best to take care of myself, but for now, I have to go." Throwing her arms around his neck and kissing him fiercely, Annika pulled back looking incredibly sheepish. "I know I probably taste disgusting right now, but please bear with it. I love you, and ... and you definitely need to return alive and in one piece."

Fin smiled down at her and kissed her softly. "I will try my best to come back to you."

"There is no 'try' in this promise. You will come back. Understood, husband?" Annika's fiery retort made Fin's heart flutter. His wife then clasped something from her cloak pocket and raised it to reveal a golden chain.

"You can't have your father know we're married. So wear your ring around your neck like I am right now, and if they try to take it from you, tell them they will be dead within the year if they do."

Fin noted the chain around her neck then and allowed Annika to pull the ring off his finger and drop it over the thin links before reaching up, clasping it around his neck, and dropping it under his tunic.

As he leaned down to kiss his ferocious wife again, he couldn't help but reply.

"Anything you want, dear."

The rain had let up so that no one needed to wear a hood, but the day remained gray all the same. Fin watched the carriage pull up to the castle from the steps.

A crowd of nobles and the kitchen aides had gathered to see him off. Hannah was tearfully holding hands with both Sir Taylor and Sir Lewis while Sir Andrews had his arms crossed and was watching the entire scene with a bleak expression. Mage Lee stood to the side of the steps, as did Mr. Howard as they masked their own emotions as best they could.

Aidan Helmer stepped from his carriage, a handsome smile on his face; he was wearing a long black coat with a matching vest and tunic. He resembled the carriage driver to the afterlife in every way imaginable, which was all too fitting. As he stared at his son with the king and queen standing behind him, the chief of Troivack's military gave a proper bow.

Eric stood holding his mother's hand, looking deeply perplexed as he watched the entire situation.

Katelyn Ashowan stood beside Captain Antonio wringing her hands and whispering prayers to the Goddess under her breath. Annika stood to the king's right in the shadows of the doorway, and Fin was incredibly grateful that she was out of his sight line ... he couldn't look at her and not betray their secret.

"Well, my son, shall we be off?"

Clutching the canvas sack packed with his clothes and the paperwork to signify his position as a Daxarian ambassador, Fin slowly stepped down the castle stairs. His pulse pounded in his ears as he passed by his friends and family, unable to look at them, or else his stony mask would slip ...

When he reached Aidan, somehow he managed to keep his expression neutral, even when anger and pain tore through his chest.

"Hopefully you've already given your goodbyes as we really do need to go." Aidan patted Fin on his shoulder, making the redhead stiffen as he gazed into his father's black eyes.

"Even if you take me away like this, you still won't win here."

Aidan laughed as his son then proceeded to climb into the carriage.

"We'll see, won't we?"

Turning to face the devastated scene he had crafted, Aidan bowed again to the king and queen, then got in the carriage without another word.

"Remind me why I can't kill him right this minute?" Norman murmured to his wife so that only she might hear.

"We need to save Charles Piereva and his wife and infant daughter ... and we need to try and find out when they are planning to attack us ..."

Norman said nothing as he stared at the dark day before him.

Of course he knew all the reasons ... but it didn't make it any easier.

Meanwhile, Annika's gaze moved to the back of the vehicle that was carrying away her husband. As it gently swayed and moved farther and farther away from her, she felt as though her world was beginning to sink into the depths of a horrid nightmare ... a nightmare where she was completely alone and hopeless. The feeling crept icily through her veins the more distant she became from the carriage, filling her with wary bitterness. For some reason, she couldn't hear anything happening around her ... Or perhaps the entire world had fallen silent as it, too, sensed the loss of Finlay's warmth.

When the carriage eventually disappeared from view, Annika finally blinked and was free to behold the new, bleak reality. Ainsley was watching her friend, her empathetic pain written clearly in her soft gaze, but Annika's attention remained fixated on the Alcide Sea where her husband would soon be adrift.

Man of my dreams ... man that I love ... father of my unborn ... Don't you dare let Aidan Helmer take anyone else from me ... or I will never forgive you.

CHAPTER 17
DODGING DRAMA

As the scenery shifted by Fin on the way to the vessel, he could feel his stomach twist in all kinds of unpleasant yet impressive knots as he thought about his wife, friends, and family …

Aidan at least had the good sense not to say anything as the carriage lurched hesitantly down the long stretch of hill toward the harbor, but as it traveled, Fin suddenly noticed a strange amount of cats appearing by the edge of the road. They all sat idly watching, their numbers increasing …

A small frown crossed over Fin's features.

Speculating why in the world there looked to be every cat in Austice staring at the carriage passing by, he waited until the only one he could talk to would appear … sensing that Kraken was waiting for him down by the harbor.

After what felt like the shortest carriage ride of his life, Fin stepped out of the vehicle quickly, not wanting to spend a second alone with Aidan longer than he needed to. He asked the Troivackian soldier, who had been accompanying Aidan during his trip, which ship they would be departing on and was directed to a large vessel on his left. It was then he also spotted a fluffy black kitten seated atop one of the dock pillars. Stepping over to his familiar hastily before Aidan had even finished climbing out of the carriage, Fin didn't waste any time in addressing the kitten.

"Kraken, what is going on with all those cats?" Fin murmured urgently as he noticed Aidan speaking with someone on the other side of the carriage.

"My pack has made a successful truce with the others of Austice in the name of justice."

Fin blinked. "What?"

"My witch, do not worry about it. Why is it you are leaving with your strange-smelling father?"

"It's a long story, but I don't have time to explain." Reaching out, he proceeded to pet and scratch his feline's head and chin.

"I do not think I understand, but if you need me ... you know to call."

"I'm going on a boat. You got scared of the water basin when the aides were doing dishes."

"A boat stays on top of water, it doesn't douse me in it."

"Not unless it sinks ..."

The feline glared.

Fin chuckled and resumed petting the cat, sensing over his shoulder his father rounding the carriage toward him.

"Stay safe, Kraken."

Dropping his hand and turning away from his familiar, Fin, wearing a rigid expression, faced his father.

"Stand up straight, Finlay! How a man carries himself is what people see during your first impressions— Oho. Is this your familiar?" Aidan tried to glance around his son, but the redhead shifted to block his view.

"I'm not going to eat him, I just wondered what sort of beast my son is bonded to."

Fin ignored Aidan entirely and began to step away toward the docks when his father's hand clamped down on his forearm like a vise grip.

"Like me or not, you will show me proper respect, am I clear?" The fire witch's voice dipped to a dangerous quiet, yet Fin gave no reaction to the order.

Instead, he waited to be released and resumed his walk down the docks.

Aidan turned a curious eye to the fluffy kitten. He noted the small spray of white fur on the beast's chest, and the shaggy tail that swished back and forth while eyeing him.

"I can tell you are going to be a large cat ... that's good. It does a witch no good to have a familiar that can easily die."

Turning to follow after Fin, Aidan only managed to take a single step before Kraken's paw swiped out and caught his sleeve, his claws digging in until they met flesh.

The fire witch rounded on the cat with a smile in his black eyes. "Yes? Is there something you wish to say?"

Kraken peered at the fire witch for a prolonged period of time, his regal aura enhanced by the magnificent puff of his chest fur. Suddenly, the feline dragged his paw through the fabric of the coat and raked it jaggedly through the cloth and down to Aidan's skin before disengaging and fleeing toward a sleek greyhound that appeared to be waiting for him. The unlikely pair before they tore off together into the crowd.

Letting out a small yelp and grasping his bleeding arm, the fire witch glared after the familiar.

I've never tried to roast a cat, but there is a first time for everything, I suppose …

"Sir, the vessel is ready to set sail. Where would you like Mr. Ashowan to be kept?" A Troivackian man who, unlike the soldiers, wore fine clothing, addressed the Troivackian chief of military.

"Keep him with the men in the hammocks belowdecks. The ambassador will be preparing meals for the crew during his stay."

With a slight bow, the assistant scurried off to inform the ship's captain of the new arrangements, weaving in and out of the Troivackian sailors as he went.

Stepping onto the dock, the heels of his boots thumping mightily as he strode toward the gangplank, Aidan Helmer smiled to himself.

It was going to be a most enjoyable week one way or another.

What the chief of military was unaware of, however, was that things wouldn't go quite as smoothly as he had expected …

The inner council, the queen, and Annika sat in the quiet council room, all dimly aware that somehow the colors of the world had been drained. Without exchanging a word, they all knew, with Fin's absence, their home was no longer as bright, or whole …

"Lady Jen— Ashowan," Norman began slowly. "You are welcome to stay here another evening if you feel the company of the queen would be a comfort to you. While technically you may be exiled from court, we can always claim you are here for further questioning regarding Lord Phillip Piereva."

"Thank you, sire. However, I think I would like to return to my estate for a few days for some … quiet time."

Ainsley reached out to her friend and gripped her hand with a sad, understanding smile, while the king merely nodded his head in agreement.

"Of course. Thank you again, Viscountess. Please send word if there is anything you require."

Releasing the queen's hand and standing stiffly, Annika dipped into a small curtsy, then pardoned herself from the council room.

Striding out into the corridor, the anxious pit in her stomach began to make her feel nauseated again, while her racing heart succeeded in making her feel unpleasantly dizzy …

"Lady Ash— Jenoure!" The queen's voice called out as Annika exited the council room, and Ainsley pursued her friend while glancing around to see if there might be any noble lingering who might overhear.

Taking a brief breath to steady herself, Annika felt the castle walls momentarily spin before she slowly turned.

"Yes, Your Majesty?" She managed to dip into a curtsy without losing her balance.

Gods I need to sit down soon … the viscountess thought to herself somewhat weakly. Physician Durand had mentioned that the dizziness was normal in her current state.

"Are you alright?" Ainsley's whispered tone and worried gaze helped Annika focus and offer a small sad smile.

"I will be. I just need to rest. It's been an unpleasant day today."

Ainsley frowned. "Your hand was burning warm, are you ill? Shall I send Katelyn Ashowan to see you?"

"I may be fighting off a small cold, but no need to bother Mrs. Ashowan. I'm sure she is more than a little occupied with worries surrounding her son."

The queen didn't appear to like that answer, and so she persisted. "Then I shall call for Physician Durand and he—"

"Ainsley, please … please, I would like to return to my estate and rest. I … I thank you for caring so much, but I would …" Annika felt her body involuntarily go lax, as a strange wave of nausea swept over her and … was Ainsley sideways?

The viscountess lost consciousness on the castle floor, while Ainsley let out a yelp and attempted to catch her, only to end up hurting herself as she still had not yet fully recovered from giving birth just over two weeks before.

The guards outside the council room doors let out a shout that had the king and the rest of the council room occupants bolting outside and immediately summoning the physicians.

It was only a few minutes before Annika managed to fight off the darkness that was forcing her body into a relaxed state. She knew that if she didn't revive herself quickly Katelyn Ashowan was going to come, and then a whole new world of stress would be flung open … stress that she could handle on a different day.

Sitting up hastily, and working on not allowing the dizziness to overtake her again, Annika's hearing gradually came into focus as the crowd of men around her and the queen tried to figure out what had happened.

"Your Majesty, my lords, I am fine. It was just the events of the day that— Ainsley! Ainsley, are you alright?" Annika then noticed her friend's pained expression while she remained crouched on the floor clutching her abdomen.

"I'll be fine; I'll just have one of the physicians— Ouch!" Norman had tried to lift her, but he was forced to place her back down.

Ainsley grasped Norman's sleeve, and he cast an appraising albeit worried glance at the lady and noted her pale face. "Our queen is in pain and in need of care! Please, there is no need for both physicians to loom over me."

"Come, Viscountess. How about we let the physicians take care of Her Majesty." Mage Lee offered his arm to Annika.

"I swear, Your Majesty, I will return to my estate and rest. There is no need for further dramatics." Annika was already nervously aware that with each passing moment, her mother-in-law drew closer …

Reaching up toward Mage Lee, the man helped to pull her upright.

"Take care of yourselves, Your Majesties. I will take my leave now, thank you for your concern."

Before anyone could object any further, clutching Mage Lee's arm, Annika dipped into another curtsy and began moving swiftly away from the scene that was beginning to draw the servants.

She had very nearly made it to the stairwell, when Katelyn Ashowan came charging up with her skirts in her hands.

"Whatever is all the commotion about?!" the healer burst out when she realized who she was about to pass by.

Mage Lee opened his mouth while casting a glance at Annika worriedly, but her sudden grip on his forearm silenced him.

"Her Majesty harmed herself and is down the castle corridor. The king cannot move her without causing her pain."

Katelyn gave a serious nod, then sprinted with impressive agility down the way Annika had mentioned.

Half pulling the mage along, Annika forced their way down the stairs as more servants ran up trying to go aid their queen.

Once in the front entranceway, Annika was grateful to spot Clara speaking with one of the footmen.

With a quick wave, and a moment of meaningful eye contact, the maid nodded in understanding and immediately sent for a carriage.

"Viscountess, are you sure you are alright? You are acting quite peculiar," the mage observed with a small frown and a hesitant tone.

The grand doors opened just as a clap of ominous thunder rang out.

"Of course, Mage Lee, I simply wish to be alone, and I know that Her Majesty will needlessly fret if I remain in close proximity. She still needs to rest." Annika did her best to give a genuine peaceful smile.

The mage studied her closely for a few moments, but after another minute patted the hand that was still clutched onto his secretly muscular forearm.

"Viscountess, do tend to yourself. I know Mr. Ashowan would be incredibly worried if he were to hear—"

"My lady, your carriage is ready." Clara appeared so suddenly that the mage gave a small start.

"I bid you good day, Mage Lee." Giving what she hoped was her final curtsy for the time being, Annika turned and left the castle without a second look back, knowing that more than a few members of the council would be questioning her strange behavior.

The storm had broken out as soon as dusk had fallen, and with it came a significant drop in temperature. With the heat fading from the air, Annika could no longer deny that she still felt uncharacteristically warm. Sitting in her bedroom chair with her arms and legs crossed, she silently turned over recent events in her mind.

Her brother Phillip was dead.

Her sister-in-law would have to be placed in hiding with her niece.

The queen injured herself.

And …

Fin was gone.

She wasn't cold, but the thought still made Annika rub her arms. Letting out a long breath, she stood and sidled over to the window where nothing but darkness and water could be seen.

I need to focus on work. That will help this time go by quickly, and there is supposed to be a letter sent to the king every day from Finlay ... I don't know if Charlie is even still alive ... or his wife, Janelle, or his daughter ...

As she began to think on how her next objective would have to be finding out how to next infiltrate the Troivackian government, a knock on her bedroom door rang out.

"Come in," Annika called over her shoulder, suspecting it was the maids to stoke the fire a little higher.

The door opened, and the footsteps drew closer to her, and promptly stopped.

Annika caught a glimpse of a woman standing behind her in the faint reflection of the window over her shoulder thanks to the firelight. It couldn't be one of the maids, they would've said something by then ...

Moving suddenly, Annika sidestepped farther away from the figure while simultaneously drawing her dagger to see who the intruder was.

The startled face of Katelyn Ashowan in the firelight had the lady immediately let out a sigh of relief.

"Good Gods, Kate!" Quickly sheathing the blade, Annika crossed her arms over her chest again, feeling all too aware of how thin her silk nightdress was. "What brings you here? I thought you'd be staying at the castle with the queen after—"

"Her Majesty is fine, she just needs a bit of rest. More importantly, Her Majesty told me you fainted from fever earlier? I am sorry that I was not able to come see you sooner. Fin visited me this morning before ... before he left. He told me you were unwell." Kate took a step forward, her hands clasped in front of her skirts.

Annika's teeth clamped together and she forced her hands to remain relaxed even though she was already bracing herself for what she knew would be happening next. She knew her mother-in-law was about to try and heal her, and if she didn't come up with some convincing lie immediately, her little secret was about to be discovered.

Her body tensed, and her mind focused intently on Katelyn Ashowan in that moment, knowing that if need be, she could always try to make yet another run for it ...

Gods, Finlay ... of all the powers your mother could possess, why did it have to be one that would tell her too damn much?!

CHAPTER 18
DOUBLE TROUBLE

I promise, I feel perfectly well again." Annika did her best to give a reassuring smile, but Katelyn Ashowan was watching her skeptically.

"I'd prefer to check for myself ... and because Fin requested it." The healer took another step closer and Annika moved a step backward.

"Would it be possible in the morning for you to examine me? I ... I'm tired this evening," Annika lied swiftly, making sure to droop her eyes.

"I see ... very well." Kate nodded quietly after a moment's hesitation and gradually began to turn toward the door.

The lady had just begun to let out the tiniest breath of relief, when the healer suddenly whirled around and lunged at Annika. One hand flew to the viscountess's forehead, and the other grasped her forearm with impressive strength as Annika reeled back trying to wrench herself from her mother-in-law's hold ... but it was futile.

The woman had a shocking grip of steel.

"Gods, you're burning hot! Why in the world didn't you ask for help when you—" Kate's words died in her throat then. Her face grew pale, as her hands then began to glow, and Annika had no choice but to remain completely frozen, albeit with an expression of open terror.

"You … You're carrying my … his …" Kate's hands suddenly dropped to Annika's swollen abdomen that she had tried to shield with her silk robe, but under the healer's experienced touch, there was no hiding it.

Tears suddenly sprang to Kate's eyes, as her chin dropped, and her voice quivered.

"There is a part of him still here … still safe …" More tears began to cascade down the woman's face as Annika felt a hard lump rise in her throat.

"I … I … it's …" Annika had no idea what to say as her mother-in-law openly wept and rejoiced at the same time.

"How could you be so far along unless—" Kate stopped suddenly. With a slight twitch of her eyebrows, the healer's entire body suddenly began to glow, casting the room in an even brighter light. Then suddenly her wide warm gaze met Annika's.

"Twins."

Annika's heart thudded against her chest.

So … it was confirmed …

Twins.

The room began to spin slightly in front of Annika's eyes as her breath came out in small gasps.

"Sit down." Kate took charge in forcing the viscountess down onto the nearest settee, immediately sensing that the expecting woman was suddenly not steady on her feet.

After a few moments of Annika gradually regaining her composure with Kate's gentle hands on both her abdomen and her shoulder, the future grandmother spoke again.

"So this was why you were avoiding touching me so much." The healer chuckled softly, while Annika still couldn't work her way past the shock of being discovered, nor the confirmation that she was carrying twice as many children as was the norm …

"I thought you were looking a little on the plump side more recently, but also thought it had more to do with Finlay's cooking …" Kate admitted with a watery smile.

When the healer recognized the distant shocked expression on her daughter-in-law's face, she decided to take the physician's approach and inform her patient of all she could regarding her condition.

"You're nearly between seven and eight weeks … It doesn't feel as though they are identical though even my magic struggles a bit with those details just yet. I am willing to bet you that one of those babes is going to be a fire witch the way it's burning hotter than the sun inside you. Thankfully the other babe won't be hurt because there are two placentas, so do not worry." When the viscountess still didn't respond, the healer continued talking. "By my estimate you are due in early spring next year—twins tend to arrive a little early."

Annika still didn't say anything, and it was beginning to concern Kate.

"You did … know … before I said anything, didn't you?"

The viscountess nodded after a moment.

"I see. Does Fin know?"

The answer took longer in coming, but eventually Annika shook her head.

"You didn't want him to worry before he left," Kate guessed quietly.

"I didn't …" Annika cleared her hoarse voice before attempting to continue again. "I didn't want him to … get excited … or worried when it was so early and with everything that is happening …"

Kate nodded in understanding. "You were trying to protect him."

Annika let out a long shaky sigh, unaware that her hands had started trembling. She clasped them together tightly as she worked to find her normal sense of self-control and confidence.

Love. Family. Vulnerability …

Her three weakest points all brewed together to make her feel wholly unlike herself.

"I'll be honest, Viscountess, you won't be able to hide this in another three weeks. Women tend to grow much faster with twins. The bright side is, if you'd like, I can tell you the genders in another two weeks or so …"

Annika shook her head. "I … I would like to ask Fin before …"

Somehow, saying his name broke her final tendril of strength, and the dark-haired beauty found tears spilling over her cheeks.

Pulling her into an embrace, Katelyn gently stroked Annika's back and hair in a very motherly manner while not saying anything more until the lady pulled back and hastily dashed away the remaining tears on her cheeks.

"I know it's frightening. All we can do is hope he makes it back and … and that you can tell him the news."

As the two women continued sharing solace with each other well into the night, the rain continued to soak the world outside, and a certain Troivackian vessel did its best to keep its bow out of the rough waters of the Alcide Sea.

～～～～

Fin awoke the next morning with a gasp, his hand clutching his chest as the vivid images from his dream twisted his heart. He had dreamt that he was peering inside Annika's bedroom window … she had been staring through him into the night looking tired and alone. He had wanted to comfort her, to call out her name, but he couldn't for some reason. Instead he had seen his mother enter the chamber. They had talked and wept, and no matter how hard he tried, the witch couldn't shout or pound the glass to let them know he was still there.

"Oyy, Helmer, your father wants you above deck," one of the Troivackian soldiers called out as Fin was wiping sweat off his face. Surprisingly, none of the men had attempted to beat him in the night, and none of them even whispered an insult … aside from refusing to call him Ashowan.

Maneuvering himself free from the hammock he had been assigned belowdecks, the redhead set to collapsing the canvas and hanging it up along with the others before following the soldier who had been sent to summon him.

The ship was still damp from the storm that had broken out, but the day that followed was sunny and pleasantly cool. Fin spotted Aidan leaning along the rail, staring out over the murky water as Austice grew farther in the distance. He wore a crisp white tunic with the sleeves rolled up, and black vest with matching trousers, setting him apart from the grubby attire of the majority of the crew.

Burying his hands in his pockets and walking over to the man he loathed with every fiber of his being, Fin cleared his throat.

Aidan turned around slowly, then chortled when he saw his son's pale complexion and dark bags under his eyes. "Not taking well to sea life?"

"You asked to see me?" Fin asked quietly instead of answering the question.

"Ah, yes. We haven't had a chance to properly talk. The storm set upon us so quickly that there was too much to do." Aidan gestured over to two small barrels facing each other where it was obvious some of the men took their breaks.

Fin obliged and moved over slowly to them as the Troivackian chief of military walked behind him, making the hairs on the back of Fin's neck prickle.

Once seated, his father's black eyes surveyed his son carefully. The fire witch folded his arms over his chest and leaned back comfortably. After a moment of silence, he finally grinned.

"I know you hate me. I know you're angry that we're using Charles Piereva and his family to bring you here, but at least we're giving a somewhat fair hearing." Aidan shrugged.

"Fair would have been *not* threatening his wife and daughter along with him," Fin pointed out flatly.

"Ahh, that is simply the way of Troivack. It is harsh, brutal … but beautiful in its efficient execution of justice." Aidan smiled charmingly, but it only made Fin's stomach burn.

"I heard you exiled that blond aide after my visit. I'm glad that she was punished for her impudence."

Fin bit down on his tongue hard enough to draw blood.

"I did hear some interesting rumors about you around the castle, you know. Some people seem to believe you are gay. Others have determined that you lost your woman—a maid serving under Lady Jenoure—after being arrested for a night. Lord Phillip Piereva reported that you had stolen away to the prince's birthday in order to spend time with a woman … I take it the maid … Clara, was it? She was the one he was referring to?"

The house witch said nothing.

"What is it you want in life, Fin?" Aidan asked curiously, tilting his head to the side.

"I want to cook," the lackluster reply did nothing but irk the fire witch.

"You can cook anywhere. Don't you recognize that you're better than what you have? I can offer you a brand-new life. Once we win this war, I will be in a far superior position, and you could take a role under me that far surpasses—"

"No, thanks."

Aidan's mouth clamped shut and annoyance flashed across his face.

"Why did you hurt Sky?" Fin questioned suddenly. For some reason, while he had his own understanding about his and his mother's subjection to his father's violence in the past, the air witch's assault haunted him …

"Ahh, so you *have* met with her. Sky was always a delicate little thing … she had great power as a pure witch, but alas she tried countless times to tamper with the greater good, and I needed to leave a strong enough impression on her that she would stop meddling."

"She went mad after what you did. She requires constant care, and—"

"Sometimes people don't grow stronger in life, and instead digress. Take yourself, for instance. I know you and your mother believe my methods while you grew up were harsh, but you are at the very least self-sufficient, and I suspect … far more well-connected than most people know." A knowing smile spread across Aidan's face.

So he's wondering if I'm the spy … this is good for Annika. It'll keep her safe.

Fin shrugged ambiguously. "It's not hard to make friends."

Aidan's eyes gleamed with interest. "Not with that face it isn't. I remember what it was to be handsome and young … I imagine it allows you in all kinds of bedchambers, and subsequently knowledge of certain secrets."

Fin wished he could kick Aidan in the groin for good measure, but he knew it was better that he was seen as a lowlife who gathered information for personal gain … so he chose not to answer.

"What could I offer you that would tempt you to take all your … *information*, and skills, and work for the King of Troivack?" The chief of military tried again, his expression growing more serious.

"Nothing that I'm aware of." There was a subtle note of irritability in Fin's voice when he answered again.

"I'd been wondering who the castle spy was, and it turns out it was my own son," the fire witch baited him, but Fin only folded his arms and leaned back, mirroring his father's movements perfectly.

"You must know that if you do not change your mind before the seven days are complete, I intend to kill you, right?" Aidan asked while scoffing.

"Can't say I'm overly surprised," Fin replied in the same monotone he had been maintaining the entire conversation and was satisfied to see his father grit his teeth for a moment as a result.

"So this is it for you, hm? You die to save some nobles as an ambassador and that's good enough for your life? You cooked, you bedded some wenches, and now you go out as a sacrifice for a noblewoman? I don't buy it for a minute." Aidan leaned forward, his elbows on his knees. "Does the king naively think I'll obey the contract? Or does he have something else planned to save you?"

Fin shrugged. "I have no idea."

A brief flash of rage passed over Aidan's face, before he suddenly broke out in a laugh that made his son's blood curdle.

"It's a pity you'll have to die like this. You're a very good spy … Not giving up any information. Willfully ignorant … For old times' sake, I'll give you a few more days to think about it. After that, I'll see to it that you die quite painfully as thanks for blasting me off Quildon."

"Even if I agreed to work for your king, you would've planned to get rid of me the moment I wasn't of any use," Fin announced unfeelingly before standing.

"Possibly ... then again, perhaps I would be willing to call it a child's first taste of power and let it go after a few years ... But you don't seem the type to change your mind easily. It makes no difference to me; I just didn't want anything troublesome getting in my way when victory is so near. You're a last-minute wild card we wanted to remove. Charles Piereva won't live ... we may allow his wife and daughter to, for a suitable price, but you'll hear all about that from my king."

Fin's ears pricked up though he did his best to maintain a controlled façade as his father slowly stood up.

If he's talking about having me killed before the week is up then ... then that means the Troivackians are intending to attack by the end of the seven days. At least I know they haven't killed Charles Piereva yet ... The realization plunged Fin into icy anxiousness. *How the hell can I save Lady Janelle and her daughter and warn His Majesty about the soldiers ... ?*

"Oh, and Finlay?" Aidan called as his son began to turn away.

The redhead looked back at his father, then received a sharp uppercut to his gut that left him gasping and clutching his ribs on the ship's deck. A searing burning pain wrenched through his shoulder where the fire witch's hand then rested, making Fin try all the harder to gasp through the pain.

"This is for your childish disrespect the past few days. Don't disappoint me again."

Then, Aidan Helmer strode off leaving his son on the deck trying to regain his breath and wondering how he could possibly survive the full week and warn everyone in Daxaria in time ...

CHAPTER 19
ROCKING THE BOAT

Fin sat in the ship's galley atop one of the water barrels, quill in hand, as two burly Troivackian soldiers watched him from under their bushy black eyebrows. A pleasant sea breeze rolled in from the open porthole, but despite this, Fin found himself sweating profusely in the small space.

I need to warn the king that the attack will be at the end of this week … But I don't even know in which city it will happen … Fin had pondered what he would write that could pass his father's presumed inspection the entire morning.

With a long sigh, he pinched the bridge of his nose and closed his eyes wearily.

"We've got other jobs to do," the Troivackian on the left grumbled, though he quickly earned a sharp glare from his comrade.

"Ah, right. Sorry. Just … Not sure what to write." Fin gave a partial smile in apology, which made both the Troivackian soldiers take a step back with eyebrows raised.

"Er … did I do something?" Fin asked while raising his eyebrow.

The Troivackian on the right cleared his throat before he stepped forward, his eyes screwed to the food storage behind Fin.

"You look like Mr. Helmer, but talk like a Daxarian."

The witch blinked. "I want to say thank you?"

Both the men shifted awkwardly, making Fin grin. "Is it that you're not used to people apologizing? Or saying thanks?"

Both the men cleared their throats again and nodded.

"Ah. Well ... if it helps, I'm considered rude by a good amount of people! So I'm not the worst of the—"

"We don't need to hear about ... about the enemy," the man on the right managed to say, his discomfort obvious.

Fin straightened and folded his arms as he gazed more directly at his two guards.

"What're your names?"

"You don't need to know," the man on the right answered for the both of them.

"Of course I don't *need* to know, I *want* to know. It's more respectful, wouldn't you say?"

Both men looked as though they had mosquitoes biting their faces that they couldn't swat away.

"You know if you don't tell me, I'm just going to give you names and you might not like them. For example, I could call you"—Fin pointed to the man on the left—"Stanley, and you ..."—Fin gazed at the man on the right who was already cringing—"Bruce."

The witch grinned up at them, waiting for them to crack their stoic silence as the duo kept their gazes fixed behind the redhead. Fin studied the men closely; the one he had bequeathed the name Stanley was slightly shorter than Bruce, his nose wide and flat, though his arms were thicker. Bruce was taller by a couple inches, but his eyes were keener ...

"Well, I suppose I better get back to this letter ... Tell me, if you had to write a letter that your king would be reading, but also most likely your mother would read it, too, what would you write?"

Stanley and Bruce stood shoulder to shoulder in silence.

"Hm ... Guess I'll tell them about my new friends Stanley and Bruce."

Both the Troivackian soldiers had their hands gripped into fists.

"Don't worry, I won't say anything bad ... I'll read it out loud to you when I'm done."

Setting his forearms on the table, Fin had an idea of how he could try and warn everyone back home ... while at the same time making the men around him less likely to report anything strange ... and perhaps just have a teensy bit of fun.

Norman frowned at the letter the falcon had delivered by midafternoon of the second day of Fin's absence. The council watched with bated breaths, each man glancing to the others worriedly.

"I … I can tell he is trying to communicate something," the king finally said with a frown on his face as he set the parchment on the table in front of himself.

"Your Majesty, might I read the missive aloud to everyone present?" Mr. Howard extended his hand to the king with a small bow.

With a short nod, Norman handed over the parchment and leaned back in his chair.

Clearing his throat, the assistant read the missive aloud to the council.

Your Majesty, King Norman Reyes,

Despite the storm of the first night, the ship remains afloat and has set a northwest course.

Even though it has only been a day, I find myself already looking forward to the lively celebration promised to me upon my return at the end of the week, as thanks for boarding the ship. I know my aides had intended it to be a surprise, but you know how devastatingly poor they are at keeping secrets.

I have made two new friends while aboard the vessel, Stanley and Bruce. They don't like to talk much, but given some time I'm sure we will form a special relationship. In fact, I'm sure in another day or two, I will be as close with them as I have been with Baron Gauva's nephew.

Give my mother my love, and let her know I am fine.

I pray to the Goddess for your safety and well-being, Your Majesty.

Finlay Ashowan

Everyone was frowning.

"A celebration? Sire, you promised him a celebration upon his return?" Mr. Howard looked up at the king, completely incensed. "You've already given him a title and a wedding! Why in the world would—"

"He's warning us," Captain Antonio interrupted, his brows knit together as his mind raced through the letter once more. "If I am not mistaken, I believe the 'celebration' is the attack. He is stating it is to be at the end of the week."

Norman straightened in his chair. "Why would you presume so?"

"Well, we didn't promise a celebration, and a 'lively celebration' suggests it is going to be … quite noisy. He also made mention that it was supposed to be a secret …"

The king let out a sigh. "It isn't much to go off, but then again I suspect his letters are being read before being sent out. We can ask the aides if any such party was planned before making a final decision."

"There is another time frame in the letter, however," Lord Fuks pointed out suddenly.

All eyes turned to the earl.

"He mentions his two 'new friends,' and says how close they will be in two days … as close as Baron Gauva's nephew," Lord Fuks reminded with a serious nod toward the letter.

"The young man who insisted he will get revenge on Finlay after he failed to abduct both him and Katelyn? When the Queen had just given birth?" the king asked as realization began to creep along his face.

"Yes."

Silence stretched on.

"Finlay might be saying he will not be safe in a couple of days … but that doesn't make sense. They intend to attack by the end of the week," Mage Lee noted thoughtfully.

"It could be that they will encounter the Troivackian king's ship in two days, and after Mr. Ashowan carries out his duties they will attempt to harm him," Mr. Howard supplied. "Though how would Helmer intend to continue to send letters if Fin is unable to?"

"Well, is it even possible for us to intervene if he doesn't? They are a day and a half ahead on their journey," the captain pointed out grimly.

Norman didn't say anything as he pondered this new dilemma.

"We will wait and see what tomorrow's letter says before making any final decisions."

"Sire, that might be too late. We may not be able to get to the viscount in time for—" Captain Antonio began before the king turned and silenced him with an oddly calm stare.

"We need to act cautiously on all fronts. We don't want to barge in if there is a chance that everything is being upheld in the agreements, and we can still save Charles Piereva and his family. We can start preparing the soldiers and knights for the end of the week, but I want it done quietly."

For a brief moment, Captain Antonio looked like he was going to disagree.

"Very well, Your Majesty." The military man bowed his head in compliance.

While no one outwardly said anything, the council men couldn't help but feel uneasy at their ruler's decision to hold off on intervening on behalf of their beloved cook.

"Ah, and one more thing. I don't want anyone breathing a word of this to Lady Ashowan, or Katelyn Ashowan," Norman announced seriously, his hazel eyes piercing each man present.

Every one of the council members stiffened.

"Both of them will try to interfere if they discover what we know. This is for not only their safety, but Fin's as well."

After a moment of tense silence, each council member bobbed their head in agreement, though all of them were beginning to feel a growing unease in their stomachs as the day moved forward.

Fin stared at the meager food offerings aboard the ship before letting out a long sigh.

Fish, of course, as well as other salted meats, potatoes, cheese, and cabbage.

He considered himself lucky that, with how few the dining options were, there was salt and pepper aboard, and even some lard. He suspected more was hidden around, but he had yet to uncover anything else.

Picking up one of the spuds, he speculated on making a potato pancake for the men, but acquiesced he'd need a flame … The ship's brick oven needed a thorough cleaning, and hours before dinner was not the best time to start such a task.

Turning around with a thoughtful frown, Fin then picked up a nearby cast-iron pot. He faced Stanley and Bruce, who subconsciously straightened their postures under the cook's gaze.

Without a word, Fin put the pot into Stanley's hands, then picked up another and handed it to Bruce. After that, he hefted the sack of potatoes over his good shoulder, then onto Stanley's shoulder, before bending down and hoisting up the small barrel of clean water in his arms.

"We need to go above deck," Fin instructed the two men who were completely clueless as to what he was doing.

"Why are we doing that? You're supposed to be sorting out the food," Bruce demanded, though despite it being obvious that he was trying to be intimidating, there was more than a little uncertainty in the man's eyes.

"I *am* going to 'sort out the food.'" Fin strode toward the door purposefully with the water barrel in his hands.

The two Troivackian men in charge of guarding him shared a brief look of confusion before scurrying after him.

"Mr. Helmer, you should be staying belowdecks," Bruce called out as the redhead proceeded to breeze past some of the soldiers in the midst of card games. When he got to the ladder, Fin shifted the barrel over his unburnt shoulder and continued on as though he had been clambering up and out of ships his entire life.

"No one will be complaining once it's dinnertime," the witch eventually replied, breathing in the fresh sea breeze as the ship creaked around him.

Scanning the deck, the Fin's gaze finally rested on the figure he was looking for.

Aidan Helmer stood speaking with a well-dressed man who appeared to be the captain of the ship. The captain wore a rich black wool coat, tan trousers, and a white tunic that was the biggest signifier of his superiority. The pair appeared to be in a serious discussion. Aidan's hands rested on his hips in a way that Fin knew to be like himself, and as he watched the way his father's face moved, and the way his head tilted, he had to admit there were a great many similarities …

Giving his head a shake, Fin strode forward until he stood only a foot away from the two men, making them immediately halt their conversation as they both turned to look at him. He set the barrel on the ground, then placed his hands on his hips.

"I apologize for interrupting the discussion; however, I was wondering if I might borrow Mr. Helmer for a moment, Captain?"

Even Aidan couldn't hide his look of surprise as he slowly crossed his arms over his chest to stare more directly at his son.

"Yes … I suppose this matter could wait."

The captain was staring back and forth between the two nervously before he slowly stepped back.

Aidan's expression was flat, and Fin could see the irritation building in his gaze.

"You are supposed to be preparing the evening meal."

"That is precisely what I am doing; however, I need your ability in order to give these men something worth stomaching."

Whatever Aidan had been expecting to hear, it hadn't been that.

"I beg your pardon?"

"The brick oven hasn't been cleaned in what looks like weeks. If I try to light it now, it will be a smokehouse down there. So for tonight, if you are able to sustain boiling water and a heated pan for these potatoes, I can prepare a better meal for the men than just salted meat and cheese."

Aidan stared at his son, completely baffled. "You … You want me to use my abilities to … boil water … for your potatoes?"

"You can call them our potatoes if it makes you feel better," Fin offered as he gestured Bruce and Stanley forward.

"Why would you come up here to ask that? Why not send one of these men to relay your request?" Aidan asked, stepping closer, his eyes narrowing.

"Because I'm doubtful you would've listened. I have your attention now, don't I?"

Fin knew what he was doing was a massive gamble, but … he needed to find ways of getting closer to everyone on the ship if he wanted to learn anything that could be helpful.

After a moment of carefully studying his son, Aidan let out a chuckle of disbelief. The smallest of calculating smiles then moved across his face.

"Very well. Let's see what I can do, shall we?"

Fin then did the unexpected.

He grinned. However, a strange sly glint in his eyes made Aidan hesitate.

"Come on down to the galley. I'm not sure Bruce or Stanley will be able to fit in there with us, though. Sorry about that, men."

Aidan turned a perplexed stare to the two Troivackians who looked openly mortified.

"We've gotten quite close, you see; they will be most disappointed to miss the show," Fin explained as he stepped past the two soldiers while giving them affectionate pats on their backs, which in turn resulted in the entire crew on deck freezing and watching the exchange as though their two comrades were naked and singing ballads.

Fin then darted back to stand in front of them, lifted the nearly forgotten barrel back up on his shoulder, and proceeded to shoot a smile and wink at the two soldiers.

Once again he startled Aidan Helmer who became at a complete loss for words as he stared at his son's retreating back. The fire witch's hands moved to his hips as he attempted to fathom just what his spawn was attempting to do … though poor Stanley and Bruce were just trying to calm their blushing faces. They also realized the only reason Fin had made them carry the potatoes and pot all the way up onto the deck and back down was so that they couldn't physically stop him leaving the galley.

"I don't think guarding the Daxarian is going to be as easy as we thought," Bruce murmured to his friend before turning and following the father and son.

Stanley frowned, but began to return back to the galley, all while attempting to ignore the strange expressions on his fellow soldiers' faces.

CHAPTER 20
FATHER SON TIME

Annika stared at Mr. Howard and Captain Antonio dryly.
The trio stood just inside the doors of her Austice estate, and to say she was annoyed would be putting it lightly.

"What do you mean there wasn't 'anything much,' in his letter?" the viscountess demanded with her hands folded in front of her skirts. The pair had come to deliver the news—or lack thereof—to her after the dining hour, and the pair did their best to keep their facial expressions composed.

"All he said was that he was doing fine. Nothing of real import," Mr. Howard clarified primly.

"I see … So the entire contents of his message were four words, and that was it?" Annika asked while taking a slow step closer and making the assistant take a tentative step back.

Captain Antonio was far harder to intimidate, and so he held his ground.

"He said he was fine, and that they had set a northwest course."

"And?" Annika's tone was gaining a certain sharpness that neither of the men had heard from her before.

"He's made friends," Mr. Howard announced suddenly, earning a dark side glance from the captain.

"Friends … on the Troivackian ship with his father?" the viscountess countered again as she folded her arms over her chest.

"Yes. He said the men were fine, and he was fine. There really was—" Mr. Howard tried once again to placate the lady but was cut off swiftly.

"Each time I ask you something, I learn that more was said. So am I going to have to keep at this all night, or will you just tell me?" There was an iciness in the woman's gaze that made Mr. Howard shiver and Captain Antonio stiffen.

"Viscountess, we understand you are worried for your husband, but there are some matters we cannot discuss." The captain was proving to be the more formidable of the two men.

"I see. Shall I call for Katelyn Ashowan to see if she thinks that is a fair judgment?"

The captain openly glared. "I will tell my betrothed myself, Lady Jeno— Ashowan."

After a moment of stalemate between the trio staring at one another but no one uttering a word, Annika finally broke off.

"Very well. If His Majesty doesn't see reason to apprise me of my husband's well-being, I suppose I cannot argue with the messengers." Turning away slowly, she could see out of the corner of her eye both men visibly breathe in relief.

"We are certain he is fine. We will take our leave so as not to disturb you any more this evening," Mr. Howard rushed on to say as he gave a low bow, then turned to exit the estate.

Captain Antonio stared at the viscountess's back a few moments before doing the same, though there was clearly something on his mind …

Annika seated herself in the office, her expression cold and murderous as she debated what her next move should be.

They were hiding something … but what? Was Fin in danger? Was he already dead? Did he have information about the war?

Clara's soft knock at the door brought her attention back to reality as the maid brought with her a cup of tea and sliced peaches. "I take it the news wasn't good?"

"They are hiding whatever news they've received," Annika replied angrily.

Clara quirked one of her eyebrows upward. "So how are you intending to find out what the letter said?"

"I could break into the castle and read it, but that'd be treason, and I don't much like the idea of giving birth in a cell. My next option is attacking the weakest link of the circle." Leaning back with her hands folding atop her swollen belly, the viscountess frowned slightly.

"So … Mage Lee, right?" Clara asked with a small smile beginning in the corners of her mouth.

"Yes, Mage Lee. He is the one who has the strongest impression of me being a delicate woman of grace. We also happen to know more than a few of his weaknesses." Annika turned with a wry grin of her own to Clara. Though unlike her usual radiant smile, this one was one of mischievous calculation.

"You mean that he and his wife enjoy … Madam Mathilda's establishment together?" the maid asked nervously.

"Not only that, but … he has a certain affinity for weddings."

Clara's gaze sharpened. "Absolutely not. I am not going to pretend to get married to get information out of him!"

Annika sighed playfully, then shook her head dismissing the idea. "Don't you remember that I already conveniently have a mother-in-law who is betrothed to a beloved captain?"

Clara's face relaxed immediately before nodding intently, her hand moving to gently touch her chin as the rest of the plan formed in her head.

"A mother-in-law who I bet is just as frustrated as you are that we aren't hearing everything …"

The two women stood at the same time and headed straight for the door, their plan abundantly clear.

Aidan skeptically watched his son flip the flattened mashed potatoes, though he couldn't deny his watering mouth as the aromas continued to fill the cramped space.

"I'm surprised you asked for my help. I would've thought you'd avoid me at every turn. So I find myself rather … intrigued," the fire witch announced in hopes of distracting himself from the mesmerizing show of the food being prepared.

"I'm an adult. When I need to get a job done, I see to it. Even if you making me work while aboard this ship as an ambassador when you already have a cook was a very strange twist." Fin answered his father casually as he then procured a block of cheese and began cutting meticulously thin pieces before slicing them further, almost as though trying to make it grated …

"You are adequately better than our ship's military cook. Besides, your guards watching you should stop any creative ideas you may suddenly spout," Aidan replied as he watched his son sprinkle the cheese atop each of the golden creations, then rested a pot lid over the pan before turning to the cabbage.

"It's a good thing I found some vinegar for this cabbage dish, but it'd be better if there were some honey I could use to sweeten it," Fin murmured more to himself than his father.

"I have some in my quarters," Aidan blurted out before realizing he had said anything. There was something strangely hypnotic about the way his son cooked. The food looked appetizing and satisfying and ... smelled like heaven ... Yet, it was all simple, poor food ...

"Might I use some? I really only require a bit despite it being for everyone. A little will take the flavor a long way."

Standing from the barrel he had been seated upon, Aidan called to the nearest soldier outside the galley doorway, telling him where to retrieve the jar. Then Aidan returned to sit on the barrel again.

"Do you drink?" the fire witch asked after another quiet moment of watching his son, the lap of waves around them and the gentle rocking of the boat somehow adding to the comforting atmosphere.

"Recently I've begun to imbibe more regularly," Fin answered as he lifted the lid off the potato pancakes and proceeded to slide them onto plates.

He handed one to his father with a fork before picking up his own and taking a bite. Nodding to himself, Fin then proceeded to cut a cabbage into quarters, cut off the stem, then sliced the vegetable thinly.

Aidan took a tentative bite of the flattened potato concoction, then proceeded to forget any previous thoughts he had as the flavors shook the world around him. It was a bit crispy, but filling, and ... even though the seasonings were basic, it still created the most complementary taste paired with the cheese ...

It wasn't until the plate was clear that Aidan even realized more than a few moments of silence had passed.

"That was ... why didn't the food at the castle taste nearly as delicious?" the Troivackian chief of military speculated curiously.

"Because I didn't want it to taste that good to you. I wanted you to take as little interest in me as possible," Fin replied matter-of-factly as he began placing the sliced cabbage into a large bowl.

"So now you want me to be interested?"

"Now I'm just doing what I enjoy. Cooking for a group that hasn't had a proper meal in, I'm guessing, close to three weeks?" Fin rested the tops of his fists against the table surface and fixed his father with a complex expression.

"I see. So this has nothing to do with the offer I made to you this morning?" Aidan asked casually as he set the empty plate on the barrel beside him.

"No, it doesn't. Why spend my last days angry and frustrated when I can cook and make new friends …" Fin shrugged before picking up another cabbage and setting to work.

"So you feel nothing about how I attacked and threatened you this morning? Just like that, you accept it all?" A cold smile spread across the elder's face.

Fin shot him a dry eyebrow raise that immediately threw the fire witch off guard.

"Tell me, Aidan. You win a war, become the head of two covens, and then what? You just let the humans rule themselves but expect witches to be superior? That makes very little sense. You create a new hierarchy in the coven pertaining to deviated and pure elemental witches, when there is already that system in existence—just not on paper. What am I missing here?" Fin resumed cutting the cabbage, his tone light, but curious.

"I intend to merge all the covens of the world. We will put ink to paper and set civilization right as it should be," Aidan explained patiently, an out-of-character serene expression settling over his features.

"What makes you think it's wrong now?" Fin asked with a small shrug.

"There are a great many useless people in power who do more harm than good. When there are beings such as ourselves who should be leading the world to maintain balance, we should be the ones to step forward and make change happen." Aidan's eyes glimmered.

"Why not work with the existing system to form something better? Why resort to the slaughter of thousands of people?" Fin was doing his utmost to keep his tone casual, but the mention of the carnage that was sure to come in a war created a pit of dread in his stomach.

"I tried already. Very few people agreed with me." A dark shadow crossed over Aidan's handsome features as his eyes stared off into memories Fin hadn't the faintest idea about.

"You mentioned useless people in power doing more harm than good. Isn't an unnecessary war more harm than good? There is always going to be someone in power whose position is inadequate for them, no matter how great a kingdom or hierarchy."

"War is like fire ... it burns away the old to make way for the new." Aidan shrugged while folding his arms over his chest. "Alright, if you think the world is fine as it is now, tell me ... why aren't there any witches who are nobility? I'll tell you. It's because even if there is one of us amongst them? They hide themselves out of fear. They are not carrying out their Goddess-given responsibility to bring us all closer to nature."

Wait ... am I the first witch to be a noble? That can't be right ... Fin hesitated for a moment in his chopping to ponder this potential discovery. Shaking his head free from the thoughts in order to stay present in the conversation, he responded with:

"Change takes time. Besides, there could be noble witches who have declared themselves, but prefer privacy from the king. It doesn't always have to do with fear. Aren't you yourself set to be given a title soon?"

Aidan let out a world-weary sigh. "I have worked years to earn my current position. I had to become a formidable force to be reckoned with if I wanted any kind of title. Yet the nobles are still wary of me. I doubt I will ever be truly accepted until they see for themselves the power of the pure witches."

"What is it that makes you believe that you are the best one to lead the covens? Or better yet, why is your plan ... your *vision* ... the absolute truth? Others feel the same as you do about many of their ideas."

"Yet none have come as far as I have," Aidan remarked, a prideful note entering his voice. "One day ... if you're lucky ... you will see what it means for a pure witch. You'll see what it is when they embrace their element. The Goddess did not give us such power in order to hide; she gave it to us to make advancements. To rule ..."

"They have never once decreed to the witches that they are meant to rule. The opposite, in fact. We are supposed to be the ones upholding the balance of the world, not forcing it to become what we deem fit."

"Isn't what we deem fit the balanced version of this world?"

"Not if it is only one of us set on burning away a significant portion of both witches and mankind alike." Fin stopped what he was doing then. There was a question he had longed to ask the man who sired him ... and he figured this was the best time to do so.

"Why ... do you like hurting people? You always toyed with and bullied my mother and me, and it wasn't to make us stronger. Mum could never fight back against you, and you knew that." The redhead kept the rage from his voice ... kept the pain, the memories ... all in order to appear as receptive as possible in hopes of getting an honest answer.

Aidan stared at Fin for a long moment without saying a word.

"There are different kinds of strength to be grown in the face of adversity. Even if to you I am the villain of your past, and coincidentally your present, I did make the both of you stronger. Right now it is unfortunate because you just happen to be in my way, and I can still beat you without ever coming close to drawing from my own life source."

The fire witch stood then, as he squared himself off with his son.

"Now. I believe I've answered a great many of your questions. Would you care to tell me about that ring around your neck?"

CHAPTER 21
INTERESTING
INTERROGATIONS

Fin's face hardened for the briefest of moments before he let out a small sigh and then donned a sad smile.

"I'm holding on to it for someone," he answered his father, referring to the band he wore on a chain around his neck. He then began to scrape the cabbage he had finished slicing into one of the bowls nearby.

"So are you betrothed? Or is that a friend's? I did hear that you are close with one of the Zinferan representatives ... it's gold from what I was told by the crew on board with us, so it can't be yours," Aidan mentioned casually, a glint of triumph in his black eyes.

"Something like that," Fin answered vaguely as he began tossing the cabbage with the vinegar, averting his eyes from the chief of military's appraising stare.

"Or"—Aidan chuckled to himself—"could it be the rumors are true that you're in a homosexual relationship with the king's assistant?"

Fin wanted to smile ...

It was too easy ...

He could somehow hear Mr. Howard's infuriated scream in his mind without any effort.

The house witch said nothing and hid his face as he worked to stave off a smirk.

Aidan stilled. "No ... you ... are you serious?"

Fin turned to face his father, his features schooled to the best of his ability. "What's wrong with being gay?"

The Troivackian chief of military's face paled. "You plan on taking a mistress to breed more witches at least, don't you?"

The cook didn't hide his disgust at the comment. "Why in the world ... would I do that?"

"Surely if he loves you, Mr. Howard must see how valuable a witch can be! I'm sure he would be understanding if you tried to—"

"Mr. Howard is not a patient man with me," Fin cut off his father, and he sincerely thought he was going to begin twitching from trying to repress his laughter.

The cook was sticking to the truth as closely as possible ... and should he ever learn of the discussion, the king's assistant would most likely commit a murder suicide ...

"It's just as well that I'll be killing you ... I don't care what your preference is as long as you do your duty and carry on the line," Aidan huffed while shaking his head incredulously.

"Ironic that you want to kill me with that outlook ..." Fin pointed out glibly.

"I can just make another child ... I've been too busy the past few years to give it much thought, but now I see it is more important than I realized." Aidan waved his hand casually as though they were discussing concerns pertaining to the speed with which grass grew.

"How wonderful. A younger sibling." Fin found himself chuckling as he then moved on to the next cabbage head.

"Yes, well, my first child was more a practice round, I suppose."

"That makes sense; as your practice round, though, my advice is to not terrorize your next offspring."

"I won't need to if I succeed with a pure elemental witch from Troivack. They are far more advanced in terms of discipline than Daxaria. Both with their education for their witches as well as their people," Aidan remarked unfeelingly.

Fin decided not to comment any further, and he was saved having to physically bite down on his tongue when the soldier from earlier returned with the honey.

All in all, Fin had managed to keep his relationship with Annika hidden, and at the same time learned more about what his father was thinking … These were all good things.

Though none of the good things changed the small detail of his pending death.

Annika sat cradling the cup of tea in her hands with Katelyn on her left, and the rest of the kitchen aides waiting. Somehow the space felt empty without Fin, even though the aides had learned their lesson, and it was kept significantly cleaner than the last time he had left them. There was just a bit of magic missing that had nothing to do with brooms sweeping the room on their own, or buckets of floating water.

However, that was exactly what made their objective so important … and so they continued to bide their time in the silence …

After a few more drawn-out moments, the faint thrum of endless talking reached their ears.

"—interesting how she didn't like it when I pointed out how everyone experiences flatulence. You wouldn't think that she would refuse my offer of creating a small breeze to clear the smell from the room!" Keith Lee opened the door to the kitchen with his father at his side, who looked stuck between a laugh and a grimace at his son's story.

"Oh my— Hello, everyone! My father said that there was an issue that we needed to solve?" Keith looked around the kitchen smiling, which was when Hannah, with visible hesitancy, stepped forward.

"Yes, we … were hoping, Keith, you might provide the knights and me with … with some … advice. We are considering opening a tavern one day, and seeing as you are knowledgeable about everything …"

The young soon-to-be mage clapped his hands in delight.

"But of course! Shall we all sit and have a cup of—"

"Well, Lady Jenoure and her mother-in-law were wanting to discuss the wedding between Mrs. Ashowan and the captain here, so we wondered if you'd like to go into Austice for a pint?" Hannah managed to smile and make it seem genuine, while Mage Lee suddenly stood impeccably straight and turned glittering eyes to the two women seated at Fin's cooking table.

"I normally do not imbibe; you know how great a responsibility it is to wield powerful magic and—"

Mage Lee clapped his son's shoulder. "Nonsense, cutting loose every now and then is equally as beneficial as practicing a regimented life. Go with them and hear what dilemmas they are faced with."

Kate shot Annika a quick look, her surprise over the bait working barely hidden.

Once the aides and knights had left with Keith leading the way, already reciting what he knew about running a tavern, Mage Lee turned to the two women at the table with a cheery smile.

"Mrs. Ashowan, you must forgive my rudeness, I completely forgot to offer you congratulations regarding your engagement to our dear captain! Are you thinking of a fall wedding? It would certainly give you enough time to arrange the guest list—and by next year we should hopefully have found a way to end the war."

Kate blinked in astonishment. She was reluctant to admit she hadn't truly believed the viscountess's insistence that the man was obsessed with matrimony.

"Mage Lee, while I appreciate and thank you for your well wishes, I'm afraid right now with us knowing so little about what is happening with my son ..." Kate's voice was disconnected and halting.

Annika reached over and clasped her hands comfortingly. "Sorry, Mage Lee. We had only just started saying how nice it would be for Fin to be back safely, and how she could even plan with him what he thinks might be best for the engagement feast."

"An engagement feast!?" The delight and excitement on the man's face had the profound effect of once again startling Kate, but the mage didn't seem to notice. "What a splendid thought! Have the feast before the war to bolster good tidings, then afterward we can celebrate with the official ceremony. I think you'd look ravishing with a bouquet filled with yellow blooms. I can even speak with Kasim about cultivating enough to—"

"Mage Lee. Please ... my daughter-in-law is distressed right now. We haven't learned anything about Fin's safety or what is happening aboard that ship with my blasted ex-husband and I ..." Katelyn trailed off as tears welled up in her eyes.

Annika knew the woman was too purehearted to fake those tears, and so she made sure to give the healer's hands an extra squeeze.

"Well ... surely the captain told you both that Finlay is fine!" Mage Lee ventured nervously. He was clearly desperate to keep the topic on wedding plans.

"But that tells us nothing! He could've been forced to write that," Annika pointed out while summoning her own tears into her gaze to back the elder even further into a corner.

Realizing that the situation was quickly spiraling out of his control, Mage Lee shifted the staff in his hands nervously.

"Lady Ashowan ... Mrs. Ashowan I ... I am sorry for seeming insensitive. I-I know Fin ... is fine! He managed to tip off His Majesty about some important information and the rest we ... I'm sure it was nothing!"

Annika allowed her tears to fall as she fixed the mage with her most heartbreaking expression.

"What was nothing? I could lose the last of my Piereva family soon; are you saying I'll lose my husband as well?"

"No, no! It was just ... he mentioned that in a couple of days that the Troivackian men might think of him ... poorly. He said it far more cryptically, though ..."

Annika's gaze sharpened, and Kate went rigid.

"What was he talking about then ... what's happening in a few days? Is it when he meets the king? Isn't he on the ship for the week?" Kate demanded desperately.

Mage Lee held up his hands in surrender.

"I do not know. We are waiting to see if he is able to reveal more in tomorrow's letter."

"Will ... will the others even tell us if he is in danger?" Annika asked quietly. Truthfully it was taking every ounce of strength she had to keep the weak façade up. She wanted to spring into action immediately and shake the mage by his robes, but she knew she had to be careful in case there was more to learn.

"I ... imagine His Majesty will let you know if the status changes! Now ... erm ... if you might excuse me. I best go see to some ... work I have to do. Right now."

The Royal Mage of the court then darted from the kitchen as hastily as was possible without flat-out running.

"I don't like this ..." Katelyn Ashowan's eyes bored into the worn cooking table in front of her.

"Neither do I. If His Majesty isn't sending a ship tonight, there isn't a hope in hell—barring a miracle—they will catch up ... Unless we go with a smaller vessel, but then we have no military power to get him back."

Annika stood up and faced the castle door, a plan brewing in her mind, when her mother-in-law's gentle touch on her forearm drew her attention back.

"Remember, everything you do now, you also risk the lives of your children."

Annika felt as though a stone had been dropped in her stomach. She still hadn't wrapped her head around her pregnancy, but to then also be inhibited in how she could protect Fin in order to take care of her off-spring? Brats she'd never met, and really, who would continue to invade her body and life … ?

She struggled quietly for a moment to think of words to say that could diffuse the healer's worries while not betraying her anger.

"Not all women … feel maternal. Or find the changes easy to accept," Kate began slowly. There was a wisdom in her stare that stunned Annika to the point where she forgot her frustration. "You have been quite successful in your life from what I've seen and heard, but … this is not something to ignore or dominate. It just happens, and you adapt the best you can."

"Do … Do the women who perhaps not feel … excited or … loving toward their children ever change?" The viscountess's heart was pounding. It had been a lingering fear in her mind since the moment she found out about her condition …

Was she going to be a good mother who loved her progenies?

"Some don't. Some most likely shouldn't have had their children if I'm being frank. And believe me, I pity those families fiercely, but in your case, I'm not worried."

"Why not? Just because Fin is good with children doesn't mean—"

"If you love Fin? You are going to adore your children. It might not be the second you hold them, or even in the first week or month but … you will. One day you will love them so much that you would risk treason just to save them."

Annika smiled a little, but she still wasn't confident about Kate's assurances. She rested her hand on the woman's shoulder, though, and with a firm tone that she hoped was convincing said, "Well, right now, I think the best thing for my children is ensuring their father returns in one piece."

Without waiting to hear if her mother-in-law had anything more to say, she turned toward the castle door to depart. Annika knew that, despite her condition, she was going to do whatever she could to keep Fin alive. No matter the cost. Striding forward purposefully, a rough plan began to form in her mind. Annika hoped that Clara wasn't finding it too difficult keeping the captain and Mr. Howard occupied. After all, odds were high that they were already aware Mage Lee would be the most likely to blurt something out ...

"Only five minutes, Viscountess. The captain will kill me if he hears I let you speak to her."

Nodding to the prison guard, but keeping her hood drawn, the lady spoke. "I only want to confirm that my trade ships have had no business with her. Thank you for your understanding."

The guard grunted, clearly not fully convinced, but he had already tried to argue with her an hour before and it had been the longest, most headache-inducing hour of his life. He then led the noblewoman down the stone steps carrying a torch high above himself, keys jangling at his side as he proceeded into the dark corridor lined with cells.

As it turned out, they didn't need to walk very far, as the very first set of bars held the occupant Annika was interested in speaking with.

"We keep her close to the stairs in case she needs to call out for help. I don't understand what ails her brother, but the man has more foam than ale in his head if you know what I mean."

Annika didn't know what he meant, but also didn't care to ask. All she was interested in was getting the information she needed.

After the guard lit the torch beside the cell, he pounded his fist on the bars, making several of the other prisoners groan and shout out over the ruckus.

"Oyy. You've got a visitor. Be nice to her and she might be nice to you," the guard called out, looking completely bored with the situation. After giving Annika a brief nod, he turned and headed back up the stairs to his office without a second look back. He didn't need or want any more trouble from the lady.

A shadow shifted in the cell after a moment, and the jangle of chains slowly drew closer until, standing in the warm firelight, with dark bags under her eyes, and her hair looking an oily mess, was Elizabeth Nonata.

CHAPTER 22
TWO SIDES OF THE
SAME COIN

"C aptain! Those two ships … they—" The first mate halted in his tracks when he realized that the captain was sitting with Mr. Helmer and the Daxarian ambassador. The captain seemed to be in some kind of trance as he polished off the plate of food in front of him.

As the man slowly set his empty dish down, a wistful smile upon his face, the first mate hadn't a clue what could've put the normally stern and cautious man so at ease … unless his cup was full to the brim with Troivackian moonshine.

"Er … Captain?" The first mate glanced around him then and noticed suddenly that literally everyone with a plate in front of themselves was in various states of peace and contentment that was borderline disturbing …

"What is it, Ewan?" The captain's soft relaxed voice drew the first mate's eyes back to his superior, though it was clear that the man was greatly disturbed.

"Those two ships that we noticed this morning have drawn closer; could it be that the Daxarian military has sent them to attack?"

The captain stood with a grunt, plucking up his small glass of wine and taking a leisurely sip before holding out his hand for the spyglass.

The first mate hastily handed him the brass instrument and waited as his superior took a leisurely glance around.

"Ewan, lad, you need to rest. That vessel to our port side is a deep sea fisherman's vessel, most likely coming out for a fine catch of mackerel. The ship to our starboard is a Troivackian merchant ship." The captain clapped a hand on his protégé's shoulder as he handed back the spyglass. "Have a plate of food and take a seat. We're talking about the tranquility of Troivackian nights to Mr. Helmer's son here. A greater quiet you've never heard when your feet is set on the central sands …"

The first mate looked nervously toward the Troivack's chief of military who was regarding the captain with a raised eyebrow and a rare, amused smile.

"Aye … Captain. I'll put Lorne on the helm."

Ewan left feeling completely baffled over his superior's relaxed attitude … tensions had been rising every day as the time for their attack drew nearer, especially with the fire witch on board … but … why was everyone acting as though it were over? As though they were on a voyage back home instead of awaiting battle?

The first mate continued to ponder this as he walked over and informed the soldier currently steering the ship he had been assigned his break. When Ewan eventually made his way over to the two soldiers who had been tasked with guarding Mr. Helmer's son, he noticed they, too, were staring around at their shipmates in confusion.

"I'm here for my meal."

The two men turned to him, both of them taking a moment to snap out of their evaluations.

"Here. Maybe you can tell us what the cook did to the food. I've not seen the soldiers this quiet since the funerals from the last civil war …" the larger of the two men explained, his keen eyes surveying the smiles and good-natured discussions wafting through every group of resting men.

The observation made Ewan even more hesitant to take his dinner from them … but then again Mr. Helmer had been with his son when he had been cooking; there was nothing he could have done to it without being noticed.

Picking up the strange crispy potato … biscuit? Pancake? Ewan took a tentative bite, and after two seconds, he felt a breath leave his body he hadn't realized he'd been holding. A breath that he felt like he'd kept locked in his chest since … since he left home.

The flavor was comforting, and yet so deeply delicious that it was also rejuvenating ...

With each bite he expected the concoction to become too salty, or too bland, but it never happened. It was perfect from the very first to the very last bite.

Turning his attention next to the cabbage, he used the blade at his side to tentatively try some of the meticulously sliced vegetable, and the moment his teeth sank into the crisp crunchiness ...

New flavors teased him under the familiar ingredients of vinegar, salt, and pepper.

"Not you, too!"

Ewan jumped. He had been so captivated by his meal that he had completely forgotten the two Troivackian soldiers were watching him.

How was it, food could make him feel so ... good? He felt at peace and comforted, and yet he also felt ... sated. Sated on a level he hadn't realized had been deprived.

"I-I ... have you two not had any yet?" the first mate asked, trying to return to the moment before his strange emotional journey.

"No. We can once we're finished, but we aren't sure we want to at this point," the shorter of the men grumbled.

"You will want to try this. It isn't poisoned; it just— It's the best meal I've ever had in my life."

The short Troivackian shoulder glanced at the dishes in front of him, then flatly back at the first mate as though he had just claimed they were eating rainbows.

"Looks like cabbage and potatoes to me."

"It is, but ... it's better. Try some now. It's fine." Ewan waved his hand encouragingly.

"Yes, Stanley, Bruce. You should eat, you've been on your feet all day." Fin appeared behind the first mate, making him nearly jump out of his skin. "Sorry, Ewan. Didn't mean to frighten you. Go have a seat and enjoy the rest of the meal."

For whatever reason, without thinking about it, Ewan gave a quick bow to the redhead before trodding off to take a seat. The action made both Bruce and Stanley glance at each other in surprise.

"Alright, you two. I can take over for now, and after you've eaten, we need to play a drinking game together; the captain says he'll even share some of his moonshine."

The men immediately perked up in excitement, before remembering they were wary of the cook.

"You're not a noble. Why are people treating you like you're … important?" Bruce asked with a frown.

Fin's eyebrows moved upward in surprise over the man's candid question. "I suppose because I don't behave like a commoner, or how you expect me to."

"You got that right," Stanley grumbled. "You should be shitting in your pants like every other Daxarian would be. Instead you wanna feed us an' share a drink, but you don't wanna become a Troivackian …"

"Why can't we be friends while I remain a Daxarian and you two remain Troivackians?" Fin asked with a friendly smile.

"'Cause … we're too different, an' we're going to have to kill you, an' most likely your friends and family and—"

"Most likely, but not for certain … A lot can change in a short amount of time. Besides, none of that is happening today, is it?"

The men both blinked and frowned in bewilderment.

"I … s'pose not," Bruce answered slowly.

"Then for today, we know we can be friends."

"So you can betray us later?" Bruce asked coldly.

"I don't attack first, and I'm too terrible at lying to betray anyone. Isn't that a relief?" Fin explained with a laugh.

Stanley's expression darkened immediately. "Troivack doesn't work that way. Only the weak trust."

Fin's smile faded as he stared at the two men appraisingly. "That must be exhausting. Constantly on guard … not having a single person you can build trust with."

"We trust that we can't trust anyone," Bruce explained with a growl.

"Well … that sounds like you're a lonely, individualistic people … but let me ask you something. If you can't trust people, and you must always stand alone, knowing that even the person at your side might stab you in the back, who is stronger? The army that isn't looking to betray one another? Or the army that believes they will die by their loved ones rather than the enemy? Which would you want to be?"

Both men were quiet for a while, but Fin waited patiently.

"I'd like to not be scared of anything. Even my friend turning on me, because I never trusted him," Bruce declared proudly.

"Are you happy then?"

"Aye," the two answered in unison.

"Well, then that is where we differ, and that's alright. However, in Daxaria I can say our mortality rate is quite a bit lower than Troivack's ... and even if we are friends today and you have a knife in my back by the day after next, at least we will have had a nice time before then. Now, grab a plate, and get going; the sun is setting and we still have to clean the galley."

The Troivackian soldiers glanced at each other, clearly ill at ease with the conversation, but one thing was certain ...

Their dialogue had definitely made them even more mystified by the red-haired cook.

Annika stared at Elizabeth Nonata from beneath the shadow of her cloak and watched as the woman tilted her head trying to see who was visiting her.

"I want to know the name of the ships you used for smuggling in soldiers." Annika lowered her voice in hopes of hiding her identity, even though the two women had never formally met.

"That information was confiscated by the king and is now a secret of the crown," the assistant recited dully.

"Are they docked now in Austice?"

"That information was confiscated by the king and is now a secret of the crown," Elizabeth repeated in the same flat voice she had used before.

"If a Troivackian warship saw that they were yours, would they see the ship as friend or foe?"

The assistant hesitated then. Finally releasing a long sigh, she leaned against the bars wearily as she looked at her mysterious visitor disinterestedly.

"Any idea where my dog went? He chased a black cat out of here a day ago when the captain came down for questioning."

"I have not heard about any kind of dog being around here," Annika said truthfully.

Though I do know a certain pyromaniac black cat ...

"I see ... find my dog. Make sure he's alright, and I'll tell you what you want to know." Elizabeth Nonata shrugged.

"Ah ... I will help you find your dog if you give me the information first."

"That isn't how I practice business. Good evening." Elizabeth Nonata bobbed her head and began to shuffle back toward her cot, her chains jangling as she moved.

Annika stood there pondering how best to handle this ... she couldn't waste time hunting down a dog ... Plus if she asked the captain about it, he would know instantly that she had been talking with a prisoner.

"Is there anything you want that I can bequeath more imminently for the information? A bath, perhaps?"

"Hm ... I suppose a reduced sentence is out of the question. The king was quite lenient given that I was not actively involved in treason ... five-year sentence for obstruction of justice and a few other trifle offenses. A bath is generous, but ... short term. A job as a maid somewhere once I leave here might be nice." The woman cited the proposition idly.

However, despite the hopeless note in Elizabeth's voice, Annika then had her answer.

"Here is what I'm willing to offer you, Nonata. You give me seven years of servitude instead of five years in this cell, and you have a deal."

The former assistant to the infamous Madam Mathilda sat up, her face openly dubious.

"For someone to make me a deal like that, you must be very powerful in either the court, or the underbelly of Austice. I'd like to know which end of the beast I'm dealing with."

"I've made my terms. Asking for more is greedy." There was a threatening note in Annika's voice despite her speaking softly.

Elizabeth visibly swallowed, then stood slowly. "I don't kill people or commit treason. I honestly didn't know what my brother had been doing, and this"—she gestured to the grimy cell—"I'd like to keep as a onetime experience."

"Fine."

"I want nothing to do with human trafficking."

"It is done. Now. Do we have an agreement?" the viscountess asked, her voice beginning to rasp.

Sidling back over to the cell door, the assistant put her hand through the bars.

As Annika reached her own gloved hand out and grasped it, Elizabeth tried to yank her forward, but the viscountess was far stronger and better trained than the woman who'd sat behind a desk most her life.

Elizabeth's head banged against the cell bars, making them ring and forcing a sharp gasp from her lips as she tried to move to instinctively clutch her head. Only, her hand was still in the vise grip of the hooded figure.

"I am not to be trifled with or taken lightly, Nonata. If you think to betray me, or flee from me after taking my deal, I will have you rot in this cell for ten years of your life. More if you think to try and pull something that harms me."

The assistant's eyes were watering from the pain in her head, but she slowly nodded.

"Do we have an understanding?" Annika asked icily, her grip tightening yet again around the woman's hand.

"Yes," Elizabeth whimpered weakly, realizing the sincerity in her visitor's warning.

"Excellent. I will return momentarily with a contract for you to sign."

Turning on her heel, the viscountess headed toward the stairs where she would commandeer a desk to draft the deal she had made countless of times with the staff members of her home. Though this one would be a little different ... After all, Elizabeth Nonata was one of the best assistants in Austice. It'd be a waste to let her talent erode away ...

"I know who you are."

Annika froze, her foot on the first stone step leading back aboveground.

She turned slowly to once again face the imprisoned woman, her heart suddenly skipping a beat.

"Oh? Who am I, Nonata?"

"I've heard about you ... you're ... you're the Dragon." Unbeknownst to the two women, there was a small shifting movement in the cell behind Annika as the man called Red sat up straight on his cot, his eyes glinting upon hearing the name of the infamous underworld figure.

A gradual smile climbed its way up the viscountess's lips, which Elizabeth only saw half of, and yet it chilled her all the same.

"That's right, and it'd be wise of you to never forget that there isn't a corner of this world you can hide, where you can be safe from me."

Red's cracked lips curved into a smile. At last ... the opportunity to make a deal with someone even his benefactor feared.

CHAPTER 23
HIDING ONE'S HEART

Madam Mathilda's ship docked two days ago and has already been turned over to the king for any documents or stowaways. Currently it is sitting at the dock with a handful of knights guarding it. However, if I find a crew, no matter how sparse, I think I might get the chance I need," Annika explained to Clara as she swept down the corridor of her keep while removing her cloak and handing it to her maid.

"I will draft the proposal for Elizabeth Nonata's release into my care for His Majesty. He won't like it, but I think my counterproposal for her punishment and subsequent use will be far more beneficial to the kingdom." The two women stepped into a small, dark room lined with bookshelves that were filled to the brim with scrolls and tomes. Near the back wall stood a large oak desk, which Annika set to seating herself at.

"Are you certain this is all it will take?" Clara asked, eyeing the scroll clutched in Annika's hand with a raised eyebrow.

"I need two people to make sure I get what I'm after ... and this information Elizabeth Nonata and that nasty man Red submitted to me is the surest way to not only do that, but also tie up some loose ends that will make His Majesty more than a little grateful." Annika grinned while she stretched her feet up on the ledge of her desk and stared at her maid.

"Now, I've never really had the natural inclination to draw attention to myself, but I think this time … I'm willing to make an exception."

Clara eyed her mistress uncertainly, but with a small sigh, she was forced to silently admit she could see how Annika's plan would indeed be successful.

So Clara curtsied to her mistress and left to carry out her tasks.

While the maid had been happy in a way for her mistress's recent marriage and announcement of her pregnancy, she had begun to worry that their days as a conniving duo were drawing to a close.

Smiling to herself as she strode through the shadowed halls of her mistress's keep, Clara couldn't help but be comforted by the fact that whether taking on the title of wife or mother, Annika would never be the kind of woman who would be content to sit on the sidelines of life.

Fin stared at the group of Troivackian soldiers with his arms folded over his chest and his ankle propped on his knee. A wry grin spread over his face, and despite the peaceful rock of the ship beneath them and the spectacularly beautiful span of a starry night sky, the men remained fixated on him.

"There's no way you can take three shots of Troivackian moonshine without tossing your dinner!" Stanley announced with a smug grin.

"I bet you I can, and if I'm wrong, I get to ask you each a question you have to answer honestly. Nothing to do with the war, I swear. If you opt out, however, I get to decide your punishment."

Fin explained his wager with a mischievous glint in his eye.

"You got yourself a bet, witch," Bruce growled despite a smile curling his lips.

Fin nodded to the barrel surface where two small steel cups had been set.

Stanley stepped forward, bottle in hand; he poured the clear moonshine into the cup nearest the redhead.

Still grinning, Fin slowly reached forward and lifted the drink.

"To all your health and happiness!" He tossed the liquor back easily.

The men all cheered and clapped.

"Lucky shot!"

"Beginner's fortune!"

"You won't make it past the second!" one of the men called out from the back of the crowd making everyone, including Fin, laugh.

Bruce stepped forward then, a hyper-demonic grin on his face as he poured the next shot to the brim.

The men began to chant in unanimous "Hohs," as though they were preparing to attack—only they were all grinning.

The witch raised the small cup, briefly glancing over his shoulder to see his father and the captain watching the whole scene before giving them a wink and tossing back the second drink.

He grimaced, slammed the cup on the table, and doubled over. After a moment, he straightened, sending the men into a fit of cheers and shouts.

"I must admit, you're doing better than I thought you would," Stanley muttered while stepping forward again.

The ship's deck fell silent as Fin beamed at the men and raised the cup again.

"A toast to your mothers, wives, and children. To your sacrifice for your country!"

The awkward silence that followed the last statement was eased by the redhead slinging back the third shot of moonshine without another word.

Immediately forgetting the moment before, the men all broke out in cheers and shouts of encouragement as Fin remained hunched over for a moment. The back of his wrist rose to his mouth, which made the crowd fall quiet once again for a moment, before he slowly stood and, finally, punched his hand into the air in victory.

The uproar was deafening.

"Your son is quite … charming in his own way," the captain noted with a small smile as Aidan observed the entire scene with his arms folded and a bemused look on his face.

"Indeed. It is quite impressive given that less than a year ago, I heard he was practically a recluse on the Isle of Quildon," the fire witch observed with a calculating stare.

Aidan watched his son's happy expression while he shared in the fun and encouraged the jubilant mood of the men, and he couldn't help but wonder what caused such a dramatic shift in Fin's personality …

Was it because he was finally with a man he loved?

Or perhaps was it that he was acting happy to make him, his father, spiteful?

Aidan frowned. Neither option seemed like a whole truth, and this troubled him greatly.

"Alright! I get to ask each of you a question," Fin announced with a slight flush in his cheeks.

The crowd chuckled then hushed as he turned to the nearest soldier. "What was the color of your mother's eyes?"

The soldier visibly balked. "My ... My mother? Dark, of course. Like any good Troivackian woman."

"Were they cold or warm?" Fin prompted a little more softly.

"She ... She was ... warm in her own way. I know she loves me but hides it as she should," the man announced with a self-assuring nod.

Fin said nothing but nodded in a vague understanding way before moving on to the next man.

"What is your favorite food?"

"We don't have the luxury of multiple food options due to our crops failing," came the gruff accusatory answer. Only it was met with a cavalier shrug from the Daxarian hostage.

"Of all the things you've eaten to date, what is your favorite then? Remember, you swore to adhere to the bet." There was a slight slur in Fin's speech, which somehow made the men more relaxed and inclined to be honest.

"Your ... Your potato flats were the best things," the soldier muttered awkwardly, as though expecting Fin to make the confession more painful.

Fin didn't say anything in response, however, and instead moved on to the next man for another strange question.

The captain and Aidan watched for a few more moments, but they eventually resumed their previous conversation. Despite most of his thoughts returning to more formal matters, the fire witch couldn't help but feel a strange tickling in the back of his mind ... he was beginning to wonder if understanding his son was something that was a little more difficult than he had originally assumed ... and he didn't care for that notion one bit.

Little did Aidan know, Fin was working his way deeper into the crowd, with the sole intention of gaining the final piece of information that would make the king's mission a success ... finding out how many men were going to attack Austice.

Fin was awoken the next morning with a searing pain in his arm, making him gasp and sit upright with difficulty in his hammock.

"You need to write your letter," Aidan informed his son casually amongst the hammocks of snoring Troivackian soldiers, a single flame extending from his index finger.

The redhead blinked and glanced around himself, realizing that it was still night.

"The sun isn't up yet," he noted, slowly clambering out of his hammock and experimentally tapping his forearm that was still stinging.

"I'm glad you inherited your mother's talents of observation. The letter needs to be sent earlier if it is to get to your king at a reasonable hour," the fire witch explained dryly while gesturing toward the ladder to the upper deck.

"The first-degree burn was necessary because … ?" Fin asked while slowly moving and keeping his gaze fixed on his father.

"A reminder that you are a little too comfortable amongst your enemies. Unless, of course, the past day has changed your mind pertaining to my offer."

"It hasn't; I just find it pointless to be stressed if there is nothing I can do about the situation." Fin shrugged as he climbed up the ladder swiftly. His shoulder was still sore from his father's first assault; the new burn on his forearm was on the opposite side, but the redhead had experienced enough of those injuries to know it'd scar without any other lasting damage.

Breathing in the cold sea air, Fin stared up at the night sky, and immediately stilled in awe. The galaxies spread before him in billions of twinkling lights with hues of different blues swept together by the Gods themselves.

"For a man with such an appreciation for life, you have a frightening lack of ambition or drive to survive." Aidan's voice beside Fin's ear did nothing to detract from the beauty of the sky.

"I will survive long enough to ensure Lord Charles and his family are safe, but I will not pretend to be confident that there won't be a cost to me. Once they are freed, I've achieved everything I ever wanted to in my life," the house witch informed his father with a sad smile on his face.

"What about that ring about your neck? Don't you have to give that back to someone?"

"They can take it back if they need to." Fin's chest ached as his mind briefly allowed Annika's smiling face to appear, then he casually moved his gaze to the horizon.

"So if I guaranteed the survival of the Piereva family, you wouldn't care if I killed you right this moment?" Aidan asked while slowly stepping forward until he stood in his son's line of sight.

"I'd rather you not as I have some people who will be sad from it, but if there is no chance of survival, and the innocent are safe, then I've done all that is important." Fin's blue eyes glowed in the light of the heavens, and his expression was serene as a gentle breeze ruffled his hair. For some reason, Aidan suddenly felt something he wasn't used to feeling … something he didn't even know the name of …

Instead of lingering in the strange moment that was somehow making his throat hurt, the fire witch turned and began striding over to the galley.

"Come on. Let's get that letter sent." Aidan turned but didn't stare directly at his son again. "We will see the Troivackian king today for Lord Charles Piereva's hearing, and after that … We will see if you are as comfortable climbing into death's carriage as you claim."

Fin watched his father's back briefly before once again looking to where the water and sky met, and in doing so, he noticed the pink glow of dawn begin to rise between them. As he beheld the beauty of the new day for a few still precious moments, Fin recognized the unmistakable streak of red emerge over the waves, and something in his heart knew then that he would be lucky to see another sunrise.

CHAPTER 24
COUNTERMEASURES

Annika stood on the docks, her hood drawn as Clara faced off with the two knights guarding the gangplank to the ship. She knew the moment she boarded the vessel, word would be sent to the king, and so, she waited.

Her churning stomach reminded her that she had eaten significantly less for her dinner the preceding night to try and deter the nasty illness she was experiencing as a side effect of her pregnancy. Dawn was just beginning to crest the horizon, and her heart was racing, despite her calm outward demeanor.

Closing her eyes, Annika focused on taking several deep breaths, honing her thoughts and her senses while doing so. She knew nothing less than a perfect execution of the plan could happen if she wanted to help save Fin.

Her husband's smile flashed in her mind's eye, and Annika nearly vomited what little was in her stomach at the sudden flood of emotion that wrangled her body.

You better be safe, Fin. If you're dead ... I don't know what the hell I'm going to do.

The sound of a carriage and hooves reached Annika's ears and immediately her skin prickled.

Turning swiftly, she saw in the light of the torches that lined the docks the unmistakable royal carriage making its way directly to where she stood.

Girding herself, the viscountess braced for what she hoped to be a conversation that would not result in her being arrested.

As soon as the polished sleek black vehicle ground to a halt, its golden handles shining in the dim light, the door opened as a silent invitation. With her back ramrod straight, Annika strode back up the creaking wooden steps of the dock onto dry land and climbed into the carriage.

Only, when she seated herself and lowered her hood, she was stunned to see the queen's annoyed face.

"Ainsley! What are you— Weren't you hurt?!"

"Oh, please. I just popped a few stitches. I'm perfectly fine as long I have a cushion under my arse," the queen quipped with a small twitch in her cheeks. Annika guessed she was still in pain but had made a special journey to see her.

"Are you having a pleasant night drive through the city?" the viscountess asked innocently.

"I saw your proposal to release Elizabeth Nonata into your custody. Norman's already suspicious of you being up to something, and he wants to question you about this. I just happen to know you better and figured you'd already be about to commit some kind of crime." Ainsley completely ignored Annika's earlier sass and got straight to the point.

"Like you would be any different in my place," the viscountess pointed out evenly.

"I'd be worried, yes," Ainsley began while narrowing her gaze.

Annika folded her arms over her chest and smiled beautifully. "Does this mean I have your permission?"

"Walk me through this plan of yours," Ainsley countered while raising a skeptical eyebrow.

"I plan to take the ship that Madam Mathilda used to traffic soldiers into Daxaria and get close enough to Fin's ship so that Raymond can go on board and find out if my brother and his family are alive and unharmed, and if so, what coordinates are the king's ship. If Fin himself is also alive and well, Raymond would stow away on the ship with him while I sneak aboard. In the middle of the night the three of us would commandeer the ship and go rescue my brother, then return home."

"Despite this plan violating the contracts Norman signed with Mr. Helmer naming Finlay as an ambassador, you think you can overtake two ships with three people? Are you drunk?" Ainsley asked patiently.

Annika shrugged innocently. "I've done crazier things."

Ainsley chuckled. "Oh sure. While I'm sure there are more logistics to this plan, I'm most curious about the insignificant detail of how you intend to go about talking your way out of charges of treason or interference of kingdom business with commandeering Mathilda's ship that is currently under our investigation," the queen pondered aloud, her tone light but her gaze hard.

"Well, now, you'll never know."

Ainsley studied her best friend for a few more moments before finally letting out a long sigh.

"No. I am not letting you do this." Knocking twice on the door of the carriage, the vehicle lurched into movement.

"Clara is still at the docks," Annika pointed out with a strained smile.

"She'll take the horses you rode back; she's a smart girl and will figure it out. Now, we need to calm you down because as much as I understand how you feel, this plan is loaded with obvious problems. Norman is handling this. You need to trust him."

"How is he handling it?" Annika demanded, her gaze sharp.

"We are supposed to receive a letter today by midday. A decision will be made afterward."

"So you expect me to twiddle my thumbs and wait?" the viscountess countered stonily.

"I hear needlework is a fantastic pastime for women of the court," Ainsley said with a dry smile.

Annika was not amused. "It's my entire family out there, Ainsley. What would you do in my position?"

"I would do my job. You need to protect this kingdom in your own way, not blindly charge into an attack that will end with unnecessary deaths."

"Then I need more reassurance on how His Majesty plans on protecting my people, because right now that is my biggest problem with it all. You expect my trust? You must give me some of yours. Isn't that what you told me when we first met?"

Ainsley's lips pursed as she studied her friend for several long moments. As the carriage turned and began heading uphill, Annika guessed they were returning to the castle. The journey continued on with the two women caught in a stalemate of silence. Annika seemed to barely blink as the carriage trundled along, and the queen appeared to be deep in thought.

By the time they pulled up in front of the castle, neither of them had spoken, yet just as Ainsley placed her hand on the carriage handle, she turned to her friend.

"Slip out in the stables and meet me in our chamber. I will have a gown prepared. Once you are dressed, I want you to meet me in the council room."

Annika gave a single nod as the monarch then exited the vehicle and greeted the servants who stood waiting for her.

Meanwhile, the viscountess leaned her head back into the soft emerald-green velvet of the seat and allowed the smallest of smiles to climb up her face as the carriage once again resumed moving.

All according to plan …

Annika held the dress that had been laid out on the queen's bed in front of herself and let out a long-suffering sigh before dropping her gaze to her bump. "You just had to be the children of an excellent cook, didn't you?" she muttered before moving her gaze over to the queen's wardrobe.

"Sorry, Ainsley," she announced to the empty room before moving over to the ornate wooden furniture.

Rummaging about, she finally found one of the gowns that the queen had to have made for her pregnancy. Turning back to the dress originally laid out, Annika pulled out one of her knives and cut a few stitches in the dress to create a small yet noticeable hole while once again apologizing mentally to her best friend.

No sooner had she dressed herself in the cream-colored gown with its incredibly forgiving waistline, when a folded piece of parchment was slipped under the door.

Meeting delayed. Breakfast to be sent, stay in passage until you hear the maids leave. Someone will knock three times when it is time to meet. Wait a hundred counts afterward before leaving.

Annika wearily pinched the bridge of her nose, then tossed the parchment into the hearth filled with glowing embers that flared briefly as it consumed the missive.

Moving back toward the passageway, the viscountess briefly wondered at what point would she no longer fit in the convenient secret entrance, and she immediately found herself shying away from the frightful answer.

As Annika strolled down the corridor having finished her breakfast, then counted to one hundred after three knocks, she found herself fighting off the urge to yawn. She had been up all night after all …

The guards straightened in her presence, but Annika could see the confusion in their eyes. No one was aware she had even arrived at the castle.

Once they had alerted the occupants of the room, she swept in with a graceful nod of thanks.

Upon entering, she was pleased to see the king, the queen, Mr. Howard, Captain Antonio, Mage Lee, and Lord Fuks in attendance.

"Viscountess Ashowan, thank you for joining us. Please take a seat," the ruler greeted while also gesturing to a vacant chair at the table.

Annika gave a curtsy before wordlessly seating herself; she ignored the questioning look Ainsley was giving her as she regarded the dress that was not the one she had laid out.

"My wife has announced that the stress over Lord Ashowan's well-being is wearing on you to a worrying degree, and that it is in our best interest to share with you what we learn in his letters."

Annika let out a relieved breath and smiled gratefully. "That would be incredibly kind of you, sire, thank you."

Norman eyed her suspiciously, but he proceeded to pick up a piece of parchment then hand it to her.

The viscountess's expression immediately warmed at the sight of Fin's handwriting. It was slanted and scrawled in its usual precise yet somehow messy manner.

After reading the letter's contents, however, her face paled. "A day or two … they're going to kill him in a day or two."

The men glanced at one another worriedly.

"Why do you say that with such certainty, my lady?" Captain Antonio asked while frowning.

"Baron Gauva's nephew has vowed to kill Fin. You should remember, Captain; it apparently happened when you arrested him."

Antonio's posture stiffened. "How do you know this, Viscountess? You were in your estate in Austice at the time."

"Fin … Fin told me everything when he came to see me. Told me about the attack, about you becoming betrothed to his mother while he was incarcerated …"

The captain cleared his throat loudly, making more than one person in attendance grin fondly at the memory.

"Lady Ashowan, we have not yet read today's missive. Are you prepared to hear what it might say?" Norman's quiet voice brought everyone back to the present, and all the men immediately sobered.

Annika gave a single firm nod, even though she was beginning to worry again that she might have to vomit.

The king studied her face, his eyebrows twitching for a moment as though he had noticed something strange on her face before finally turning his gaze to the scroll that Mr. Howard was handing him.

Unfurling the parchment, everyone held their breaths.

To the King of Daxaria, Norman Reyes,

I am well and intact, the starry sky this early morning was beautiful to behold, and the red sky of the morning promises an equally vivid sunset. I will be sad to miss it as I will be spending my day with the King of Troivack, though I look forward to commencing with the hearing so that I might be able to send you good news soon regarding Lady Jenoure's family. Last night I enjoyed a night of drinking and camaraderie with the Troivackian soldiers aboard my ship, though they claim it'd be even more fun if their entire family could've properly initiated me to their circles. I imagine it'd be a rousing good time if they were all together, perhaps it was better that it was only half of them I was subjected to. I'm not sure I'd survive their toasting drinks otherwise.

I must go now, as I am about to meet His Majesty Matthias the Sixth, and I am certain that meeting the leader of a foreign nation will be a memory to last a lifetime.

Send my mother my love, and remind my aide who is tending to my cat in my absence that it is perfectly acceptable that he should be allowed to sleep in the bed. He is a wonderful companion that I hope will remind him of me while I'm gone.

Stay safe, Your Majesty.

Sincerely,

Finlay Ashowan

Norman frowned at the page, but both the captain and Annika looked pale.

"The red sky … the red sky is a warning. He is saying he will not live to see the sunset once he meets the king," Antonio announced quietly.

"He … is telling me his familiar will remind me of him when he's gone," Annika added on, her voice coming out as a croak.

Every eye swiveled back and forth between the two.

"Why … both of you … explain," Norman demanded with a frown.

174

"Your Majesty, it is a saying that the Zinferans often use who sail. 'Red sky in the morning, sailor take warning.' The latter half is that 'red sky at night, sailor's delight.' However, he mentioned not being able to see it this evening. Judging how Mr. Helmer most likely read these, I don't think he cares about the blatant hint. As long as there is deniability."

Norman nodded before letting out an agitated breath and turning to Annika.

"He ... I ... told him I did not want the feline in our bedchamber while we sleep. No one has been placed in charge of the familiar, and so I can only assume ..." Despite the viscountess trailing off, everyone understood without needing to hear more.

"Something else bothers me, though; he referred to the Troivackian men he was drinking with by saying only *half* were present," Lord Fuks noted with a frown, worry beginning to glitter in his eyes.

"Gods ... do you think he is telling us that the whole of the Troivackian army isn't attacking one place? That means we have to divide the numbers and guess where they might attack!" Mage Lee balked as he finished connecting the implications of their guess.

"Most likely Xava, as it is easiest to get to after Austice and would allow them to unite to overcome our east and south forces," Norman interjected while shooting Mr. Howard a meaningful look that had the assistant reaching hastily for his inkpot to send word to the military post in the western city.

"How are we going to save them?" The calm, yet dangerous voice of Annika Ashowan interrupted the discussion, bringing everyone's minds back to the viscount.

The viscountess went on, "Sire, it is clear that they mean to execute him, and my brother's family; if they aren't going to uphold the legalities of the hearing or Fin as an ambassador ..."

Captain Antonio leaned forward, his chest armor glinting in the light.

Ainsley turned to her husband and rested her hand atop of his in the quiet that followed their vassals' queries.

"I think it's time we told them."

The king gazed back at his wife, and the worrying news of the multiple oncoming attacks slowly ebbed from his thoughts as his focus on the task at hand returned. Nodding in agreement, he squeezed the queen's hand quickly before facing the council with his head held high, and the slightest upturning of his mouth softening his otherwise serious stare.

"Yes, I believe now is a perfect time to let you all know my ... backup plan to protect Lord Ashowan, and to give us a fighting chance in this war."

CHAPTER 25
TROIVACKIAN HOSPITALITY

After plating the last fillet of salmon, Fin noted both Bruce and Stanley standing by the galley exit with their hands folded over their fronts instead of being seated on the ale barrels. Knowing what this meant, he slowly placed his knife down and removed his apron.

"Have either of you met the Troivackian king?" the redhead asked while placing his hands on his hips.

"No. Neither of us have had the honor," Bruce answered shortly.

"Do you think the Piereva family is still alive?"

"Depends … His Majesty is not always predictable," Stanley explained with the smallest of shrugs. Oddly, the man did not appear all that pleased with the notion of an entire family being murdered …

Glancing out the round window to his right, Fin did his best to appreciate the beautiful shimmering water that spanned as far as the eye could see, knowing that it might be the last beautiful thing he could behold.

For the thousandth time, he felt himself silently apologizing to Annika for not being able to save her brother …

"Are you aware that you may not survive this?" Bruce interjected suddenly, his hesitant expression negating some of the condescension in his tone.

He'd always had a hunch … but, regardless of the certainty of his death, Fin knew he was glad to be standing there instead of Annika. Even though it looked as though his worst fear was coming true and he would not be able to save her family, he also knew that even if he hadn't gone, Annika still would have. So if at the very least he had managed to save her … at least it was better than doing nothing.

Giving Bruce a small smile of appreciation, he shrugged. "I'll fight to get the Pierevas to safety until my last breath, but … regardless of whether or not I succeed in doing that, I recognize that even trying will cost me my last breath."

Then, without any further ado, Fin plucked up the book with loose pages that carried the paperwork he required for the hearing and strode out of the galley. Idly, Fin noticed a slightly smaller ship had pulled alongside their own, and a lifeboat had been prepared on deck where his father and the captain of the vessel waited with a man he had not met before.

"Another spectacular meal, my boy! It was a fine lunch!" the captain greeted the cook before turning to the newcomer. "Mr. Kraft, this is Mr. Helmer's son, the ambassador from Daxaria. Finlay, this is your father's assistant. He has been busy reviewing paperwork regarding the coming siege of—" A sharp look from Aidan had the man clamping his mouth shut.

Fin raised an eyebrow but turned his attention to the slim Troivackian man beside his father. He wasn't quite as tall as the Daxarian witch, but he had intriguing eyes. The left was a dark brown with a splattering of gray, while the right was a bright blue with flecks of light green and gold. His face was a mask of indifference as Fin blatantly studied his face.

"Mr. Kraft here is a deficient witch just like yourself, Fin," Aidan explained while noting his son's careful examination of the assistant.

Fin proffered his hand to the fellow witch, who ignored it while studying him in turn with his head tilted over his shoulder.

"Are you certain he's a witch?" Mr. Kraft asked as his eyes began to shimmer.

Unable to hide his shock, Fin's eyebrows shot up. "Are you … are you able to identify abilities?"

"Sharp just like the man who sired you, hm?" Aidan clapped a hand onto the cook's shoulder. "Mr. Kraft here can see a witch's magical aura as though they were using their full abilities. It's handy knowing someone's power level and element."

Fin still hadn't managed to school his expression, when the assistant suddenly grasped his outstretched hand.

All at once, it felt as though the cook had been stripped down and he couldn't hide an inch of himself. The shimmering in Mr. Kraft's eyes intensified, and the man's apathetic expression melted into one of astonishment. Slowly, he released Fin's hand and straightened his shoulders before going completely still.

Aidan chuckled after a moment of silence passed between his son and assistant. "If I didn't know better, Mr. Kraft, I'd say it was love at first sight. Sorry to say, Fin, my assistant is more interested in the fairer sex."

The assistant's gaze hadn't moved from the house witch despite his superior addressing him, and for whatever reason, Fin felt as though he were holding his breath.

"Mr. Kraft?" Aidan's voice had turned wary, making the man blink at long last before turning to his superior.

"Do not let this man return to Daxaria." Mr. Kraft's hard stare made Aidan hesitate for a moment with a small frown before glancing briefly at Fin.

"That was never the plan, Mr. Kraft, so there is no need to worry. Now, shall we? His Majesty is waiting."

The assistant managed to give a small bow of his head before climbing aboard the lifeboat.

Fin followed suit while trying to shake off the peculiar encounter he had just experienced and ignoring his father's troubled expression.

It wasn't until the lifeboat had safely been lowered onto the water that the redhead even remembered to be anxious as one of the Troivackian soldiers began to row them over to the king's ship.

The sky was beginning to grow overcast, and the inky water that had been calm an hour before was becoming somewhat choppier. Casting his sights to the distance to try and view whether or not another storm was on its way, Fin then noticed the Troivackian merchant ship that seemed to have drawn closer to them that morning. He then set to looking for the fishing boat that had also been spotted again earlier that day.

"Suspicious how those two boats haven't left our sights," Mr. Kraft suddenly noted as though reading Fin's thoughts.

"It is indeed, but I can handle them if the Daxarian king sent them to interfere," Aidan remarked casually. He clearly wasn't overly worried about any potential interference. "Though it would be odd that the king would invest such resources for the sake of a cook."

"From what I've seen, I don't think it's that strange at all." The assistant's gaze was once again fixed on Fin, making him lean back and fold his arms over his chest subconsciously.

Aidan turned to Mr. Kraft, clearly annoyed. "If you're going to keep behaving so peculiar, I'll ask: What did you see? I thought you said there wasn't any aura around him."

"That's because his power has compiled within his being. Once I shook his hand I could see it in him. It's as though he's sucked it all in and has locked it away. The power I saw …" Mr. Kraft's eyes rippled again. "… was unlike anything I've ever seen from a deficient witch."

Clearly displeased with this report, Aidan's black eyes shifted over to Fin, his expression hard and appraising. "It doesn't matter if he's useless the second he is outside of his beloved home."

Fin gave a single shoulder shrug. He didn't really feel the need to defend himself.

Not to mention he was slightly more preoccupied with his pending death …

So the rest of the boat ride passed without another word, as each man remained deep in thought as the creaking wood of the ships they rowed between echoed ominously …

The faces of the knights that stared at Fin were far less complacent than the soldiers aboard his father's vessel. Every man present stared at him coldly, as though ready at any moment to relieve his neck of his head.

Aidan stepped forward and bowed, before straightening and fixing the men with his charcoal gaze.

"Are His Majesty and the prisoners belowdecks?" the fire witch asked as waves of heat began to roll off him, making the knights who failed to greet him involuntarily wince.

"Our king is in his cabin with the Piereva family. He wants to speak with the ambassador alone," one knight replied gruffly, which succeeded in making Aidan frown.

"Why does he need him alone?"

Neither of the men who had stepped forward to acknowledge the fire witch answered.

Fin, however, stepped closer; one hand was tightened into a fist inside his pocket while the other held the documents he had to show the king.

"Are you two showing me to His Majesty or—"

Aidan's hand shot out, grabbing his son by the front of his tunic and jerking him toward himself.

"You will not bring shame to me in the name of spite. Understand?" The fire witch's quiet words were laced with implicit threat as the house witch fought off the urge to land a blow of his own on his father. The knights watched completely nonplussed.

Fin shot a brief steely glance at Aidan before turning back to the military men, who met his gaze straight on.

"Come with us."

The cook stood perfectly still until his father eventually released the front of his tunic and allowed him to follow the men.

One of the knights had already begun marching across the deck, while the second waited for Fin to walk past him, then proceeded to follow behind.

They guided him over to the steps that led down into the ship's cabins, all while passing impressively large soldiers and knights who were silent but watched closely as the Daxarian was escorted by.

After descending belowdecks, Fin walked to the end of a long narrow passage and halted before a door at the end, while the knight at his front knocked.

"Your Majesty, the Daxarian ambassador is here to meet with you."

"Send him in." The deep baritone voice that resonated from behind the door had Fin stand a little straighter without it being a conscious decision. The knight who had knocked then stepped clear of the door and immediately rested his hand on the hilt of his sword strapped to his side.

Slowly, Fin forced his feet to move forward, and grasping the handle, pushed the door open to reveal the master cabin.

Its back wall was made of windows, and underneath was what looked like a comfortable bed. There were shelves along the entire perimeter of the room, and a fine burgundy, patterned rug that nearly covered the entire floor space. Standing against the ship's wall to his right was a slight man with thick black hair cropped short and an equally short beard; his eyes were blindfolded and his mouth gagged. Beside him huddled on the ground was a woman whose eyes were also blindfolded, but there was no gag as she whispered soothing words to a teary-eyed infant in her arms that couldn't be older than a year …

Fin's eyes stayed stuck on them for an entire moment, rage coursing through him as his hand clasping the book of documents tightened until the leather creaked.

Then he turned to face the large intense presence in the center of the room that was watching him. Seated at a round table with a map spread out, his dark eyes unreadable, was the Troivackian king.

Fin stepped in and closed the door behind himself before bowing and straightening with great difficulty.

"Your Majesty, I am Finlay Ashowan of Daxaria, and I am here as an ambassador to represent King Norman Reyes in this hearing regarding Lord Charles Piereva."

Matthias was larger than most Daxarian men, like almost all Troivackians, but his black beard was cropped close to his jaw, and his handsome face so motionless and cold, he could have been carved from stone. He surveyed Fin without betraying a single thought. A beautiful sword lay on the table within reach, and judging from the powerful build of the man, Fin had no doubts that he could wield the weapon masterfully.

The witch stood waiting for the ruler to say something, and after several moments he began wondering if it were rude to continue staring directly at him, or if it would be better for him to gaze around the room.

"You're nothing like your father, are you?" The calm voice startled Fin out of his steady stream of panicked thoughts.

"Aside from looks, I don't believe so. Though admittedly, my mother believes my stubbornness comes from him ..." Fin hadn't the faintest idea why he would even mention such a thing, as his heart raced and stomach twisted.

"I see."

As the king slowly stood, he reached over and grasped his sword. "You've heard that this man here, Lord Charles Piereva, is a spy I discovered? He would gather information from the now deceased Lord Phillip Piereva, then come running to Daxaria to report his findings."

"So they say," Fin managed while feeling a trickle of sweat run down his back as every muscle in his body remained tense. "However, His Majesty has sent me with all shipping records from Troivack to Daxaria and vice versa. Here it does not list Lord Charles Piereva as a passenger, anywhere, and—"

"I'm well aware that your king has sent you with what he believes to be firm evidence in support of Charles Piereva. However, he has already confessed to selling secrets to a mercenary in Daxaria. He is my citizen and it is my right to rule his sentencing as I see fit. Whether it be a confession of duress or not," the king continued, already sensing the argument that Fin was considering making.

"The question now is, what will you give me if I spare his wife and child?" The king began strapping the sword to his side.

Fin stood up straighter in alarm as he glanced at the Troivackian family that collectively trembled ...

"P-Please, whoever you are ... Please give him anything ..." Charles Piereva gasped.

The king, displeased with the outburst, stormed forward, grabbed the lord by the back of his neck, and proceeded to half drag him out of the room.

When he returned, Fin's heart had tripled in speed and his mind was racing.

Gods, why can't I have any sort of magic in a time like this?!

"Lord Charles Piereva is going to die in a manner befitting his crimes. He will have stones tied to his feet, and he will be lain to rest on the border of Troivack and Daxaria in the Alcide Sea."

A small sob escaped Janelle Piereva's mouth as she clutched her daughter closer to her.

"W-Why don't you tell me what you want? I'm sure I can—"

"I want to know who the spy is. I want to know who it is that Lord Charles was reporting to," Matthias responded with an eerie calm.

"Then you'll spare his wife and daughter? What guarantee do we have that you'll do that?" Fin demanded while still trying to think if it would be possible to save Charles ...

"You would have my vow of honor. Do you know what that is, Ambassador?"

Fin frowned and shook his head.

"It is a vow more important than a Troivackian's life."

Fin stared at Janelle Piereva, his uncertainty and desperation clear as he watched the mother rock her daughter silently while she wept.

"You can ask the traitor's wife if you like. Even in this circumstance, all Troivackians know the weight of this vow. As much as we love our ... conniving methods ... we all follow our own individual honor, and so to make a vow on that is without tricks. It is one that claims you have the strength, regardless of the odds or betrayals, to see what you promised through to the end."

"Is ..." Fin licked his lips, his throat growing dry as he finally, with great clarity, realized what he could do. "Lady Janelle, is it true ... what the king says?"

The woman nodded frantically, her breath still coming out as half sobs.

"There you have it." Matthias stepped closer to Finlay, his boots thudding against the planks.

Letting out a long breath, Fin closed his eyes and, upon opening them again, did the only thing he truly believed could save as many people as possible.

"I am the spy. I'm the one who has been feeding information to my king."

Matthias's expression barely shifted, as though he had had some inkling of this all along ... that is, until the witch spoke again.

"However, it wasn't Charles Piereva who was my informant ... it was my father, Aidan Helmer."

CHAPTER 26
RISING TIDES

Matthias fixed the witch with his dark gaze before turning and strolling over to his window, the air delicately still after Fin's announcement.

Picking up a crystal bottle that clearly held Troivackian moonshine, the king poured himself a hefty drink in his goblet.

The witch remained silent, his blood roaring in his ears.

The monarch slowly returned to the center of the cabin and gently set the goblet on the table before he turned and pummeled a mighty blow into Fin's gut, immediately cracking a rib and dropping him to his knees, unable to draw a proper breath.

"I had wondered if there was some truth to Lord Phillip's ramblings … but in this moment, whether you are lying to save Charles Piereva's family makes no difference to me."

Fin felt the sting of a cold blade at the back of his neck and immediately felt his heart skip several beats.

"What is your father's weakness?"

Still working on getting air back into his lungs, the witch took a moment to answer, only to feel the edge of the blade rest more heavily against the back of his neck.

"He's a fire witch … so his counter element … is water," Fin finally managed to gasp out beneath the pain.

"So if he were to be deposited in the middle of the sea, there is nothing he could do?"

"Yes. Though, I tried that once and he still somehow survived." The blade left Fin's neck, and the king's boots appeared in his line of view from the floor.

"How did you manage that? I was under the impression he hasn't seen you in years."

Slowly, Fin straightened, wincing as he did so before he began to move to stand, only for the edge of the king's sword to appear against his throat.

Snapping his blue eyes upward to the monarch, the witch noted that the man looked to be in complete control. There wasn't an ounce of passion in his face as he plainly showed how easy it would be to continue hurting the redhead, or even to just kill him instantly.

"I shot him off the island we lived on when I was eight years old. Magically."

The only movement in Matthias's face was a black eyebrow that rose up. "I was also told you are not very powerful. Are you exaggerating this feat?"

"No. I'm a house witch. I can only use magic in my home, but I can protect it." Fin watched as his words made the king frown and take a step back.

"How is it you and your father began this deceitful arrangement?" the king asked calmly, despite an ominous shadow growing behind his eyes.

"I-I reached out to him when … when I was hired as the Royal Cook. I wanted to tell him I'd made something of myself, and he … asked me to relay information as 'the dragon' to the king. I-in exchange for becoming ennobled a-and wedding a wealthy woman … W-which is why Viscountess Annika Jenoure was his target in coming aboard this ship in the first place … He would've … suggested himself as a husband." How Fin had come up with such a convincing lie on the spot was nothing short of a miracle, albeit one that signed and sealed his execution.

The king said nothing for a long time as he sifted through the information, but after thoroughly examining its validity, he gave a nod. "The implications of your magic I would like to ask you more about; however, we are pressed for time. I have a war to wage, and you have now served your purpose. I will spare Lord Piereva's wife and child as I vowed, so please keep in mind your death did have some worth."

Despite the blind terror of the moment, a strange pull at the back of Fin's mind made his vision go blurry for a moment, making him blink rapidly and frown in an attempt to focus on the king.

"What is happening to your eyes?" Matthias demanded when he noticed a strange milky film begin to sweep through the witch's gaze.

"I … I don't know …" Fin closed his eyes and shook his head trying to clear his sight, when all of a sudden his vision turned inward, and he found himself suddenly staring at Annika.

She was sitting in the council room back in Daxaria, and she looked … terrified. She *was* terrified; Fin could feel her fear and worry as dark shapes around her that he couldn't see clearly spoke to her …

A sudden pain tore through his chest and made him cry out, pulling him from his vision; yet just before he lost sight of her for good, Fin realized that Annika had turned and looked directly at him and had screamed …

When his vision cleared and he had once again returned to the ship, Fin found himself lying on the cabin floor, blood pooling from his chest as the king's polished black boots faced him.

"You can't magic your way out of this situation, Mr. Ashowan. Casting spells on me with your unnatural gaze is not acceptable." Matthias crouched down until he could make eye contact with Fin, whose face was draining of more color with every weakened beat of his heart. "Death's carriage comes for us all one way or another. You bear death with dignity, which is more than I can say for most men; you have my respect," the king stated calmly as he watched the life ebb from the witch's eyes.

Fin, unable to speak, felt his body growing colder, and his vision beginning to darken as the pain racked his body, nullifying almost any coherent thought, but as his grasp on the mortal world began to weaken, he managed to spare two final thoughts.

Annika … I'm so sorry … Then, reaching out to the tendril of connection between him and his familiar that was already beginning to fade, he tried to relay what was most likely his final request. *Kraken? Please take good care of my wife and my mother … please …*

The council room had fallen into a silence after Annika's anguished shout had rung out. It had been incredibly strange; her eyes had suddenly taken on a milky appearance, and all color had drained from her face …

"Lady Ashowan, is everything alright?" King Norman asked while Ainsley immediately stood and walked over to her friend.

The viscountess didn't speak as she allowed her head to fall into her trembling hand for a brief moment as she blinked and gradually had her vision return to her.

"Fin … I saw … I saw Fin," she whispered, her voice hoarse as bile began to rise in the back of her throat.

"Gods, you are burning up! Mr. Howard, please summon Mrs. Ashowan or Physician Durand immediately," Ainsley ordered as she rested her hand over her friend's suddenly clammy brow.

The assistant wasted no time in rising and immediately stalking from the room to hastily summon the nearest healer.

"What was it you saw?" Mage Lee insisted, though his voice was quiet.

"He … He was just staring at me, and then there was blood … Your Majesty, how long did you say it'd take them to get there?" Annika's panicked expression made Norman lean back in his chair with a frown. He had never seen her look fearful in all his time of knowing her …

"They assured me they'd remain less than an hour away at all times. I sent them my orders more than an hour ago by now … I'm sure they will intervene any moment now."

Annika nodded, but she couldn't fully regain her composure as her temperature seemed to be increasing even more. Reaching for the goblet of water on the table, she tried to stave off the sense of doom in her gut, as the men and queen all exchanged grave looks.

After several long moments, Katelyn Ashowan burst into the room with Physician Durand on her heels.

Both greeted the nobles with a hasty bow and curtsy before Katelyn was up and off again.

"Mrs. Ashowan, it is not necessary for you to take over all my patients you know!" The normally easygoing physician was shouting as Kate reached Annika's side in record time.

"Come, Viscountess, I think it is time you rested." Kate gingerly placed a hand on Annika's back and gestured toward the doorway where Physician Durand stood with arms folded over his chest.

"Perhaps, Mrs. Ashowan, we should allow my appointed physician to attend to the viscountess," Norman interjected when he noticed the bags under Kate's eyes.

The witch, however, didn't seem to hear him as she regarded Annika's sweaty brow with a frown before resting her hand against her skin.

"Gods … Mr. Howard, there is a boy here in Austice I need you to summon immediately. Please tell him I need him. I will write down the directions for the messenger." Kate was clearly in her physician's mindset as she straightened and moved immediately to the king's side where she reached over to the stack of parchment beside the king without permission and quickly picked up his quill to scrawl a hasty map.

"His name is Urick Jelani; his aunts will allow you to take him as long as you say I am the one to have summoned him." Kate handed the note and map over to the assistant who was watching the woman command him with a vaguely impressed and hesitant expression.

"What … What is wrong with Lady Ashowan?" Captain Antonio interjected while eyeing the king apologetically over his betrothed's lack of mindfulness around the ruler.

Admittedly, everyone was more than a little perplexed as to what was making the normally considerate and respectful witch behave in such a way over her daughter-in-law.

"She needs to cool down. The boy I have summoned makes ice."

"An ice bath?! In her condition? Mrs. Ashowan, that is not something that I can allow you to order. She must rest in bed with plenty of fluids and—"

"This condition isn't like others." Kate cut off Physician Durand sharply, with everyone in the room watching the entire scenario unfold with growing bewilderment, as Annika herself straightened in her chair and reached out to touch her mother-in-law's hand. She was trying with all her might not to appear distressed as the two physicians were dancing closer to revealing exactly which "condition" she was in.

Not wanting to add any more chaos to the already tense atmosphere, Norman spoke up with the intent of settling matters. "Mrs. Ashowan, I cannot have you ignore the Royal Court Physician's expertise without explaining your reasons to him. If, after hearing your explanation, he does not think it is in Lady Ashowan's best interest, then we will defer to his decision."

"I trust Mrs. Ashowan," Annika piped up, forcing herself to sound more in control than she felt. She was terrified of what was happening to Fin, and trying to maintain control of the situation, but what on earth was going on with her brats? She felt as though she had a small sun inside of her …

"Well, we agree that she needs to be lying down, do we not?" Kate turned to Physician Durand, her tone somewhat quieter than before.

The man nodded slowly and gestured toward the door.

"No, I'd like to stay and hear what is happening." Annika shook her head and immediately took another gulp of water.

"Absolutely not. You look as though you are about to pass out. You just spontaneously started sweating— Wait. Does this have something to do with magic?" The queen turned to Kate with a frown and explained what had happened.

"Lady Ashowan just claimed to have seen a vision of the viscount. After that, she immediately became ill."

Kate's face drained of color before she turned to her daughter-in-law.

"What did you see?" Her voice was hushed, and everyone immediately stiffened.

"Something bad," Annika replied while already reaching to refill her goblet again. For a moment no one dared to breathe as they waited to see how the healer would respond.

"Viscountess, come with me. You need to lie down." Kate's face was still pale, and her hands folded over her skirt were gripping it until her knuckles were white.

"I already said I—"

"Now. You could harm yourself." There was a hardness in the healer's tone that no one had ever heard from her before.

"I will be fine! I just am warm and—"

"Oh, my … Gods. He didn't," Mr. Howard interjected suddenly with an astonished half smile as he stared at Annika with a light in his eyes that the viscountess did not like one bit.

"Mr. Howard, I don't believe anything is funny here," Ainsley reprimanded sternly.

The assistant turned to the viscountess once more and bowed his head. "My lady, I apologize. I do not mean to make light of the situation. I was merely … taken aback."

Norman eyed the man oddly before turning to Annika.

"Viscountess, I will send word of any news we hear. For now, please rest. No arguing."

For a moment it looked as though she were about to argue again; however, one look at Norman's firm gaze told her it was futile. So, with a small sigh, Annika conceded to a retreat as she slowly stood and curtsied.

"Very well, Your Majesty."

After the viscountess had exited followed by the court physician and Mrs. Ashowan, Norman and the queen turned back to Mr. Howard.

"What was that about?" the monarch demanded without hiding his displeasure. "You do realize that Mr. Ash— I mean *Lord* Ashowan and the Pierevas may be dead right now?"

At this the assistant bowed his head again, his expression dutifully somber.

"I apologize, Your Majesty. I truly was just taken aback for a moment. I, too, hope that they reach him in time …"

"What took you aback, Mr. Howard?" the queen asked while facing the man squarely.

The assistant shifted in his seat and glanced around at everyone uncomfortably while also once again trying to prevent a small grin.

"Does anyone else find it interesting the way both Mrs. Ashowan and Physician Durand mentioned Lady Ashowan's 'condition'? Not to mention how insistent Mrs. Ashowan was to take care of her daughter-in-law?"

Everyone except Ainsley continued frowning in confusion. The queen's face fell into astonishment.

"They were discussing Lady Ashowan's visible illness. Of course Mrs. Ashowan is going to fuss, she's already worried about her son," Lord Fuks interjected while reaching for his own goblet of water.

"Not to mention … Lady Ashowan seems a tad … well. Uh …" The normally droll assistant grew sheepish. "Well, she seems a little … filled out."

"Mr. Howard, please speak plainly; this is getting— Oh." Norman's face suddenly fell. One by one, the men around the table's expressions all moved into awkward realization.

"It could just be that she is eating too much of his cooking," Captain Antonio attempted while clearing his throat.

"She didn't wear the dress I picked."

All eyes moved to Ainsley whose face was still frozen.

"Pardon me, Your Majesty?" Mage Lee leaned forward.

"She … I … her dress was … different." Ainsley waved her hand dismissing the question as she realized that she couldn't out the fact that her friend had been brought to the castle while acting as the Dragon.

"It would also explain why Mrs. Ashowan was so adamant that her condition was unique. It could be that the viscountess is going to have a witch," Lord Fuks pointed out with a twinkle in his eye.

"They must have been together longer than we originally thought … I wonder when she's due?" Mage Lee pondered aloud.

"Oh Gods … a small version of Finlay Ashowan running around here?" Mr. Howard shook his head wearily as many of the men around the table were unable to fight off small smiles.

"Norman …" Ainsley whispered under her breath as she turned to stare at her husband, her worry written all over her face.

"If we fail to get any of them back, she ... they ... would be alone." Mage Lee voiced everyone's shared thoughts quietly, the sadness descending upon everyone as they realized what Fin's passing would mean to his family.

His children never meeting their father ... Annika widowed twice ...

Norman glanced around the table at everyone's somber expressions and felt his heart grow even more heavy with the new responsibility upon him.

"There is nothing we can do, but wait," he managed bleakly.

"And hope. Hope that he comes out of this alive ..." Ainsley pointed out while reaching out and grasping Norman's hand.

"Sometimes, though ... sometimes it's the hope that is what makes the fall much worse." Mr. Howard's solemn observation wasn't what the council members wanted to hear in that moment, but every one of them couldn't help but feel the same.

All of them had just realized precisely how high the stakes were to have their beloved cook returned alive and well, and they knew that the aftermath if the king's plan failed was going to be hell.

CHAPTER 27
SLIPPING AWAY

Your Majesty! A deep sea fishing vessel is heading straight for us! Mr. Helmer says it has been near their ship since they left Daxaria. How would you like us to proceed?"

Matthias looked up from the redheaded witch bleeding on his cabin floor at the knight who had barged in.

"Is Mr. Helmer able to set it aflame?"

"He says not yet, but it is moving unnaturally fast ... another Troivackian merchant vessel is nearing us as well, and there seems to be some kind of scuffle on the deck between the crew, but they all look Troivackian."

The king frowned. Just what in the world was happening?

As he stepped over the unconscious cook and made his way back above deck, many of his men were standing at the ready with their eyes fixed on the fishing vessel.

"Here is the spyglass, Your Majesty." The captain of the vessel hastily handed over the item.

Scanning the horizon, the king regarded the fishing boat that was moving abnormally quickly toward them. In fact ... within a matter of minutes they would be within shouting distance.

"Helmer, once that vessel is within your vicinity of attack, I want it burned to ash unless they run up the white flag."

"Yes, Your Majesty. Might I ask where Finlay is?" the fire witch requested idly as he turned his sights to the fishing boat.

"Most likely dying or already dead on my cabin floor."

The immediate hesitation on Aidan's face surprised the king greatly.

"You were going to have him killed regardless," the monarch pointed out while turning to face Aidan's profile.

"I'm aware … it just feels … anticlimactic I suppose. Ah … We also threw Charles Piereva overboard as you requested." The chief of military shrugged and turned his attention back to the boat nearing them. Raising his hands, two balls of fire ignited, yet as he cast them to directly catch the sails of the vessel, two pillars of water suddenly burst from the sea.

Everyone leapt back in shock.

"Mr. Helmer, I take it?"

The fire witch whirled around to find himself staring at two women and one man who had appeared behind them while they had been focused on the vessel. The knights all had their swords drawn, yet the trio didn't seem all that concerned.

"Ah. Witches," Mr. Kraft announced loudly enough for everyone to hear as he regarded one of the new arrivals who had long wavy auburn hair, then the brunette woman with a snake tattoo wrapped around her upper arm, and finally, the man with his ebony skin and short white curly hair.

"Who are you to trespass on the King of Troivack's vessel?" demanded one of the knights.

"We are here to collect a member of the Coven of Wittica after we received word that he was in grave peril. We mean no harm so long as we may retrieve the ambassador Mr. Finlay Ashowan uninjured." The brunette woman spoke with a haughty eyebrow raised.

"There is no Finlay Ashowan aboard this ship," King Matthias informed the trio while drawing his sword. "You will leave my vessel immediately or—"

Aidan cast another fireball at them before the monarch could finish his threat, only to have the man with ebony skin snap his fingers and send the flames soaring upward on a great gust of wind into the sails of the very ship they stood upon.

The chief of military waved his hand and immediately had the flames snuffed out, but the damage to the sails had already been done. They no longer resembled stuffed pillowcases filled with wind but rather fluttered frantically, their singed edges sending ash lazily adrift across the decks.

"You were taught to be careful when fighting with fire, Mr. Helmer. Particularly on a boat in the middle of the sea." The witch with the auburn hair stepped forward. "Now. Before there is more damage done, where might we find Finlay Ashowan?"

The king once again opened his mouth to respond, when the captain of the vessel spoke up.

"Your Majesty! The merchant ship has been heading toward us this entire time! I thought it was going to veer off but ... I believe it is going to crash into our port side by the bow!"

Everyone, including the witches, turned to stare at the merchant vessel that had most definitely drawn closer during the confrontation, and due to Aidan's ship being off to the starboard, and the fishing vessel lying directly in front of them at that time, there was no way they could avoid collision.

Snatching the spyglass from the captain, Matthias looked for the traitor who was about to crash into his vessel by the helm. Only, no one was at the helm. Everyone was in the midst of a particularly bloody brawl. The only creature by the helm was a greyhound that ... was chewing on one of the spindles of the wheel and not letting go.

Baffled by the strange sight, he roved the spyglass over the rest of the ship and nearly missed what he thought had been a lifelike figurehead at the bow, but no ...

Squinting a little harder, the king finally could make out ... a cat.

A fluffy black cat with a small white patch on his chest was sitting at the bow of the ship, his whiskers fluttering in the sea breeze as the beast stared *directly at him* with his sharp green eyes. The gaze was so ... intelligent, that somehow ... it almost seemed as though the feline knew exactly what was happening.

"The ship is being steered by a dog," King Matthias announced as he lowered the cutlass and turned to the three witches who all wore matching expressions of bewilderment. "You mean to tell me this is not your doing?"

"No. Now either surrender Mr. Ashowan to our care or—"

Aidan stepped forward and flung out his arm; a ring of fire crackled into existence that coiled around the three witches, making them all cry out. A wave of magically summoned water suddenly cascaded over the edge of the ship, lurching the entire vessel onto a forty-five-degree angle, subsequently tossing most of the knights into the sea. The king, Aidan, Mr. Kraft, and a handful of men managed to stay aboard by grasping onto the railing they were thrown against.

"Vera, go find Mr. Ashowan. Chima and I can handle the nasty little firefly we seem to have on our hands," the witch with the snake tattoo hastily ordered her auburn-haired companion as she then swelled water beneath the boat, forcing the vessel to once again be level, but also causing the men in the water to be swept farther from their ship.

The witch named Vera began to step toward the entrance to the cabin when the king drew his sword, and with speed that was almost inhuman for his size, he lunged toward the woman.

That was when the Troivackian merchant ship collided with the vessel, sending the king back several steps; the witch, however, had vines sprouting from the pockets of her cloak, snapping around any ledge or spindle they could and holding her into place as she then continued her descent belowdecks.

Aidan regained his footing and straightened while facing his opponents. Heat rolled off him, drying him instantly as his eyes and aura began to glow like a blacksmith's coals.

Tensing his hands at his sides, fire burst out as he once again cast rings toward the two witches, only this time the white-haired man was suddenly flying high in the air, dodging the attack effortlessly before casting a concussive air strike at Aidan that hit him firmly in his gut, making his powers extinguish immediately.

"As powerful as you are, Mr. Helmer, you are far outside your element," the witch named Chima called out calmly.

Another wave of water rose up and swept the fire witch and remaining knights off the ship, leaving only the king on board clutching one of the ropes.

The dark-haired witch nodded to Chima as they turned toward the cabin together, intending to join Vera, when a sudden magical blast of air blew them both backward.

Standing on the top deck was an elderly Troivackian man with one milky white eye, and the other dark like his brethren. He wore a dirty, stained cream tunic, and a tattered gray robe, but in his hand he wielded a gnarled staff with a shining crystal at its top.

"Goddamn mages," Chima hissed as her lips curled.

The pair squared off with their new adversary when a fluffy streak of black fur darted past all of them and dove into the galley belowdecks.

———~~~———

Vera had just finished checking the second cabin along the narrow ship corridor when the sound of galloping paws reached her ears.

Poking her head outside of the room that looked like a cramped office, she realized that a fluffy black cat was frantically pawing at the door at the end of the hallway.

Frowning, but deciding to trust her instinct, Vera strode over to the door and pushed it open.

The stench of blood filled her nose as her gaze moved swiftly around what was clearly the king's quarters. She froze when she noticed the smeared path of blood that led to the body of a man who was undoubtedly Finlay Ashowan.

"Oh, Gods ... the ship lurching so much must have moved him," she uttered panickedly to herself as she immediately moved to the figure's side and dropped down beside him.

Noting the bright red hair that matched the King of Daxaria's description, she held her breath as she reached out and gently rested her fingers on the side of his throat.

Staring earnestly at the handsome pale face, Vera felt her heart constrict as she waited for any sign of life.

The feline that had led her to the witch was already rubbing his head against Fin's and chirping worriedly.

"You're his familiar, aren't you?" Vera asked quietly as she continued waiting to feel some kind of pulse.

The cat turned its green stare to her, and she was alarmed to see tears in its eyes.

"E-Excuse me ... are y-you here to save us?"

Turning sharply at the quiet voice of a woman, Vera then saw the blindfolded speaker, huddled under the table in the center of the room with an infant clutched to her chest.

"Gods ... You must be Lady Janelle Piereva. Yes, please come with us." Vera sent a vine over to the woman and had the blindfold lowered immediately.

As soon as Lady Janelle laid eyes on the scene before her, however, she immediately closed them again.

Vera wished to comfort her, but the more important matter at hand was whether or not she could find a pulse.

Another moment passed, then another, and then ... she felt it. The faintest beat of his heart.

Regarding the gash in Fin's chest cautiously, Vera immediately tore the hem of her skirt and pressed it to the wound before then summoning her vines to coil around his body to hold it in place.

"Lord Ashowan, you have a great many people waiting for you," she whispered before having her vines carefully roll him over onto his back.

Standing up, she then turned to the feline and Lady Janelle. "Guard him. I can't lift him on my own, I'll need help."

The fluffy beast seated itself dutifully beside his witch and stared at Vera keenly, as though saying, *Hurry up.* Whereas the lady shifted forward to sit nearer Fin's body though she still couldn't bring herself to look at him again.

Running back down the corridor and setting foot on deck, Vera was momentarily distracted by the elderly man in sandals who was flying through the air, over the rails, and into the water. That is, until the spinning staff landed with a clunk on the deck mere steps in front of herself.

Looking up toward her colleagues, her expression flat, she said, "Mage?"

The two nodded before rolling their eyes. "Mage."

Letting out a disappointed sigh, Vera then remembered the dire straits the house witch was in.

"Lor— Mr. Ashowan appears to be near death. I can't move him. Come, Lady Piereva's with him!"

Chima didn't say a word as he hurried past her to descend below.

"He's in the room at the end of the corridor! Hurry!"

Turning her attention back to Cora, the brunette witch, Vera stepped forward.

"I don't know that he will make it back to shore, so we need to go as fast as we can to return. How much magic has Chima used?"

"A fair bit, I won't lie … I don't know that he will have enough in him to make it all the way to Daxaria in one go, but we can always send a message to the shore and see if they can send a ship to—"

"Why are my feet wet?" Vera interrupted with great alarm.

"Remember how that ship hit this ship?" Cora asked dryly. "The men we've cast off are boarding that ship over there … it looks like they will start firing arrows once they get organized."

"Right."

Chima appeared again then, floating the redhead carefully while the black feline trotted beside him, and Lady Piereva's shoulders hunched protectively over her daughter.

"You weren't kidding. I don't even know if this man will make it to see nightfall. I'll meet you two down in the boat. We need to move now," Chima informed them grimly.

"Bring the boat to the other side; otherwise, those knights are going to tear apart our sails. I'm shocked they haven't started firing at Isla yet," Cora commanded while moving to the other side of the sinking ship.

"She's probably hiding, which is best … she is still a bit young to see this." Chima nodded to the bloodstained witch.

The women shared a knowing look before turning back to the task at hand of successfully escaping the Troivackian ships and making it back to Daxaria.

Vera used her vines to swing down to the small fishing boat that they had been hiding on during the previous days, while Chima floated down with Fin, Lady Janelle with her daughter, and Kraken. Cora leapt into the water and allowed a small swell to carry her over the edge of the fishing vessel.

"Right. Chima, send a message requesting a physician to meet us at our coordinates. Don't lie about his state, though … we need someone as fast as possible. Even if he does make it, I … I don't know if he will ever be quite right," Cora ordered while checking Fin's wound briefly. "I've only learned the preliminary of wartime medicine, but even I don't think there is much hope here."

The air witch nodded stiffly after casting a brief, somber glance at the poor man on the deck of their ship and did as he was ordered.

Panting, Annika tried to slow her racing heart as the heat in her body grew more fevered despite lying down in her old bed. Katelyn pressed a cool damp cloth to her forehead while behind her, maids were rushing in and out as they proceeded to fill a tub with chilled water.

"Physician Durand went to personally escort Urick here. Just take deep breaths. You need to calm down," Kate soothed as Annika remained curled on her side.

"What … What is happening? Why do I feel like I'm on fire?" the viscountess asked as she began to once again try and sit up, only to have her mother-in-law gently push her back down. The healer lowered her head so that when she whispered none of the maids might hear.

"The magic of the fire witch in your body is growing agitated by your panic. Calm down, it could hurt you or the other babe if you don't. Unless they both are fire witches, but I'm doubtful of that."

"I thought … I thought witches don't have their powers emerge until they are older?"

"That is true, but usually there are hints. When I was pregnant with Fin, for example, I made the best food I'd ever been able to in my life. It was strange because cooking has never been my strength …"

Annika smiled sadly, but slowed her breaths. "How do I not be worried?"

"You need to think of the children right now. You cannot afford to be anxious or to … or to even grieve should the worst happen. You need to save the last parts of him"—she touched Annika's thickened middle—"no matter what." Kate grasped the viscountess's hand and squeezed it tightly. "Just focus every ounce of your love on them."

Annika could feel the healer's desperation and realized that the order was also a plea from a mother who was deeply terrified that the children the viscountess was carrying were all she'd have left of her own son …

Another hour passed, and Annika was already in the tub, her temperature gradually cooling, when they began bringing in the ice.

Incredibly, it didn't even feel all that cold as Kate saw to at least three buckets being added to the tub.

Yet another hour passed, and by that time the viscountess's temperature was once again under control. Her mother-in-law even deemed her condition safe enough that she could leave the tub and dress herself again. Annika had just turned to ask Kate if she might thank the witch named Urick, who had selflessly come to lend her his power, when a rapid knock at the door rang out.

"My lady! The king has summoned you and Mrs. Ashowan immediately." A guard's voice called from outside the door.

Both women stared at each other nervously before they then hurried unceremoniously from the chamber, back down the corridor toward the council room.

The second Annika burst into the room, she felt her heart stop. Everything seemed devoid of warmth in that long agonizing minute as she noticed everyone's pained and saddened expressions.

"Oh, Gods … no. Please … no." The broken voice that came from Kate made Annika's throat suddenly close, but she couldn't move. She had somehow become rooted to the spot.

"The good news … is that Lady Piereva and her daughter are alive and well. Lord Ashowan … is … was … alive when they sent word about an hour ago. They are requesting a ship be sent out to meet them with a physician; however, the damage done to … done to the viscount they indicated to be … dire. They suspect he will pass this evening, and even if we manage to meet them while he is alive, he will not ever fully recover." Norman's voice was grave and anguished. "And unfortunately … we were not able to save Lord Charles Piereva in time."

Katelyn trembled, her arms wrapping around her middle as broken sobs tore from her throat.

Antonio was up and across the room in a matter of moments as he wrapped her in his embrace.

"We'll send our fastest vessel with you on it, lass," the captain murmured quietly into his betrothed's hair.

"Annika?" The queen's gentle voice did little to break through the darkness the viscountess had fallen into.

She was unaware that she had turned gray in complexion as she stood like a statue by the council room doors, her mind unable to properly function …

"We need to act quickly if there is even the slightest chance, please, Mrs. Ashowan. We know that you are the only one who could ever hope to heal him." The king's soft insistence succeeded in pulling Kate from her haze of grief.

"I-I will … I will go. I know a … I know an air witch who can move the vessel quickly … She resides with the boy, Urick."

Norman nodded and locked eyes with Antonio, who didn't need any spoken orders before he gave Kate's shoulders one final squeeze and dropped a kiss onto her forehead. Then with impressive speed for his age, he took his leave from the room to carry out the king's command. Kate followed the captain without a second look at the men of the room, her hands still gripping her upper arms, as she stumbled in his wake, presumably to prepare any tools she might need.

Annika remained motionless in the deathly silent room, until the queen stepped forward and slowly reached out to touch her friend's shoulder. The viscountess jerked away at the last second.

Turning around without a word or a curtsy, Annika left the room, and on numb legs, she walked down the corridor to the castle stairs. Descending down to the main hall, Clara suddenly appeared by her side.

"My lady, is everything alright?" The maid glanced around nervously at the number of nobles and servants who were watching the viscountess, who appeared ghostlike, and were beginning to whisper to one another.

Annika didn't say a word and instead headed to the kitchen.

She ignored a number of servants and knights trying to stop and question her, and when she finally reached the kitchen, she found the aides all gathered around, hurriedly preparing dinner. For some reason even Jiho was present, his sleeves rolled up and his tunic sooty as he added another log to the fire while pointing out that there was a bit of mold on a corner of cheese Hannah was about to cut.

The aides didn't even notice Annika for a moment as she watched them all work, chattering idly amongst themselves, but the first to notice her was Sir Lewis.

"Viscountess? What is—" the knight began to ask, making everyone stop what they were doing and look up. Seeing all their faces, but not one of them being Fin's, Annika burst out in tears as she gently slumped against the kitchen wall and slid down to the ground while clutching her face.

Everyone looked at her and stilled in alarm, until Jiho stepped forward, his hands limp at his sides. Understanding filling his face, followed by great pain; when he spoke, the Zinferan's voice was hoarse.

"I'm so sorry … Viscountess."

CHAPTER 28
A HIGH PRICE

Annika didn't remember being moved, or when she fell asleep. All she knew was that she woke up in her old chamber in the castle, with Ainsley beside her on the bed, sitting with her back against the headboard.

As the viscountess slowly sat up, her eyes feeling almost too swollen to be open, the monarch turned with a start.

"How are you feeling? Are you well? Do you need Physician Durand?"

Annika shook her head, and instead, she stood and crossed the room to retrieve a goblet of water.

"Gods, you need to let me do that! You gave the kitchen aides a fright when you said nothing while crying, then you fainted …"

Annika glanced at the window and noticed it was deep into the night already.

"Did Mrs. Ashowan leave already?" Her voice rasped, but she didn't pay it any mind.

"Yes. Before sunset they left. I suppose the witches from the coven set out glass orbs as they traveled that resemble fishermen markers … they apparently can transmit messages faster, so we will be hearing regular updates about when they meet up as well as how … how the viscount is."

Annika nodded.

"Why didn't you tell me about your condition?"

The viscountess's eyes snapped over to the queen who visibly recoiled under her friend's hard stare.

"We … we all somewhat guessed after Physician Durand and Mrs. Ashowan's argument earlier," Ainsley explained, feeling awkward.

"I see." Annika moved over to the window and gazed out over the twinkling lights of Austice toward the sea. For some reason, lately, she felt rather pointless … and it was an entirely novel sensation to her …

"When are you supposed to deliver—"

"They're due to arrive in early spring."

"That means it is relatively— Wait. They? As in, more than one?!"

Annika didn't answer, but she could hear her friend rise from the bed.

"Gods, no wonder Mrs. Ashowan was fussing like a mother hen with you! Twins!"

"Yes, and because of them I can't do a Godsdamn thing to save my husband, and my last and only decent brother … is dead." The anger in Annika's voice made Ainsley hesitate.

"Nothing could have changed the Goddess's will. This was … These children are a gift from the viscount."

"I don't want this gift! I *want* my husband *back*! Charlie didn't deserve to die … And Fin especially doesn't deserve to die! Charlie always risked his life when he reported to me, but Fin? He … He was kind. He was a good man, and he … He was … everything. Hope … warmth … home. He was … Fin was … supposed to be *my* home." Annika's fury and pain had merged together, and she felt it bursting forward.

"I know it isn't fair, I know—" Ainsley's words of comfort were stopped abruptly as a golden light suddenly shone brightly around the viscountess. "What …"

Annika stared down at herself, her eyes wide, but then noticed a ribbon attached to the glow pouring from her … it flowed out the window through the starry sky toward the sea …

All at once, she realized that the light was her connection to Fin. Some strange innate part of her knew …

The ribbon weaved out into the inky night until it was lost in the darkness. Staring out in awe at the horizon, the two women remained silent. Until … they noticed the golden light was fading. Off in the distance, the ribbon was disappearing.

"No. No … why would it … No!" Annika watched as the ribbon faded away closer and closer to her, until at long last, it reached the shine around her and … then that, too, was gone.

It was then she knew, without a doubt, Finlay Ashowan, was dead.

Katelyn boarded the fishing vessel in a hurry. They all had seen the golden stream stretch across the sky, illuminating the inky waters in its magical glow. Unsure of what it was at first, the healer had stared at the heavens with Adamma Jelani at her side, as Sky stood at the stern of the ship pressing them hurriedly across the Alcide Sea. It wasn't until the captain of the ship called out that the fishing vessel was in sight that Kate guessed what she was seeing.

Hope filled her for a brief shining moment … before she noticed the light surge brilliantly, then begin to slowly disappear.

By the time she was aboard the fishing vessel, in her heart, she already knew what she was about to find.

Four witches stood around Fin, his face gray and lifeless, his clothes covered in his blood. They had rested his body on the storage box by the bow … and had waited.

Kate stepped over to him stiffly, her legs already threatening to give out from under herself. With shaking hands, the healer reached out and touched the sides of her son's head, gently stroking his fiery red hair.

For a moment, he was a small unconscious boy in her arms again, and she could hear herself saying the same words she had uttered on a particular rainy day …

"Oh, my sweet boy," Kate whispered as she sank down to her knees on the ship's deck, completely oblivious to the bowed heads around her.

Slowly, she lowered her forehead to his as she closed her eyes, tears once again slipping off her cheeks.

Reaching out with her magic, she felt the lifeless shell under her grasp.

She felt the burn wounds that were fresh … and healed them. They would appear as old scars that wouldn't alarm his wife should she happen to see them on his body …

She then noticed the cracked ribs as her magic moved deeper under his skin. She healed those, too, because … because she needed to. She needed to do something.

When it came to his chest, the wound that had cut the veins to his heart and lungs, Kate let out a small angry cry.

He had died in pain … and alone …

Slowly, she worked her magic, healing the tissue and circulatory passages, the lungs …

Then the brain.

The blood- and breath-deprived brain that, even if she had reached him hours sooner, would've meant he'd never be the same again.

His small smiling face as he would wait for her to try his latest recipe flashed in Kate's mind.

His scream when he had blasted his father off their island.

The tears he'd wept when his best friend, Ian, abandoned him and the children had stoned him …

The day Jiho arrived and became his friend.

The day he had left to go work at the castle, the broom she had made him firmly in hand.

A house witch should have a fresh broom for every new home. It only makes sense, she had prattled on, not knowing why it had mattered to her so much at the time.

The day Fin left for the ball, looking like a noble, his eyes full of hope …

His wedding day, the expression on his face when he saw Annika at the end of the aisle.

His back as he climbed into the carriage with his father …

"You don't deserve for things to end like this," Kate whispered as more tears fell.

Her magic began to glow around herself again, as she began reviving his mind. Every wrinkle, every curve of gray matter …

Please … Goddess … please. I am willing to pay the price … but please give him back.

Fin gazed at the beautiful forest before himself, then glanced down at his boots. He was standing on a dusty dirt road, and when he looked back over his shoulder, he could see a rickety black carriage rolling away. The driver had his back turned to him and wore a black hat that covered his neck and head entirely.

The strange thing was … Fin couldn't see around the carriage. There was emerald-green grass on either side of the road, but it would just roll away ahead of the carriage out of view.

Slowly, he turned back toward the trees and stepped off the road.

A stag loped out of the woods before him, and the two locked eyes for a long moment, before the beast turned back and disappeared amongst the foliage.

Sliding his hands into his pockets, the redhead stepped farther into the woods, marveling at the ginormous trees and beautiful flowers that were sprinkled along the soft moss.

"This is unbelievable, I'll have to tell … have to tell …" He frowned. There were people he needed to tell about this, but who again?

"Finlay."

The house witch looked up and felt his entire being instantly become at peace.

The woman before him with her olive skin and flowing chestnut hair with golden streaks through it, her eyes swirling colors of gray, green, and gold, stood waiting. Her hands folded over her golden loose gown as she smiled warmly down at him, a sprinkle of freckles across the bridge of her nose making her appear more approachable …

Fin didn't know how he knew she was the Goddess, but it seemed the most obvious thing in the world to him as he slowly knelt down and bowed before her.

"Oh, goodness, stand back up, child."

He obeyed, his heart and mind in complete harmony as he stared up into her face, and smiled.

"You do not need to be sent to the Grove of Sorrows; you have led a kind and good life, Finlay Ashowan. As a descendant of my daughter, the first witch, you have borne your gifts with dignity and respect."

Fin bowed his head in thanks.

"Before you move farther into the forest, would you like to ask me any questions?" she asked, her voice melodic and beautiful. As she spoke, the deer Fin had seen before slowly trotted to her side from the foliage.

"My family, and friends … I … can't … recall them …" Fin frowned as he failed to bring a single face to his mind.

"Ah … sometimes when one dies painfully, the carriage driver tries to ease their suffering. Normally as you move deeper into the forest, the more you come to forget, but you must have been very worried," the Goddess explained kindly as the stag at her side suddenly shifted into the form of a man, though his antlers remained. A deep green coat clad his shoulders, and a loose black tunic was draped over his torso. The fine garments framed a crystal that hung around his neck against his chest. He had long brown hair, and dark eyes like the deer that watched Fin expressionlessly.

A strange glow behind Fin suddenly brightened, making him turn around.

Squinting at the ethereal light, unable to determine what he was witnessing, he returned his attention to the Gods.

"I thought we might have more time, Finlay Ashowan. However, I may have to send you back." The Goddess stepped closer to him and rested her hand on his shoulder gently.

A strange power filled Fin's body … one that made his vision and awareness suddenly sharpen.

"Why … Why might you do that? I just got here. I thought anyone who crosses into the trees can never return."

"We owe a great debt to your bloodline. Though it has not come to pass yet for you, time moves differently here. Do you not wish to return, Finlay?" the Goddess asked, her eyes shimmering in the growing light from behind him.

"I don't know if I do," he answered honestly.

"Then you don't need to," the Green Man announced with a slow regal nod of his head.

"You are welcome to stay in these woods and find your family and friends who have parted from you. I'm sure they would love to meet you."

"What debt could you, the Gods, owe a mortal?" Fin asked suddenly as he stared into the unfathomable eyes of the Goddess. He knew if he stared long enough, some part of him would go mad as the whole of the universe would unfold before him …

"A child of yours saves a being very dear to us," the deity answered with a beautiful sad smile.

"Child? … I-I don't have a child. Do I? I would remember a child … I'm a house witch; that would be important."

The Green Man stepped forward; the crystal that hung around his neck was beginning to twinkle.

Fin didn't know why his eyes were drawn to it in that moment, but suddenly a thousand images burst out of the stone.

He backed up in awe as he stared at …

Annika.

His mother.

His friends …

"It's everyone." Fin felt his heart fill with love, and … worry. Fear … they were in danger, and he wasn't there anymore.

Memories began filling his head like warm tea being poured into a cup, and as his heart skipped a beat, he stared at each moment from his life and felt tears in his eyes.

"Are you still uncertain about whether or not you'd like to return?" the Goddess asked patiently.

"Well, if you say a child of mine helps you, then I have to …"

"This child already exists, Finlay. You don't have to go back should you like to stay," the Green Man informed him with a genial look.

Fin felt himself go still as his gaze dropped from the pictures back to the Goddess.

"What?"

"The child …" She pointed to a different image then, one that wasn't from Fin's memory.

Annika stood in front of a mirror, her stomach swollen, her face stressed as she struggled to pull down her gown over the bump before she turned to the wardrobe and drew out a dress that looked larger.

"S-She's … with my … Annika and my … they'd be alone …" Fin stammered, his entire body suddenly awash with shock.

The light behind him grew even brighter.

Before he could say anything else, the Goddess gently rested her hand on his chest.

"I think I can see the decision in your eyes." She smiled again. "Remember, Finlay. Your home is sacred, and it doesn't have to be about the place, so much as where those you care for are."

Then the Goddess dropped a kiss upon Fin's brow and gently pushed him backward into the encompassing white light; their Godly faces were the last thing he could see as he felt himself being consumed by a pure magic …

Fin's eyes flew open, and he sat up with a gasp, then winced against the twinge in his chest.

Where was he?

It was nighttime.

He was on a boat.

Turning his head, he squinted against the light of a torch that was held up by a stunned man with ebony skin and white hair. Fin then stared at three women who, again, were strangers. A strange weight against his foot made him drop his gaze to see a furry black thing staring off to the side by his feet …

"Kraken?!" Fin exclaimed, blinking in confusion, but the familiar didn't move. His eyes were fixed on …

When Fin turned again, he saw Captain Antonio cradling something in his lap, his head bowed.

"Antonio! What in the Gods is—"

The military man straightened to look at him, his cheek damp with tears, and that's when Fin saw who he was huddled over.

There in the captain's arms was his mother.

Only ... she wasn't awake ... or moving ...

"Captain, what ..." Fin felt himself grow nauseated. No one around him seemed capable of speaking, and he felt a creeping suspicion climb up from his toes and wrench his heart.

Slowly, Antonio laid Katelyn on the deck, carefully arranging her hair around her face and resting her hands over her chest.

"She's gone, Fin." The captain's voice was quiet in the night. The waves lapped against the boat, and yet everything was ... still.

CHAPTER 29
COPING MECHANISMS

The rulers of the continent stood silently at the top of the stairs to the castle. Annika stood several feet to the side of the queen as knights in two rows lined the stairs leading all the way down to the ground. Mr. Howard, Mage Lee, and Lord Fuks stood at the very bottom of the stairs wearing morose expressions. Everyone waited under the cloudy sky without a word, the dark mood of the day smothering.

There hadn't been word sent from the witches since the captain and Kate had set off to meet them, and everyone grimly assumed it was because Katelyn Ashowan had been beside herself with grief over the loss of her son.

A messenger had relayed to the king that the ships had returned and that Captain Antonio was on his way back up to the castle with Lady Piereva and her daughter, but nothing else was communicated.

The queen cast a sad glance at her best friend, but Annika kept her eyes fixed on the drive, waiting ... Waiting to see her husband's remains.

At long last, the inconspicuous black carriage crested the hill and made its way slowly to the front of the stairs. Even the driver looked grim.

Annika's heart pounded in her chest, as she tried to focus on remaining as composed as possible ...

Captain Antonio was the first to step from the carriage, his face pale and the usual light in his lone blue eye extinguished.

He stood alone and stared at the second carriage that had followed his while standing completely still.

All sounds ceased, and aside from the faintest of breezes that gently tousled his long gray hair, nothing dared to shift him from the center of all attention.

When the second carriage stopped, the driver stepped down, and the captain nodded to the nearest knight, who immediately went to assist.

As they opened the carriage door and slowly pulled out the long stretcher with the body covered in a white sheet, Annika felt pain surge through her chest.

"Men! Hero's Salute!" Captain Antonio roared as he raised his hand to his brow. The knights then drew their swords in perfect unison, the tips pointed to the sky.

As the knight and footmen carried the stretcher up the stairs, Annika could feel her stomach twist sickeningly, and as a result, the magical heat from her unborn once again flared. Swallowing with great difficulty, she struggled to focus on each breath.

The king and queen stepped aside and dutifully bowed their heads as the body was carried past them into the castle.

In the haze of emotion and dwindling control, Annika vaguely recalled thinking that the figure on the stretcher seemed far too small to be Fin …

"Good Gods, what—!" Mr. Howard's exclamation drew Annika and the monarchs' attention.

There, at the bottom of the stairs, his hand raised in salute to his brow, was Finlay Ashowan.

Alive.

King Norman was still in shock when he received Fin in the seldom used throne room. It was customary to receive the body of a fallen hero with the utmost decorum. The body upon the stretcher beside the redhead was still wrapped in the white sheet, the identity of the individual unknown as everyone failed to mentally grasp how the cook was alive …

The king saw to Fin's report alone, however, sensing that perhaps it was for the best.

Oddly, not only was the house witch alive, but … he was healthy. Fin looked exhausted, pale, and there was a strange glow in his blue eyes that seemed ethereal … as though a white flame flickered behind his gaze at all times …

But he was standing. His tunic was stained with enough blood to warrant a man's death, yet he seemed perfectly fine on his own two feet. Though, there were shadows around his eyes and mouth that had not been there before.

"Lord Ashowan, what … has happened? Last we had heard you were, well … dead."

Fin's hollowed gaze when he stared up at his king was made all the more eerie by the strange magical shimmer behind his eyes.

"I was. I'm told I … I died last night." His eyes dropped down slightly for a moment, as though haunted by a memory.

"Then are you … is this … witchcraft of some kind? Are you passing a message from the grave?" Norman asked quietly.

"My … my mother … cursed me." Fin's voice had become hoarse.

Norman frowned; there was something he was not understanding …

"Your Majesty, for a witch to cast a curse, it means they have exhausted not only their magic, but also their life. Their spell becomes permanent."

The king's face slowly stretched into astonishment blended with understanding as he recalled the information and shifted his gaze to the body wrapped in the sheet.

"Your … Mrs. Katelyn Ashowan … brought you back to life by sacrificing herself," the king sounded out, his words sounding distant to his own ears.

"Yes." Fin bowed his head. "Your Majesty, the Troivackian military will be upon us in a matter of three days. I do not know where precisely, but I would presume both the cities of Austice and Xava are in their sights given that the king's ship met with Aidan's within a day's sail."

Norman nodded seriously. "Thank you, Lord Ashowan. I am sorry that your time aboard the Troivackian ship came with such pain. Your mother was … was one of the best women I've ever had the privilege of meeting. She truly was a hero of Daxaria, and I will see her honored as one. On a more personal note, she was a warm, strong individual that we were blessed to get to know. I am deeply sorry, Fin." The king stood then and stepped down from the dais until he was only a few feet from the house witch.

When Fin finally raised his tear-filled gaze to the ruler, Norman bowed deeply to him.

"I can't ever apologize enough."

Sobs racked Fin's body as he covered his face with his hands, unable to maintain his composure.

Slowly, and hesitantly, Norman reached out and hugged the young man, his voice cracking.

"My friend, I am so sorry."

Annika sat in her chamber with her eyes closed. She was trying to focus on calming herself down so that the blistering heat that raged through her would subside.

Her sister-in-law had been delivered to her estate and was being tended to dutifully by her staff … unfortunately, Annika wasn't sure she had the capacity to offer Janelle a shoulder to lean on as she was still reeling from shock.

Fin hadn't even spared her a glance as he had slowly entered the castle, his face marred with weary distress.

He's alive, and right now that is the best thing to focus on …

Annika had just succeeded in becoming mildly warm as opposed to sweltering when the chamber door burst open. Clara rushed over to her and immediately dropped down to her knees.

"It's his mother. It's Katelyn Ashowan."

Annika's eyes flew open. "What?"

"It was his mother's body they brought back. I overheard one of the knights tasked with contacting the coffin maker about it …"

Annika's face morphed into one of deep sorrow and pain. "Oh, Gods no … he has to be devastated. She …"

The healer's smiling face and gentle touch appeared in Annika's mind, and she felt her throat closing.

"Gods, she was a good woman … but how …" Annika dropped her forehead to her hand and allowed the tears to spill from her eyes.

After a few moments of the two women silently mourning the beloved witch, the viscountess raised her gaze. "Where is Fin now? Is he still with the king?"

Clara shrugged, while looking apologetic. "I don't know. It was difficult enough getting that information."

Letting out a long breath, Annika stood with a new objective in mind.

"I need to help with the funeral, and I need to find my husband."

Clara rose with her, though even the normally cool maid had to wipe away a few tears from her own cheeks. "I will speak with Kasim about flowers."

"I will go see the queen to find out if the debriefing has concluded." Annika and her servant gave each other reaffirming nods, and both set off with their objectives fixed in their minds.

Hannah's vise grip around Fin was commendable as Jiho sat quietly weeping behind her. Sirs Taylor, Andrews, and Lewis bowed their heads as a show of respect for their friend's pain.

"I w-wish I could do more to help," the blonde gasped through her own watery sobs.

"I understand ... nothing more can really be said at this point," Fin acquiesced quietly.

"H-Have you seen L-Lady Asho—"

"No. I haven't. I need ... time before I am alone with her," Fin interjected, his voice hoarse.

"She ... She was so b-broken when w-we thought you'd died, though ... y-you should g-go s-see her." Hannah finally released the cook and pulled back while still grasping his arms.

"It's ... It's complicated. I will try to see her a bit later ..."

"Fin ... that's ... that's too cruel," Jiho finally spoke with a small frown. "She literally collapsed from grief when she thought she'd lost you."

"I-I can't ... see her yet. She ... they ... don't deserve ..." Fin trailed off, unable to look at his friend as he swallowed back his next words.

"Cook"—Sir Taylor stepped forward then—"I lost my mother when I was younger than yourself; she passed while giving birth to my youngest brother. They both died ..." The large burly man's blue eyes dropped to the floor. "I know the world seems empty and uncertain now, but your wife will help. Family always helps."

"Why do you think I'm here with you all now?" Fin replied with a sad smile. Sir Taylor's gaze snapped up to the redhead's, and the two shared a silent moment of understanding before Hannah released him and stepped back while dabbing her cheeks with the back of her wrist.

"Yes, we are your family, but Fin? So is she. I don't understand why you are being pigheaded about her again—"

"Annika's pregnant," the witch announced suddenly.

Everyone immediately became speechless, and their jaws dropped in shock.

"I don't want the moment she finally tells me to have any ties to the conversation we will have about my mum dying. I want … I want every moment of my child's existence to be a happy one. From the moment my wife tells me, until I die."

No one said a word for several long moments.

Jiho was the first to come to his senses. "You already know, though. In her condition to have gone through such stress … Fin, you can't—"

"I just need a bit of time alone. Please. I want to see her … desperately I do, but let me just have a bit more time. I know it makes me selfish, and coldhearted even, but … at least until tonight. I need to grieve my mother, and not feel any kind of happiness."

Jiho's shoulders slumped forward in defeat. The Zinferan wordlessly nodded, and he slowly collapsed back into the kitchen chair with a single nod.

Fin then turned to the kitchen door and slowly trudged out of the room, his hands in his pockets, looking like the loneliest soul in the world.

Clara gently closed the greenhouse door behind herself and was setting an impressive speed as she marched back toward the exit of the courtyard, when she happened to career into none other than the king's assistant, Mr. Howard.

"Oh, my apologies." She curtsied dutifully.

"Not a problem, no harm done. Were you just in the greenhouse tower?" Mr. Howard asked while straightening his tunic.

"I was, yes." Clara kept her head bowed.

"What a funny coincidence, I was just on my way there myself. Was Kasim—"

"He has already gone home for the day," Clara interrupted calmly.

"Ah, unfortunate. I will have to speak with him tomorrow then. Well, good evening." The assistant nodded his chin to the maid and directed his toes to walk away, when he suddenly frowned and turned back to her.

"How is Lady Ashowan faring? I heard her health has been less than ideal with all the chaos as of late."

Clara kept her face bowed down to avoid eye contact. "My lady is managing to be quite resilient. She is searching for Lord Ashowan even now."

"Ah, yes ... I'm surprised he isn't with her already. I know his mother's death was a tragedy; however, given her condition she—"

Clara suddenly straightened and gazed directly into Mr. Howard's blue eyes.

"Condition?"

The assistant let out a small pitying sigh. "Yes, I am sorry to say His Majesty, the queen, and a few others are aware of what ails the viscountess. We are all quite happy to hear Lord Ashowan's marriage has been blessed with a new family member so swiftly, though—"

"Family member?" Clara's slow smile was peculiar, and Mr. Howard wasn't at all certain he understood its nature in its entirety.

"Yes ... we all discovered she was expecting her first ... child ... with— Why on earth are you looking at me like that?"

The infamously emotionless maid to the viscountess was looking gleeful. Normally she would never share any personal information about her mistress; however, it seemed the majority of the news was already shared.

Her eyes sparkling with mischief, Clara leaned in a little, which in turn made the assistant do the same.

"The viscountess isn't expecting *a* new family member."

Mr. Howard's cheeks flamed red. "Oh ... no. I offer my deepest apologies. I never should have said anything when it had not yet been officially announced from the lady. My sincerest—"

"The viscountess is expecting twins."

The assistant's eyes bulged, and his mouth froze in place.

"The ... th-that witch ... has made ... *double* ..."

"Yes. I don't doubt we will be seeing two very troublesome future nobles in the not-so-distant future. How wonderful, wouldn't you say?" Clara's delight over the response she was getting was foreign to her. She normally hated gossip, but the assistant's well-documented irritation with the Royal Cook just made the opportunity too ... delicious.

"I ... I think I'm going to bed with a bottle of wine now. Good evening." With that, Mr. Howard turned on his heel and scurried away, his complexion as white as a sheet while the maid allowed herself to laugh. Though admittedly it sounded more like a cackle ...

CHAPTER 30
ENDURING EMBRACES

Fin stared at his reflection in the mirror for a long while. Standing only in his trousers, he regarded the new marks on his body with barely any emotion, save when he looked at the ancient magic symbol burned into his left pectoral ... the symbol of his mother's magic and mark of her curse over his heart. Not far from the mark was the thick ropy scar where the Troivackian king had stabbed him to death.

The burn scars on his shoulders and arm made him let out the smallest annoyed sigh. Then he noticed under the first wave of his hairline what looked like two thin birthmark lines running parallel to each other. They were not obvious to see unless one really looked under his hair at his scalp, and Fin was momentarily puzzled until the vivid memory of the Goddess's lips gently brushing his head flashed into his mind.

"Thought just my eyes were different ..." Fin muttered to himself as he turned toward the steaming tub that sat in the center of the chamber the king had provided for him to bathe and don a fresh set of clothes.

The chamber door suddenly opened and closed, startling the witch back a step. He then recognized the swish of silky ebony hair, and olive skin, and immediately felt his heart ache.

Facing Fin squarely, the viscountess's expression was a mask of calm composure, but her dark eyes contained a sea of emotions varying from worry, pain, relief, and hesitancy.

"You're quite bold," the lady whispered, the intensity in her gaze making it difficult for Fin to swallow.

"Annika—"

"You greet your kitchen aides before your wife?"

Fin winced, still unable to meet her stare. "I'm sorry."

He expected her to be angry, and he knew she had every right to be. He also expected her to tell him he was being selfish, but then ...

She had him in her embrace.

Her faint spicy smell wafted up to his nose ... her form felt ... warm ... inviting.

"I'm so sorry about your mum," Annika whispered into his chest, and somehow, all tension melted from Fin's body as he collapsed into his wife's hold and allowed himself to be soothed by her.

After several moments where neither of them moved or spoke, Fin at long last took in a deep cleansing breath, then pulled back enough to plant a kiss on the top of Annika's head.

"What ... What happened?" she asked, her voice still slightly muffled from having her face pressed into his chest.

Fin wearily stepped back and gently clasped her upper arms, staring morosely at her. As he stared, however, Annika's eyebrows twitched.

"Why are your eyes ... ?"

"I died."

The viscountess blinked in shock.

"I saw the afterlife ... I met the Gods ... and then my mother cursed me and brought me back to life while sacrificing herself," Fin recounted the story as quickly as possible. Not wanting to have to dwell yet again on the painful reminder that his decisions led to his mother's death.

"How did you die?" Annika asked while refusing to release her husband from her arms.

"The Troivackian king ran me through with a sword when I ... when I ..." Fin frowned suddenly while staring at Annika curiously.

"I saw you get hurt," the lady began slowly after taking a guess at what was going through his mind. "You saw me, too, I take it?"

Fin nodded while his brow remained furrowed. "I've never been able to see a loved one in a vision while not at home before ... nor have they ever been able to see me in return."

"You've never been married before, either. Is it possible that change has something to do with it?"

Fin considered the notion for a moment before nodding. "That could be it. I do think that when a person has found their true home, they always have a connection to it …"

Annika's brows lowered thoughtfully before glancing at the steaming bath beside them. "Get in, I'll wash your back for you."

The witch gently reached up and pulled his wife's hands free of his waist while stepping back.

"I need time to—"

"What is this?" Annika's eyes swiveled immediately to the magic symbol burned in Fin's chest, before she noticed the stab wound. Her small hand immediately flew to a place beside the scar, her breaths growing ragged as she surveyed the damage inflicted upon her husband.

"Gods … I'll have to kill him …"

"You're going to kill the King of Troivack?" Fin asked with an empty smile. The expression dropped, however, when he looked in Annika's eyes and saw that she was entirely serious. "Don't try to kill the king."

His wife raised an eyebrow, her face becoming blank as she said nothing in response aside from, "Get in the tub."

Fin grimaced as he once again found himself wanting to try and twist a guarantee from her that she would not seek vengeance on his behalf. However, he was weary … both in soul and in body, and while he had intended to send Annika away to spare her from the burden of his grief …

He instead wound up being wordlessly bathed by his expecting wife. Then Annika carefully and lovingly dressed him before pulling him over to the bed and gently pressing him back onto the soft coverlet.

"Sleep. You look like you haven't had a proper rest since you were last on Daxarian soil."

Fin opened his mouth to object until Annika flopped down beside him and nestled in closer.

The witch suddenly felt the small telling outward curvature of her belly, and his body stiffened.

How had he not noticed before?

How was she already showing when it was still so early?

… And why did she feel like a human bed warmer?

Fin was pondering these questions silently, unaware that darkness was already creeping into his vision, pulling him into a sleep he didn't know he was capable of finding.

Within minutes, he was in a deep rest, and shortly after, his wife joined him. Both were completely unable to resist the quiet comfort of each other's presence after the traumatic events of the previous days.

The military men marched through the streets of Daxaria and began going door to door to inform the citizens that the Troivackian army was likely going to attack by the end of the week. Most of the men in the city were already enlisted in the army, and any of the wives who did not have children or elderly parents to mind were welcome to stay in the makeshift campsite on the castle grounds that was going to be constructed to help tend to the wounded.

Meanwhile in the king and queen's chamber, the couple faced their son with their infant daughter resting in her mother's arms.

Eric's hands were balled into fists at his sides and his cheeks were tinted pink.

"I won't go!"

"Sweetheart, all the noble children are going, including your friend Morgan! We will send for you as soon as it is safe for us to be with you."

"Why isn't Lina going!" the young noble demanded, as his fear made his heart skip several beats.

"Your sister and mother will join you in another week. For now, Lina is too young to travel on her own, and I need your mother here to organize the camp and provisions while I work with the captain to set up our lines of defense."

"Then … then I can stay and help Mother! I-I should learn about war stuff, too!"

"Eric … you are the future of Daxaria. It is your duty to remain safe until you are old enough to rule, do you understand?"

"I'm not a child!" the boy cried out while hastily using his sleeve to wipe away his running nose.

"Yes, my son, you are." Norman stepped forward and knelt before the young prince before resting his hands on his shoulders. "There is nothing wrong with being a child; in fact, it is far more important than you know. You are entitled to your childhood, Eric. All boys and girls are, and it is the adults' responsibility to protect those childhoods. When you are grown up, then it will be your job to protect the younger ones."

Eric sniffled more before his father reached up and gently brushed his golden curls.

"You need to take your childhood to grow big and strong, because not only are you meant to one day protect the children, but everyone in Daxaria. So you, more than anyone, need time to become as wise and good as possible. Can you do that for me?"

The eight-year-old clearly wanted to argue with his father, but he eventually nodded.

"Thank you, Eric. Your mother and I are so proud of you." Norman scooped his child up in his arms and gave him a strong hug as the boy clung onto his tunic and sobbed.

Ainsley sniffled behind them, and even the princess began to cry out, making the father and son pull apart and carefully include the women in their embrace.

"It's okay, L-Lina!" Eric announced, forcing a cheery tone through his tears. "W-When you come, I'll make sure you have a cradle and … and that everyone is nice to you!"

The infant's eyes moved to her brother and immediately grew transfixed, her small brow occasionally furrowing as though she were trying to understand what he was saying. Her adorable expression succeeded in making Norman and Ainsley share a loving wordless glance as they basked in their precious family moment.

Sadly, a knock on the chamber door shortly after the happy moment signaled the end of their time.

The king reluctantly stood and crossed the chamber, opening the door to reveal Captain Antonio.

"The men are in Austice and should have alerted everyone by tomorrow morning. We have set up roadblocks, and knights have been assigned to guide the traffic into the woods," Antonio announced with a small bow.

Norman nodded seriously. "Excellent. How are the preparations for Katelyn's burial?"

The captain stiffened for a moment before tonelessly answering, "By tonight everything should be prepared."

"I'm sorry we couldn't give a proper funeral and period of grieving for her, Antonio. She deserves—"

"It is the way of war, Your Majesty. I understand."

The king gave a slow nod but eyed his friend worriedly. "How is Lord Ashowan? He is aware we need to announce to the nobility by tomorrow morning his new status if he is to be permitted in all discussions pertaining to the battle?"

"I have yet to inform him. I will go now to see if I can find the viscount." Then, with another brief bow, the captain excused himself and strode purposefully down the corridor, his blue cape swishing behind him.

Fin drew the fine black coat over his black tunic and turned to leave the chamber, glancing back tenderly at Annika's sleeping face. His wife had been busy from the moment he'd returned, it seemed. Not only had she prepared most of the arrangements for his mother's funeral, she had also brought several changes of the clothes she had purchased for him to be taken to the castle.

Stepping out into the corridor, he magicked the door to remain locked unless Annika herself opened it, guaranteeing her privacy.

As he moved down the corridor, he began to grow increasingly aware of the stares the maids and nobles were giving him.

No on knew Fin was a noble yet—they were still adjusting to the knowledge of him being a witch—and now … now he was dressed in all black clothes made with quality material. He was certain he looked quite strange to them. Even though he understood this, their scrutiny was uncomfortable.

As he rounded the corner, he headed toward the king's council room, trying to avoid the curious gazes that seemed to be multiplying around him.

"FIN!"

His nerves already on edge, and dreading the uninvited encounter, he realized that the shout had come from none other than Eric who was streaking down the corridor to him.

The young prince immediately threw his arms around Fin's waist and hugged him.

"I'm so glad you're back! Everyone's going crazy!"

Patting the boy on the back, Fin couldn't help but smile ever so slightly at the child's affection.

"Crazy how, Eric?"

"Well, Mom and Dad are sending me away to one of our keeps in the country with some of the other noble children … and the entire city is disappearing into the woods! Everyone is scared, and all my friends and their mothers are crying."

Fin grimaced. He could feel the tension in the air as battle drew closer … despite being back home, he couldn't shake the cold darkness enveloping the castle.

"War is a frightening thing," he finally said as Eric pulled back and stared up at him.

"Your eyes are different," the boy observed with a small frown.

"Ah … sorry about that."

"It's okay. I'm just glad you're here! Mom and Dad were really worried about you. Lady Jenoure seemed to keep fainting places and scaring the maids … Mr. Howard is drinking in his chamber and saying strange things about a 'lifetime of headaches' and 'one was bad enough' …"

Fin blinked in surprise. "You seem to know a lot about what's going on around here."

"Ever since that Mr. Helmer man left, no one has really noticed when I'm around … it's been great!" The boy smiled excitedly up at Fin, who, despite himself, couldn't help but laugh a little.

"I'm glad you're having a good time … I need to go see if I can speak with your father, but Eric?"

"Yeah?" the boy asked, grinning cheekily.

"Thank you."

The prince's confusion was obvious on his cherub face.

"I've been having a … a bad week. Seeing you helped me feel a bit better."

The boy beamed proudly for a moment before his expression fell into a look of concern. "Why was your week bad?"

Reaching out and tousling the prince's hair, Fin answered, "Don't worry about it."

Then, striding the rest of the way over to the council room door, the house witch hesitated and turned to look at Eric's back as he happily bounced down the corridor.

I wonder if my child will get to be friends with Eric … they'd be pretty lucky if that were the case.

CHAPTER 31
GREETING THE SUNSET

The camp will be set behind the castle. Viscount, you are confident you can provide the shield should Troivack's military make it this far?" The king turned toward Fin with his hands clasped around his back, his chest plate armor glinting in the late-afternoon sun as a small crowd moved with the leader around the back of the castle.

"I can. I can maintain one longer if I'm not expelling anyone from the vicinity. If I have perhaps thirty minutes the day of, I can make a barrier that will not permit anything in. I can maintain that type of shield for a few hours. Though I don't know how it will fare against magic attacks," the redhead answered seriously before glancing over to the captain who nodded at him in understanding.

"Perfect. We are doing our best to arrange wagons for those unable to travel by foot on their own, but it could take a few days. Having a safe campsite is a great help," Mr. Howard contributed, though Eric's intel from earlier appeared to be correct as the man sported purple-stained lips and a small flush in his cheeks. The king seemed to be in a forgiving mood, however, and overlooked his assistant's obvious hangover.

"Captain Antonio, assign at least a hundred men to assist in the moving of any invalid citizens to the site to be settled," the king addressed the military leader.

"Yes, sire."

"In your estimation, Mr. Howard, has the new Duke of Iones had any problem handling of the men?"

"To be frank, most of the men appeared relieved that it was Lord Harris taking over, Your Majesty," the assistant said as he nodded seriously.

"I am pleased to hear that. Lord Fuks, have supplies been distributed, or are we still waiting on the delivery carts to be organized?"

"They are currently being loaded. The provisions in Austice are already being passed out as people exit the city, and Xava should have theirs by the end of the week. Rollom will receive theirs from Sorlia around the same time."

"Lord Ryu, have we yet confirmed when precisely the Zinferan military will be joining us?"

"At best, they will arrive in Rollom within two weeks. Xava, most likely a week," the Zinferan lord replied while giving a slight bow toward the Daxarian king.

"That is ideal, particularly if they intend to strike Austice first. I want to thank you again for volunteering to act as the diplomat between your emperor and myself during your stay here," Norman replied with a regal tilt of his head.

"Of course, Your Majesty. Thank you for allowing me to formally be accepted as a Daxarian noble. The emperor is most pleased with this compromise," Jiho replied with a polite smile and humble nod of his head.

"I, too, am grateful for this outcome. Now, if you are able to be frank with me, would you mind letting me know if there will be any lingering resentment following this deal?"

Lord Ryu's polite smile dimmed slightly as he replied. "The emperor's pride was prickled; however, the additional five percent of tax trade added to the deal for another five years helped numb the sting. Lord Nam, on the other hand ..." Jiho cleared his throat a bit and glanced down with a small grimace.

"I understand. Well ... another problem for another day." Norman sighed briefly before swiftly moving on to the next topic.

"Mage Lee, how many mages have confirmed their involvement in the war."

"At this time, Your Majesty, twenty. Three are here in Austice, four are in Sorlia, two in Rollom, one in Xava, and the last ten are coming straight from the academy. My son, while not a fully qualified mage, has been permitted to use his skills to assist the kingdom."

"Thank you, that will serve us well. I take it the news that the Coven of Wittica is taking part was … accepted more or less?"

Mage Lee grimaced and gave a noncommittal shrug.

"There won't be any internal fights at the very least?" Norman tried again, the tension in his voice noticeable.

"I do not believe so, Your Majesty. So long as the witches themselves behave."

Fin shot the mage a sharp look, which the elder ignored entirely.

Norman decided to not comment further to avoid any additional risk of a fight between his vassals.

"Excellent. Lord Ashowan, when are you to meet with the coven members?" Norman's gaze softened when it moved to the witch. It was clear he didn't like forcing Fin to work so soon after his mother's passing.

"Tomorrow after the meeting with the Daxarian nobles," the redhead replied calmly, his eyes shimmering even more so in the late-afternoon sunlight.

The king nodded. "You are welcome to use either the banquet hall or the council room to receive the coven members, but please inform Mr. Howard which you choose so that he can schedule the meeting with the catapult unit without conflict."

"Yes, Your Majesty."

Norman fell quiet then as he gazed at the men surrounding him. Everyone stood with either blank or darkened expressions, each man clearly burdened yet persevering the best they could.

"I want to thank you all for your combined efforts in making Daxaria ready for this war. As nobility, it is our sworn duty to protect not only our loved ones, but the citizens who make up the backbone and heart of this kingdom. You have all borne your responsibilities with honor, and I couldn't have prayed for a better grouping of men to endure the hardships to come." The king bowed to the group. Fin shifted uncomfortably, until he noticed everyone placing their hands over their hearts and slowly descending to a knee.

He followed suit and listened as everyone but himself and Jiho called out in unison, "For our king, and Daxaria our home, we serve."

Norman let out a quiet breath and lifted his eyes to the sky, his heart beginning to race as the reality of battle began to descend upon him.

"Well, men, let us retire for our dinner and convene for Katelyn Ashowan's funeral at dusk."

~~~~~~~~

Ainsley watched as her best friend frowned at her reflection in the mirror and immediately began stripping off the black gown that was far too tight.

"You know … I've been thinking …" The queen leaned back in her chair while gently patting the princess's back who was cradled asleep in her arms. "When I came and stopped you from boarding that boat to save Finlay, none of your household servants were present. The same ones you claimed were integral to your plan …"

Annika didn't even hesitate or show any reaction as she pulled another one of Ainsley's maternity gowns over her head.

"They had to pack, they were going to come within the hour."

"Mm-hmm … that could be … or … you made the whole thing up."

The viscountess was growing breathless as she tried to grab the black ribbons dangling at her back, and as a result swore colorfully.

"Why would you say that?" Annika eventually managed to say as she finally grasped the silky material and proceeded to tie a perfect bow.

"Well, for one thing, it isn't like you to have such a half-cooked plan. At first I figured it was because of your potent love for our dear cook—or viscount rather. Then when I learned of your matronly condition, I wondered if you were experiencing the intellectual muddle that some women experience."

"I am, after all, expecting double the normal amount of infants," Annika reminded the queen once she had finished tying the dress and stared satisfied at her appearance.

"Or … in true Annika Jenoure fashion—"

"Annika Ashowan," the viscountess interrupted with a small smile.

"Yes, yes, in a far more likely method … you pretended to be acting impulsively to make us inform you of our plans. We've never withheld information from you before …"

"Or treated me so delicately for that matter," Annika pointed out dryly.

"Precisely … you were able to learn everything by creating that wave. However, what I am still unclear about is what you stood to gain from contracting Elizabeth Nonata under your care."

Annika turned to her best friend and smiled prettily. "I haven't the faintest idea of what you are talking about. I am so glad, my dear friend, that you worry about me, though."

The queen's eyes narrowed. "Mind yourself, Lady Ashowan. If you take advantage of the liberties we've given you and move against our words, it does not bode well for our trust in you."

Annika's gaze sharpened. "I will remind you then, Your Majesty, that in my time of need you two were the first to go against my trust and underestimated me after years of my service and loyalty. What I said in the carriage still holds true."

Ainsley leaned back in her chair, clearly taken aback by the viscountess's words. Despite them being said in a lighthearted tone, there was a subtle edge to them.

After a moment of careful thought, the queen spoke. "You have my apologies for violating the mutual respect shared in our dealings. In my defense, I will point out that you fainted on two separate occasions, and nearly gave yourself heat stroke from stress."

"I did not behave inappropriately, though."

Ainsley let out a hesitant sigh. "No, you did not." After another momentary pause, the queen's face broke out into a faint smile. "Do you think you can handle being the mother to one or two witches?"

Annika grimaced. "Not at all. It's horrible enough what happened to Fin's mother … but even finding a governess will most likely be the death of me if one or both of them are keen on setting the keep on fire."

Ainsley chuckled. "Yes, I do suspect you will have your hands full."

Shaking her head wearily, the viscountess nodded toward the chamber door.

"I will meet you at the funeral. I'll take the passageway to leave. The nobles are already perplexed about why I've been present at the castle so often when I was supposed to be exiled."

"Once they discover the identity of your new husband they will be far too distracted to think about that."

"Yes, well … until then." The viscountess nodded to her friend and swept over to the secret panel.

"Annika?"

The Troivackian beauty looked over her shoulder as she opened the secret door.

"How is Fin doing? Norman said he … that he'd died."

Annika's face tightened, and her hand slid from the panel slowly. "He's … different. It's hard to tell how much of that is the horrors and pain he is carrying from his time on the ship, and how much is the shock and grief from losing his mother."

The queen nodded, her face openly anguished. "Whatever you need, I'm here for you."

Annika gave a tight smile of thanks and then disappeared into the passage without another word.

The crowd stood on the cliffside where there was a wide swath of lush grass that lay south of the city of Austice—and most likely wasn't too far from Annika's estate.

A rectangular hole had been dug, and at its head stood a large rock that towered over everyone. In the face of the stone it read:

Here lies Katelyn Ashowan, beloved mother, healer, and betrothed. A hero and witch of the highest order.

Twelve decorated knights stood facing one another, their swords drawn to create an aisle. Beside the empty grave stood the king and queen, and toward the end of the row of knights were the rest of the inner council, the newly ennobled Lord Harris, and the kitchen aides—including Peter, who had been released from his cell shortly beforehand.

Twelve witches from the Coven of Wittica had arrived and wordlessly surrounded the entire ceremony in a perfect wide circle.

A sleek black carriage slowly glided over to the site and pulled to a halt at the end of the aisle of knights. Out stepped Finlay, who handed Annika out of the carriage, followed by Captain Antonio, and finally, Jiho.

Moving to the back of the carriage, Fin, the captain, Jiho, Sir Taylor, Sir Lewis, and Sir Andrews lifted the casket over their shoulders.

Slowly, they carried the body of Katelyn Ashowan to her grave. A cool breeze and the crash of waves far beneath them were the only sounds in the quiet clearing.

They carefully lowered the wooden box, until roots magically wove up from the ground, flowers blooming from them as they tenderly wrapped the coffin and gently lowered it into the shadowy ground. Adamma who stood in the crowd nodded to the king through her tears, as Sky wept beside her.

Hannah moved up the aisle clutching a bouquet of exquisite flowers that were so large they required her to use both her arms to carry.

She handed them to Fin while dashing tears from her cheeks with the back of her wrist. Giving her shoulders a quick squeeze in affectionate appreciation, he took the flowers and stepped toward the grave, his throat aching and his stomach a black hole.

"Goodbye, Mum. You were … you were my one and only family for most of my life and … and"—the tears were spilling from Fin's eyes as he forced out the final words—"you were my first home."

Laying the bouquet on the casket, he stepped back, and Annika's warm hand found his.

Fin's blue gaze remained fixed on the coffin, but he squeezed her hand tightly, his gratitude for her support clear.

The king stepped forward and spoke to the crowd of Katelyn's kindness, quiet strength, and heroic feats. A representative of the Coven of Wittica presented herself and acknowledged the healer's outstanding contribution to not only the humans of Daxaria, but to the coven as she modeled what a witch was meant to contribute to the world. They lit a magical flame atop the large stone that would burn for three days. The ring of witches then bowed, and while facing the stone and coffin that held Katelyn Ashowan's remains, everyone present slowly lowered themselves to kneel for a long respectful moment of silence.

When the ceremony ended and the attendees gradually began to leave to return to the castle, Fin remained standing at the grave that had been filled with fresh earth, flowers already magically sprouting around the rock and plot. His eyes remained fixed upon another bouquet that had been rested against the stone by Antonio …

Annika stood by the carriage that had arrived from her estate to take them back, but she waited patiently, knowing that her husband needed more time.

Staring at the grave, Fin absentmindedly reached up and loosened the cravat at his throat before dropping his hand over his heart where his mother's symbol had been burned.

"I promise, Mum, I'll take good care of my family. I'll make you proud. I just … I wish you were still here. I wish you could've met my … my …" Fin trailed off, unable to speak the words. Instead, he managed to say, "I'm so sorry. I never … I never wanted you to have to pay for my ambitions." Slowly, Fin lowered to his knees in front of the stone, the sea breeze in front of the colorful sunset tousling his hair.

"You were the best mum I could've ever had. You always encouraged and pushed me … even when I didn't really hear you. Or even when I took you for granted. I will never forget you or stop loving you … I promise."

Staring out over the water where the Troivackian warships would inevitably appear, Fin felt the pain of his grief somehow slowly melt away into a sense of peace.

"I'll make sure you didn't die for nothing, Mum. I'm going to make sure we win this war, and I … I know I can do it."

A stronger gust of wind whipped around him then, as though his mother were trying to tell him from the forest of the afterlife that she believed in him and would always be with him one way or another, come hell or high water.

Fin closed his eyes, allowing his tears to fall, and at the same time feeling his guilt ease away with the winds that caressed his cheek as softly as his mother's hand once did not so very long ago.

CHAPTER 32
NEW HEADACHES

Fin stared at the clothes before him and let out a long-suffering sigh.
He was not used to having to dress like a noble and wasn't entirely certain he was looking forward to the experience in a long-term capacity.

"Would you like my advice?" Annika asked from behind him as Clara added the finishing touches to the elegant updo the viscountess was wearing for the council meeting.

"That'd probably be a good idea. In the future, could we ban all lace cravats? I just know I'll feel like a bloody cupcake wearing it."

Annika smiled before rising and crossing over to the various tunics laid out before him on the bed.

The colors ranged from black, cream, navy blue, and even a forest green.

"Hm, you wore the black coat with silver designs yesterday. I think the cream coat with matching trousers will make you feel more approachable. A black tunic underneath, however, with perhaps a gold-embroidered cravat will still make you look quite imposing—this one doesn't have lace or ruffles, and it matches the gold on the coat."

The viscountess turned to look at her husband and noticed the vacant expression that tended to befall most men when their women began explaining the style choices presented and the logic behind them.

"Sounds good, I'll do that then," Fin said after a moment when he realized Annika was staring at him with a bemused smile.

The viscountess stepped in front of him, filling his vision, and gently reached up. Freeing the gold chain with his wedding ring from under his tunic, she smiled gently. "Thank you for keeping this safe, but I believe it is time we wear our rings once again."

Fin raised his hand and covered Annika's before tenderly clasping her fingers and kissing them. "Will you help me take this off then?"

Smiling even more beautifully, his wife proceeded to wordlessly remove the golden chain and slip the ring free of the golden links, only to place it back on his finger.

Fin then did the same to her, his hands gently brushing the back of Annika's neck, making a small rush of goosebumps spread over her flawless skin. Once he had returned the wedding band to her own finger, Fin gently cupped her face and planted a kiss on her lips.

The move was intended to be pure of heart, but it was rapidly shifting to one of a different nature when an irritated throat clearing reminded them both that Clara was still present.

"I hate to hinder your morning *activities*, but I believe you both need to finish getting ready quickly if you are to make it to the meeting on time."

Annika and Fin immediately parted and, after sharing a nod of understanding, resumed their task of getting ready for the meeting that neither of them were entirely certain would go well.

Another hour later, both Fin and Annika were loaded into the carriage and about to depart to the castle, when Clara, who had been pulled aside by a worried-looking maid, waved to the coachman to prevent him from leaving.

As Clara rushed forward while frowning, Annika leaned out of the small window worriedly.

"What's wrong?"

"It would seem there has been an ... occurrence in the poisons room," Clara whispered with a small frown.

Annika's dark eyes widened in alarm. "What do you mean 'an occurrence'? Is anyone hurt? Only four people, myself included, have access to that room. Did someone sneak in?"

Clara's eyebrow twitched ever so slightly. "Not someone, but rather ... something. I believe it is the viscount's cat, Mistress ... only there are ... several cats that have come and gone in that room, even some rats. We aren't certain what has been done, but for now we've posted guards to prevent them from getting in."

"What has Kraken done now?" Fin interjected suddenly, the edge in his voice razor-sharp.

"Er … I shall tell you on the journey." Knocking the top of the carriage, Annika hastily signaled their departure before turning to her husband.

"Fin, there has been … a great deal about your cat that I believe we should discuss."

The witch waited quietly, his eyes focused on his wife with his brows lowered seriously.

"For one, he started that fire that led to the Troivackian soldiers being discovered."

The viscount folded his arms and nodded wordlessly.

"You knew about that?!" Annika spluttered with the intent of saying a great deal more, when the carriage began to wind down the steep hill away from the estate, making her immediately grow pale and queasy.

"Are you alright?" Fin asked as he noticed the dread on his wife's face.

"F-Fine, just … just the heat getting to me, I suppose," she lied while battling the nausea that threatened to cast out her breakfast.

The witch watched her worriedly without a word, knowing full well what ailed his wife but wanting her to tell him on her own time.

"Perhaps we … perhaps we discuss your familiar a little later today," Annika finally managed as sweat beaded along her brow.

"Of course."

The couple fell silent for a few moments as the viscountess did her best to take slow breaths like Fin's mother had taught her while trying to keep her eyes fixed on a still point.

"You look beautiful today … like a member of royalty," Fin said quietly as he eyed her gold-and-cream gown with its voluminous skirts and strand of pearls woven into her hair. Gold dripped from her ears and adorned her fingers … Annika had never worn so much jewelry in all his time of knowing her, but he presumed that she wanted to look as imposing as possible.

"Thank you. You look wonderful, too. It's amazing how well it suits you, to be honest."

Fin cringed but forced a smile best he could. "I don't feel that way, but … oh well. I suppose I'll grow used to it."

"Well, it's wonderful that you have someone going through the exact same thing in that regard. Lord Harris, I heard, drove one seamstress half mad with his outrage over her prices."

"Is that why you ordered my wardrobe for me?" Fin asked wryly, making Annika smile.

"I had a few reasons, but it did occur to me that spending our money may be a little foreign to you in the beginning."

"I'm more than a little … unsure of looking at our finances," Fin admitted with a sigh before he reached up and rubbed the back of his neck, which immediately reminded the viscountess that it was only a week ago that he was still a cook.

"Don't worry, I've managed successfully for a while now. We can look at the fiscal details once life settles a bit more."

Fin nodded and turned his attention out the carriage window. In truth, he, too, was feeling somewhat unwell at the thought of his public reveal that day, but …

One way or another, it was going to happen whether he was ready, or not.

"Lords, I want to thank you for welcoming the new Duke Iones into our meeting so graciously. His Grace has taken the militia serving under his house's name firmly in hand just in time for the war, and your continued support I'm sure will prove beneficial long term," Norman announced while gesturing toward Lord Harris, who was tugging at the lace cravat at his throat while giving a quick wave above his head to the other members of nobility in the room, which was received with various reactions.

The group had gathered in the throne room, which told the men there was something of ceremony to be addressed.

"However, it is my honor to inform you that there is another man who has recently joined the rank of nobility. We unfortunately needed to keep this from you and the general public until now."

A wave of whispers swept around the table.

"Pray tell, who is this man?" a voice called out closer to the doors to the throne room.

"He is the new viscount who has wedded the former Lady Jenoure and thus has inherited house Jenoure as his own," Norman announced carefully while staring unwaveringly at each man present who shifted dubiously in their seats.

"Your Majesty, a viscount? Whereas before he did not have a title?! This individual must have quite a substantial backing of wealth or prestige to be—"

"Ah! I understand! Captain Antonio, you've finally received the honors. This I accept wholeheartedly. Though, when did you wed Lady Jenoure?" Lord Laurent burst out, causing a rush of sighs and guffaws of relief to break out.

"I've not yet accepted a title, Earl Laurent," Antonio interjected gruffly.

The room fell into an awkward silence once more.

"Then … who … who is it?" another lord inquired, growing more puzzled by the moment.

Norman lifted his gaze to the guards at the door. "A man who is responsible for saving many of our lives, including Lady Jenoure's sister-in-law and niece. He brings with him a different kind of power to our ranks. My lords, it is my pleasure to introduce Lord Finlay Ashowan. Husband to now Lady Annika Ashowan."

With a nod to the guards, the door to the throne room opened revealing the viscount with his viscountess on his arm.

The pair were dazzling in their fine clothes and good looks, and there was something strange about the former cook's eyes that stopped any audible reaction from the group for a long moment as the pair strode forward only a few feet so that the majority of the room could easily see them.

Fin took the stunned silence as an opportunity to address the crowd of nobles after his gaze had swept around the room appraisingly, while Annika's chin remained raised proudly. Her beautiful face was as cool and poised as ever.

"My lords, it is an honor to address you again. I hope that you can find it in your good natures to accept my presence in your ranks," Fin recited the practiced line and followed it up with the equally rehearsed regal nod of his chin.

"Oh … my …"

"Gods! Absolutely not, Your Majesty! This is madness! *He is a cook!*"

"When did this happen?!"

"*Silence!*" the king's voice boomed, and from his throne he looked incredibly imposing. "As you all are aware, Lord Ashowan is responsible for saving hundreds of lives as I mentioned before. He also has been secretly helping us gain insight into Troivack's plans for this war and has spared thousands now because of it. Not to mention …" Norman continued, his eyes flashing before he reached a hand out to Mr. Howard who pulled out a small scroll that he then deposited in the king's hand.

"It was because of Lord Ashowan that the former Duchess Iones was discovered as the one responsible for shipping in the brunt of the

Troivackian soldiers on her own personal vessels. He learned this after he managed to persuade Madam Mathilda to reveal that the man Red we had apprehended had been hired as a former employee of the duchess to carry out various crimes. One of these was the arson case that led to the death of Lord Harris's own mother!"

The room remained hushed for a moment as each nobleman present struggled with the information presented to them.

The truth was …

Annika had been the one to discover the information the night she had tried to commandeer a ship, though she didn't mind the credit going to her husband if it helped the Daxarian nobility look upon him more favorably.

In actuality, her plan the entire time had only been to be read Fin's letters and sit in on the council … however, learning that the infamous Dragon was making deals in the dungeon had prompted the man named Red to make a deal of sorts … in exchange for the information, he would never be put to death, and after fifteen years in a cell, he could appeal to be released … Though one of the judges for that hearing would be none other than Lord Harris.

Red was not aware of this detail.

"Does the cook have any nobility in his blood? Isn't his father a Troivackian noble?" a marquess called out, drawing everyone's attention to their original outrage.

"He is not," Finlay announced, though his tone had become frighteningly icy.

All eyes moved back to him, though for some reason the men all felt distinctly ill at ease at seeing Fin's somehow formidable presence.

"My father is not of nobility; His Majesty bestowed this title on me generously without worrying about my parentage."

"Y-Your Majesty, why not a baron title? Why would he inherit Lady Jenoure's status?" Earl Laurent stammered.

"Your Majesty negotiated us down from a dukedom to a viscount is why, my lord. We would not have accepted anything less." An elderly woman with intense brown eyes and a tall lithe body stepped through the doors behind Finlay and Annika. Her posture perfect, her gray hair pulled back into a bun, and a strange air about her in her long forest-green robes made her … intimidating.

"My lords, I am here on behalf of Eloise Morozov, our coven leader. My name is Donna Bieren, and I am here to confirm that Lord Ashowan has been selected to act as the official diplomat between the Coven of Wittica here in the court of Daxaria. He will be the voice of our people and will be instrumental in all negotiations going forward."

"Wait … does this mean … ?" the same marquess as before began.

"With the ennobling of the witch Finlay Ashowan, you have the strength of the Coven of Wittica in the upcoming war at your side." Donna gave a slight curtsy to the king, then to Fin.

The council room fell into a wordless stupor for a long period of time.

Unable to take the awkwardness, or the stiff formal clothes, Fin finally turned to the coven elder, who clearly had only come to help smooth out the king's announcement.

"Thank you for your support and attendance." He gave a small bow and watched as the woman almost smiled. A prickling along his skin told Fin that she was a force to be reckoned with, and he wondered what element of magic she was …

"I will take my leave now and return to organizing the witches who have volunteered to fight. Your Majesty, lords …" Donna Bieren gave another slight inclination of her head, then exited the hall in the quiet, clearly not seeing a point in waiting around for everyone to collect their thoughts.

"Does anyone have any further questions?" Norman asked, while a small quirk of his lips indicated he was giving a small smile of celebration for quelling his vassals.

A tentative hand extended into the air. A young baron with a kind face looked at the king sheepishly.

"Yes, Lord Haversher?"

"Er … how does marrying Lady Jenoure come into all this?"

"I can answer that one, Your Majesty," Fin interjected, which once again drew every eye to him. The new viscount met the gaze of the baron who had spoken unwaveringly.

"It came into all this because I happened to fall in love with him," Annika interrupted unapologetically while smiling demurely, which instantly charmed at least half the men present.

"—And I'm not crazy enough to ignore the viscountess … at least not for a third time," Fin teased, shooting the baron a smile of his own, making the poor young man blush.

"Wait … *you* rejected *her* before agreeing?!" Lord Laurent exploded in disbelief.

"Twice," the witch recalled as Annika confirmed by holding up two fingers.

"Gods, man, you should've gotten on your knees and begged her!" another lord exclaimed in awe.

Fin glanced at Annika with a raised eyebrow, who shot him an equally amused expression before the redhead looked back to the nobles. "What can I say; being infuriating is part of my charm."

The king's expression was less than impressed with the retort as Mr. Howard at his side began shaking his head; he drank deeply from a wine goblet that no one had seen in his hand when they'd first entered …

While a great many murmurs broke out amongst the nobility, Fin cast a small warm smile at his wife before giving a cheeky wink to Mage Lee, who immediately scowled in response.

It was beginning to occur to Norman that Finlay Ashowan had been a hassle when he had been a mere peasant … just how exasperating was he going to be as a noble?

CHAPTER 33
DOUBLE DUTY

"Finlay, my boy … I've been meaning to ask you something," Lord Fuks began slowly.

Fin looked over to the earl expectantly. After the meeting with the courtiers had ended, the inner council had been requested to proceed to the council room on the second floor, along with Annika.

"What is it?" he asked patiently while noting that Mage Lee and Mr. Howard were sharing similar looks of uncertainty.

"Are you … not … going to be the Royal Cook anymore?" Mage Lee managed to speak for them all to save the others from having to ask the question that felt a little ridiculous to be raising in light of more serious events.

The witch's eyebrows jumped upward as his gaze moved over to the king who also looked a little stricken by this inquiry.

"I … er … don't know? I can't really do other duties and be the cook, but I know it'll be hard to get another person capable of taking over here so last minute. I know everyone is getting really tired of stew, but at least there hasn't been another poisoning incident …"

The memory did not help the morale of the men around the table.

"I think we can discuss this another time. For now, there is the matter of testing out your abilities, Viscount, and seeing how the knights can best support your magic when defending the castle," said Norman, rerouting the conversation back to more pressing matters, though his gaze bore a brief twinkle at the far milder topic of replacing Fin as the Royal Cook.

Fin nodded, then glanced over at Annika, who was frowning and staring at the table, deep in thought.

Gods … is she feeling unwell? I wish she'd just tell me about her pregnancy so I could ask her directly about these things … Fin found himself thinking fretfully.

"Lady Jen— Lady Ashowan?" The king noticed what had distracted the witch.

The viscountess's head snapped up, her expression clearing immediately. "My apologies, Your Majesty. I think I should return to my estate and make sure that everything is in order. There was a slight disturbance before we left."

Fin stood with his wife, intending to escort her out, when the king called out again.

"Lady Ashowan, I … I know you and the viscount have only just been reunited; however … do you not think it wise to join the families that are evacuating?"

Annika's gaze sharpened. "Your Majesty, I intend to stay right here. Thank you for your concern."

Giving a hasty curtsy and not waiting to hear any follow-up queries that could easily turn to demands, Annika then hurried from the room, leaving the men behind her to exchange knowing glances, save for Fin who was staring after her worriedly.

When the viscount did turn his attention back to the inner council, he noticed Mr. Howard and Mage Lee giving each other a meaningful look and immediately narrowed his own gaze.

"How has the viscountess been feeling?" Lord Fuks asked in a light tone, which made Fin turn ever so slowly from staring at the mage and assistant to the earl.

Without answering, he glanced over to the captain, then to the king who was also staring at him sympathetically.

"Did she tell all of you already?! She hasn't said a word to me!" Fin suddenly burst out exasperatedly while sitting back down gracelessly.

The council let out a collective sigh. "No, she didn't tell us. We found out rather by accident, but … then how is it you learned of it if she didn't say anything?" the king replied, equally confused.

"The Gods told me." Fin's flat reply was met with stony silence.

"The … the Gods told you?" Mr. Howard repeated dumbly.

"Yes. Before the Goddess shoved me back into my body." The witch didn't seem to care at all that he was stunning the group of men around him as his thoughts remained fixated on the dilemma pertaining to his wife.

"Were … were they nice?" Lord Fuks asked pleasantly.

"He meets the literal creators of everything, and you ask if they were nice?!" Mr. Howard's incredulous shout as he exploded from his seat somehow didn't seem to bother the earl in the least.

"They were lovely. The Green Man seems a quiet sort …" Fin replied casually, while also ignoring Mr. Howard.

"Well, that's a good thing to know." Lord Fuks grinned and leaned back in his chair. "I'd hate to die and then find out I'm stuck for eternity in the woods with nasty folk."

"No, no, perfectly fine pair. The Green Man seemed to like showing off his chest a bit much for my taste, but, the Goddess was … well … a Goddess."

The men were unable to move for several long moments.

"And the deities told you that the viscountess was expecting … huh." The captain's face was blank as he blinked only once while in profound thought.

Fin nodded then pinched the bridge of his nose. "Pardon me, Your Majesty, I think I need to demand my wife tell me what's going on. I'll be right back. This is all just too absurd." The witch stood and bowed sloppily before darting to the door and taking his leave.

The men present glanced at one another briefly, then immediately scrambled to the door in Fin's wake.

They did not want to miss a moment of the conversation.

"Annika!" Fin called as he spotted the hem of her skirts begin to disappear around the corner of the stairs. He broke out into a run as he desperately tried to stop her from gaining any more distance.

Annika, who had just stepped a toe down on the third step, turned in surprise at the sound of her husband's call and saw Fin clasping the wall as he took a couple quick pants to regain his breath.

"Is everything alright? I thought the meeting would go on a little bit—"

"I know you're pregnant," Fin blurted while bending forward and lifting Annika off her feet into his arms. He stumbled back with her onto the second floor while holding her in a tight embrace.

Annika was so stunned by the sudden announcement, she couldn't think of anything to say in response.

When her husband finally placed her down, there was a bit of pink in his cheeks and ... the entire inner council was standing a little ways down the corridor watching.

The viscountess did a double take to register her audience of the king himself, Captain Antonio, Lord Fuks, Mr. Howard, and—

Was the blasted mage weeping *again*?

"Did you tell him?" she demanded of them, color rising in her cheeks.

"No, Viscountess! The Gods told him!" Mr. Howard called out gleefully ... he seemed excited about something.

"Annika, I know why you didn't tell me sooner. I know you didn't want to burden me after I returned and my mother was dead, and part of the reason I didn't want to see you was I knew I wanted to be completely happy with you about the child and—"

"The child?" Annika asked faintly, before she suddenly winced as though bracing herself. "About that ... well ..."

"Is everything alright? Did something happen?!" Fin's face shifted to morbid worry, and he immediately began looking around them for a private room to talk in.

"Viscountess, can I tell him? I really want to tell him!" Mr. Howard called out again. The man seemed to have gone a bit mad recently ...

The witch cast a very disturbed look at the assistant before focusing once again on his wife.

"Fin, there isn't *a* child ..." Annika explained while lowering her voice to a near whisper.

Her husband's look of anguish nearly broke her heart. "What? But I—"

The lady blushed brightly under the many eyes watching her. "It's ... It's twins."

Fin's expression froze.

"What'd she say? I couldn't hear over this blubbering mess here?" Lord Fuks called over to Mr. Howard who was already basking in the radiance of Fin's catatonic state.

"Twins. The viscountess is expecting *two* little redheaded hellions!" Mr. Howard announced loudly, while smiling with a hint of madness appearing in his eyes.

There was another beat of dumbfounded silence.

Then the king, the captain, and Fin all wore identical expressions of severe shock, leaving Mage Lee to cry even harder, Lord Fuks to look impressed, and Mr. Howard to declare it in years to come as one of the most amusing moments of his life. At long last, the know-it-all cook was struck speechless, and for once he was the one a step ahead and had nothing to do but bask in the glory.

"Are you sure you're alright?" Annika asked again as Fin sat in the emptied council room.

"I should be asking you that, don't you think?" her husband pointed out with a small smile before reaching out and taking her hand. "I wondered how you could already be so bi—"

Annika's narrowed gaze had him clamping his mouth shut. Fin cleared his throat.

"So my … my mother told you that it was twins, and that one or both were most likely going to be a fire witch?"

The viscountess nodded.

"I see … Well … I love you." Fin stood up then and pulled her into another embrace, startling the poor woman for the second time that day.

"I love you, too," she murmured into his tunic.

"Excellent, now I need you to promise me that if the fighting reaches Austice, you will leave."

Annika stepped back, glaring openly up at him.

"No. I will stay here. I fully intend to kill the King of Troivack. I was not making that vow lightly."

"I know you weren't, but you have to—"

"If you say 'protect the children,' I will kick you. Everyone is saying that to me, and that is not the only thing I can do just because you got carried away the night of the masquerade!"

"I— Wait, the masquer— That's when … ? Gods … you'll be giving birth in early spring …"

"Finlay! Focus! Stop treating me like a bloody mare that is only used to breed!" Annika snapped angrily. "I know everyone means well, but just because I am having children doesn't mean I'm not a person anymore, and so help me Gods if you try to send me away without any regard for my opinion, I will imprison you where no one can find you for the rest of your days!"

Fin stared at Annika who looked quite sincere in her threats, and after a moment of studying her face, he let out a long weary sigh. "I won't insist you leave, but please … please don't actively engage in combat, either."

Annika folded her arms over her chest. "Fine."

"Good. Now, I need to go attack the knights with magic, but I will be back at the estate later this evening."

The viscountess nodded. It was clear she was not happy with the turn of the discussion.

Leaning down and planting a quick kiss on her cheek, the witch left the room, and as he did so he sent a quick prayer to the Goddess that his wife would calm down by the time he saw her again …

Fin stood in the center of the circle of knights who all joked around with one another and occasionally glanced cockily in his direction. These men appeared to be handpicked by the captain … meaning they probably were some of the best fighters under Antonio's guidance.

The witch had changed into a plain tunic and trousers, and while many of the men present would have seen Fin at his mother's funeral, and would have therefore heard he was ennobled, it didn't necessarily mean they would immediately respect him.

Captain Antonio then strode over to the group and handed the knights their real swords instead of the wooden training ones used for when they taught their squires, effectively silencing them.

"Captain, what is the meaning of this? You know we could injure Lord Ashowan," one knight pointed out, his tone mocking as he gestured to the man they had all been astounded to learn was married to the former Lady Jenoure.

"That 'lord' is a viscount. You will treat him with the deference he deserves, understood?" The inherent threat in Antonio's words was not ignored.

Everyone present once again fell silent and turned their attention to Fin, who was already mildly embarrassed by the exchange.

"Then … why the swords, Captain?" one of the other knights asked, confused.

"I'm sure you all remember that it was also announced that Lord Ashowan is a witch. He will be one of our key figures defending the castle when the Troivackians arrive in a few days, so we will need to see how we can best work together to be the most effective."

The men shifted quietly then, their previous confident attitudes things of the past.

"Er … what kind of magic do you do … my lord?" one of the younger men asked nervously.

"I'm a house witch," Fin answered tonelessly. "Usually I am more effective with cooking, but in this case … any help is good in a war, wouldn't you say?"

"We'll see about that," Fin heard a knight close to his left mutter under his breath, but when the witch's gaze cut over to him, he saw the man recoil under the strange gleam in his eyes.

"Now, men, we are going to try and train as much as possible over the next day and a half to help increase our odds, but on the morning the Troivackians are due, I want you all to rest. You know we will need to conserve our strengths," Antonio announced while striding out of the training area to watch from the tall chair that was positioned near one of the borders so that he could get a better view on group maneuvers.

The men all turned their attention to Fin then, and they slowly lifted their weapons.

"I want you all to attack me at once," he instructed calmly.

The knights broke out laughing.

"You take us so lightly, Lord Ashowan? Remember you were fighting against knights less skilled than us the last time you were in this ring," the same knight who had taunted Fin before jeered at him.

This time, the witch didn't let the comment slide as he turned and faced the man with his eyes already beginning to glow even more brightly. "While that is true, I have no intention of holding back or fighting fairly. Not with the war about to start."

The knight's smug expression morphed into a frown. "Don't say we didn't warn you."

Fin smiled coldly. "Likewise."

With a roar, the soldier called out to his comrades, "Alright, men, attack!"

They each lunged a single precise step, and then each proceeded to be blasted two feet backward onto their backs by a sudden explosion of blue lightning in front of them.

The ring was silent as the knights all slowly recovered from the shock and gradually stood back up with new wariness.

Glancing up at the captain, whose blue eye was slightly widened, Fin called out, breaking into a slightly friendlier grin, "I don't even have my frying pan, yet!"

CHAPTER 34
BACK TO BASICS

The knights were far quieter as they worked on coordinating their attacks against Fin's magic, yet as they went along, they also asked very helpful questions such as:

"How do we fight against a witch from Troivack if they ..."

"How can I get around ..."

To which Fin had very little he was able to help with. He had never considered the combative side to magic, and he really was more interested in shielding and neutralizing those who had sought out to attack ...

It wasn't until the captain stepped forward from his vantage point with an idea.

"Fin, you mentioned that you are able to do long-term charms in your home that are far less of a drain on your magic."

The witch nodded while rubbing his eyes wearily. Constantly battling using small bursts of a shield was already beginning to wear away on him. It was hard controlling how far back each knight would go so as to not fling them out of the ring.

"What if you managed to magic particular spots long in advance? Say, one spot the soldiers will sink into the ground up to their knees, or another area they—"

Fin's head snapped up, a smile lighting his tired features.

"Captain, that's brilliant. I don't know how that will affect me long term, but if it was a single use of my magic instead of me having to repeat the spell, that should help. I also don't know what would happen to me if a bunch of charms ended up going off at the same time … but I think it is a better option."

The captain nodded and addressed his men then who were all dripping with sweat and panting heavily.

"Alright, men, go to the rain barrels. We will train tomorrow, but after that, you rest. Good work today."

Fin nodded to each of them, though the gesture went mostly ignored, which gave him a somewhat uneasy feeling in the pit of his belly.

"It's more about their anxiety over the war than you. Don't worry too much," the captain explained after he had climbed down from his seat and joined Fin's side.

"I'll try not to." The viscount sighed. "I think I'll head back to Annika's estate and find out what the problem was with Kraken this morning." Fin turned and began to walk away expecting to then bid the captain farewell, only the man instead fell into step beside him.

"I think you mean, *your* estate, Viscount," Antonio reminded with a firm tone but a kind glint in his eye.

Fin tried to smile, but he failed as he quickly glanced at his feet.

"I suppose so. I feel … more like an imposter right now than I do a proper noble if I'm honest. I've never felt so … out of my element," he tried to explain, looking at the captain again, the bags under his eyes somehow appearing darker.

Antonio squared off with the witch, halting their trek across the castle lawn.

"Adjusting your scope to such a grand change will be difficult for you. Especially after losing your mother and standing to lose so much more. Your home is no longer a single room, nor are you safe behind closed doors out of sight. You are a leader now, Lord Ashowan."

"I don't know that I should be, though. I have no training for this position, and I know next to nothing about what I should be doing. At least as a cook I was able to learn more about inventory and expectations from Luca the previous cook before coming here."

Antonio gave a small smile. "I wouldn't worry. Your wife was managing splendidly long before you came into the picture, and I think you just need to remember what you are bringing to the position. Part of the reason for His Majesty's decision to elevate you was that you are meant to be different. You have a strength that is not like other nobility, and knowledge most others don't have."

"I can make a terrific pie, but—"

"Lord Ashowan, how is it you thought of creating a protected union within a brothel?" the captain interrupted with an arched eyebrow.

"Oh … that was because that was similar to what the coven arranged for some of its members after so many hostile takeovers of their government a century or two ago. The abandoning posts until demands were met? That was how part of the treaty between Daxaria and the Coven of Wittica came to be agreed upon. They get tax breaks in exchange for their continued work."

Antonio straightened in surprise. "Their continued work … ? What work?"

"Remember how I mentioned some of the most-skilled people in the kingdom were, in fact, witches? When they weren't happy with their treatment, all those witches who lent their powers and skills that added to the accomplishments of the kingdom—"

"… ceased to work," the captain finished in growing awe. "Gods … that was why the blacksmith Theodore refused to make anything for anyone in the beginning of his career."

Fin smiled and nodded.

"But do you see, Viscount? That is precisely what I mean. You've brought equality, and balance, to those you encounter because you are able to implement this unique knowledge."

The witch dropped his gaze to the ground.

"I've also been speculating how it is that you seem to have the strangest … persuasion over people. Every exchange you've had, you generally seem to come out with the most favorable dealings …"

Fin glanced up at Antonio, revealing that he was equally curious about the man's theory.

"I think it's because there is something about you that makes us all think of home. You carry an essence that makes us all sense and in turn crave a place that is whole. Something about you makes us want to embrace the harmony you suggest as it could draw us closer to that place. That home …"

Fin's cheeks flamed red as he turned and resumed walking.

"As someone who is not on that side of my, what was it Mr. Howard calls it?, 'chaotic mischief that leads to a ghastly mix of problems and solutions,' I can't say for sure."

Captain laughed. "Ah, right ... the assistant did say something to that effect ... I honestly can't tell if you are the bane of that man's existence, or if he really *is* trying to hide his feelings for you."

"So Mr. Howard does prefer men?" Fin asked with moderate curiosity.

"Who's to say other than him? He is married to his work and gives no indication that he has any preference, though you have made us all wonder ..."

Fin laughed and continued striding toward the front of the castle where he would have the very awkward task of ordering someone to fetch him a carriage to return back to the estate. One day he hoped he could learn to ride a horse and not have to feel so ... cumbersome and noticeable.

It was yet another area Fin needed to develop, which only reminded him of his new burdens as a nobleman; that is, until the captain's words began to churn to life in his mind.

Perhaps there was an easier approach ... and maybe it would help make the transition feel less like a fish learning to fly.

Gods, I hope things start to fall into place a little easier ... otherwise I might have to be the only viscount in history who left all his duties to his wife in order to stay a cook ...

As Fin stepped down from the carriage, he was surprised to see servants standing outside waiting for him. They were already bowing as he approached, and he once again needed to fight off showing the intense discomfort he got from their display of formality and respect.

"Where might I find my wife?" Fin asked one of the stewards who straightened as he spoke.

"In your bedchamber, my lord."

"Ah, thank you ... what's your name?"

The man's thick gray mustache bristled. "Dirk, my lord."

"Thank you, Dirk. Has she had dinner yet?"

"I do not believe so, my lord."

Fin nodded, then turned away from the stairs, as he felt himself reach a very important conclusion.

If I have to change my scope of what my home is ... as well as what kind of viscount I'll be, then the most logical place to start ... would be the estate's kitchen.

Once Fin had reached his destination, he greeted Raymond and the handful of maids in the room who were all talking amongst themselves.

"Greetings, Viscount." Raymond was the first to acknowledge his new master and bow, which in turn made the maids curtsy to him.

"Good evening, everyone, I ... I am going to have to ask you to leave the kitchen." There was a note of uncertainty in Fin's voice as his stomach roiled at executing his unfamiliar authority, but ...

I need to start feeling like I belong here.

The servants glanced at one another warily, then all vacated the room quietly while once again issuing bows and curtsies.

Fin shifted awkwardly, only moderately relieved that none of them had sought to argue with his request.

Once the door was closed behind them, and he was alone in the kitchen, the witch let out a long breath ... and immediately felt tension melt from his chest and shoulders.

Rolling up his sleeves, Fin stepped behind the cooking table that already had the beginnings of a meal started.

"Looks like ... cabbage salad and ... carrot soup," he murmured quietly to himself.

Reaching out, he began to clear a space for himself on the table. He then picked up a bowl and began measuring out flour, then salt, sugar, and yeast ...

As he worked, Fin slowly found an old spark of joy igniting in his chest. There was a comforting rhythm to the task that was familiar to him and truly made him feel whole.

Glancing up briefly with a smile on his face, he noted the beautiful sunset setting the kitchen ablaze.

As he then thought, *Better start caramelizing the onions,* a pot floated down from its hanging place by the hearth and rested atop the grill.

Fin turned suddenly, realizing what he had done. He jerked his chin toward the paring knife that lay harmlessly on the table beside the carrots, and with his heart hammering in his chest, he nodded to it.

The vegetable and knives sprang into action immediately. Matching Fin's own masterful pace when doing the task himself, he could feel the gentle rise of magic as it trickled through him until it overflowed and began streaming wider and wider throughout the room until the entire space began to fill with it. Ginger root floated over to the table. A wooden spoon dove into a churn of butter and magically tapped the dollop into the pot, making Fin smile again as a swell of emotions rose within him.

I guess I'm heading in the right direction.

~~~~~~~~~

Annika looked through her lists of poisons that had been disturbed by her husband's familiar, Kraken. She sat on the couch in front of the hearth paging through the inventory that Clara had double-checked for her while she'd been at the castle, and she grew more and more perplexed.

"He really did just disrupt ... this one barrel ... but why? It wouldn't smell appealing to them ..."

The viscountess's mutterings were interrupted by a soft knock on her door.

"Come in," she called out without tearing her eyes away from her page and her mind continuing to wade through the possible explanations in the face of the new mystery.

That is until the door opened, and Annika's senses were assuaged by the most mouth-watering aromas she could've imagined.

As soon as her eyes landed on Fin and Clara holding trays laden with food, Annika had no doubt about who was responsible for the fare.

"I thought we might eat in here today," Fin greeted.

He looked tired ... but there was something in his face that seemed more at ease. Something that looked a little more like the Finlay Ashowan before his time aboard the Troivackian ship.

Annika set her papers aside and waited as he proceeded to use the small table in front of the fire to lay out their dinner.

Once he had completed the task with Clara's help, the maid excused herself, leaving the couple alone.

"This smells incredible, Fin." Annika looked over the colorful food before her and noted the orange-colored soup with its faint aroma of ginger, then the cabbage salad that looked crispy and fresh, and finally the strange fried bread that looked diabolically delicious.

"Thank you. I figured it had been a while since I'd been able to pre-pare a meal for us on my own."

Annika would have replied, only she had already dug into her dinner with great enthusiasm.

"I was able to use my magic in your kitchen," the witch informed her quietly, his gaze fixed on the fire.

The viscountess stopped her chewing and turned toward her husband, her face growing still.

After swallowing what was in her mouth, she spoke.

"Does this mean you can no longer use magic at the castle?"

Fin shook his head. "I don't think that is the case. I just wish I had more time to grow comfortable with having a wider area I think of as home. I don't know if I'm weaker with a wider radius that includes more people. After all, if multiple people are scared or in danger, there's no telling what will happen to me. Then there's the worry that I may start losing the sense that the castle is my home as I grow attached to this estate here."

Turning to face him more, Annika reached out and took his hand. "War brings out emotions you don't even know you have. It brings passion, rage, and violence. You might find yourself developing a very keen sense of just how big your home is once the fighting begins ... I remember never feeling like my father's household had any meaning to me ... until a civil war broke out and it was my father's men against those who wished to hurt us."

Fin listened quietly.

"Once it was clear that those who stood beside me wanted to protect the same thing, even if it was for different reasons ... I felt more a part of the family than I ever had before."

"I don't really like the idea that violence is what unites a home ..." the witch admitted while giving his wife's hand a gentle squeeze. "I think I'm still overcoming my experiences with people and witches from the coven who made me an outcast for most of my life. You yourself said part of your pull toward me was that I seemed as alone as you felt. I don't really know what my new personal house rules are with all these places and roles getting jumbled together, and somehow despite having more than one home, I'm feeling more misplaced than ever."

"I can understand that, but ... do you still feel alone even though ... you've already started your own family?"

Fin grew thoughtful as he regarded Annika seriously for quite some time.

He still hadn't told her one of their children was supposed to help the Gods in some fashion, but at that moment, it didn't seem as important.

Instead, he pondered how she was right.

He still felt adrift in a wide world, even though everyone had made room for him. Everyone in the castle and the estate had welcomed and invited him into their households. He even had children on the way who would need him as a father.

Pulling Annika into his chest, Fin closed his eyes and tried for the first time to sense his children and what they might be craving. It seemed a strange thing to do at that moment and yet ... he was beginning to suspect it may be the small things that would help him find a way to anchor himself.

Breathing slowly, he reached out with his magic. He could feel the warmth of the room, felt the furniture react to his awareness, could sense that Annika was craving the carrot ginger soup fiercely, and then …

He felt a strange yet strong desire for peaches.

Underneath that sensation there was another craving. One that was quieter and harder to discern … A craving for herb bread and butter.

Fin opened his eyes while smiling. The cravings felt stronger to him than the queen's had when he'd sensed the unborn princess, perhaps because of his filial relation to the two he was connecting with.

"What is it?" Annika asked when they'd pulled apart and she stared up at his warm expression.

"Tomorrow I'll give you a bushel of peaches and bake you all the bread you want."

His wife's shocked expression made Fin laugh as he once again pulled her into his arms. "At least I know one thing about my place in all of Daxaria … it is going to have to be very close to you three."

CHAPTER 35
PREPARATIONS

Striding into her chamber while polishing off the crust of herb bread in her hand from her morning breakfast, Annika froze when she realized that the room was not empty like she had been anticipating.

Janelle Piereva stood waiting, her gaunt face and deadened stare regarding Annika emotionlessly. The viscountess hastily finished her food and dusted her hands of crumbs before closing the door quietly behind herself.

"Might I ... have a word with you, sister?" Lady Piereva curtsied, briefly, and straightened again.

"Janelle, how are you faring? Is there anything I can do for you?" Annika began immediately.

Since arriving no one had seen hide nor hair of the woman as she remained locked in her room, mourning the death of her husband ... barely even managing to care for her daughter.

"You ... You were the one Charles was reporting to, weren't you?" The hollowed voice that came from Janelle made Annika's heart beat faster.

The worst part was ... she knew she still couldn't tell her the truth; otherwise, she'd risk endangering her all over again.

"What do you mean? Finlay Ashowan was the one who—" Annika's pained expression was completely genuine, but her sister-in-law was not having any of it.

"Don't … don't lie to me. Charles wouldn't risk his family just for the sake of rebelling. He would only do something so stupid for you. For the only family member he never could protect while growing up."

The viscountess felt her throat ache and her stomach turn at the woman's words. "Charlie would come here and I would give him money, but I never—"

"Was that it? Did Phillip cut us off so horrifically that Charles came to you for help? Did you exploit him to spy for you in exchange for keeping us taken care of?" Janelle's eyes glimmered, and her voice was quiet, but it still made her sister-in-law wince.

"No. Charlie came here to receive the money himself because otherwise Phillip would've heard about me transporting the gold to him and interfered. You know this. I loved my brother, and I never—"

"You're the coldest woman I've ever met." Tears spilled over Janelle's cheeks. "Did you not even bother to mourn the only family you have left? You didn't come to check on me or your niece yourself for a full day! You didn't cry for any of your other brothers, either … I thought you cared for Charles."

"I am mourning Charlie best I can but—"

"There is always something. Always some selfish reason for you." The widow moved to breeze past Annika, only the viscountess grasped her by the arm, firmly halting her in place.

"My older brothers, save for Charlie, were not worth mourning. You did not grow up in my keep, Janelle. Now before you start casting judgment, I want you to think very carefully about how little you know."

The darkness in Annika's eyes when she gazed at her sister-in-law visibly shook the woman, but she continued on … she had had enough stress and guilt to last a lifetime.

"Stop making me your enemy. It is King Matthias and Troivack's chief of military that are responsible for this violence. I will see to it that you are safely hidden here in Daxaria and provided for comfortably."

"I am not staying here. I am going home with our daughter where I can give Charles a proper funeral!" Janelle cried angrily.

"My brother is going into the ground one way or another. If you choose to return, you and your daughter will be buried right beside him and I won't be able to do a thing to help."

Lady Piereva wrenched her arm free from Annika's grasp, as she looked with pure hatred at her sister-in-law.

"I hope that you remain alone for the rest of your life. No man or child should have to suffer your heartlessness."

Janelle stormed from the room, and the viscountess said nothing in defense as her heart thudded in her chest.

Annika stared after her sister-in-law, knowing her anger came from a place of deep grief; perhaps when the war was over she could tell her more, and help her understand, but for now …

All that mattered was that she and her child were safe.

Even if her words cut the viscountess deeper than she could admit.

Giving her head a shake, Annika squelched the urge to succumb to tears. Grieving would have to be stored for another day … a day where she could properly send her prayers of thanks to the only brother to ever show his little sister that she at least had one blood-bound family member who cared.

Fin stood at the crest of the hill of Austice with the castle behind him, his eyes glowing and his arms outstretched. Off to the side, Mr. Howard regarded him with his usual look of irritation and mild contempt.

"Are you aware that you have flour on your tunic?" the assistant asked dryly.

"Can't say I'm surprised. I had to bake Annika some bread this morning."

"You do realize you have servants now who can do that for you, right?" Mr. Howard stepped closer to where Fin was working and noticed the strange ancient symbol that was glowing on the lawn.

"We both know mine is better," the witch answered without bothering to look at the assistant.

"Was it your massive ego that seduced your wife, or was it the food I wonder …"

Fin's eyes narrowed as he turned his gaze to the exhausted assistant who didn't appear to care the slightest bit that he had irked the new viscount.

"So what is this trap supposed to do?" Mr. Howard asked, turning his attention back to the scroll of parchment that had been stuck to a piece of sturdy wood to enable him to take notes and walk freely.

"This will collapse into a pit that will be approximately twelve feet deep and will span the width of the castle," Fin replied while turning his attention back to his task.

The assistant looked up at him in great alarm. "Where does that start?"

Fin pointed a few feet down the slope of the road leading down to Austice where another symbol glowed.

"Good Lord, that ... if timed right ... could take out—"

"Exactly. We've also been able to set up a few traps throughout the city that don't require magic, just with some ingenuity from the knights."

The assistant looked impressed as Fin then turned back to the castle while rolling up his sleeves. He had a few more places he needed to go to set more deterrents to their unwanted guests, and not all could simply be a massive hole.

"By the way, Kevin, how did you know that Annika was having twins?"

Mr. Howard tripped as he walked beside Fin, his head jerking upward to stare incredulously at the man who had addressed him so casually.

"Did you just ... call me ... by my first name?"

"Well, I'm your superior now, aren't I?" Fin's smile was devilish, and the assistant didn't like it one bit.

"I'll have you know, Ashowan, that were it not for my talents, your ennoblement would still be bogged down in a stack of paperwork so thick that your children would not only be born but also fully grown by the time it could ever come to fruition."

The witch stopped, and with his hands on his hips he turned to stare at the assistant whose cheeks were tinged with red.

"You reeaally don't like being called Kevin, do you?"

Mr. Howard almost looked like a child he was so flustered. "I just don't appreciate your attitude this morning!"

"You could've been ennobled at some point I'm sure; why haven't you been?" Fin asked suddenly, curious.

The assistant immediately made a face of disgust. "Ashowan, the responsibility, and the stress? Terrible. I prefer to be one of the highest-paid noncourtiers who has great influence and perks with none of the downsides."

" ... You raise a good point. Truthfully, I hadn't really wanted to be a noble."

"You don't say?" The assistant rolled his eyes, then noticed Fin's unimpressed expression. "Becoming a Royal Cook and being a house witch doesn't exactly scream 'I want to be a lord.' You can't fault me for stating the obvious."

Fin rubbed the back of his neck and resumed his walking toward the castle with the assistant at his side.

"Do you want to get married at some point?"

"Absolutely not." Mr. Howard's response was incredibly quick. "I've had two relationships in my life and they were all suboptimal. No. Work, wine, and good food are my life objectives. Though I greatly look forward to watching your struggle with whatever beasts you've bred."

Fin was in front of the assistant, his eyes glowing with magic in a heartbeat. "Talk about my family like that again, and I will make it my life mission to ensure every drop of wine you taste be sour."

Mr. Howard faltered, and with a sudden grimace, his shoulders slumped forward. "My apologies, that was perhaps a bit too uncouth. I blame the stress of war."

The viscount nodded his forgiveness then continued on toward the castle.

"So how did you know about the twins?" Fin asked again, looking for a change of topic.

"Oh, that maid who works closely with the viscountess, the one from a fallen noble family? Clara, I believe. Anyway, she took great delight in telling me when we happened to cross paths."

"Clara was a noble?!"

"Yes, she and her sister Farrah are now servants, however, to pay off their father's vast debt … Farrah is Prince Eric's governess currently."

Fin recalled the woman who seemed wholly unprepared to mind a child, and as he thought back, he recognized the similarities in the shape of her forehead to Clara's.

"Huh … why did Annika hire her?" the redhead wondered aloud.

"I believe Clara begged her for her job, and somehow the two formed a bond …"

More like Annika was impressed over some kind of cunning ploy Clara attempted, the viscount theorized silently to himself.

"Ashowan, I must ask …" There was a strange waver in Mr. Howard's voice that drew back Fin's attention. "What was it like … when you died?"

The witch looked at Mr. Howard and, suddenly, with great clarity, realized that the threat of thousands of deaths was weighing far more heavily on the man than he liked to let on.

"I won't lie; getting stabbed to death was more painful than I could've ever imagined. Then it felt like I was growing weaker … then it felt cold … and dark. It was …"

Fin trailed off, his eyes growing haunted.

"Anyway. Then, next thing I knew, death's carriage had dropped me off in front of the forest, only I couldn't remember anything or anyone. I was just in a beautiful place that felt warm and peaceful. I could be alone, or I could wander around and find someone to talk to if I wanted ..."

The men had reached the front steps, but they had stopped before mounting them to prolong their privacy.

"You won't really remember the pain or the ones you loved so that you don't worry about them ... The Gods only allowed me to remember because they gave me the choice to return."

Mr. Howard appeared deeply distressed. "Did you know what ... coming back would mean?"

A shadow of sharp grief moved through Fin's features. "No. I didn't know coming back meant my mother would die. Honestly, if they hadn't told me about Annika being pregnant, I don't think I would've returned even without knowing what it would cost my mother ... I'd done everything I felt I needed to do. As much as I wanted to end my father's terror, I'm not a killer. The only man I ever killed was in self-defense during the raid in the inn, and I'm sure when this is all over it will continue to haunt my mind."

"I notice you use past tense when talking about stopping your father," the assistant observed carefully.

Fin fell silent for a long moment and turned his eyes out toward the city of Austice. "He's caused a lot of pain, and ... I don't even want to try and figure out what he would do if he found out about Annika and our family. If there were a way to bind him to no longer cause danger that did not entail death, I'd still consider it. Sadly, I know that he will never stop."

Sensing a touchy subject, the assistant averted his gaze from Fin and began mounting the castle steps.

"Well, Ashowan, you're going to have to figure out what you want done with him soon. By tomorrow, the ships will arrive, and one way or another, the beginning of the end will be upon us."

The camp for the expected injured had been set up behind the castle and was already bustling with people who were waiting on carts to move the elderly, or sick, or children whose sole parent was a soldier.

Night had fallen around them, and while there were torches lit and food being passed around, the darkness that grew in people's hearts and minds could not be quelled easily.

Fin was exhausted by the time he arrived at the camp to meet with the king, but he knew everyone was just as, if not more, tired.

"Your Majesty, everything is set. Mr. Howard is finalizing the official report of what I have set up around the castle grounds and will have it for the captain and knights to review tonight. I will need to go to sleep soon so that I can be ready for tomorrow." The viscount addressed the monarch who was seated beside his wife as they spoke with local merchants around a campfire about using their carts.

"Yes, thank you for your hard work, Lord Ashowan. Ruby arranged for you and the viscountess to take over one of the more spacious quarters that one of our courtiers has vacated," Norman explained, his weary gaze in the firelight barely even registering the witch.

"Thank you, sire." Fin bowed to both the rulers and turned to head back to the castle, when he saw something that stopped him in his tracks.

Slowly striding across the camp, he walked to a particular small tent laden with blankets and pillows, where a group of children all sat in their sleep shirts, staring up at three familiar knights who each held a child on their laps as they appeared to tell them all a bedtime story …

"—and then, he fled from the ball before being caught by the wicked brother who was momentarily distracted by the bard." Sir Andrews stopped his enthusiastic tale abruptly when he noticed Fin standing with his arms crossed and an interested smile on his face at the mouth of the tent.

"Then what happened?!" one of the little girls in the front row squeaked as she clutched her well-loved stuffed bunny toy to her chest.

"Ah … er … then the … poor soldier … punched the brother in the face …" Sir Andrews continued haltingly. Unsure why his presence had unnerved the knight, Fin continued listening, but he soon understood once he heard the names of the characters in the story.

"—Then Fred and Annie lived happily ever after!"

It dawned on Fin that the story was based on a very real couple … and suddenly he understood why Sir Lewis and Taylor were trying desperately to stop laughing at Sir Andrews's red ears.

"They didn't even kiss!" the little girl with her bunny exclaimed disappointedly.

"Eww! Who needs kissing? Why didn't the brother fight him back! One punch and that was it? Too easy!" A little boy with dirt smudged on his cheeks had sprung up in the middle of the group, his fists pumped into the air.

"Well, there were a few more details …" Sir Andrews cleared his throat awkwardly as Fin leaned his shoulder against the tent post.

"I think it's time for sleep, everyone," Sir Lewis announced, earning several loud disagreements.

"Why do we need to sleep when the soldiers might come get us?" a different little girl with messy dirty blond hair asked, her eyes wide and fearful.

"If you don't get some sleep and the soldiers come, you won't be able to run as fast as you can away from them, that's why." Hannah's voice made Fin jump as he realized she had joined him at his side with a tray loaded with what looked like a jug of warm milk and honey, with several wooden cups.

"While I pour this for everyone, why don't we have Sir Taylor sing us a lullaby, hm?"

The boys groaned, while the girls stared adoringly up at the knights, bringing a smile to Fin's face.

Sir Taylor nodded to Hannah with a friendly smile, then, lowering his gaze to the children, began to sing.

As the song carried on, Hannah's voice joined ... her gentle soprano nowhere near as powerful as Sir Taylor's bass, yet gradually, one by one, the children's eyes began to grow heavy. The pull of the soothing tones was too comforting and warm to win against.

Fin didn't know why, but the sight of the kitchen aides singing and caring for the group of children somehow made him want to cry.

There was something loving, sad, and precious ...

"They've been practicing a lot the past few weeks."

Fin turned to look at Peter and Lord Harris as they strolled over to where he was standing.

Peter, who had been the one to speak, fixed Fin with a somber gaze as he stepped forward and lowered his voice. "I'm sorry I was not more careful with your secrets ... thank you for insisting to His Majesty I should be released."

Fin nodded, "I know it wasn't done on purpose, and besides ... you're the most talented of the aides when it comes to cooking. Can't have the courtiers starve to death. "

The swell of appreciation and gratefulness in Peter's eyes made Fin smile in understanding as the aide then dropped his gaze to the grass and gently scuffed his boot against the ground.

"So," Lord Harris asked, clearing his throat. "Think we're ready to face them?"

Fin stepped away from the tent and turned his eyes toward the Alcide Sea where there still weren't any signs of ships. "One way or another we're going to find out, but I hope so."

The three men fell silent as they each drifted into their own anxious worries of the hard times nearing them that made them reluctantly realize their peaceful days in the kitchen had come to a close, and things would never again be as they once were.

CHAPTER 36
A SLOW BURN

King Matthias of Troivack stood by the helm of the ship, watching the single fire at the top of the city of Austice. A flickering eye from the castle, beckoning them closer …

Night cloaked their fleet, but the dawn was only a couple hours away. As he thought of the King of Daxaria's face last they'd met, he smiled slightly while relishing how he was going to show Norman Reyes what true strength was.

It had been six years before, when they'd convened on Daxaria's shores to discuss trade increases, only to reach a stalemate when Matthias had been forced to reject King Norman's counteroffer …

"*I will increase trades for food supplies for three years only, but in that time, you must decrease your military expenditures and instead use some of the funds to help your farmers to replenish their soils, and lower their taxes so that they have the strength to work their fields without starving,*" *Daxaria's king explained sternly, his hazel eyes betraying no flicker of leniency in his decision.*

Matthias shook his head as his mind passed through the memory. Then he squinted his eyes as he recalled his own firm no and how he had left. He had spent the entire journey home thinking that the smug

265

imposter king would have to learn the hard way not to force others to rule as he did.

"Your Majesty, it is time to ignite the torches to signal the men onshore," the captain announced from the helm a few feet behind the king, pulling Matthias free from his memories.

The monarch turned to glance at Aidan Helmer who stood over the captain's left shoulder.

"Light them."

The fire witch gave a brief bow of his head, before displaying an arrogant half smile that sent a ripple of magic across the entire fleet of Troivackian warships, each with a lantern hanging from their figureheads; they all burst into flame.

Everyone waited with bated breaths. Waited to hear the beginning of the chaos they had orchestrated for years …

The men who had successfully stayed hidden despite Earl Piereva's carelessness with his own unit of men lay in wait on the shores and should have been surprising the Daxarian military and reducing their numbers. Aidan recalled only the single unit being behind bars when he had visited the men during his time in the castle.

Yes, this was going to be a glorious beginning that would bring pride to their hearts.

Then everyone continued to wait, in a growing uneasy silence.

As the fleet drew closer, they realized that there wasn't really any sound or cries of shock at all, which, given that there were supposed to be a thousand men swarming the city, made no sense.

Occasionally they believed they'd hear the ringing of steel or a short cry, but that was all.

"Mr. Helmer, when was the last time we received any correspondence from the men in hiding?"

"In Austice we heard word from only a small unit that they were well, but that there was some concern over the others. Though when I visited only one unit was behind bars."

Turning toward the fire witch, the king's expressionless face appeared all the more ominous.

"You did not think that their lack of confirmation was strange?"

"The men had said that during the kingdom's preparation for the war, there was a chance they'd no longer be able to communicate. More soldiers and people were growing suspicious of anyone Troivackian—"

"This should have been brought to my attention, Helmer." The displeasure in the king's voice made Aidan's coal-black gaze momentarily glimmer in the dark.

"In the unlikely event that they have found every single one of our soldiers, we can still take the city in a matter of days."

"You discuss the potential loss of a thousand men as though it were trivial." Despite speaking quietly, Matthias's presence was somehow becoming larger …

"What I am saying is, not all hope is lost. We must look at the greater picture."

The torches at the front of the ships burned a little brighter.

"If this is the only army we have—" Matthias began to say before the fire witch cut him off.

"—We will still conquer Austice. I also happen to know a certain healer witch that, once captured, can be made to restore our men," Aidan cut off the ruler while casting a look over his shoulder at the ship directly behind their own. It carried their secret weapon that would ensure victory for them.

"You better be right, Helmer."

As the Troivackian king turned to stare at the Daxarian shores, he began to feel uneasy. He found himself thinking of his two young children back at his castle and wondered if he had appointed the right advisers for his eldest son. Especially in the event that he … perhaps … didn't make it back after all …

Fin didn't know when exactly he had fallen asleep. All he knew was that it was shouts within the castle that woke him and Annika up with a start. Leaping to the window before the witch could even swing his legs over the edge of the bed, the viscountess surveyed what had started the call.

"The ships have appeared on the horizon. There is a row of lights … which isn't very inconspicuous …"

Fin's mind had already snapped to attention, and he was in the midst of pulling on his tunic when he realized what exactly was happening.

"They are signaling their soldiers onshore to begin the attack."

No sooner had the words left Fin's mouth, when the distant sound of shouts and steel meeting steel could be heard, but then … the quiet returned.

Quickly throwing on his black coat over his tunic, Fin swept out of the chamber, leaving Annika to hurriedly begin dressing herself.

As he moved down the still darkened corridor, he lit the torches as he approached them. More for Annika's sake than his own. As his heart pounded and his fingertips tingled, Fin could sense every stone in the entire castle regardless of whether or not it was cast in shadow beyond his sight.

Had he always been able to do that?

Fin had always been aware of the furniture and knew that it acknowledged him, but now it felt like his skin was prickling with new awareness … as though he was a part of the castle.

As Clara appeared at the end of the hallway, Fin strode purposefully up to the woman and gently clasped her arm.

"Get Annika out of here by any means necessary if the fighting reaches the castle. She promised me she would, but I want your word that you will keep her safe." Fin's gaze that had grown strange with the flickering light behind his eyes following his death had an even eerier shimmer to them when the world was cast in darkness, which made the maid swallow firmly before replying.

"Yes, my lord," she agreed quietly. Clara stared up at him briefly, silently wondering if she would ever get used to her new master's obvious new mark of supernaturalness … Lowering her gaze once more, she curtsied to further confirm her promise.

Satisfied, the witch released her and continued down the hall to the stairs.

He passed by a handful of people—a few knights and a couple of maids who had bravely decided to stay and help—but once Fin had set foot outside the castle, he found Mage Lee and Jiho already on the steps silently watching the crest of the hill.

"Where is the king?" Fin asked as he looked around them.

"His Majesty is waiting in the camp for the captain's report. There must have been another unit of Troivackian knights that were missed," Mage Lee observed somberly.

The viscount felt his teeth grind.

"The witches should be hidden under the docks. It's more likely that the unit will try to find the soldiers or knights to try and overtake them. Though they may be a little … surprised to find our city deserted." Lord Fuks suddenly appeared from the castle behind them. The man for once was not wearing an excessively billowing coat.

"I see. So ... for now we wait until the ships reach us?" Fin asked, his heart galloping in his chest.

"That is all we can do until they are within range of the fire and air witches," Mage Lee pointed out patiently.

Fin's eyes grew fixed on the ships that were difficult to count from such a distance without a spyglass.

"I don't like waiting," he muttered after a few tense moments ticked by.

"Don't wish for violence to hurry," Jiho reminded him quietly. The Zinferan had his long hair tied back, but instead of donning his usual blend of Zinferan and Daxarian styles, he wore the traditional garb for Zinferan soldiers. A spear, which was his weapon of choice, was leaning nearby, against one of the carved stone trees in the castle's front. The man had come fully prepared to be in the thick of battle, but he was rightfully wary of it all the same.

"I'm not wanting it to happen. I just don't like the uncertainty ..." Fin replied slightly louder as he watched the line of ships slowly advance closer to them.

"By the way, Fin ... if you happen to die again and leave Annika a widow ..." Jiho started, his light teasing tone earning a good-humored glare from the redhead. It was then Lord Fuks quietly joined them to watch the ships. Oddly the man failed to add anything to the conversation as he, too, grew lost in deep thought.

After a brief nod to the earl, Fin regarded his friend again, his tone wry. "You want to raise my children for me? Good luck."

"I would rather— Wait. Plural? Children? Not child? Oh Gods, no. Twins? No. I'll just try to have one of my children marry one of yours and call it a day." Jiho shook his head, his expression mortified.

Mage Lee couldn't help but chuckle while Lord Fuks smiled.

"You need to actually have children then, and for that to happen you'd actually have to be interested in someone who isn't my wife."

"You raise a good point. Mage Lee, do you happen to have—"

"I have a son," the elder replied a little too hastily, before adding, "At best, a daughter of yours could marry him."

"Hey now, Lee, no need to be so testy. Though, Jiho, would you really want Keith wedded to a daughter—making him your son-in-law? No offense, Lee."

"I take plenty of offense, you redheaded buffoon. Stop nattering like old maidens about who will marry who and talk about something else, will you?" the mage huffed while giving the smirking friends a warning glance.

Sighing, Lord Fuks stepped between Mage Lee and Fin and wrapped his arms around their necks. "It's been an honor getting to work with you all. If I die on this hill today, I'm glad I do so with friends at each of my sides."

Fin shot a smile to Jiho, then the batty old man who had flashed him his fruit basket the first day they'd met, then he noticed Lee watching him.

The elder held out a gnarled hand to him.

"Ashowan, we've had our spats but ... I do consider you a friend."

Overcome with the moment, the witch reached out and shook his hand. The two shared a meaningful look. Upon releasing the mage's hand, Fin then proceeded to wipe his palm on Lord Fuks's coat in feigned disgust.

Lee, noticing the physical slight, immediately grew incensed. "Oh, you son of a—"

"Witch! What is that there?" King Matthias pointed to the nearing shores of Daxaria. The sky was turning a delicate shade of blush pink as the sun crept closer to the horizon behind them, but clear as day, there were several balls of fire dotting the entire perimeter of Austice.

Aidan frowned as he marched forward and snatched the spyglass from the captain.

Squinting into the instrument, he swept it along the edge of the nearing city and felt anger burn through him.

"They've ... They have fire witches directing fireballs in catapults toward us. I imagine there are air witches there prepared to help them with their distances." Lowering the spyglass, Aidan turned to see the King of Troivack staring at him with his usual unreadable and infuriating gaze.

"Are you able to disperse the flames?" the king asked briskly.

"Perhaps half of them." The fire witch then turned and began striding back from the bow to the stern of the ship.

"Helmer, what is it you are planning?" the king called out, his silent footfalls easily closing the distance between himself and Aidan.

"Most of our plans aren't going as we hoped. So I'm going to improvise a real surprise for them."

"I thought you only wanted to bring *that* out after most of Austice was ablaze."

"Like I said. Plans changed. I'm going to destroy the castle and grab that healer. While there I'll find out exactly what's going on ... they should not have been this prepared. I just need your men to rush the streets toward the castle so that you can join me. I doubt I will need long."

The king felt the overwhelming urge to snap the neck of his chief of military for the thousandth time in a matter of a week. The man who had for years given careful thought and planning to the war was now quickly becoming a liability. The fire witch hadn't conferred with him, the king, on anything of import for weeks ... and as time had passed it had become clear that Aidan Helmer was planning a coup of his own. Then of course there was the confession of Finlay Ashowan, the fire witch's very own son, that he was in fact leaking information to Daxaria ... The problem following that realization was that the chief of military had become ridiculously difficult to kill ... especially because ...

He gave them an edge that *no one* could have prepared for.

A loud whistle pierced the air, along with the creaking and splintering of wood.

The Troivackian king sighed. Aidan Helmer needed to die, but it could wait a day or two.

As Fin sipped his coffee on the castle steps, he listened to Captain Antonio relay to them all that they had captured the unit of Troivackian soldiers that had remained in the city successfully without any casualties to themselves. The entire inner council with the addition of Jiho had gathered to be briefed, and to share a quick breakfast, not that many of them could stomach much.

So far, their strategizing was working remarkably well. They had foiled what would have been a devastating surprise attack, and they had formed a strong alliance with the coven that was ideally going to torch most of the ships before they could anchor.

A strong start indeed.

"What in the world is that?!" Mr. Howard's exclamation as he looked past the group toward the fleet that was almost within firing range immediately snapped everyone's attention back to the incoming army.

Everyone swung around, their stomachs leaping to their throats.

However, all they saw was the first wave of fireballs being launched.

Granted, half of the missiles wound up in the sea, but they had anticipated Aidan Helmer's interference on that.

The men watched several ships go up in flames in a moment of silence as the first waves of death spread before them.

"No, not there! Oh … GODS! LOOK!" Mr. Howard's tone of sheer terror drew everyone's eyes to him as he pointed to the sky.

When the men followed the assistant's direction, they all froze.

"How is he … WHAT?!" Mage Lee spluttered in panicked disbelief.

"Ashowan, did you have any—" Norman asked with rising intensity while reaching for the hilt of his sword, as did the captain whose lone blue eye was fixed on the sight before them all.

"I had no idea!" Fin's heart rate tripled in speed as he stared at the calamity before them. "I-I honestly had NO idea … How …"

Mr. Howard turned on the witch, his hysterical alarm making the man's hands tremble as he roared his next words.

"YOUR FATHER BROUGHT A FUCKING DRAGON?!"

Fin couldn't bring himself to reply as he numbly watched the largest creature he had ever seen in his life soaring above Austice, his father on its back.

When his brain finally began working again, Fin's only coherent thought as screams began to ring out around him was,

We're done for.

CHAPTER 37
SNAP CRACKLE BOOM

Fin's mind was exploding with the panic and fear of everyone gaping at the dragon flying straight toward them. His own hands were trembling, and his mind had gone blank as the king roared orders at his side and Captain Antonio drew his sword.

Mage Lee had grabbed Fin's shoulder and was shaking him profusely, which succeeded in making the redhead turn his head to face him, the screams in his mind slowly losing their volume as the sounds around him began to filter back in.

"—an we do?!"

"What?" the witch asked dumbly.

"*What can we do?!*" Mage Lee repeated as the flapping of great wings drew closer.

Peering back up at the dragon that was nearing, its ruby scales bold against the pale morning sky, something occurred to Fin then.

"If it's a dragon ... it could breathe fire at us ... but why isn't it doing that?"

Mage Lee opened his mouth to snap a reply, until he realized it was an excellent question.

The king appeared back at Fin's side in time to hear the query. "It might be him demanding an immediate surrender, or … he wants *something* to remain uncooked."

"Well, he might … have some trouble getting down here …" the witch announced faintly.

Everyone save for Captain Antonio, who was already commanding knights to ready spears and crossbows, turned to look at the viscount who remained paralyzed with his eyes fixed on the great beast that, until a few moments ago, he'd never believed to still roam the earth.

"Ashowan, make some sense, man! What do you mean he's going to—" Mage Lee demanded as the dragon soared over them circling to land, when all of a sudden the beast's nose rammed into an invisible barrier that sparked a couple times, and then …

A shield of blue lightning exploded into the sky, its dome-shaped existence revealing itself all around the castle grounds and spreading into the king's forest.

Rearing back at the surprising obstacle, the dragon's large golden eyes surveyed the barrier, and it immediately charged it once more.

Everyone fell silent as they realized the dragon kept bashing against the shield of blue lightning wrought with ancient symbols, but it remained unable to break through.

The group turned in awe toward the witch who was glowing, his eyes shimmering more brightly than before. There wasn't a soul present that could deny the impressive tsunami of his power encompassing them all that started and ended with their house witch … and it gave them the tiniest bit of hope.

Aidan gripped more firmly to the rein around his familiar's neck, as well as its back with his thighs, as the dragon once again drew back with the single-minded intention of attempting to overwhelm the impressive magical shell that had spread completely over the castle grounds.

Once he had secured his position on his back, the fire witch could see the full scope of the shield laid before him, and even he was unable to mask his utter disbelief.

"What in the …" Aidan's heart thudded in his chest as his shock and ire mixed dangerously. "*How* … ?"

He began to try and figure out what exactly was happening, when he noticed the symbols wrought throughout the blue lightning … it was the same symbol that was scorched into the earth of his old home on Quildon as he was sent flying through the air, the sight of his young son's face screaming up at him, his eyes filled with—

"Fin's alive?!" Aidan roared in shock and fury as he strained his eyes through the lightning to try and see where his troublesome offspring might be standing.

He couldn't catch a glimpse of his son from his height, and the barrier itself was filled with tight symbols that only hindered Aidan further. Gritting his teeth as his familiar continued to try and claw its way through the lightning, only to be met with resistance, Aidan immediately began to reassess his position.

"He can't keep this amount of power up forever, and when that shield is gone, I will let you eat him," Aidan hissed to his familiar as he jerked the reins to force the dragon to fly back.

"Fire on my order!" he shouted while raising his fist in the air. Staring down at the massive dome, Aidan felt the heat in his body burn even hotter.

Impressive, my son, but not even you can win against a dragon.

"Fin ... by chance ... was this on the list of traps you had Mr. Howard submit?" Norman asked in obvious wonder, his arm hairs rising.

The viscount was visibly strained as his magic thrummed around them. However, he finally managed to reply after swallowing with great difficulty. "It ... was."

"In the future, 'magic shield' is a little ambiguous for all of ... this." Norman gestured around in a small daze. "So nothing can get in?"

"Not ... as long ... as I maintain it," Fin ground out with great difficulty.

"How long *can* you maintain this?" Norman finally turned his gaze back to the dragon as it let out an earth-shuddering roar of frustration and swooped backward for some reason, which was filling everyone with dread.

"Hard ... to say ..." Fin gasped as the cries of children rang out from somewhere on the castle grounds.

A burst of fire erupted from the dragon that had everyone shrieking again. Yet the flames didn't make it past the shield.

"Maybe an hour ... at most," the witch added as a thin sheen of sweat spread on his brow.

"Is there any way for us to help you, Viscount? How can we communicate with the rest of the army and witches with this shield up?"

"Ashowan, why won't my magic work outside the shield?!" Mage Lee demanded frantically while shaking his staff with the dormant crystal at its top.

"We just need … to get rid … of … the dragon. No one can come in, but you can … leave here. No magic comes in … or goes out …" Fin managed to explain as the glow around him grew a bit brighter.

"Mage Lee, come with me. We need to find some way to dispose of that creature before it flattens us." Norman nodded to the mage who was only just managing to regain his wits.

"How long do you think it will be before he turns that dragon on Austice?" Norman asked Mr. Howard, who began walking alongside his king on trembling legs.

"Depends on whether or not the dragon has a limited amount of fire. Then there is the matter that a blazing city could prove problematic for the army that is on its way here …" The assistant pointed toward the boats nearing the docks; it was at least good to see that a great number of them were on fire.

"Your Majesty, we need to request a wind and a water witch. They might be able to help the viscount from the other side of the barrier. From within the barrier I can't cast any magic to the other side. It honestly is quite incredible that Ashowan is able to nullify magic use to some degree," Mage Lee interjected while jogging until he had caught up with the king.

"We have massively bigger matters to discuss right now, Lee. For example, what do we do *here* when Fin runs out of magic. We need to send someone out to summon two of the coven members," Norman ordered as he moved purposefully toward the shield that looked incredibly … unwelcoming.

Another blast of fire from above rained down, halting Norman in his tracks. " … Then again they can probably see what's happening. Alright, let's get some of our archers at the ready."

Aidan's fury was unending as the shield continued to hold, and his familiar's fire dwindled down. The dragon most likely wouldn't be able to breathe fire for another three days after all he had used over the course of an hour …

"How the hell is he still holding it? I don't even see signs that he's using any of his life energy …"

The fire witch was just about to turn the dragon to Austice, where he himself would rain down fire on his enemies, when he noticed then the symbols had begun fading in patches of the shield.

It was beginning to weaken!

With a cruel smile, Aidan reared back, and steered the dragon toward one of the symbols that had almost faded to nothing.

With its great leathery wings pounding the air, the beast charged once more, and at long last, burst through the shield. Behind them the remaining blue lightning faded away.

The dragon let out a triumphant roar, and Aidan laughed delightedly as the ground raced up to meet them, when a sharp sting in his shoulder had his head snapping around. He noticed a cloaked figure in one of the castle windows ducking for cover so quickly that he didn't get a glimpse of their face, but the blood blooming on his tunic indicated he'd just been grazed by an arrow.

Hastily, Aidan began pulling the dragon back up to the sky, the fire witch noticed the spears and arrows that were pointed in his direction from the men on the ground, and he immediately scattered them by hurling a large ball of crackling fire at them from his hands.

Then a burst of wind nearly knocked him from his seat, and it succeeded in throwing off his trajectory, but the fire witch held fast with his thighs, and with another great swoop, landed his familiar far enough away that it would take archers and soldiers a long while to reach him.

He dismounted, magical heat glowing in his hands.

"I've come for my wife!" he shouted at the nearest figures. "Hand her over, or I will barrage you all with—"

A jet of water stung Aidan's face, knocking him back against his familiar who began growling, its yellow eyes fixed on the Daxarian Royal Court Mage who was strolling toward them with the crystal atop his staff glowing.

Two members of the Coven of Wittica weren't far behind him.

"So that's how it's going to be, is it?" Aidan muttered with a bloodthirsty smile. "Have it your way."

Mounting his familiar yet again, the fire witch took to the sky and proceeded to rain down fire. Some of it was extinguished by the mage, while one of the coven witches drew water from the air and shielded the barrage from their position on the ground. As heat met water, steam rose into the sky with a hiss and subsequently blocked Aidan from view.

The fire witch scanned the grounds intently as he resumed his search for the son he should of drowned as a child.

At first it seemed that Finlay was hiding, until a flash of red hair caught Aidan's eye, revealing that his offspring remained standing, though slumped against a pillar at the front of the castle, clearly weakened. Everyone had run toward where the fire witch had first landed on the far back lawn of the castle, leaving Fin alone to catch his breath.

"There you are," Aidan crowed happily.

Coming about and dropping to land in front of the castle with impressive speed, the fire witch dismounted the dragon, but as he climbed the steps he found guards rushing him with their swords drawn.

Aidan held out a hand, intending to burn them to a crisp, only when he tried to do so, a significantly smaller version of the same shield from before appeared, its blue lightning crackling smartly at him.

The fire witch's smile disappeared as he turned on his son, who had straightened. His hand was extended, but he was pale and visibly shaking from the effort.

The guards cheered Fin on, only to stop abruptly when the fire witch once again began to rapidly cast flame after flame at his son.

With a grunt, the house witch deflected each fireball as his father drew nearer and nearer. Sweat dripped down the sides of Fin's face as he struggled to keep an eye both on the dragon that was rearing up on its hind legs toward the guards and his father's unending assault as the man continued closing the distance between them.

Aidan at long last reached his son, and without a moment of hesitation, grabbed him by the front of his tunic, his hands burning away the fabric until it seared Fin's skin.

Letting out a garbled yelp, Fin felt his knees weaken as he was thrust back into the stone pillar behind him.

"Where's your mother, boy?" Aidan demanded, his voice unnaturally quiet and his black eyes glittering with the pleasure of violence as he let his burning hands press even more firmly against his son's blistering skin.

Staring through his pain into the fire witch's black eyes, Fin's memories of the last time his father had gripped him like this on Quildon surged forward. The burning hands scorching his skin, the pouring rain, and the scene of his mother's body being thrown to the ground appeared clearly in his mind's eye. His anger surged as he remembered the sinking helplessness he'd felt … the fear that choked him …

I'm not that scared child anymore.

Through the pain, Fin clamped his lips tight, and he stared infuriated into the glowing black ember eyes of the man who sired him. His mother's smiling face flashed into his mind, and suddenly he found himself standing back up, his sweaty forehead pressed firmly against his father's while he snarled back at him.

"My mother is somewhere … where you … will *never* … be able to touch her … *again*. Now, get *out* … of my *home!*"

Lightning filled Fin's eyes, and his father's hands burst into flames, effectively setting his son's clothes ablaze.

Releasing a shout that could only be described as pure primal fury and pain, lightning touched down around them. With an explosion of magical air and static that cracked loudly enough to sound as though the world had split in two, the dragon and Fin's father found themselves being launched back off the castle grounds, over the city of Austice, straight into the oncoming Troivackian ships.

As Fin fell to his knees, the flames consuming his tunic, engulfing him in unworldly pain, he found himself too weak to put them out. Instead, he fell onto his side; a familiar darkness was creeping upon him … he'd used far too much magic …

I might not be able to use magic … for a few days … was the final thought in his head before he succumbed to the comfort of unconsciousness, despite the smell of the fire climbing up his arm and neck until it met his hair being incredibly off-putting …

The guards who had witnessed the entire scene rushed forward with shouts for a physician and water, each man pulling off their helmets as they bolted toward the witch who had saved their lives. The two guards both determined that no matter what, the former cook would wake again to hear their thanks.

CHAPTER 38
RECOVERY TIME

A idan seethed as the physician stitched his shoulder closed. Fortunately, while the wound was deep, it hadn't done any permanent damage. In fact, considering his abrupt return back to the ships, he was remarkably lucky to have returned with only a few scratches and bruises aside from the arrow wound.

When the fire witch had been launched back toward the Alcide Sea, he had been about to crash headfirst into the masts of one of the ships, when an air witch from the Coven of Aguas had caught him and managed to reroute him and slow his descent.

His familiar, the dragon, was taking up the entire deck of the vessel beside Aidan's, and while sunning himself, was clawing at every inch of his being in an effort to rid himself of the salt that had worked its way under his beautiful scales.

"I hear the king's ship will reach land in another two hours or so. Will your beast be back on its feet by then?" the physician, a reedy man with a pair of small wire spectacles, asked as he took a dampened cloth and cleaned more blood off the fire witch.

"He'll need a day to warm himself properly. Then I am going to raze this city to the ground and have him tear down that castle until it is nothing but rubble," Aidan declared as the heat in the ship's cabin rose drastically.

"All the witches aboard our ships are rather surprised that there is a Coven of Wittica member powerful enough to have expelled you both off to this distance. I know nothing of magic, but was it truly so impressive?"

Aidan's ire tripled. "It was a grossly mismanaged use of power. He will probably be unconscious or unable to use magic for days as a result."

"Hm ... even so. Against a surprise attack from a dragon, they did buy themselves a day as you say."

"Not from the soldiers and our own coven they didn't," Aidan snapped back while pushing himself to his feet. "I am going to confer with the captain and the coven elders now. You said they'd assembled on the deck?"

"Yes, sir. Be careful about reopening your stitches if you can. I'm afraid that while no permanent damage is done, it will scar."

The fire witch didn't bother responding as he stepped out of the cabin and began climbing up to the deck where three Troivackian witches, along with his assistant, Mr. Kraft, stood in a circle. The human military captain, however, had placed himself off to the side, his gaze fixed on the nearing shore.

"All finished?" the air witch, an older woman with long white hair, leathery olive skin, and milky eyes asked as she leaned heavily on her staff.

"Just a scratch. You have my gratitude for catching me," Aidan remarked quickly before turning his gaze to the military man who still hadn't joined them. "Captain Orion, come here," the fire witch ordered darkly.

The captain turned his scarred face to Aidan and glowered. The two had never gotten along.

Nonetheless, he moved wordlessly over to the witch's circle.

"I told you not to let your son return to the shore," Mr. Kraft began calmly.

"That power was from a single witch?! Including the shield? A fire witch?" the water witch elder, a woman with long flowing black hair, and unnaturally bright blue eyes set against her olive skin, demanded with great alarm.

Aidan felt angry waves of heat roll off himself as his black eyes met hers, making her stiffen before he then looked to his assistant. "I did not *let* him return. He was dead and forcefully removed."

Mr. Kraft only responded by nodding his chin briefly in apology, before turning his attention to the water witch. "Mr. Helmer's son is a house witch, Ms. Lozitta."

"A ... house ... witch. Do you mean to tell me that that was the work of a deficient witch?" The third and final woman present, an earth witch, asked her question with a mixture of astonishment and wonder on her warm yet lined features.

"He's my son, so even as a deficient witch he bears some amount of power," Aidan replied before straightening his shoulders. "We need to discuss how we will combat the Coven of Wittica members onshore. It is hard to say how many members are in the city, but while I was at the castle, I only noted two aside from my son."

"It is … surprising the coven has begun to move on its own accord with the Daxarian monarchy. One begins to speculate what they received in return for their contributions," the water witch pondered aloud before continuing. "The landscape is to our advantage. I will flood the city and wash as many of their soldiers away with it as possible. Ms. Aetos, if you manage to simply block the archers, that will be beneficial. The witches under your command can help create larger waves and spare some of my own as well. We can see about potentially freezing the water to further incapacitate them."

"There is a chance we will inhibit the Troivackian soldiers in doing this; however, they can always stay on the ships," the earth witch added with a serious nod.

"The soldiers came for a war, and a war is what they will be getting," Captain Orion interjected with a growl. "You witches keep underestimating Daxaria from what I've been hearing. They have their own hags to combat you, what about them? Not to mention, making that hill pure ice is going to be a problem not just for the Daxarian army, but our own."

Aidan turned to face the man and glared down his long nose at him. "The fire witches along the shoreline have ceased their firing, which means they are either running out of magic, or waiting until we are in front of the docks. In which case, we will have our own fire witches taking care of them. The air witches are capable of flying over the firing squad. Some may even be able to carry the water witches over. From there, we battle, but our objective of flooding the city will be met one way or another."

"What of the men?" Orion insisted again.

"They'll have their war. They'll be the scavengers to pick off any nuisances to save our magicks. Don't worry, Captain. There will be plenty of bloodshed as we pillage the entire kingdom." The fire witch's black eyes glowed faintly before he turned and stared at the nearing shores.

The rest of the coven did the same, except for Mr. Kraft, who was watching the captain carefully. He could see that as confident and powerful as Aidan Helmer was, his growing desperation for victory and absolute power was beginning to create more enemies than even he may be able to handle.

Not to mention the matter of his son, Finlay Ashowan, who by all accounts, was far more powerful than anyone had anticipated.

With his mouth hanging open, Norman watched the two ships that the dragon had totaled upon his crash. The king was in similar company, though, as Mage Lee and Mr. Howard stood shoulder to shoulder behind him in equal awe.

"Godsdamn … I might have to agree with Ashowan for once," Lee muttered to himself as he recounted the viscount's many smug comments on the superiority of witches.

"Lee, what're the odds that that beast is dead?" the king called over his shoulder.

"I doubt it's dead, Your Majesty, but it most likely won't be able to fly at us again today. It was just submerged in the sea. Red dragons like that one, I learned long ago, are incredibly sensitive to cold water temperatures … I also heard that the salt is rather itchy on their scales …"

The mage was beginning to shake his head and come back to the present as he stepped in front of the king.

"Alright … and what're the odds Aidan Helmer is alive?" the king asked next.

"Less likely … unless a witch or mage aboard one of the ships managed to save his fall."

"Call me mad, but I get the distinct impression that the fire witch is a lot harder to kill than most …" Mr. Howard added dazedly.

"I hate to say it, but I'm inclined to agree," Norman admitted, his fingers longing to curl into a fist.

Just then, Lord Fuks came darting out from the front of the castle toward them, showing off a frightening speed for a man his age. "Sire! Ashowan is unconscious and burned up badly! He's been taken inside!"

Everyone save for the captain, who was in Austice commanding soldiers, immediately broke into a run.

As soon as they maneuvered their way through the growing crowd of witches and soldiers at the front of the castle, they burst through the front doors. Norman was surprised to see upon entering, however, that a ring of people surrounded someone lying on the floor.

Norman's heart skipped a beat when he noticed the worn leather boots on the body he glimpsed between a set of maids. He immediately pressed through the final row of spectators until he was in the center. Physician Durand was kneeling on the floor beside Fin and was in the process of removing what looked to be the singed remains of his black tunic while Annika had his head in her lap with a cold cloth pressed to the side of his face.

"What is his condition?" the king demanded as Mr. Howard and Mage Lee began directing the crowd away frantically.

"Severe burn wounds down his arm, his chest, and right side of his neck and face. He will be in immense pain upon awaking, and I doubt he will be able to—"

Physician Durand's explanation was cut short as Fin suddenly drew a very loud gasping breath, and his eyes flew open, bright with pain.

"SON OF A MAGE!" he shouted, his hands balling into fists at his side.

"Oh Gods, we need to apply ointment and administer something for the pain. We may need to hold him down—"

"Wait a moment," Annika interrupted suddenly as the physician began to reach for his leather satchel he had brought with him. Her eyes were fixed on Fin's bare chest where the strange magical symbol over his heart suddenly grew darker.

They all then noticed that, beginning from the symbol, the burned flesh was beginning to … heal, and a golden glow was emanating from Fin's skin.

Everyone watched in awe as the healing moved up farther over his chest, then his neck and face, and eventually down his arm until it reached the very tips of his fingers. It was a golden glow that those once taken care of by Katelyn Ashowan recognized immediately. The entire time, Fin drew shaky breaths and grimaced as the pain gradually subsided.

After a matter of minutes, every speck of burn on the redhead was completely healed, and aside from old scars, there wasn't any sign of new damage.

"How in the world did this happen?" Physician Durand murmured in awe.

Fin lay on his back staring blindly up at the ceiling for a perfectly still moment, before Annika bent down and gently kissed his forehead. The physical touch made him reach up and grasp his wife's hand that still had the cool cloth pressed to his face. Tenderly stroking the back of her hand, he then slowly sat up, not bothering to care that he was bare chested in the castle's front entrance.

"I think … this is my mother's curse …"

"Well, that is quite the curse, Lord Ashowan." Physician Durand chuckled in wonder.

"Do you mean to tell me that you now possess the ability to magically heal yourself?! What about others?" Mage Lee demanded excitedly.

"Her dying spell was to bring me back alive and healthy, so I think it would … just apply to me," Fin replied; then he added dryly, "But I can't say I've tried it out extensively the past three days."

"I thought her death gave you life! But this …"

"Her death was the trade to retain balance, but the exhaustion of her magic in the process … must have had its own results," Fin speculated, his brows knit together as he stared at his perfectly mended hands.

Standing up carefully, the witch let out a long breath before the group was interrupted once again.

Captain Antonio burst through the front doors.

"Your Majesty! The Troivackian ships are set to arrive in the next hour or so. I saw the dragon and Helmer sailing across the sky; just what— Viscount, where is your tunic?"

Fin cleared his throat awkwardly and was thankful when a shy young maid reached out and handed him a peasant's cream-colored tunic. The material felt more like what he was used to wearing, and he was grateful for it when everything else in his body felt strange …

Going from blinding pain to feeling perfectly fine again in a matter of moments was more than a little jarring.

"We all just discovered that Lord Ashowan here is a mite harder to kill or injure than before thanks to … you called it a curse?" Mr. Howard remarked while still examining Fin's torso and arms interestedly.

Antonio's lone blue eye fixed on Fin and frowned. "I'm not sure we can afford an explanation for that statement at this time. Right now, I'm here to report that the witches and soldiers have all retreated up the hill. No one should be in the city at this time. I have commanded all archers to be at the ready at all times and to aim for the eyes of the beast. There also—"

The captain halted his report as a growing roar outside the castle's front doors reached their ears.

"What is that?" Annika asked, looking worried as she grasped Fin's hand.

"It sounds like … it sounds like … the men are all yelling something?" Mr. Howard noted while frowning.

Norman stepped over to the doors, Antonio at his side. After sharing a concerned glance, the two men tentatively pulled them open.

Before the castle steps were the knights, common soldiers, guards, and the Coven of Wittica members. They were all facing the doors shouting at the top of their lungs, their fists and weapons thrust in the air as they called out over and over ...

Fin stepped forward, Annika's hand in his own as he faced the thousand or more people who filled the castle grounds, and every single one of them boomed even louder as he stepped into the light.

It took him a moment, but Fin finally understood what they were all chorusing ...

"*HOUSE WITCH! HOUSE WITCH! HOUSE WITCH! HOUSE WITCH!*"

Despite their impassioned shouts, they weren't out for Fin's blood ...

No. They roared in celebration for him.

They cheered and rallied for the witch who could take on a dragon—and win.

The same one who had saved the guards from a fire witch, and who also happened to be the best cook in the entire kingdom.

Their very own house witch whom they believed in with all their hearts.

CHAPTER 39
THE DARKEST NIGHT

Fin stared out over the sea of faces cheering him. The shock rendered his mind blank, as he blinked at them all, unable to say a word, until Annika broke his stupor.

"Why are we glowing?"

Snapping his head back to glance at his wife, the witch looked down and realized that a pale magical light was emanating from both of them. Frowning, he tried to fathom what on earth was happening, when Eloise Morozov, the leader of the Coven of Wittica, stepped forward from the crowd and mounted the steps up to him.

"Lord Ashowan, if I may speak with you privately, I believe I might be able to offer some insight."

Fin gestured for the group to return back to the quiet space of the castle, but the captain and king excused themselves to convene with the knights.

Once the castle doors were again firmly shut, Eloise regarded the glow around the newlyweds with a slight frown mixed with a small suspicious smile.

"Lord Ashowan, before agreeing to have you act as a diplomat on behalf of the coven, I did extensive research on the notes you submitted to me and have given your unique gifts a great deal of thought ... You mentioned before that the people of your house *feeling* at home gave you more strength and endurance … therefore, more power. My estimation of why you are aglow right now is that everyone out there who is cheering for you is feeling … more aware and proud of their home, thanks to you."

Fin's eyebrows shot upward as he recognized what she was saying.

"So … I'm … powering up thanks to them rallying around me?"

"Not just around you, but the joining of hands between witches, and humans of all classes … they are all fiercely protective of Daxaria right now, and I imagine your fight with the dragon and your father gave them a great deal to feel good about."

The witch nodded again, but Annika was still confused.

"Why am I glowing, though? In fact … this isn't the first time it's happened … a few times when I was around Fin it'd happen and I thought my eyes were going bad …"

Eloise Morozov chuckled. "I think, Viscountess Ashowan, that you are the reason Lord Ashowan's power was able to start growing."

Annika blinked several times. "I don't understand."

"I think you are the roots Lord Ashowan has placed down. You are part of why he is able to absorb the feelings around him; because he has settled down with you, he has fully begun his very own home."

"So I'm a root? Like a carrot? Or beet?" the viscountess asked flatly.

"Roots to a mighty oak are important, Lady Ashowan. Now, onto a few more important matters given that we are about to be swarmed with Troivackians … Might I speak with your husband privately?" The coven leader looked to Annika and smiled kindly.

The viscountess shot her a dubious look before turning back toward the doors. She gave Fin's arm a quick squeeze, and the two shared a meaningful glance before she then took her leave.

Fixing Fin with her stern gaze, Eloise's expression grew devoid of mirth. "That was … an unwise management of your magic. There were better ways to get rid of the dragon and your father. If it weren't for everyone outside, you would be powerless now for the next few days. Did your tutor not talk to you about how to ration your magic more efficiently?"

"Er … no? In his words, 'What would be the point? You'd just have to wash dishes by hand for a while.'"

The earth witch opened and closed her mouth without a single word being formed, until at long last she sorted out her thoughts. "A tutor of our coven said *that* to you?! How old were you?" she demanded, clearly outraged.

"Twelve," Fin replied before aiming to change the subject. "In my defense, I don't think a single person here anticipated a bloody dragon showing up."

Eloise balked for a moment, but quickly regained control of herself. "That is true ... there hasn't been a sighting in over a hundred and fifty years. We speculated that there could theoretically be one in the Troivackian mountains ages ago ... Regardless, I—"

"That shield wasn't meant to keep out that kind of assault. The ground outside of its perimeter was supposed to cave in and consume the soldiers. The shield was only set up to deflect arrows or spears, perhaps a unit of men at most. Not a hundred-fifty-foot legendary creature," Fin added while straightening his shoulders and crossing his arms.

Eloise sighed and rubbed her forehead. "The problem is that we don't know a great deal about dragons anymore. To find the records we would have to go back to the Isle of Wittica and research ... but we don't have that luxury. Lord Ashowan, can you confirm you've regained some of your power?"

Fin paused for a moment and reached out with his magic to see if he still could sense the castle the way he had that morning ... and found he could. Just as well as he could before.

He gave a brief nod.

Eloise gave a strained smile. "Well, the Goddess gave us that blessing at least. Remember, the best witches are strategic in their use of their powers. Use as little power as possible while having as large an effect as you can. Sometimes even just nudging a spear tip a few inches is all that's needed. Now, shall we see how we compare against the Troivackian Coven of Aguas?"

Fin smiled, though he felt weary already, and gestured toward the castle doors. "You go ahead. I need to go see about the children on the castle grounds. I need to find out how to smuggle them out of here safely and quickly."

The earth witch smiled grimly and gave a small bow of her head before leaving. Her heels echoed out against the stone in the eerily still castle that was normally bustling with life.

Fin took a deep breath in through his nose and did his best to sort out his thoughts. Everything felt ... dark. Strange, and dark, and he didn't like it at all ... He just wanted to be back in the kitchen making food for everyone, looking forward to a warm night with Annika beside him ... He wanted his mother safe on the Isle of Quildon, his father gone ...

Dropping his eyes to the floor, he moved his hand over his chest where his mother's symbol was burned. He let it rest there a moment, before turning and setting off toward the children's safe spot …

His kitchen.

Fin arrived in his former workspace and felt a tightness in his chest he didn't care to think about just then. The group of children were all quiet, a haunting fear in their eyes that had no business tainting their innocence. Hannah was in the middle of hugging one particular child while Sir Taylor stood just behind her wearing his armor, his expression somber.

Everyone turned and looked at him with a start, and then they surprised him thoroughly by all breaking out into maniacally happy smiles.

"MISTER!" one of the boys burst out while showing off his two missing front teeth.

"It's 'lord' dummy! He's a viscount!" one of the little girls chastised while punching the lad in the shoulder.

"I thought he was a cook! My dad said he makes great food but has about as much right to nobility as a chicken!" another younger child chirped brightly, clearly unaware of the insult they were repeating.

Hannah was visibly trying not to laugh; meanwhile, Sir Taylor looked pained.

Staring down at the children, Fin slowly moved farther into the room, his hand gently resting atop his beloved cooking table.

"It's alright. I feel more like a chicken than a noble, anyway."

The group of children all burst out in giggles, which was rather infectious.

The viscount knelt down so that he was eye level with them, a shadow of a smile on his face. "I hope you all are going to be leaving the castle now. I hear you are all going to board a wagon and will be traveling north toward the mountains?"

"We are, though we don't know why we have to … you're going to protect us no matter what!" The same toothless boy from before stepped forward confidently.

"Well, that's because while I'm busy fighting, Hannah and Sir Taylor are going to take you far away to make sure you don't have to see bad things."

The little boy frowned, displeased with the explanation. "I'm not scared, though!"

"I know, but a lot of adults are, and they don't want you to see." Fin decided to mix a little truth into the response.

"Is it true you're a witch?!" a little girl with long dirty blond hair asked excitedly. "I've always wondered if I was a fire witch. Especially because Da always says his relationship with my mum has always been heated! That's how I know."

Fin didn't have the heart to disagree with her earnest declaration.

"Yeah! I think my grandma was a witch! She had warts, and Mum always says she was frigid!" a little boy chimed in eagerly. "Like an ice witch!"

"My grandpa has to be one, too! He always says the best way to get a woman is to blow smoke up her as—"

"Who knows! They could all be witches!" Fin blurted out loudly in an effort to stop the runaway carriage wreck that was unfolding before him.

He then stood and fixed both his former aides, who were struggling not to laugh, with a complex expression.

"Hannah, feel free to take the frying pan to defend yourself. Sir Taylor … I'm surprised you volunteered to be their escort," Fin admitted.

"It was only going to be Hannah leading them out … Peter voluntarily returned to his cell to ensure he remained free of suspicion. Sirs Lewis and Andrews can't, and … a true man protects the weak," the knight explained with a stern bow of his head.

Pride in the knight before him shone in Fin's eyes before he stepped closer to him. "Well … it's great that you did." The viscount then dropped his voice so that the children around him wouldn't be able to hear.

"The Troivackians will reach shore soon. They'll arrive at the castle in a matter of hours on foot, so I recommend you all leave as quickly as possible."

Sir Taylor nodded seriously. "I will guarantee their safety no matter what. Sirs Andrews and Lewis are skilled archers, and they will aid you in taking down the dragon."

"Yes, I was surprised to learn Sir Lewis was such a skilled marksman," Fin commented before turning to Hannah who had strode over to them. "I will see you when this is all over."

The blonde threw her arms around his neck, squeezing him tightly.

"Ms. Hannah, he's married!" one little girl shrieked out, making the adults laugh.

"It's okay, Patty, he's like my brother, and I quite like his wife," the blonde replied when she had pulled free of hugging her friend while wiping tears from her eyes. She then fixed her beautiful big blue eyes on the redhead. "I heard your father hurt you; are you alright?"

Fin smiled down at her with pain and affection radiating from his eyes, but he didn't answer the question. He never liked lying, so instead he replied with, "Stay safe."

With a final farewell, Fin exited his kitchen and strode down the garden path he had tread more times than he could count since arriving in Austice to rejoin the battle preparations.

Gods ... I would prefer preparing for a hundred Beltane festivals than this ... I'm not a soldier. I'm not a killer ...

As Fin neared where Norman and the captain stood conferring, knights stood at the ready nearby, crossbows in hand, prepared to assume their new defense positions when the dragon inevitably returned.

"We can't spare too many men to just focus on the dragon, they will be overwhelmed. Even with the witches' aid, we cannot."

Fin overheard the captain explaining while handing Norman a parchment that presumably held the numbers of knights, common soldiers, and then inexperienced civilian volunteers.

The king was opening his mouth to reply, when a hawk suddenly appeared above them, causing a flurry of men to suddenly fall silent.

Confused, Fin watched as the bird flew straight down to Captain Antonio, who was ready and waiting, his expression already grim.

Moving even closer, the house witch watched as the military man unfurled a small missive that had been strapped to the bird's leg before he raised his bright blue eye to his ruler, his expression filled with anguish.

"The Troivackian military didn't attack Xava first like we had expected ... They attacked Rollom and the southern islands first."

Fin felt his world suddenly shift as his heart for the briefest of moments missed a beat.

Rollom had been one of the places that made very little sense to attack first ... for one thing it was the nearest point of Daxaria to Zinfera, and the Zinferan army was due to arrive in less than two weeks ... For another, the rocks were dangerous and the weather unpredictable in the coming fall.

Only a fisherman who had lived there his whole life would have been able to know how to safely navigate around them. Transporting soldiers aboard a single vessel would have been dangerous enough, let alone an army.

"The aunt of the king." Annika's quiet voice drew everyone's eyes to her. Most people had forgotten she was even present as she blended into the shadows.

Her brown eyes were fixed on Fin as she gave him a concerned look he didn't fully understand. The viscountess then stepped forward and bowed her head before the king.

"The viscount told me months ago that a woman who had been banished from Troivack was on the island of Quildon. I believe it is the former Troivackian princess ... Nora Devark. It is possible she had a hand in helping them learn the waters as her husband and sons are all experienced fishermen of Quildon."

"Gods, you mean Nora Corway? Her husband and sons were all experienced in sailing around the rocks ... It would make sense that they'd be able to map out the safest path for the Troivackians." Fin recalled the large family of twelve boys with a pang in his gut. Despite the eldest boys being his tormentors growing up, the idea that they were the ones responsible for the deaths of thousands of innocent souls sickened him.

Everyone fell silent as the weight of this discovery settled over them. They all knew that while there were knights and soldiers in every city, Rollom would be sieged with great ease if half the Troivackian efforts were targeted there.

"Goddess ... may you guide the people of Rollom to safety in the forest of the afterlife ... and please forgive me for my shortcomings." Norman's quiet prayer was the only sound that could be heard as agony swept across his face. The deaths of countless innocent Daxarian civilians, without any chance of defending themselves, would've taken place in a matter of hours ... and no matter how much one prepared for war, nothing could take away that inevitable burden.

From any of them.

CHAPTER 40
GETTING THE BARREL
ROLLING

The pounding of hundreds of feet sounded down the docks of Austice's shores. There was no need to try and be quiet. Despite night surrounding them, torches were lit, and dark intentions were in the minds of the Troivackian men as they moved forward, preparing themselves for the barrage of attacks.

However, everyone gradually began hesitating in their journey once they began climbing the streets toward the castle and realized … there wasn't a soul around.

As the men all glanced at one another, all equally disturbed, cries began to ring out into the night from their comrades traveling up one of the other narrower streets parallel to them.

Captain Orion, who was leading the charge up the center road of Austice, didn't know what was happening. There wasn't the singing of steel or the scuffling footwork of a fight … so what in the world was—

"SIR! WATCH OUT!" one of the men cried out as five ale barrels were suddenly released from some sort of tether that was still smoking … as though a fuse had been lit moments before. The barrels came crashing down through the men. Many were able to dodge, but in the crowd of bodies, not everyone was successful. It was then they learned that the barrels were not, in fact, empty, and they had gained a fair bit of speed rolling down the hill.

"These traps are childish," the captain snarled under his breath as he took stock of the fifteen men who had been injured. No sooner had the military man reset his sights on his journey back up the hill than he heard the faint rumbling and … what was that sound?

A distant shout in the night suddenly reached their ears. "FLOOD!"

Orion's eyes widened as he saw, too late, the gleam of gallons of water surging toward him under his torchlight.

Aidan stood on the ship deck, shoulder to shoulder with the elders and his assistant, as they watched what had been their plan hours before … be turned completely against them.

"Your son takes after you more than we realized," Mr. Kraft observed casually.

Aidan turned to verbally reprimand his assistant, only to hear the crackle of water turn to ice.

Closing his eyes, with his hands clenched into fists, the chief of Troivack's military felt his rage boil. "We will warm the ice so that the men don't freeze to death, but that uses up quite a bit of our magical reserves. We can wave for a cease-fire for the night to collect the bodies and begin again at dawn. By then my familiar should be prepared to attack once more."

Aidan tore himself away from the ship's railing, already dreading having to deal with the Troivackian king's ire.

At the very least they had received the good news that Rollom had fallen completely into their hands. Once they took Austice it would be easy to eliminate Xava and then, ideally, negotiate a fair surrender for Sorlia. The most beautiful city in all of Daxaria with bountiful fields …

"That also means rest for the enemy as well," the earth witch elder reminded Aidan.

"True, but they used up far more of their reserves than we have. Even after a night of rest, they will not be able to fully recover," Aidan pointed out while regaining his composure and straightening his shoulders. "No, tomorrow they will be tired, and if we continue to whittle away at their magicks we will have the upper hand. I'll take my familiar and drain even more of their power while trying to find where they stowed my wife. I doubt she would've fled with the others. She'd want to stay close by to help with the healing …"

"Mr. Helmer, despite her being a deficient witch, you are exerting a great deal of your energy on locating your wife," Mr. Kraft noted while jotting down a quick note in his small journal.

"Deficient or not, she can heal what should kill a witch or human with ease. It is an incredible power to have on your side. Though never ask her to help you sober up. Learned that the hard way. Once I came home from a night drinking at the neighbors, and Fin had made this incredible—" The fire witch suddenly stopped his reminiscing as an unfamiliar feeling shifted through his chest. He hadn't realized he'd been starting to smile at the memory.

A faint cool breeze rustled the sails in the quiet as the elders listened intently.

"It's been a while since I've thought about them in a favorable light, I suppose. Regardless of her inadequate methods of curing a hangover, Kate is a valuable asset," Aidan finished instead, resuming his former air of superiority.

The assistant nodded along, though he would be lying if he were to say he wasn't intrigued.

For as long as he had known Aidan Helmer, not once had he spoken fondly of his time in Daxaria.

What the fire witch hadn't revealed, however, was the strange ominous feeling he'd had when he'd looked into his son's eyes earlier.

Fin's gaze had had a strange glimmer to it that Aidan had only ever seen in one man before … a man who had died and returned miraculously to life. It was more than just that, though … he had also glimpsed an endless well of grief in Fin's expression. Not merely hatred and anger toward his father, but something else that made Aidan uneasy, though he didn't want to admit it …

"They've called for a cease-fire to collect the dead." Captain Antonio explained the missive that had been delivered via wind magic.

"Oh, thank the Gods. That means Ainsley can leave in peace with Lina." Norman rubbed his eyes while his elbows were pressed against his knees.

Everyone was exhausted by the day's events, and no one had relished the thought that they would have to be fighting all night, too.

"Sire, we've received confirmation from the knights in Sorlia. They are already en route to try and lend aid to the city of Rollom," Mr. Howard announced while striding forward with a small missive strip in his hand.

"Good. I've ordered only around fifteen percent of the military in Xava to go help Rollom. I won't send more in case they are planning to attack Xava in the near future as well."

"Fortunately, our roads system is confusing, so it might buy us some time," Lord Fuks thought aloud.

"No, my father knows the roads well. It was one of the many things he used to go on long rants about because he often got lost while trying to recruit—" Fin stopped himself from continuing. They didn't need to hear any more in-depth explanation of the bad news he had just delivered.

Instead, the viscount continued resting with his back against the castle wall, his eyes heavy. Annika had gone elsewhere when a carrier pigeon had arrived from her estate in Austice. Apparently there was another disturbance that required her attention … Fin hoped it wasn't anything too serious.

"Lord Ashowan, you need to sleep if you are to recover more of your magic." Mage Lee's quiet voice made Fin jerk his head up suddenly. Had his eyes been closed?

"Yes, we will all take advantage of this small reprieve. Fin, did you set up the alarms should the Troivackians try to attack us despite the cease-fire?" the king asked kindly.

The witch nodded while covering his mouth and yawning.

"Good. Now go get some sleep. I'm going to try and convince your wife to leave with Ainsley."

Fin smiled gratefully as he slowly managed to stand once more. His body felt as though it had been filled with lead, and the next time he blinked, he feared he might pass out.

In fact, it wasn't far from what happened as Fin took two steps and stumbled. Mr. Howard was the one to catch him and haul him back onto his feet.

"Come now, let's set you up amongst some potato sacks so you'll feel right at home," the assistant muttered with a grunt as the two struggled to leave the camp.

Norman watched Fin's retreating back for several moments before turning to Mage Lee, who was still staring after them.

"He really did use too much magic today. Even if he regained some of his power, he will have sacrificed a great deal of stamina," the mage explained quietly.

"I'm worried about him, too." Eloise Morozov appeared suddenly then, her expression firm as she gave a quick curtsy to the king before folding her arms across her chest. "Forgive my intrusion, but we are relying heavily on a witch whose ability is so far removed from warfare, it is incredible that he isn't already unconscious with no hope of waking in the foreseeable future."

Norman fixed the leader with an interested stare as he slowly straightened and tilted his head. "Ms. Morozov, we know very little about witches, and furthermore, the viscount has not spoken a word about any of this to us. Would you perhaps enlighten me?"

The witch nodded, her confidence and steady nature reassuring. "Lord Ashowan will continue to deplete his magic more quickly than the rest of us because this is the antithesis of what the Goddess gifted him with. There is a reason his most powerful move is expelling threats from his space. Danger and harm do not exist in a harmonious home, and right now, this is not a home. This is a battlefield. Lord Ashowan either needs to be tasked with something else, or we need to try and do things his way, by his rules."

"You want us to … bake … the enemy … pie?" Lord Fuks asked slowly, earning a look of agitation from Mage Lee. The earl had sounded incredibly intrigued, as though he were willing to accept the notion as a reasonable solution.

"No. Either we reassign the viscount and fight without requiring anything from him aside from his traps— A wise idea. Or we do things Lord Ashowan's way. Whatever that may be. I've heard rather strange stories from the knights here … a drinking competition that somehow led to one of the knights becoming a duke? Then there is the mystery of how Lord Ashowan and his wife fell in love … and of course I've heard stories about a series of fountains around the gardens. Yet no one speaks of the mysterious tenth one …"

Norman let out a small snort as Mage Lee blushed a crimson red.

"Yes, I … will admit. Whenever we have done things the viscount's way, things have always … gotten better." The king let out a long sigh. "However, I can't risk every life in Daxaria on his outrageous luck. He may not even have any ideas on what could turn this all around."

Eloise bowed her head. "I defer to you, of course, I was just offering my input. Lord Ashowan is an incredibly powerful witch, but … a sword when attempting to sew a tapestry is the wrong kind of steel."

The men shared meaningful gazes in light of the coven leader's wisdom. They knew she was right.

It was not going to help anyone if they merely burned away Fin's ability to defend.

Just as Norman was opening his mouth to speak, the viscountess suddenly rushed into their midst.

"Has anyone seen Fin?" she breathed, a missive clutched in her hand.

Captain Antonio stepped forward worriedly. "He went to sleep. The man is barely conscious; is something amiss?"

Brandishing the message in her hand, her beautiful brown eyes wide and incensed, she burst out, "I want him to summon that damned cat of his."

Norman was on his feet in an instant. "What did that spawn of Satan do now?"

Eloise Morozov blinked in confusion. Why were they all so distressed over a cat?

"Apparently a clowder of alley cats have torn through my keep and disrupted not only sensitive powders I carry, but our food storage! That little beast has already burned down a building! I don't want—"

"*He did what?!*" the king boomed, the crazed glint in his eyes matched only by Annika's as everyone around them faded more into the background.

"Is there … something wrong … with this familiar? A *cat*, correct?" Eloise was beginning to wonder just how sane the king and viscountess were.

"Fin's familiar," Mage Lee interjected quietly. "His Majesty and the feline seem to be at … slight odds with each other."

"*Slight* odds?! That wretched beast has wrecked numerous pairs of my shoes and clawed up our bed frame. Not only that, but he is persistent in stealing my dinner rolls, and at one point drank a goblet of wine he purposefully knocked over—"

"I beg your pardon … are we still talking about a cat?" Eloise was at a true loss as to what was happening.

"I would like to go back to Kraken burning down a building. What was that about?" Captain Antonio insisted with a deep frown.

"The fluffy beast is the one who set the fire that led us to discovering the Troivackians!" Annika explained briefly before turning her attention fully to the king who looked as though he were only just getting started on his list of grievances pertaining to her husband's familiar.

"Fin is able to speak with him, and I want to know what the hell this cat is doing! I swear, that animal has known everything going on and—"

"Wait a moment ... Is this cat black, fluffy, white patch on his chest and another on its nether region? Green eyes?" Eloise Morozov asked suddenly.

Everyone's heads whipped around in unison to stare at her. It was more than a little disconcerting ...

Clearing her throat and blinking several times as she recovered from the unstable energy directed at her, Eloise straightened to her full height and addressed them all. "It's just ... the witches who were sent to rescue Lord Ashowan mentioned that part of the reason the mission went so smoothly was that a cat bearing that description, and a greyhound, appeared to have somehow steered a ship into the one the viscount was being kept in. The ship the animals were aboard collided with the Troivackian king's and sank two vessels as a result. Now I'm hearing Lord Ashowan can even fully communicate with his familiar? This is incredible! There are so many questions witches have never been able to ask and learn of our companions!"

No one said a word for a moment as they all instantly became desperate for answers, yet one thing had become abundantly clear ...

The familiar named Kraken seemed to be up to something, and given his track record, it probably had something to do with protecting his beloved house witch. What that meant for the rest of them, however, was not as easy to guess.

CHAPTER 41
BACKFIRING

Fin groggily opened his eyes, his entire body stiff and heavy as though he had been working tirelessly for days and days on end. Which in a way was true …

As he yawned, and tried to bring about another adrenaline rush to carry him through, the fact that dawn had not yet begun made it all the more difficult to be roused.

"Oh, thank Gods, you're awake! I'll alert His Majesty and Captain Antonio!" Annika's breathy panicked voice made Fin blearily turn his head to stare quizzically at her. She looked exhausted, and pale, but there was a frantic energy about her that helped pull him up into a sitting position even though it made his chest throb.

"What's going on?" he managed to ask while stifling a yawn.

"Honestly, if I didn't know that you required sleep to regain magic, I would've shaken every tooth you possess from your head," the viscountess muttered, not having heard her husband's question as she wrenched open their chamber door and informed a guard who had been posted outside their chamber.

"Annika, love, what is going on?" Fin tried again, swinging his legs over the edge of the bed.

"We need you to summon Kraken and ask him our questions, because we think that blasted cat— Sorry," his wife added hastily. "We think he is up to something. Fin, were you aware that not only was he present at the time of your rescue, he is responsible for sinking two ships in the process? We aren't even sure how he managed it! Then there is the matter of burning down that building with the Troivackian soldiers and—" The witch slowly stood and crossed over to his wife who was already pacing with her brow furrowed.

"I understood about a quarter of what you said, but I will summon him. Where are we supposed to meet the king?"

Letting out a long breath, Annika finally stilled herself and looked up into her husband's face.

"His Majesty is out giving a speech to the army before they all return to their posts. We're anticipating the dragon returning."

The viscount bowed his head morosely before letting out a long weary sigh and closing his eyes. He reached out to feel Kraken's presence and found …

Fin frowned.

"What is it?" Annika asked while grasping the witch's tunic sleeves a little tighter.

"He's … it feels like he's deep in the king's woods for some reason."

"What?! Hours ago he was in the estate! Remember how Clara mentioned a disturbance in the poison room?"

The witch nodded slowly. He was equally perplexed.

"When they reviewed the inventory, they found that he interfered with one *very* dangerous poison. It's an extract obtained from a fish with spikes that swells, then releases a poison through its points. I was worried at first that Kraken might've harmed himself, but I'm starting to suspect he knew *exactly* what it was. We call it tetrodotoxin."

Fin felt his sluggish mind begin to resume its normal functions as he recalled his familiar mentioning he had learned a great deal about poisons during his stay at Annika's estate …

"You mean from puffer fish? I've cooked them before … What could he potentially do with their poison?"

"Many things, yet we can't know for certain until we speak with him. Did you summon Kraken?"

"I will now. This is unbelievable. He was just a small kitten a few months ago, how in the world did he become so …" Unable to think of a proper term or description for the feline, Fin failed to finish his sentence;

he instead let out an irritated sigh through his nose before once again closing his eyes and, this time, summoning his familiar.

"It's done. Let's go meet with the king. Kraken will be able to find me no matter where I am now that I've called."

"MR. HELMER! MR. HELMER! QUICK! THERE'S A PROBLEM WITH THE MEN!"

An air witch that Aidan couldn't remember the name of bolted up to him on the ship's deck, while two other witches were close behind, along with one of the king's personal guards.

"What is the meaning of this?" the fire witch demanded, placing his hands on his hips. It was not yet dawn, and he had just been tending to his familiar and ensuring that the dragon was indeed ready to fly again. Even without its fire, it could still do plenty of damage.

"It seems … as though … I swear it sounds mad! Yet, it's true! I-I-I don't know how else to say this."

"Well, *someone* will tell me what is happening, and they will do so quickly."

The king's guard, a man who, like his brothers-in-arms, was stoically serious, regarded the fire witch with the briefest moment of hesitancy.

"There was … a swarm of cats."

Aidan didn't say anything for a moment as he stared blankly at the hulking mass of muscle that didn't show any sign of jesting.

"A clowder of cats, yes, go on?"

"A clo-oownder?" one of the younger witches present asked, confused.

"A clowder. It is what one calls a group, or in this case, 'swarm' of cats."

"Er … right …" The air witch who had first spoken decided to try and continue, though he was a little surprised that his superior was so accepting of the strange event. "Well, the *clowder* of cats swarmed the camp. At first we thought it was some dock cats, but then we realized we were completely surrounded … it felt as though there were more than a hundred of them. We found it a bit strange, but got distracted when we started seeing rats everywhere as well … The knights and soldiers were too busy chasing the vermin out that they didn't notice the cats kept swiping any exposed flesh they could reach. We thought they were aiming for the rats!" At this, even Aidan looked confused, but the air witch had committed to telling the whole tale and could not be stopped for questions.

"Then ... about ... thirty minutes ago, the men all started experiencing very severe symptoms that indicate they've been poisoned. Vomiting, passing out, other ... things ... it's a mess! The physician here thinks that the cats ... that they had poison on their claws." The poor witch looked more and more nervous as he told what felt like an absolutely outrageous nonsensical tale.

Aidan looked to the king's guard and noticed that the man wasn't refuting or disagreeing with any of the account.

"The men on the ships appear unharmed, but all the soldiers on land are ... incapable of fighting."

The fire witch was already in motion as he began striding off the ship down the gangplank toward camps along the border of Austice.

"I want numbers, and I want them now. How many men do we have that can fight, and what antidote is needed?"

"The physician doesn't have enough materials with him to cure everyone; it's a very specific poison. The Daxarian army will slaughter us at this rate. Especially because I heard word from the messenger who issued our cease-fire that the house witch is not only awake, but still possesses some power ..." The air witch huffed as he raced after the fire witch on the dock.

The poor lad then almost careened straight into the fire witch's back due to his sudden stop.

"The ... *house witch* ... is not only *awake* but he has magic left?!" Aidan's black eyes flared, and a surge of heat pulsed from his body.

After a moment of incredulousness, he shook his head, regaining control over himself. "It won't matter. There is no way he will be able to last for long at this rate. He's most likely running on reserves. One good battle and he will either die or collapse at the very least."

"Y-Yes, sir ... that is most likely true ..." the air witch conceded quickly as the king's guard joined them.

"His Majesty is speaking with the physician now. I was told to escort you there." Aidan didn't bother to hide his scowl as he failed to quell the surge of heat rolling off his being, and he waited for the guard to step in front of him to begin leading him to the monarch as rank dictated.

The guard eyed Aidan's back disdainfully before stepping around him and leading the way to his king. Before Troivack's chief of military could begin to follow, the young air witch behind him dared to whisper to his comrades then.

"It was so strange ... it's like the rats and cats had plotted it out! But how in the world could that have happened?!"

Aidan felt his patience near its breaking point as he, too, wondered how such a strange phenomenon had occurred … but at the same time he knew without a doubt his son had to be involved somehow.

Then he reached the camp where the Troivackian king stood talking with the Royal Physician who had joined them for the war. Matthias's legs were braced apart and his arms were folded across his chest; it was clear he was irate. Mr. Kraft stood at his side, his face expressionless as ever, his long blue coat rumpled after hours of work through the night condensing all the reports they had received from the army in Rollom.

By the time Aidan reached the meeting, King Matthias was already in a black mood.

"You, witch. I'm about to consult a Godsdamn mage because no one seems to have any clue how this happened," Matthias growled dangerously while casting a murderous glance at the fire witch.

"That would make two of us," Aidan informed the monarch, his voice louder than usual. "There is no record of such a strange occurrence of two species uniting and seeming to conveniently poison an invading army. They're beasts. I suspect a witch of some kind has a hand in this."

"Ah, it must be Mr. Helmer's son," Mr. Kraft observed with a sudden nod of understanding.

Matthias snatched the front of the assistant's coat and hauled him up off his feet until Mr. Kraft was an inch from his face.

"If you know anything about this, I suggest you speak quickly."

To his credit, the assistant managed to keep his voice calm, though his cheeks turned the shade of parchment paper in the torchlight as he stared into the dark, deadly gaze of the king.

"I haven't any idea how this would have been accomplished. I only know that the house witch possesses unlimited power."

At this Aidan straightened. "What? You never mentioned this to me."

"We all assumed he was dead until recently, and then we were busy," Mr. Kraft replied while daring to shift his eyes from the king, who still had him in a steely grip, to the fire witch.

The monarch gave the assistant a firm shake, which nearly jostled the man's spectacles off his face. Mr. Kraft's attention swiftly returned to Matthias.

"What does 'unlimited power' mean?"

"Well … only if he knows how to use it properly. His magic is based on a sort of instinct, or feeling, people get. It cycles back to him as much as he puts in. To completely drain him, he would have to be working against the nature of his power. The animals uniting together for a common cause, I really do not know how that was managed, but … everything that has been strange about this war has started and finished with Mr. Helmer's son."

Matthias turned slowly to Aidan, a predatorial glint in his eyes that was not lost on the fire witch.

"How strange … that your son predicted the soldiers being found here. Even more peculiar that he managed to be rescued and survive on your watch, quite easily I might add, while two of my ships were sunk."

"I am not a Daxarian spy; I—" Aidan's fury was evident as he began to bark his defense. However, the king only continued his list while moving stealthily closer.

"—Then we have this atrocious show of the majority of the men being poisoned, your dragon runs out of fire … it is all quite convenient. If I were a betting man, I'd say a strategic thinker could play both sides of this war and come out a winner either way it ends."

Aidan then noticed the king's knights beginning to surround him.

"Don't be ridiculous. I provided you with insight and communication with your exiled aunt. That alone allowed Rollom to fall within a day. The Coven of Wittica would never have—"

The knights lunged toward him, but the fire witch had been prepared.

"NO!" He exploded, flames erupting around him, forcing the men to leap back away from him at the last second.

With the fire surrounding him, Aidan moved toward the king again, fury in his eyes. "If you think your metal-clad humans are capable of taking me against my will, I will show them how melted steel feels against their flesh."

The king said nothing as he watched Aidan's face amongst the flickering flames.

"I will retrieve my wife before dawn and have at least a unit of men healed and ready for battle."

"A convenient way to flee to safety," the king observed coldly.

"That weak-hearted *boy* only escaped from me once before because I was surrounded by nothing but water for leagues. He survived what I did to him yesterday because that is precisely how talented his mother is. I will get her and return. You will see the truth of what I am saying soon, mark my words."

"Oh, your words are marked, without a doubt." The king smiled, the murderous intent in his eyes enough to even make Aidan second-guess himself for the briefest of seconds.

Glaring, the fire witch strode away from the camp back toward the ship where his dragon waited, a ring of flames encircling Aidan as he moved to ward off any ambitious attacks.

"You, assistant," King Matthias called to Mr. Kraft who watched the whole scene with great interest.

"Yes, sire?"

"What are the odds that Mr. Helmer's son destroys him before I do?"

The witch stared after Aidan for a long thoughtful moment before replying.

"It is tough to say for certain. While the house witch is powerful, his magic is weak to conflict and violence. Mr. Helmer, well … he feeds off it."

The Troivackian king's lips curled upward to form an ominous smile. "Then I suppose the pleasure will be all mine."

CHAPTER 42
ENTANGLEMENTS

S ire, there is a fire near the docks of Austice!" one of the lookouts atop the castle walls with a spyglass pressed to his eye called behind himself to the captain and king, who were conversing about whether or not to place more archers on the crest of the hill or the castle walls. At hearing the soldier's call, however, both immediately ceased their conversation and stepped forward frowning, their breaths coming out in faint puffs in the chilled night air.

"We still have an hour until dawn," Norman began as Antonio took the spyglass and looked for himself.

"Ah, it … it isn't a blazing fire; it merely appears to be … moving and not growing … It's boarding one of their ships now …"

The men were still watching, perplexed over the strange display, when they were interrupted.

"Your Majesty, I was told you wanted to see me as soon as I was awake?" The viscount's voice interrupted the newfound mystery and instantaneously shifted their focus.

"Yes, Lord Ashowan, have you summoned your familiar?" Norman demanded urgently.

"I have. I'm not entirely certain what time he will be here, but it should be— Gods, that's the dragon!" Fin's exclamation made everyone turn back around in time to see the great beast in the paling starry sky.

"ARCHERS, READY! SPEARS UP, MEN! REMEMBER, GO FOR THE EYES OR GENITALS!" Captain Antonio roared as the soldiers on the castle walls stood at attention.

The dragon soared over them out of reach, a terrifying roar shattering the quiet night as the beast swooped around one of the towers and surprised the archers, knocking them and a portion of the wall over with its tail. Shouts and crumbling stone dust filled the air immediately.

Chaos reigned over the former quiet as the dragon then barreled through the glittering peak of the green house's tower, shattering the glass at the top, exposing it to the outside. As the beast began to fly away from the scene of destruction to inflict damage elsewhere, a wave of vines and branches burst out of the greenhouse, immediately lassoing the dragon's tail and stopping it from pulling away.

"What— Fin, is that you?!" Norman rounded on the house witch who watched with a small awed smile.

"No, Your Majesty ... I believe that's the Royal Botanist."

"*The Royal Botanist is a witch?!*" the king shouted over the din of battle around them.

"Ah ... shit. Should have kept that to myself. Forget I said that!" Fin called back while watching the dragon's struggle with the earth witch's beloved plants.

Giving a small laugh of astonishment as the dragon was pulled lower and lower, Fin turned to the nearest stairs to try and find where he might be more useful, completely forgetting that the reason he had been summoned to the castle walls in the first place was because of his familiar ...

And said feline was beginning to trot through the forest toward the castle.

As Kraken felt the powerful magic pulling him forward, consuming his mind, he smirked to himself as the forest rustled around him.

Don't worry, witch. All will be well soon.

Aidan turned in his saddle and snarled at the net of plants that continued to tie more and more restraints around his familiar's limbs; he immediately sent a stream of fire down to burn them to a crisp. He was succeeding with great efficiency, too, when a sudden burst of wind nearly knocked him from his seat.

Turning to look down where the attack had come from, his eyes widened briefly and then a cruel cold smile stretched across his face. "It's been a while, Sky."

The white-haired witch was staring up at him in the growing dawn amongst the soldiers firing crossbows with the aid of four witches at each corner of the castle walls.

Sky, however, stood alone, her cheeks streaked with tears as she raised her lily white hand and suddenly gripped the air as though she were grabbing ...

Aidan suddenly couldn't breathe.

He tried to take in a clear breath over and over and failed.

His black eyes descended to Sky's pale blue ones, which remained unerringly fixated on him.

With his lips beginning to turn blue and tremble, Aidan raised his own hand and sent out a stream of flame that forced the air witch to dive away.

Immediately Aidan gulped his first sweet breath of air. Wasting no more time, he sent another rain of fire down toward Sky, forcing her to use all her attention and magic to avoid it.

When he was certain she was properly overwhelmed, he returned to his familiar.

Glancing back at the dragon's back end that was once again being seized by the multiple ropes of trees and vines from the destroyed greenhouse, Aidan created a column of fire hot enough to melt and warp the glass around the plants, forcing them to either burn, wilt, or recoil away. It was enough to free his dragon from their hold, and so he urged his familiar back to the sky with a shout and squeeze of his thighs.

As they began to rise above the castle walls once more, a concussive burst of air struck him, then forced Aidan to flip his familiar to take the brunt of the attack in its belly. The beast wheezed audibly, and again, Aidan was almost shaken from his saddle as even more vines danced out of the tower greenhouse.

"*Godsdamn* this," the fire witch hissed before conjuring an explosion of flames in the sky over the castle, the heat wave forcing everyone to dive for cover or immediately be burned to a crisp.

Aidan pulled the dragon to fly low toward the south of the castle, and shortly after aimed their descent near the outskirts of the king's forest where the archers would have a significantly harder time without the high ground.

As he descended, he spotted several witches already running or flying toward him, and to them, he sent a similar fiery explosion that knocked them all to the ground. Once Aidan had landed, he remained mounted and waited for the next wave of attackers.

Only he was suddenly launched from his seat and thrown to the ground unceremoniously from behind.

Rising to his feet on a surge of hot air, Aidan turned with fireballs gathering in each of his hands. He was immediately doused with water as he faced off against the infuriating Royal Mage of Daxaria.

Mage Chad Lee.

"I give you credit for not running with your tail between your legs, but you'll die quickly." Aidan threw another fireball at Mage Lee, only to have it redirected into the trees. Unfortunately, it sent a good many trunks up in flames, and the fire appeared to be spreading rapidly.

Aidan continued bombarding the old man on every side, until all there was … was fire.

Even when Lee managed to extinguish some of the flames, the steam still stung his face and obstructed his view.

"Now, you're close to the king from my understanding, so tell me. Where is my wife?" Aidan smiled down at the mage who was on his knees sweating and panting as the heat surrounded them, stealing the breath from his lungs.

Lee said nothing, only began uttering his magic words and extinguishing more of the heat around himself.

With a sigh, the fire witch grabbed the mage by the front of his tunic and hauled him up closer.

"Answer my question and I might let you live."

Lee glared at the fire witch as sweat poured down his brow in the unforgiving black clouds of smoke around them.

"Very well. To be honest, I was hoping you'd be stubborn." Aidan smiled again, but as he did so, he found himself suddenly …

Underground.

The earth opened up a hole just his size beneath his feet … and completely swallowed him.

Lee gaped at the dirt that was still churning from its meal, before then lifting his chin to stare at his savior. He met the warm gaze of Adamma Jelani briefly before she continued launching patches of earth up into the blazing trees, smothering the flames until at least the area around them was safe to exit.

"Thank you," the mage managed briefly before coughing violently.

The earth witch wordlessly pulled Lee toward the castle, and they were nearly at the final ring of trees as Adamma patted his back carefully. "Come, you need water and rest. Help is coming, but we must—"

The dragon reared up before them, then landed on all fours with a trembling thud, its great yellow eyes shimmering with the reflection of the forest fire behind them. The beast's lips peeled back, as though smiling, revealing fangs nearly as long as a man's entire arm.

Behind the duo, the earth began to heat … And crack … and slowly fall apart around a very angry fire witch.

The dragon opened its mouth, ready to take a gruesome bite out of the mage and witch, when an arrow suddenly whistled through the air, piercing its eye.

Roaring in agony, the beast began to thrash around.

Aidan, with a surge of flames, burst the last couple of feet out of his hole and glowered fiercely in the direction the arrow was shot. Locating the cloaked figure, he recognized them as being the one to shoot his shoulder the previous day.

Coward. Seething, Aidan turned his full attention to the figure. *They do not reveal themselves to me because they know their only hope of survival is escape.*

As though the mysterious assailant had heard his thoughts, the figure suddenly lowered the crossbow and straightened. Aidan watched with a raised eyebrow and a fireball growing in his right hand as the hood was drawn back to reveal …

Lady Annika Jenoure holding a crossbow.

"I'm the only Godsdamn Dragon here," she muttered as she swung the weapon over her shoulder with ease.

Both of Aidan's hands fully ignited as he felt white hot rage feed the desire to murder the woman point-blank, when he was suddenly launched backward by a burst of blue shield.

Fin strode forward from the direction of the castle, his eyes glowing as he stepped in front of Annika and continued to walk toward his father who was already back on his feet laughing.

"I wondered when you were going to come. Let's try this again, shall we? Where is your mother?"

Fin stared at his father stonily. While his insides raged about Annika and his children being in danger, he decided to not give the fire witch the satisfaction of his full wrath as a strange cold clarity seeped into his mind.

"Why do you want to know where Mum is?"

"Still call her 'mum'?" Aidan laughed, while behind him both Lee and Adamma were frozen in place before the beast whose other great yellow eye scowled threateningly at them. He appeared even more dangerous despite his injury.

Fin tilted his head and waited for the answer to his question. The longer he kept his father talking, the more time they would all get for another witch or two to join them to help. Fin knew he hadn't recovered enough of his magic to hold off his father for long.

"She'll do the work she has avoided doing her entire life. Serving the pure elemental witches as she should!" Aidan finally responded while staring at his son with great amusement. "It's no use lying to me, so may as well tell me where she is. You were always terrible at hiding your nonsense."

Fin stiffened at the phrase that had been said to him many times in his life … but as a result, he stepped closer. Somehow, the truth of his mother's whereabouts seemed the most fitting answer to his father.

"My mother is dead."

Aidan's features stilled, and his black eyes searched his son's face for any sign of deception.

"Kate … Kate's dead? How? With her healing, she should—"

"That is not your business," Fin replied evenly as he felt the heat around them begin to rise.

Aidan snarled, an odd glimmer appearing in his eyes … They could almost be mistaken for tears …

"Boy, you will tell me exactly what happened or you—"

It was then the rustling of ground foliage in the forest could be heard coming from the eastern tip that was closest to Austice and away from the blaze that was rapidly spreading. It wasn't a single animal, either. It … it sounded like a wave of rustling amongst the smoky trees drawing nearer.

Both Aidan and Fin turned toward the woods to see Kraken suddenly emerge.

The two men stared, both perplexed by the handsome cat's appearance.

Kraken, however, let out a long meow that echoed through the trees … leaving the fire witch and house witch for once in a similar headspace …

Utter bafflement.

CHAPTER 43
KRAKEN VERSUS
THE DRAGON

Fin frowned down at his familiar in confusion, as more cats suddenly began to appear from the forest underbrush.

"How many cats do you own?!" Aidan burst out incredulously.

"I swear I only own that one," Fin spluttered, pointing at the fluffy black familiar at his side, unable to mask his own confusion.

"Doesn't matter, I suppose. There's always more than one way to toast a cat, after all." Aidan's hands once again ignited with fire as he turned toward the growing sea of felines that were bypassing the fire witch entirely. "I know you had something to do with the poisoning last night."

The last remark his father made gave Fin pause. "Wait, what was that about poisoning?"

Kraken addressed his witch then. "*You take care of your sire cat. My comrades will handle the overgrown lizard.*"

"What? What do you mean? What do you mean your comrades will—" Fin didn't have a chance to finish his question before his father tried to toss an explosion of fire at the army of cats, which Fin barely managed to snuff out.

"Your magic won't last forever, son. You've used far too much already," Aidan taunted, turning his attention back to Fin. "Besides, why are you wasting your time? We both know your ability makes it impossible for you to kill me. So why not—"

Fin's eyes suddenly burst into lightning as a blue spherical shield encompassed his father entirely.

Cursing loudly, the fire witch brought his hand up, intending to unleash his own power against the barrier ... only to find his abilities didn't seem to work within the sphere.

"You cannot hold him for long in your condition! What are you doing?!" Annika rushed forward to her husband's side as Aidan shouted and carried on his tirade.

"I don't need to outlast *him*. I just need to make sure *they* finish whatever it is they're doing," Fin ground out in response. The effort of restraining his father was creating unbelievable strain on his already weakened magical abilities.

Turning to see what her husband was referring to, Annika finally noticed the wave of cats that were in the process of swarming the dragon.

"Wh-What?! Wait ... why are there rats with them?!"

The dragon's head dove into the flood of animals, its jaw opened wide, only all cats leapt out of the way perfectly in time, while a single group of strangely plump rats were swallowed instead.

"Why were they just waiting to be eaten?!" Annika burst out as her grasp of the situation continued to grow even more distant.

"*Witch, please tell your mate that these rats volunteered their noble sacrifices for this moment.*"

"What?!" Fin demanded while nearly losing his hold on the sphere containing his father. "How are rats going to kill a dragon?!"

Kraken didn't say a word, and yet within a minute the dragon slowly, but surely, collapsed.

"*Your beloved coffee kills lizards. Your mate's minions discovered this at the estate, and they even added tobacco to make it more ... effective on the intrusive small lizards in their midst. I knew your sire human didn't smell right, and when I discovered this pompous reptile was going to ruin my dinners, I broke into your mate's hideaway food space for the goods.*"

Fin released his father from the shield, too shocked and drained to maintain it. Aidan, instead of resuming his attack, immediately bolted to his dragon's side, sending at least a hundred cats fleeing upon his approach.

"In exchange for the sacrifice of fifty rats, us cats will share our food with them and not hunt their kind for a year. Be prepared for the repercussions of this, because this agreement was no easy feat to obtain. I have no regrets and will not apologize for it."

Fin stared after the sea of cats and remaining rats that dispersed through the forest, as his father continued inspecting his familiar with growing agitation.

"You … killed … a dragon," he finally managed to say, his voice still weak with disbelief.

"I have clawed my way to my current position over the past few months, and I'll be damned if some senile familiar thinks I will relinquish my place as the head of the pecking order. It had to be done."

Staring down into the bright green eyes of his cat, Fin's mind failed to wrap around the full extent of what was being said as days of exhaustion clouded his mind. Fortunately, Kraken took pity on him and added on a final meow of wisdom.

"While some familiars are mirrors of their witches, others are strong where their masters are weak. You are the Ruler of Homes. You bring peace, and much more. I am war, chaos, and seductively fluffy. Together, my witch, we are unstoppable. Now a good day to you. I expect fresh cheese bread and a grilled salmon every night for dinner as thanks. Oh, and congratulations on your future kittens!"

As Kraken began to saunter away, Annika stood at Fin's side perplexed, and desperately wanting answers, about what in the world had just transpired. Turning to her husband, she opened her mouth to begin asking her questions, when a fireball that appeared out of the corner of their eyes had Fin grabbing her and turning his back to the flames to protect her.

The blast had definitely been aimed at her.

Gasping and shaking in pain from the stinging heat and blistered skin, Fin slowly turned around. He ignored Annika's horrified gasp when she laid eyes on the burned flesh on his back; he instead faced his father who appeared to have gone mad with fury over the death of his familiar and was bearing down on Fin, flames once again in his hands.

"YOUR *CATS* ARE RESPONSIBLE FOR THE DEATH OF A THOUSAND-YEAR-OLD—"

Kraken's words rang in Fin's head …

You are the Ruler of Homes … Rules for my home …

Fin took three strides forward and seized the front of his father's tunic, stopping his shouts. He hauled Aidan up to stand nose to nose with him, while the fire witch returned the favor and grabbed what remained of his son's shirt.

Behind him Annika was about to pull out one of her hidden knives and aid her husband, when, sensing this, he shot her a brief look over his shoulder that clearly indicated he did not want her doing a thing. Facing his father once more, ignoring the pain that seeped down to his very core from his back, Fin managed to smile.

"I am the ruler of my home."

Aidan laughed, but the redhead continued.

"I'm the Ruler of my home, and in *my* home"—Fin's eyes suddenly filled with white and gold magic—"*you*, Aidan Helmer, are banned from using magic."

A strange ringing in the air pierced everyone's ears within the castle grounds. As its frequency grew louder and louder, Aidan's fire extinguished as his hands moved to his ears; and a gentle wave of power rippled out of Fin, bringing silence over the grounds once again.

When the fire witch realized that the noise had stopped, he lowered his hands from the sides of his head and seized his son's tunic again only ... there wasn't any fire. No spark ... not even a surge of heat.

"Wh-What ... ? How ... How did you ... you ..." Aidan stared down at his hands, his eyes wide, his forearms trembling as they flexed and strained with the effort of trying to summon his element.

Fin grabbed Aidan's forearms and shoved him to the ground.

"All this time I've never fully accepted that ... in my house? *I* set the rules."

Aidan didn't seem to even hear his son as he continued to stare at his hands that remained horribly normal and unmagical.

Fin took a small breath in, when he felt Annika's tentative touch on his arm. He didn't show any sign of registering this, however, and instead addressed his father yet again. "The coven will come for you in a moment. Excuse me."

Turning around and striding away with Annika at his side, Aidan was left to stare at his son's retreat. His anger surging as he watched Fin's bloody and charred back, Aidan suddenly stilled when he noticed the angry red and blistering skin beginning to mend itself, healing into fresh healthy skin as though he hadn't been burned at all—save for the tunic that was little more than a rag.

It was then Aidan realized exactly how his wife died.

The magnitude of his losses descended upon him in a sickening realization that began to consume him until he was left with nothing but the helpless action of seizing the grass beneath his hands in clumps—and screaming.

As they walked away from Aidan Helmer, despite his shouts echoing across the grass, Annika glanced poignantly at her husband without slowing even for a moment. His blue eyes blindly fixed ahead of himself as he walked.

"Fin, I didn't know you could do something like that … what … was that?"

"It's as I said. I am the ruler of my home. I am connected with every stone, every apple, and every hearth. If one of these parts of my so-called element is not abiding as nature dictates it should, it is up to me to bring it back to balance." As Fin explained, several coven members rushed by him toward Aidan, only sparing the viscount brief glances of awe and confusion over what he had done.

"Are you alright?" Annika asked quietly as they moved closer to the sound of shouts and clamoring as the knights and soldiers prepared for the Troivackian soldiers that were beginning to gain ground up the streets of Austice toward the castle.

"There isn't time for me to find out right now, and you …" Fin stopped after they rounded the bend and stood in front of the castle, turning to face his wife. "… It is time for you to leave. The Troivackians are nearly here and you promised me."

Annika stilled, and her face became a mask of impenetrability.

"OYY!"

Both Fin and Annika jolted at the interruption, then looked over and spotted Sirs Lewis and Andrews jogging toward them. The kitchen aides were nearly unrecognizable in their full armors, and it made things feel even more out of place.

"Fin! You need a sword if you're going to fight. The captain wants to know if you have any magic left, and— Wait, what happened to your tunic?" Sir Andrews paused and raised an eyebrow at his superior's bare chest.

Letting out a long breath, and his heart beginning to hammer against his chest once more, Fin grimly began to brace himself for more combat.

"My tunic was a casualty of stopping my father. I'll go grab a new one and a spear and be at the front hill."

The two knights nodded in understanding before Sir Lewis turned toward Annika. "My lady, perhaps you should go hide now ... Some maids are in the cellars, and some are in the stables waiting to leave just in case things start going south."

The two knights then noticed the crossbow she had in her hand and shot her questioning stares.

"I will see where it might be best. Stay safe, sirs." Annika bowed her head regally without offering an explanation for the weapon she carried.

While Sirs Lewis and Andrews turned and jogged back to relay the witch's message, Fin began to walk toward the nearest castle entrance.

"Fin, wait," Annika called out, stopping him as she then darted to him, her arms flying around his waist as she held him close. "You aren't allowed to die again."

Raising her stern brown eyes to his blue ones, Annika lifted herself up onto her tiptoes and gave him a quick kiss before she released him. Fin's face filled with stress and apprehension; she gave his hands a final squeeze before releasing them.

"I'll be waiting for you after."

Unable to say anything to properly convey his feelings, Fin sufficed with giving his wife a slow nod before he turned and resumed his harried pace to try and find another tunic and weapon before the physical battle began.

Guilt brewed in Annika's stomach as her gaze moved down to the polished crossbow in her hand that still held three arrows.

Sorry, Fin ... Man that I love ... man of my dreams ... I hope you can forgive me breaking my promise ... but after what the Troivackian king did to you and Charlie, there is no chance in hell I'm letting him live to see the sunset.

Lifting her hood back over her ebony tresses, Annika turned to take the parallel path her husband was to take toward the front lines of the war.

CHAPTER 44
THE BEGINNING
OF THE END

Scrutinizing the wall of soldiers before him, Fin clutched the short sword in his hand tightly, his palms already moist with sweat. The Troivackian soldiers stood united as a wall before the castle grounds, the air heavy between them all. While it was clear their numbers were reduced, the average size of their soldiers both in height and width aided their intimidating presence. At their head stood King Matthias, his thick brows lowered over his eyes as he beheld his enemies.

The tension continued to grow as both Matthias and Norman beheld each other. The smell of smoke from the king's forest only aided the hellish mood.

Then ... the final moment of silence passed.

With a fierce roar, Matthias thrust his sword into the air and began charging up the hill leading his men.

The Daxarian soldiers at the forefront held firm, not moving a muscle.

Once the Troivackian soldiers were within range, however, the front line of soldiers stepped aside to reveal their archers ready, arrows notched in their bows and crossbows.

"FIRE!" Captain Antonio roared, and immediately a cloud of arrows split the distance between the two groups and struck down those without shields, or those who were not quick enough to raise theirs.

The Troivackian men who made it through the first barrage began to speed forward, their swords raised, when all of a sudden, the ground rumbled beneath them. At least a hundred men fell into the pit Fin had bewitched immediately, followed by another fifty who had not been able to stop their charge in time to avoid the fall.

Fin's complexion grew pale as the magic used for the trap began to drain out from his being, forcing him to shake his head to ward off a wave of dizziness.

The Troivackian king had been one of the ones to almost fall in, but an air witch at his back managed to cast him across the ridge, saving him from a broken leg or neck.

Matthias soared through the air, his eyes burning with intensity as he landed softly, then took off like a panther toward Norman who had stepped forward, his sword at the ready.

The arrows resumed their flights, some aimed at King Matthias, but he blocked the three that would have struck his chest, while also ducking his head behind the wooden barrier. Somehow, despite having to use his shield, he never faltered for a moment in his pace as he drew closer and closer to Norman.

Behind Matthias, more of the knights and soldiers were being cast over the chasm with the help of the Coven of Aguas members. Soon Matthias's comrades were falling in step behind him, joining their king's side to at long last do battle face-to-face.

The Coven of Wittica members behind Norman began casting their spells to stop the Troivackian king, but for each one they cast, the Troivackian witches managed to counter.

Matthias was bearing down on the Daxarian king only a few strides away, his target unmistakable. The witches and archers then grew more concerned over accidentally striking their own people and halted their attacks. Sensing this, the Troivackian king threw his shield aside triumphantly, his speed barely slowing.

With his sword gripped in his hand, Matthias reared up to strike; Norman stood at the ready.

An arrow suddenly whistled past Norman's ear, close enough that he could feel a small sting near its top, but he was too stunned to care as, in the blink of an eye, the arrow pierced through Matthias's throat, stopping him literally dead in his tracks.

The oncoming soldiers didn't stop at the sound of their king's blood-filled final breaths, nor did anyone spare a moment to glance up to see the small cloaked figure standing at the top of the castle steps holding a crossbow.

As the fighting commenced, the cacophony of steel clanging and men's horrified shouts echoed through all of Austice.

Fin managed to physically duck blows and avoid being stabbed, but he could feel his energy waning and knew he didn't have long before he'd fall unconscious after using too much of his magic.

The redhead also had zero doubts about who it was that had shot the Troivackian king dead. Despite having told Annika to stay hidden, he realized she had chosen to enact her revenge for her brother and himself. He knew this for the simple fact that no one else would have been brazen enough to take a shot so close to Norman's head.

Fin was moving slowly, but steadily toward the stairs of the castle where he was certain Annika was still taking active part in the fighting as an archer. Right when he was a few feet away from the bottom step however, a Troivackian soldier managed to catch him off guard and cut his side, making the house witch leap back, his movements significantly sloppier thanks to the blow.

With a grunt Fin backed away from the soldier who was smiling and showing off several missing teeth. Even as he stumbled, Fin could feel the wound beginning to heal, and so as the soldier tried several more times to finish him, his reactions grew *more* agile, puzzling the soldier sufficiently.

However, despite healing, Fin was not a soldier, and he had depleted his magic.

The Troivackian bested him easily. With a wide swing that tricked Fin into believing his abdomen was the target, he instead found his feet being swept out from under him.

Rolling quickly to try and stand up, Fin felt the sting of the blade by his throat, and for a moment, his world froze. It felt as though there were no sounds as he waited for his blood to cover the ground. He winced in preparation to once again set foot in the forest of the afterlife, when the feeling of the weapon against his skin disappeared.

Scrambling to his feet before he could be trampled, Fin shifted his grip on the handle of his sword, wishing he could have a moment to dry his palms. Only he found himself staring at the backs of two very familiar

Troivackian men who continued fighting others around him ... but Fin's former attacker lay on the ground.

"Stanley ... ? Bruce ... ? What are you ..." Fin blinked up at his former guards from his father's ship in utter shock.

"When this is ... over ... make sure we eat your cooking once more before we face death's carriage," Bruce shouted over his shoulder as he knocked to the ground ... another Troivackian soldier.

"What are you doing exactly?!" Fin demanded, fully confused as, from his position that was being guarded by Stanley and Bruce, he gazed over and noticed more familiar faces from the Troivackian crew, and all of them ... were fighting *against* the other Troivackians, and the battle was turning very favorably toward the Daxarians.

"The way our country lives is killing us. Troivack is a great kingdom, but ... it isn't becoming greater like it should," was all Stanley managed to say as the fighting continued.

Fin wasn't sure if he had hit his head and was imagining what he was seeing, but he also didn't have long to consider this as he found himself once again being forced to dodge the earnest advances of yet another Troivackian soldier.

Within two hours, the remaining Troivackian soldiers found themselves on their knees, their weapons on the trampled grass, and their hands behind their heads.

Norman wiped the blood dribbling from his mouth and nodded to Captain Antonio, who was sweating heavily but remained unharmed.

Fin sat on the castle steps, his forearms leaning against his thighs, his hands trembling as the adrenaline soared through his body.

Annika was seated beside him, her head leaning against his shoulder as they stared across the ground littered with bodies.

"We can move someplace else as soon as you can stand," the viscountess whispered as Norman discussed how many knights were to be sent to Rollom with Mr. Howard and Lord Fuks who had reappeared once the fighting had ceased. Earl Fuks apparently had lost a few fingers in an unfortunate encounter with a soldier, though in his usual fashion, only said, "Don't worry, I've still got the important one," while wriggling the middle finger on his left hand, then adding, "Besides, I hear women love men with battle injuries."

Fin wasn't as capable of taking the results of battle so breezily. As he slowly raised his head and gazed out at the carnage, he felt a lump form in his throat.

"I ... I could never get used to this. I didn't kill any of them on purpose. Only tried to knock them down."

"You helped the best you could," Annika soothed while giving his arm a squeeze. Her own gaze was indifferent to the scene.

Turning to face his wife, unaware that a tear or two had begun rolling down his face, Fin regarded her somberly.

"It was unacceptable the risk you took with our children's lives today. During the rest of your pregnancy, if you think to do something like this again, I will lock you in a room if I have to. I will never tell you how you should care for yourself, but never again will I let you gamble their lives as well. Understood?"

Annika immediately grew taken aback as she pulled away from her husband and peered into his glimmering blue eyes. She had never seen him angry with her, and she could tell he wasn't fond of the experience either.

"I'm sorry," she croaked, emotion suddenly seizing her.

Fin nodded, his face still moderately stern before he then leaned forward and kissed her forehead. "I'm going to take a nap ... but when I get up ... I'm making dinner for everyone here. If anyone is looking for me, can you tell them that?"

Annika nodded and gave a sad smile as her husband patted her hand gently, then stood and retreated back to the castle without another glance over his shoulder.

Turning back to stare over the battlefield, the viscountess felt herself go still as her hand then moved to her swollen abdomen unconsciously.

"I'm sorry to you two as well ... I ... uh ... ugh. I am sorry you aren't getting a better mother, but I promise that ... that I will protect you. I will do my absolute best, so please don't ... please don't hate me, and forgive me if I don't show I care as much as you need."

Letting out a long sigh, the viscountess then wrapped her arms around her middle.

"Also ... to one or both of you ... if you are in fact a fire witch and turn out to be even an eighth of the pig slop your grandfather was, I am not afraid to submit you to proper Troivackian child-rearing, understood?"

"Already threatening the unborn? Goodness, motherhood really isn't every woman's calling, is it?" Clara appeared behind Annika from within the castle carrying a flask of water.

Annika rolled her eyes in response and took a drink. "Glad to see you finally picked the lock of that wardrobe."

Clara shot a sidelong glare at her mistress before deciding to ignore how she had spent the battle imprisoned thanks to the viscountess's insistence that she not leave until she had killed the King of Troivack. Instead, the maid seated herself and addressed the previous topic.

"You know … it isn't like you didn't have arsehat family members, too. In fact, I think aside from Lord Ashowan's mother, the number of horrible people your children are related to far outnumber the good. Meaning the odds of your brats being proper beasts are quite—"

"Clara?"

"Yes?"

"Shut up."

As Norman took stock of the rows and rows of the dead, he felt the expected sense of loss and failure settle in his chest. No one truly came out victorious in wars …

With a long sigh, he closed his eyes and tried to fight off the aching in his bones from countless hours awake and physical combat.

"A bath has been drawn, Your Majesty," Mr. Howard announced to him quietly.

"Thank you. The soldiers have been locked up?"

"Yes, sire."

"You said that Mr. Helmer is alive, but not a threat?" Norman opened his eyes again and turned to face his assistant squarely with a frown on his face.

"That is correct. The coven is discussing how it was even possible, but they think the viscount somehow made a binding magical rule that his father cannot use magic in his son's home, which logistically makes things … tricky."

Norman nodded. It would mean Aidan Helmer had to be kept nearby until his execution. A deeply unpleasant fact. Not that the man would be living long regardless …

"Is Fin also the one responsible for slaying the dragon?"

Mr. Howard suddenly grew stiff and uncharacteristically awkward as he became very interested in a pile of abandoned weapons several feet away.

The king frowned. "What happened?"

Clearing his throat uncomfortably, the assistant shuffled his feet slightly. "Well ... er ... that is where the eyewitness's accounts and the ... reports from the Troivackian side grow ... strange."

Norman waited, though his patience was wearing thin.

"It was actually the, er ... his, uh ... It was Kraken."

The monarch straightened, too confused and taken aback to immediately understand. "What was Kraken?"

"The ... the cat. The one you refer to as ... 'the greatest menace in Daxaria'? Yes, that one ... he somehow struck a deal with the city rats, had about fifty of them stuff themselves with coffee grounds and tobacco, only then to be voluntarily eaten by the dragon. It poisoned the beast and well ... yes. We now have a giant dead ancient dragon on the castle lawn."

Norman looked at his assistant blankly. He was so motionless that he didn't even blink, and Mr. Howard was growing increasingly worried that the news had pushed the king to his breaking point.

Then Norman suddenly burst out laughing. He laughed and laughed until his face was bright red and his sides ached, drawing several confused glances from knights and soldiers around him.

"Wait until you hear about him poisoning most of their men ..." the assistant added while daring to give a small smile.

The king's baffled expression returned, and then he proceeded to listen to the incredibly outlandish, and yet somehow believable, story of how a single cat brought about the downfall to the Troivackian army.

An hour later, Norman entered his chamber, rubbing his right shoulder carefully to try and ease some of the pain, when he stopped in his tracks.

There, on the velvet cushion where his crown rested, sat the very cat that he had been hearing about.

Kraken's fluffy chest fur was puffed up magnanimously, and his green eyes were bright and keen as he regarded the monarch interestedly.

With a long sigh, followed by a small chuckle, Norman slowly stepped over to the feline.

"I hear I have you to thank for helping us win today."

The cat continued to study him.

"Well ... thank you. I know we don't get along, and that you did everything for Fin, but you helped my people, and for that I will always be indebted to you." Bowing to the familiar, Norman then straightened and smiled.

"Perhaps we got started on the wrong paw so to say …" Reaching out, the king allowed Kraken to sniff his hand, then Norman began to tentatively pet the beast's silky head.

"See? This isn't so bad. Perhaps from now on we can—OUCH!"

The familiar had bitten the king's hand hard enough to draw blood, but what Kraken hadn't anticipated was the explosion of movement from the noble as he seized his hand, making Kraken leap clumsily off his pillow.

"YOU RUDDY FLEABAG, I WILL SEE YOUR WHISKERS PLUCKED FROM YOUR HEAD YOU—SON OF A MAGE!"

Kraken hadn't recovered from his initial blunder and tried to jump to save himself, only he launched himself crookedly and … landed directly in the king's bath.

With a great roar, the cat bolted from the tub, sopping wet, and fled from the room just as a maid and two guards were arriving.

"Is everything alright, Your Majesty?!"

Norman glared at the puddles across his castle floor and said tersely, "Everything is fine, thank you. I'm going to have my bath now."

Clutching his still bleeding hand, the king turned to face the servants directly. "Also, if any of you happen to let a cat into this chamber ever again, I will have you mucking stalls until the day you die."

The servants glanced at each other in worry and confusion, but decided that the battle had taken its toll on their usually calm and compassionate king, and so slowly closed his door to give him privacy without another word.

CHAPTER 45
SETTLING A SENTENCE

With the dead awaiting burial, and the remaining Troivackian soldiers locked away, some of the knights and soldiers had immediately set off to go help Rollom in the south. The ones to remain did so to ensure there were no further issues with the Troivackian captives or any other surprises.

By sunset, the banquet hall was packed with soldiers, nobility, and servants. Some were seated on the floor talking and laughing heartily, while others mourned together. Norman sat on his throne observing the wide array of emotions in his people. The ones who couldn't fit in the banquet hall had set up the camp once again outside, and many were delighted to hear that their beloved former cook was in charge of the meal.

When the banquet hall doors opened once again, platters of food magically drifted in carrying salads, golden creamy mashed potatoes, boats of gravy, and then came the meat. How Fin managed to create what looked like meat chunks fried with assorted vegetables in as little time as he had, no one knew, but many toasted to the house witch and his health.

The entire meal wasn't fussy, but it did bring with it color and warmth to not only the banquet hall, but to the hearts and minds of the survivors, a momentary respite and comfort from the darkness that had swept up onto their shores.

Mr. Howard's cheeks were already bright red from the ale, and even Mage Lee's son and wife seemed a little friendlier. Mage Lee himself was still requiring rest after his fight with Aidan Helmer, but it was assured he would make a full recovery.

As the hours ticked by, and Norman found himself surprisingly still conscious, he felt a gentle presence stir beside himself.

Looking up after a moment, he realized that it was the Coven of Wittica's leader, Eloise Morozov.

"Your Majesty," she greeted with a small curtsy before gesturing to the vacant seat beside the monarch in a silent question.

It was normally Ainsley's seat … the king smiled a little sadly as he felt the pangs of missing his beloved and their children. He nodded nonetheless to signal the witch could sit.

"I have questioned Aidan Helmer regarding his knowledge of the dragon. Asked about where the beast had been found, and if there were perhaps other ancient beings still alive that we had been presuming dead," the earth witch began slowly. "However, he doesn't seem to be in his right mind. Babbling about his magic, and curses, and then randomly shouting about beasts."

Norman nodded. "I am afraid I will not allow him to live to see midday tomorrow, so I hope that you—"

"Sire, I … I know I have no right to ask this, but perhaps in a month, we might be able to—"

"Speak with the Coven of Aguas and see if he said anything to them, but he has cost many lives and ruined several families. He will pay with his life, and there is no amount of pleading or bargaining that can change that. He is too conniving to be left to his own devices for another month."

Eloise Morozov opened her mouth to try a new angle when Norman cut her off once again.

"Ask the viscount's familiar if he knows anything, or if he can find out more. He is the mastermind behind most events as of late."

The earth witch looked caught between a laugh and serious consideration. "Yes … Kraken is without a doubt outside of what is considered a 'normal' familiar, but then again … Fin is outside the norm of witches. According to our past records, while there have been mutated witches that have communicated with their familiars, none of them have been as … clear and well-spoken as Kraken. Perhaps it is because of how well Lord Ashowan and his familiar suit each other."

The king nodded, his eyes still moving through the crowd.

"I look forward to working more closely together in the future, Your Majesty."

Norman cast a wry glance at the woman and nodded again. "I thank you for your cooperation. I hope you are fully prepared for working with Lord Ashowan."

The coven leader gave a small curious frown, but decided not to comment any further on that topic.

"Can you imagine if there are more beasts like that dragon just roaming around unseen? It all seems so … fantastical," Eloise mused more to herself than the king.

"Well, if there are more of them, let's just hope that Kraken is able to handle them."

At this, the coven leader, and even Norman, succumbed to a good chuckle.

The following morning, the King of Daxaria sat upon his throne in the official hearing room and waited. With him, lining the walls were his courtiers, as well as their wives who chose to remain behind during the war to tend to any of the wounded.

No one breathed a word, and everyone in the crowd, dressed in their glittering jewels and fresh tunics, was collectively grim. Some had wounds that were sewn closed or stood on rough crutches, but all of them awaited without a word of complaint.

At long last, the doors opened to reveal two guards escorting none other than Aidan Helmer. Troivack's former chief of military looked sullen. His face had smudges of soot, and his black eyes had somehow lost their sheen; instead, they were matte, and sunken. Gone were his former confidence and swift steps. Replacing the arrogant witch from the day before stood a man who had had his very essence burned free of his body.

The two knights escorting him forced Aidan to his knees in front of Norman.

"Mr. Helmer. You are hereby charged with the mistreatment of a Daxarian ambassador aboard your vessel, and the subsequent death of a hero of Daxaria. Furthermore, your attempt to abduct a Daxarian citizen during war has only been tacked on, but quite frankly, your death sentence was sealed the moment you returned to our shores and blackmailed, murdered, and tormented my people."

Aidan said nothing from his position on the ground.

"Do you have anything to say before we lead you to your execution?"

"I do," the fire witch announced darkly, his eyes finally rising to stare hatefully at Norman.

"Then you will say it to the Viscount of House Jenoure; it was a special request of his as the newly appointed diplomat of the Coven of Wittica."

Aidan frowned. "Viscount Hank Jenoure died more than a year ago."

"Ah … I suppose you haven't heard …"

Norman nodded to the knights at the doors, who couldn't contain their smiles as they opened the doors once more.

Aidan didn't turn to see whoever entered and instead fixed his eyes on the steps leading up to the dais the king sat upon as he pondered who this new pompous human diplomat could be. That is, until a pair of leather boots and bejeweled white shoes appeared in his line of vision.

Raising his gaze up, Aidan's eyes widened when he looked into his son's cool gaze. Fin was dressed in a fine black coat with gold-threaded designs around the cuffs and buttons. Under the coat was a snowy white tunic and tan trousers. His hair was washed and swept to the side, and the glint of a gold wedding band on his hand drew his eye next … but only because it was a hand that held …

The hand of Viscountess Jenoure.

"Mr. Helmer, the inheritor of the Viscount House Jenoure was Lord Finlay Ashowan. Official diplomat between my court and the Coven of Wittica. I believe you have already been acquainted with his wife, Lady Annika Ashowan."

Aidan frowned at the stunning woman standing at Fin's side. Her dark hair was swept over her left shoulder, while gold dripped from her ears, and a magnificent white dress draped over her body. Her dark eyes seemed sharper than he remembered …

He then glanced at the nobles around him in the room, and his thoughts were abundantly clear to Fin.

"This did not happen last night. Everyone here has known for quite some time. I was ennobled and married before I even stepped foot on your ship." The viscount's icy tone made the room grow even more still.

"I thought you were in a sordid love affair with the king's assistant," Aidan noted with a raised eyebrow. "At least that was what you hinted."

"You hinted what—?!" Mr. Howard's outburst must've been silenced by the king, because his exclamation was cut short.

Annika's dark gaze brightened for a moment, yet when she spoke, her tone was cold, yet somehow ... dangerous. "How is your shoulder, Mr. Helmer?"

The fire witch's eyebrows snapped up, as he suddenly remembered the archer who had clipped his shoulder ... and then how he had seen the viscountess firing an arrow straight into his familiar's eye ...

"I see ... that you have gotten somewhat better at hiding your nonsense, Fin." Aidan's lips curled.

"You will address me as Lord Ashowan, Mr. Helmer. Now, what is it you wanted to share with His Majesty? As the diplomat acting on behalf of the Coven of Wittica, I am who will be handling these matters."

A glimmer of Aidan's former cockiness flashed across his face as he smiled. "Call you 'Lord'? Or else what? I already have a death sentence."

The cool edge of a blade against the back of Aidan's neck made him straighten his shoulders fractionally.

"Or else we won't hear what you have to say," Fin explained, staring down emotionlessly at the man who sired him.

The fire witch's lip twitched. "Very well, *Lord* Ashowan." The clear mocking in his voice failed to evoke a response. "I wanted to let your king know that without me alive, you will never know just what ancient beasts still live. I know more than you could possibly dream, and with me dead, the war that will fall upon not just Troivack's lands, but Daxaria's, Zinfera's, maybe even Lobahl's ..."

There was a dramatic pause where the fire witch laughed, a sound that made most people want to back away.

"It might not be this year, or next, or even in ten years ... but mark my words. Your children will see the ancient ones return. You will all live to see each pathetic human life extinguished, because only the truly strong can survive what is to come. I tried to prepare the world for the rebirth of true power, but ... I suppose you'll all be content knowing you've brought the sea of blood to your children's doorsteps. All so that you might kill me."

Fin stared down at his father's twisted face and tilted his head to the side as ripples of uncertainty ran through the crowd.

Then after another brief moment of thoughtful silence, the viscount addressed the courtiers.

"If they are to come, true strength lies in uniting all we have. Not dividing."

Then he turned back to Aidan. "You terrorized my mother's past and trespassed on her present. Therefore, the man whose future you stole when you decided to use me in your games will be the very one to introduce you to your own end."

Once again, the fire witch was frowning in confusion, when Captain Antonio stepped forward, his gaze sharp.

"Captain Antonio and my mother were to be wed, and she was supposed to have a life where she no longer had to be lonely and could have someone care for her the way she deserved to be. He will be your executioner," Fin explained, his grip on Annika's hand tightening a little as he spoke.

The fire witch didn't say anything, only glared up at his son.

"Goodbye, Aidan."

As the knights dragged the fire witch from the room, everyone could see him beginning to grow pale as the captain then moved past Finlay, his lone blue eye trained on Aidan Helmer with cold intent. He only paused for a moment to speak over his shoulder to the redhead.

"Do you wish to see it happen?" Antonio asked gruffly.

Fin's voice didn't waver in the slightest when he answered. "No, and thank you, Captain."

The military man gave a firm nod, then continued out of the room, his deep blue cloak swishing behind him.

Stepping aside to make way for their king, everyone bowed as Norman rose and took his exit to watch over the proceedings of Aidan Helmer's demise. Some nobles elected not to go, others wished to be certain he was dead. However, regardless of which they chose, all filed from the throne room.

At long last … it was going to be over.

Never again would the fire witch disturb their home with his greed and terror.

After a few moments, when it was just Fin and Annika left in the official throne room, the two turned to each other and embraced.

"There are still the soldiers in Rollom, but … for at least a month … might we hold off joining the army, and simply rest?" the viscount asked his wife as she tenderly lifted her hand and touched his cheek.

"My dear, by then I don't think I'll be allowed to travel. Remember, things will be over sooner if we do not put things off. However, I … I think I should stay behind even if you leave with the king's next wave of knights," Annika replied with a small tired smile.

Fin gently reached out to touch her rounding middle through the many layers of her dress, and he let out a long breath. "I know. I'll try not to be gone for too long. I don't know why I didn't realize that leading the knights of the house to aid the battle would be expected ..." The viscount allowed a cheeky smile to touch his face. "Are you sure you don't want to give up on being a noble and just be a cook's wife?"

The lady's grin warmed considerably. "You're still a cook, Fin. You just also happen to be wonderfully wealthy with a few more responsibilities, thanks to me ..."

Dropping his forehead to touch his wife's, Fin then drew her closer. "Just a few more, hm?"

Annika gave an ambiguous single shoulder shrug as she feigned looking innocent. Fin laughed.

"To be honest I'm not sure which will be more chaotic ... the war, or our twins ..."

At this, Annika gently cuffed the back of his head, making him laugh again before kissing her soundly.

When they pulled apart, Fin held on for just another moment longer, not ready to let her go yet. "Stay safe, and I'll be home before you give birth. No matter what, I will be there. I promise."

Annika squeezed him tightly and buried her face against his shoulder, settling into the space where she belonged.

"You better be back soon ... Clara's already ready to kill me ... you'll need to hold her back when I'm too fat to defend myself ..."

At this Fin couldn't help but succumb to even heartier laughter as he held his wife and enjoyed a rare, wonderful moment of peace.

Soon, all would be right in the world again ... Just a little bit longer.

CHAPTER 46
PUSHING THROUGH

Norman stared around the table at his inner council members seriously as the stewards completed their task of pouring wine for everyone, as well as setting out other small refreshments for them.

Captain Antonio looked grim in his seat, while also remarkably ordinary for once ... Instead of donning a fine tunic and fitted black leather vest, or gleaming armor, he wore a simple white tunic and brown trousers. Lord Fuks, looking as bright-eyed as ever, was struggling with his bandaged hands to lift the wine goblet to his lips. Mage Lee looked exhausted, and for once leaning on his staff didn't look to be a production.

Mr. Howard's complexion was pale, the circles under his eyes deep, as were the lines in his forehead.

Fin wore a black tunic with brown trousers, his traveling cloak already clasped around his shoulders as cool autumn winds whistled between the castle stones.

"We will take back Rollom, and then I will remain there to rebuild the city," Norman began, his deadened gaze meeting everyone's. "Once it is safe, Ainsley and the children will join me there. It may be years. Mr. Howard and Captain Antonio will join me permanently, while Lord Ashowan will return to Austice once we have vanquished the last of Troivack's soldiers. After the viscountess gives birth, it will fall to him to manage the witches who are remaining here to offer their assistance in precautionary defense. Coven Leader Eloise Morozov will be helping establish Fin's authority as the coven's diplomat and therefore will be spending a few weeks to months in each of our four fair cities to ensure it is a smooth transition. Lord Fuks, you are to advise and monitor the viscount's decisions. Mage Lee, you, too, will remain here to keep an eye on the viscount and lend assistance when needed."

The group collectively nodded.

"I'm afraid this will be our final meeting together." Slowly standing, Norman managed a warm smile to those around him. "I could not have asked for a better inner council during these times. You have all served me honorably, and I will never be able to thank you all enough."

Everyone bowed to their king, wordlessly accepting his praise.

"Your Majesty ... If I may ... ?" Lord Fuks suddenly interjected, his eyes twinkling.

Norman nodded permissively.

"I need to know ... why did you risk sending our dear cook on the Troivackian vessel—even with the witches on the nearby boat? It seemed a little odd to me ..."

At this, Norman managed a strained smile. "Ah ... well ... I had a couple reasons for that decision. Almost all of which came to be fruitful. My biggest regret, however, is that it came at such a high cost."

Fin said nothing, but his face did grow a little paler as he sat waiting expectantly.

"For one, I did not wish to send Lady Annika Ashowan to her death. Finlay truly did have a high chance of surviving ... We also needed to try and rescue the remaining members of the Piereva family. Subsequent to those reasons, we also needed more information on their army, as well as a sense of their timing. Lord Ashowan's involvement aided all these motives. Especially as it was also a way to form concrete ties with the coven, while at the same time having firm grounds to ennoble our former cook here." Norman paused then, and a small blush crept into his cheeks. "Then there was the possibility ... that the viscount could somehow ... persuade some of the Troivackians to be more harmonious in nature ... given his previous track record."

At this, even Mage Lee cracked a smile.

"I was surprised when fifty Troivackian men suddenly turned on their fellow soldiers during the battle yesterday, but I'm given to understand that ... my particular estimate did indeed come to be accurate. Though,

Viscount … I have a message from two of those soldiers." The king turned to his vassal wearing a puzzled frown. "Two soldiers named Rhett and Dylan, though they said you knew them as Stanley and Bruce?"

Fin suddenly grew sheepish, and the men around the table could only speculate why.

"They requested that you write a letter on their behalf during a hearing for their fates?"

The house witch nodded with a small smile. "I will … I honestly didn't think one night of drinking and flirting with the men would—"

"You flirted with them?!" Mr. Howard burst out incredulously. "Here I was thinking the bard was terrible for sleeping his way around the castle, but you—"

"Kevin, it's too late to want me back. I'm married and it's wrong," Fin interjected while shaking his head with mock rejection.

Everyone shifted in their seats as they tried not to laugh.

"It's 'Mr. Howard' to you," the assistant grumbled darkly.

"Back to more … official matters," Norman said, clearing his throat loudly, though amusement still glittered in his eyes for a moment. "The King of Troivack was planning on leaving a handful of his nobles to seize control of the kingdom and then proceed with having them rule our land as an extension of their own for our fertile fields and resources. Once we beat back the last of them, we can negotiate their penalty—and how we can stop their entire nation from starving. They were resistant to my ideas before, but we will not be reentering those meetings with the intent to negotiate after we win this war."

No one said a word, only waited for the king to continue. "As Charles and Phillip Piereva were the last technical male heirs to the earldom, Lord Charles Piereva's wife inherited the house title and wealth. We will need to have her decide, though, whether or not she is willing to return to the land given that she will most likely be forced to remarry quickly due to their inheritance laws. Mr. Howard, please make sure to record this topic when we eventually begin our rendezvous with the remaining Troivackian leaders."

The assistant was already scribbling away.

"Excellent. Now, are there any other matters we need to address?"

"Er … I have a question … ?" Fin raised his hand tentatively.

"Yes, Viscount?"

"What are we going to do about the very large dead reptile on the lawn?"

At this there was a beat of silence before Norman spoke again. "What does the Coven of Wittica believe we should do?"

"Hide the corpse. People have enough on their minds without thinking about ancient beasts. It will also allow us to study its physiology and compare our historical records."

The king nodded. "Very well. Draft up the official paperwork of the exchange, but please make sure that all their findings are shared and transparent with myself."

Fin nodded.

"Now, I believe we should see to packing and getting on the road by morning," the king announced imperially until Fin stood suddenly.

"Sire, what if we … er …" Fin picked up the goblet of wine and downed its contents before clearing his throat awkwardly. "Because it is unlikely we will all be back in the same place for a long time … what do you all think about having one more evening of …" The witch trailed off as the wine bottles on the table magically drifted into the air and began topping up everyone's goblets.

The men all raised their gazes to one another, as boyish smiles began spreading over each of their faces.

Camaraderie and good humor suddenly began to lighten the heavy atmosphere of the room, and the fire in the hearth crackled merrily behind them all as though promising that their evening could indeed be a good one.

"I suppose … one night to let off steam before rejoining the battle doesn't change the schedule. After all, we're all mostly packed, anyway …" Norman began slowly while raising his goblet to his lips.

"Not to mention the viscountess is probably not going to say anything if we happen to … borrow … a bottle or two of her private stock of moonshine," Mr. Howard noted casually.

Fin's grin turned cheeky. "Very well. Perhaps go ask my aide, Peter, if he also has any of his family's absinthe to spare."

The assistant launched himself out of his chair and was halfway across the room before the witch had even finished speaking.

Chuckling to himself, Fin turned to his right to see the captain studying him carefully, his lone blue eye somehow darker …

"Ashowan … are you … really alright? Your father was beheaded this morning," Antonio observed carefully while turning to face Fin who was seated to his left, making the room once again stiffen.

Fin's smile faded from his face as he lowered his gaze to the table.

"I ... I don't crave violence or revenge. I know he needed to be stopped, but to me ... I suppose he was dead to me long ago." No one spoke as the witch clearly was bracing himself to say a little bit more. "There is too much happening to properly process it, admittedly, but ... if I'm being perfectly honest ... I don't want the last night I have amongst friends for a long time to be lost because of Aidan Helmer."

Even saying his name brought back an unpleasant wrenching of Fin's gut.

The captain nodded. "I, too, do not feel taking his life was sufficient for the pain of losing Kate, but ... at least he isn't a danger to us anymore."

Everyone stayed silent for a long thoughtful moment, until, with a shake of his head, Fin grabbed his goblet and lifted it to the air.

"To Daxaria, the best home I could've asked for!"

Six months later ...

Pulling up to the castle doors of Austice on a snowy white steed, Fin lifted his hand, bringing the knights following him to a halt. Dismounting swiftly, and walking purposefully up the steps, Ruby, the Head of Housekeeping, rushed out to greet him in the sunny, yet damp early spring day that wasn't all that unlike the day he had first arrived as the new Royal Cook ...

Pulling off his leather gloves, the sword clipped at his side now like a second limb, he nodded to the servants that lined the steps and bowed to him.

"Viscount! Viscount, oh thank the *Gods* you are here! The viscountess and her maid are trying to throttle each other, and no one can tell when the pains are coming, but poor Physician Durand cannot examine her properly at this rate!"

Fin frowned. He had only felt Annika's initial panic when the labor pains had started, but he couldn't sense anything else ... perhaps the birth hadn't really started?

He had received word late the previous night that she had first felt the contractions, but he had already known and had been in the middle of saddling his horse when the messenger had come to tell him.

As Fin strode through the castle, he noticed several smiling faces greet him and many people waved to him excitedly.

"Better get up to the fourth floor, Viscount! You can hear the screams from the stairs!" Lord Fuks's chipper voice rang out as he passed Finlay in the great hall. The man didn't even break his stride despite not having seen the witch for half a year.

Fin broke out into a jog, and by the time he was sliding into the corridor near where his wife was supposed to be giving birth under the Royal Physician's care, he witnessed Clara being thrown with great force out of Annika's chamber.

The maid looked unhinged; her normally neat hair was disheveled and her cheeks were tinged with pink. She was in the process of rolling up her sleeves and muttering expletives while Mage Lee and Keith, who stood outside the door, tried to hold her back.

"CLARA!" Fin shouted out, slowing his speed down as he approached the scene with a small amount of hesitation.

Fortunately, his shout seemed to snap the woman out of her haze of ire.

"Viscount! Thank Gods you made it in time," she breathed and groaned at the same time, her eyes closing.

"Yes, thank the Gods you are here. I never knew that the ladies of the court had even *heard* such colorful language, let alone … this!" Keith admonished, his eyes carrying a haunted look that immediately brought many questions to Fin's mind.

Stepping around the two mages, Fin threw open the chamber door in time to see Annika gripping Hannah's shoulders and letting out a loud moan of pain as she swayed her enormous rounded middle back and forth.

The blonde grasped the viscountess's shoulders and swayed with her as though the pair were in a strange dance.

"Ah, Viscount, thank Gods you've arrived." Physician Durand was standing beside the hearth, his face already matted with sweat that he was attempting to dab away with a clean linen.

Annika, standing in nothing but her night shift, with her long black hair woven back in a loose braid with several flyaways, looked up immediately at hearing the announcement of her husband's arrival.

"You're here!" she cried out, grateful tears springing to her beautiful eyes. "Godsdamnit, where've you been?! This hurts, Fin! Gods, it hurts so much. Why the hell did you have to look so damn good at the ball …" she whimpered nonsensically, making the physician and Hannah both look at Fin with wry amusement.

Clearing his throat awkwardly, the house witch unclipped his sword from his belt and stepped forward to take Annika's hands off Hannah's shoulders. "Where is the queen? Wasn't she supposed to be helping you?" he asked, lowering his voice as he marveled at the sight of his swollen wife.

"She's calming Eric down … he seems … traumatized about people giving birth …"

Fin nodded in understanding. "Is Kraken there with him?"

"Yes, though … I won't lie it was strange, but it URGAAAAGHH—" Annika shrieked, her grip on his shoulders becoming impressively painful.

"Viscount, could you please get her on the bed for me to examine. Her fight with her maid prevented me from checking her progress."

"That frigid bitch started it! Saying I'm carrying on like a Godsdamn brood cow! I'LL CUT *HER* LIKE A COOOOW—OWOWOWOWOWOWOW!"

Tears were running down Annika's cheeks as she doubled over her middle.

Fin and Hannah wordlessly worked as a team to maneuver his wife back onto her bed where Physician Durand checked how close she was to giving birth.

"Alright, Viscountess, we still have a ways to go. I imagine by nightfall you will be ready to pu—"

"I HAVE TO DO THIS UNTIL NIGHTFALL?!" the normally composed viscountess roared, making the poor man jump.

Fin began rubbing soothing circles around her lower back, making her moan in appreciation, her previous gusto immediately deflating.

"It's alright, love. We know you can do it," the witch soothed while trying to settle his own nerves.

Despite having assisted in countless births, Fin had to admit this one was more than a little nerve-racking as it was not only twins, but *his* twins.

"Exactly! Look, Viscountess, there's no other way out of this one, you're just going to have to shove those little witches out at some point. So just suffer through best you can," Hannah crowed, smiling confidently and placing her hands on her hips.

Annika fisted the front of Fin's tunic and dragged his face down until it was mere inches from her own.

"Get me your Godsdamn frying pan. I am going to need to hit something if I'm going to keep doing this."

"A perfectly reasonable request! I'll go get that for you!" Hannah skipped out of the room cheerily.

Fin, on the other hand, gulped. Perhaps Hannah wasn't the best influence on his wife who also happened to be a little too deadly a woman when she wasn't crowning ...

In her current state?

The viscount eyed the physician apologetically. Physician Durand looked mildly put off by the expression, but slowly resumed checking on Annika's progress.

Maybe I should see about funding the man's retirement ... or perhaps just have one of the knights loan him a helmet ...

CHAPTER 47
FIN

It was the dining hour, the sun was setting in a blaze of magnificent golds and red, and the castle servants and courtiers were in jovial spirits ... all save for the Viscountess Ashowan.

With Physician Durand positioned down by her legs and Fin sitting behind his wife holding both her hands as she bore down and worked to push out the first of their children, anyone in the fourth-floor corridor could hear her shrieks and grunts.

"Oh Gods, I never knew how distressing it was on the other side," the queen admitted as she wiped her sweaty palms on her mustard-colored dress and once again brought a damp cloth to Annika's forehead.

"Not ... HELPING!" Annika shouted as her eyes squeezed shut and she gasped through yet another burst of pain and pushing.

"My lady, you are very nearly there, I believe I can see the head of the first babe!" Physician Durand called out encouragingly as the viscountess dropped her head back onto Fin's shoulder while he whispered words of encouragement and assurance.

"Alright, give one big push!"

Annika screamed bloody murder, and poor Keith, who sat outside of the door with his father, succumbed to tears while swearing over and over he would never be able to have children knowing how awful it sounded.

"The head is out, my lady! Another big push … yes … yes … splendid, Viscountess! The babe is free!" the physician cajoled as he immediately wrapped the first of the couple's children in a snowy white towel while the unmistakable raspy cries of a newborn babe drifted alongside Annika's pants.

Fin's eyes were glued on the tiny bundle in Durand's arms, his heart thundering in his chest.

"Viscount, Viscountess, you have a daughter!" the physician smiled as he presented the new parents their child, her small resilient shrieks and waving fists an excellent sign of her splendid health.

Letting out a weakened sob, with trembling arms, Annika reached out to take her firstborn eagerly.

"She's … so tiny …" she managed weakly as Fin stared starstruck down into his daughter's tiny face. She was immediately beginning to calm down in her mother's arms, her eyes struggling to open in her new bright world.

"She …" Fin trailed off as he reached around his wife and gently touched the infant's hand, making the small girl ever so slowly frown, then peel open one eye … and then the other.

"Oh my!" The queen gasped from the bedside as both Fin and Annika gazed in equal astonishment into the bright golden eyes that peered up at them. There was already a magical shine in their depths that was incredibly striking …

"I take it … you … are the fire witch," Annika whispered as she tenderly reached her hand up and brushed her thumb against her daughter's cheek.

Both the viscount and his wife stared down into their child's beautiful eyes that resembled the brilliant sun that was still in the process of settling into the horizon. The world felt whole and still as the beginning of their new family wrote itself forever in their memories and hearts.

"Alright, Viscountess, we're about ready to begin pushing again!" Physician Durand chirped happily.

Both Annika's and Fin's stricken expressions lifted to stare at the elder, who may have been somewhat optimistic about how the news would be handled.

Then, in perfect unison, the couple burst out, "Son of a mage!"

"Congratulations, Finlay, my boy! Two children, healthy and happy!" Lord Fuks clapped Fin on his shoulder as the men all stood outside the banquet hall wishing happy tidings to the new father.

"Aside from Lady Ashowan's screams permanently making me grand-childless ... this is indeed a joyous occasion!" Mage Lee admitted with only the barest hint of agitation in his voice. Meanwhile Lord Fuks set to packing a pipe of his finest tobacco for Finlay before handing out the dried leaves for the others to enjoy.

Fin accepted the pipe and with a snap of his fingers had it lit and was puffing gratefully with a smile.

"I didn't know you enjoyed pipe tobacco, house witch," Lee noted with vague interest as the young lord leaned against the wall to his side and settled into his smoke.

"I didn't used to, but being away from Annika during her pregnancy and chasing out the last of the Troivackian soldiers proved to be slightly more stressful than I anticipated."

"Were you able to use your magic in Rollom, after all? His Majesty was rather vague with his correspondence out of fear the missives would be intercepted," Lord Fuks asked curiously.

"Ah ... about that. After a bit of trial and error ... yes. Though now that I'm no longer residing there, I don't think I can use long-range magic. About halfway back up the continent I could feel myself lose connection with it. I think I'd have to visit the city again to reestablish that connection, but even so ... His Majesty counted it as a very promising development. I'll be doing annual tours of the cities and establish a governing office of witches in each one to ensure that education and work is being fairly corroborated between Daxaria's citizens and our own kind."

Lord Fuks let out a long whistle, while puffing away on his own pipe. "You sound like a proper aristocrat, boy. With far too much work to do and an unnecessary do-gooder outlook to boot."

Fin laughed and rubbed his eyes wearily. "Yes, well ... I want to try and unite and make Daxaria as strong as possible if what Aidan said before he died is true. And I have two children to think of now, after all."

The trio fell into an amicable silence for a moment before the earl suddenly burst out, "By the way! I want you to know I've thought of some names for your new family members! Names that will make them unfor-gettable and a lesson in mental and emotional fortitude! As you know, my name is already perfect for forming such wonderful characteristics. Now the last name Ashowan does prove to be quite the weakness in such an endeavor, however—"

"Lord Fuks, I, er, *appreciate* the thought but ... uh ... I don't think we need—"

"Nonsense! No need to be modest. My idea centers around the use of both the first and middle name; we can think about changing your last name later. What about Patricia Enis! I know it doesn't sound all that funny, but when you take the first letter and pair it with—"

"House witch!" Lord Fuks was saved from finishing his explanation much to Fin's immense relief by the arrival of Captain Antonio, Mr. Howard, His Majesty King Norman Reyes, and the kitchen aides who were all striding alongside the group, talking excitedly.

Fin straightened with a warm grin.

"These kitchen knights here tell me you are officially a father!" Norman greeted Fin with a broad smile, while Mr. Howard looked as though he were bracing himself for a death sentence.

"I am indeed. A beautiful daughter, and a handsome son, who already scared the mead from us when he didn't feel like crying upon being born."

Captain Antonio's face split into the brightest smile since Kate's death, as tears glistened in his blue eye.

"Congratulations, Viscount." The military man bowed, perhaps to hide his show of emotion.

"I see the worries have already begun," the king noted while nodding to the pipe in the viscount's hand.

"They have indeed." Fin chuckled self-consciously while straightening his shoulders.

"At least one of them is a girl," Mr. Howard began despite his pale expression. "Lady Ashowan should be able to teach her how to be a well-behaved child …"

Fin decided perhaps it wasn't the best time to inform the assistant that it looked as though it was his daughter who without a doubt was a fire witch …

"Tell me, what're the names of these new nobles?" Sir Taylor boomed happily.

"Sir Lewis and I have bets that you'd name at least one of them after a vegetable," Sir Andrews pointed out jovially.

"Or fruit! Fruit is not out of the question. I can just see little Blueberry being a butterball of terror," Peter mused while nodding to the group.

Mr. Howard began to look a little green.

Deciding to save the assistant from dwelling on the potential problems his offspring would cause, the witch informed everyone of the names that he and his wife had chosen.

"Our son we've named Tamlin, and our daughter ..." Fin trailed off and shifted his gaze to the captain while giving him a meaningful smile. "We decided to name her Katarina. Not exactly my mother's name but ... we wanted it to be close."

The men all silently nodded in agreement.

It was incredibly fitting.

"Well, then, a toast to their long and healthy lives!" Norman announced while procuring a flask from his side.

"Long, healthy ... and hopefully *quiet* lives ..." Mr. Howard muttered before pulling out his own flask and taking several deep gulps.

Fin muffled his laughter as he began thinking how he needed to return to Annika's side. He found himself already missing the sight of his new family ...

Sitting in the rocking chair before the hearth, Fin rocked back and forth with the two infants in each of his arms. While Tamlin slept soundly, his daughter peered around the room, completely alert.

Annika slept peacefully in the bed several feet away, and all was quiet. The residents of the castle had long gone to bed, leaving only a handful of guards and servants awake in the balmy spring evening.

"I think you're going to be our resident troublemaker," Fin observed with a heartfelt smile down into his daughter's face as her eyes struggled to fixate on his features.

From the bed Annika rolled over at the sound of her husband's voice, immediately making Fin feel guilty about potentially waking her.

"Come with me ... I'm going to show you the best place in all of Austice," he whispered down to his children as he slowly stood.

Moving over to Annika and planting a kiss on her temple, the witch then quietly left the chamber, using his magic to open and close the door behind himself, and proceeded through the sleepy halls.

Not a single soul passed by the father and his children as they made their way down the stairs, down the east corridor, passing by the rose maze that stood budding proudly in the moonlight.

Breezing by the servants' dining hall, Fin then magicked open the door to their destination: the kitchen.

Stepping quietly into the room, Fin magically lit the candles and hearth, and, feeling his heart fill with happiness and comfort, he moved over to his old beloved cooking table.

That was when he discovered Kraken fast asleep in one of the chairs.

The great furry beast let out a long yawn, showing off his long and pointy fangs.

"*Good evening, house witch, how is— Oh!*"

The feline slowly sat up and stretched before leaning forward and sniffing the two bundles in Fin's arms carefully, his whiskers gleaming in the firelight.

Kraken blinked up at the new father, who beamed proudly.

"*Congratulations on the new kittens, witch. I will alert my followers that we have new soft humans to keep a close eye on.*"

Fin's face fell to a frown. "Your followers? Just what exactly have you become?"

"*Ruler of the underbelly of Austice. Though do not fear; I will expand my radius of power. I have almost grown to my full size now. Few will challenge me these days.*"

Fin blinked and shook his head. "Just be careful."

"*Of course, witch. Now … if you will excuse me … I think I hear a tasty mole out in the gardens …*"

Then with a graceful leap from his perch, the great Kraken loped off toward the garden door, which Fin magically opened and closed for him.

Letting out a long sigh, he wondered if he'd ever get around to hearing the full story of how his familiar seemed to organize and overtake the cats and rodents of the city … but decided it wasn't going to be that night. So he turned back to his sleeping children once more and was unable to fight off the smile that immediately sprang back to his face.

"This is where everything truly began for me. I met your mother in this room … I met the prince and the king in this room … In fact, I think I met every single new friend in the castle in this room … save perhaps for Lord Fuks. A word of advice? Do *not* laugh at his name no matter how much you want to. Katarina, if it were up to him you would have a name that would have you rebelling against me the minute you figured out what it meant."

Fin laughed softly, and Tamlin's eyes slowly began to open as a result.

Moving his attention over to his son, the redhead smiled thoughtfully.

"You look like your mother, and you seem remarkably composed like her already."

Dropping a brief kiss onto his son's brow, Fin slowly seated himself on the tall chair that sat at the cooking table.

"Just remember to be honest and trust those whom you love, and who love you back." Fin watched as the boy began to coo and sigh contentedly in his arms.

"I want you both to know … you are the final missing pieces. You are why I grew my power. You are what completes my home here with Annika …" He let out a long breath as emotion welled up inside his chest. "So I promise … I will keep you safe, and you will always know you are loved, and that you are never alone. I will do everything within my growing abilities to make sure, witch"—Fin nodded to his daughter before his attention moved to his son—"or not a witch, you will always have a place to belong."

Basking in the warmth of the moment and the night, Fin slowly rocked his children, feeling both whole and wholly unprepared for what fatherhood would bring. After all, it was only a year ago he had arrived thinking he would spend his days making delicious meals, and doing nothing else …

Knowing how incredibly lucky he was, the witch sent a silent prayer of thanks to the Goddess and the Green Man for bringing him to the castle and helping him overcome his demons to embrace Annika and his promising future.

The babes then began to squirm in his arms, signifying their need to be fed.

Alas, the food they required was one even the great house witch could not procure.

"Better take you back up to your mum," Fin said with a sigh and a smile as he carefully stood back up. His arms were aching from holding his children, and yet even though he could use magic to lessen the burden, he knew he didn't want to let go of his children just yet.

When he moved toward the castle door, Fin cast one last long look at the kitchen and knew down to his very core that whether it be in the castle or elsewhere in the world, as long as he was with his children and wife, he was exactly where he was meant to be.

As he closed the door behind them, the hearth flickered down, and the candles snuffed out.

"Just promise me one thing …" Fin's quiet voice murmured in the darkness. "Be friends and love whomever you want, but … never become a mage."

EPILOGUE
NOBLE ACKNOWLEDGMENT

Eric stared down at the two infants fast asleep in their bassinet and tilted his head while staring perplexedly at them.

"Is something wrong?" Fin asked the young boy who was nearing his ninth birthday.

The prince had been beside himself with excitement to meet Fin's children and had even tried to kidnap his baby sister from her nursemaid in an attempt to steal away to the viscount's keep for a secret meeting.

Suffice it to say, Eric had almost been banned from meeting the twins as a result, so it was particularly strange that he wasn't responding as jubilantly once he finally laid eyes on the children.

Annika glanced at Ainsley, who stood behind her son looking equally puzzled.

"It's just ... I thought that twins were supposed to look identical." Eric sighed, his shoulders slumping.

Everyone broke out into good-humored smiles.

"There is such a thing as fraternal twins where they look nothing alike. After all, didn't you hear that there is a boy *and* a girl?" Fin asked with a chuckle as Eric looked up at him with open disappointment.

The boy's eyebrows shot up. "I just heard them say they were twins! A boy and a girl?!" He looked at the sleeping infants with renewed interest. "Which one is the girl and which one is the boy?"

"Do you see the one with black hair? That's Tam, he's the boy. The one with lighter hair? That's Katarina," Annika explained while resting her hands on the edge of the bassinet and smiling down at her children.

The prince was about to say something else, when Fin's daughter stirred, a long yawn stretching her small rosebud mouth.

"Ah, the child who never sleeps …" Annika sighed wearily while Fin rubbed her back in sympathy.

Then the small infant opened her eyes and Eric fell completely still. "Wh-Why are her eyes *golden*?!"

Fin smiled at the queen who was staring at his daughter with equal admiration despite having seen her before.

Her expression was identical to her son's, amusingly enough …

"She's most likely a witch. A witch can have unique physical characteristics associated with their element," the viscount explained while placing an arm around his wife.

"Whoooaaa, that's amazing! Can she make giant fireballs?! Can she become a sun?!"

Fin was having a hard time keeping a straight face, and even the queen had to resort to biting her lip.

"Er … it is too early to know, Eric. She most likely won't show any power until she is a few years older."

The prince was disappointed all over again. "Well … what about him?" he asked, pointing at the still-sleeping boy halfheartedly.

"We aren't sure about him yet. He's incredibly quiet … we honestly thought he may be a mute until one day he saw Annika and me all the way across the room hugging and he started screaming bloody murder. Scared the shit out of—"

The queen shot the redhead a warning look over his language.

"Ah … I mean … we were … *startled* …" Fin cleared his throat guiltily.

Eric stared at the slumbering child for a moment before growing bored and moving his attention back to Katarina, whose golden eyes were fixated on him.

Reaching out with his index finger, the prince bowed.

"Lady Ashowan, lovely to meet you. Please don't set me on fire."

Unable to stop himself, Fin burst out laughing while Annika looked mortified, and the queen appeared mildly concerned.

"Don't worry, Eric, I'll make sure she doesn't grow up to be that kind of person."

The young royal nodded, a mature expression suddenly overtaking his childish features that had already aged significantly in the span of a year.

"I know you will. Just like Alina is the best princess in the world because she has me, and Mom, and Dad. Well ... I'm glad I got to meet them before we have to leave ... again."

Eric's moment of wisdom had passed, and instead the look of a child on the brink of complaining took its place.

"I'm sorry you have to leave Austice," Fin said to Eric as Annika bent down and picked Katarina up who, for once, wasn't squirming like a worm to look around at everything. "But I'm sure you'll like Rollom. The Alcide Sea on that side of the continent is beautiful, and who knows! Maybe one day you'll get to live here again!"

The prince began to fiddle with the corner of the sheet in the bassinet. "Maybe ... Even Morgan is going to Sorlia so I can't see him, either."

Just then, the swish of a fluffy tail swept by Eric's leg.

"KRAKEN!" the boy burst out excitedly before swooping down and picking up the familiar to cradle him against his chest. "I haven't seen you since the babies were born! Where were you?!"

The feline blinked slowly up at the eager face, then released a small chirp.

"He says he had to guard my children." Fin gave a small apologetic smile.

Annika stepped forward then and slowly crouched down, her daughter cradled in his arms.

"Your Highness, I am sorry I frightened you during the birth. I'm sure it didn't help that we refused visitors for a while, but I—"

"Three months." The bitterness in Eric's tone was followed immediately by a look of guilt that he then chose to hide by burying his face in Kraken's magnificently fluffy chest.

"I ... I am very sorry. It was just that ... I didn't feel like myself for a long time, and I needed to get used to having two children."

Shyly, the curly blond head lifted again. "I'm sorry, too ... it sounded scary. I was just worried."

Annika smiled kindly. "Thank you for worrying about me."

Ainsley's proud expression made Fin grin as the pair watched the two talk, when they were all suddenly interrupted.

"Your Majesty, my lord, my lady," Clara greeted quickly. "Duke Iones has arrived unannounced to meet the new Ashowan family members."

Both Fin and Annika let out a long breath, sharing weary smiles of understanding.

"Ever since the word got out that people can meet them, it feels like we are hosting nonstop," the viscountess explained while slowly straightening and patting Katarina's back unconsciously as the child began to squirm.

Fin looked to his wife. "How about I take Kat, and you and Her Majesty enjoy some time to yourselves. Clara, you're fine with staying with Tam while he sleeps, aren't you?"

The maid's blue eyes cut to the sleeping child warily. "He won't need to be changed, will he?"

Fin chuckled while Annika shot him a grateful smile and handed him their daughter. "If he does, go and get his wet nurse."

Clara was visibly on edge, but somehow, she managed to dip into her usual graceful curtsy. "Yes, my lord."

Giving Annika another peck on her cheek, Fin then bowed to the queen and began to leave the room when suddenly Eric moved behind him.

"I want to go with you," the prince murmured quietly, while glancing briefly at his mother with an obvious expression of guilt.

Fin looked to the queen, who smiled in understanding and nodded.

"Well, let's not keep Lord Harris waiting, shall we? So tell me, how are your swordsman lessons going?"

Fin and Eric disappeared through the doorway, with the lad's happy chatter echoing back up the corridor all the way until they reached the bend that would take them to the stairs.

Both Annika and the queen excused themselves to the solar, and once the door had been closed behind them with the warm afternoon sun casting the room in a comforting glow, Annika half melted, half collapsed into the nearest sofa.

Ainsley regarded her friend sympathetically before primly seating herself beside the noblewoman.

"Do you remember when Eric was four or five years old ... and we had just met, and you said to me—"

"Oh, for the love of— Are you really going to say 'I told you so'?!" the viscountess blurted out with a look of utter disbelief.

"Ah yes, I remember *exactly* what you said ... 'Children—if I should ever suffer having one—and one is the most I will endure, will be cared for by their wet nurses and not bother me until they can speak. At least then I can teach them something worthwhile.' So imagine my surprise that the formidable and cold Annika Piereva—then soon-to-be Jenoure, and now Annika Ashowan—is keeping her *twins* in a bassinet in her chamber because 'the wet nurse won't tend to them right.'" Ainsley's glowing smile succeeded in making Annika cover her eyes with her hand in an effort to hide from its glory.

"Blame Hank. He started turning me soft. Of course, Fin just had to come along ... Then the Gods decided to give me two children at once, and on top of that, one of them doesn't seem to need more than a couple hours here and there *at most*."

"It could be worse ... Tam could be the same way, or you could've had triplets ..."

Annika's face grew ashen. "Don't even jest. No more children after these two. None. Zero. I am done."

Ainsley's devious smile only agitated the viscountess further, and so she set to changing the topic as quickly as possible.

"In more important news ... you are leaving Austice for ... how long do you suppose?"

The queen let out a long, sad sigh as she leaned back into the couch cushions and, glancing down at her lap, gave a small, sad smile. For a moment, she once again looked like the timid shy young woman Annika had seen in portraits.

"I don't know how long. We first came to Austice because we realized that, for a military city, it was outrageously corrupt and not at all organized. Things have improved significantly, but even if we have retaken Rollom, there is much that needs to be rebuilt, and we need to restore order there as well. It's a fishing city, but there have been a couple of mines discovered that hold real promise ... Ah. But you're the one who told us about those, so it isn't a surprise."

Annika nodded seriously. "Yes. Particularly this new type of steel we could wield. Stronger than most, yet not overly heavy ... I am waiting on the reports from my blacksmith and mercenaries to tell me what they manage to accomplish with their findings. The collaborative effort with the witches could yield some incredible results."

The queen nodded.

The conversation quickly descended into further talks of business and politics, topics Annika had sorely missed despite loving her children wholly.

As the sun began to settle itself in the arms of the horizon, a small knock on the solar door ended the conversation between the best friends.

"My lady, the viscount sends word that dinner is prepared. Her Majesty and the prince are of course welcome to stay," said one of the younger maids, who had entered and curtsied to them with her head bowed.

"Very well, we will be down to join them momentarily," Annika replied before having to stifle a yawn.

The maid took her leave, and the two noblewomen rose to their feet, while both stretched in very unladylike ways.

"By the way … what happened with your sister-in-law Janelle and her daughter? Last you told me she was furious with you …"

The viscountess's face grew still for a moment as she straightened her shoulders and glanced out the window at the setting sun. "She still refuses to speak or have anything to do with me. Even though it isn't safe in Troivack for her, she is insistent on returning and intends to live hidden from the court … she still blames me for Charles's death."

Ainsley wordlessly reached out and gently patted her friend's shoulder.

"Maybe in time she will grow less angry … especially if she learns exactly how much you were supporting them."

Annika let out a long sigh and shook her head. "Regardless of whether or not Charlie spied for me, I would've sent them the money. He just was a true Troivackian and refused to live off the funds I provided without doing anything to earn them."

The two women exited the solar then, each deep in their own thoughts and worries; that is, until they entered the dining hall and were greeted with the smiling faces of their loved ones … and Lord Harris who appeared to still be struggling with how to dress like a noble.

He wore a bright green patterned tunic that clashed terribly with his skin tone and brown trousers paired with a cream coat that had black designs around its buttons and on its collar …

All in all, a mash-up of everything, and unfortunately no one had been able to bring themselves to tell him.

"You look like a court jester," the prince suddenly announced as the platters of food magically floated onto the table.

Apparently, a child prince was less concerned about offending the duke's sense of style.

"Eric! That was incredibly rude! Apologize this instant!" Ainsley demanded, her gaze already apologetic.

To his credit, Lord Harris laughed while watching Annika struggle to hold her daughter who had glimpsed the shining cutlery and dove for them.

"It's alright, Your Majesty. I ... erm ... I miss dressing in peasant clothes, if I'm honest. Noble fashion is just a headache to me." The former kitchen aide shook his head as though chastising himself. "Ah well ... perhaps I should just lean into it and get a hat with bells on it. What do you think, Your Highness?" the duke asked with a cheeky waggle of his eyebrows.

Eric pondered the suggestion for a long moment, but he seemed caught between wanting to answer and knowing his mother would scold him again.

"I, for one, think it'd be great fun if everyone could tell where you were at all hours of the day," Fin volunteered with a bright grin.

"Yes, it would certainly help me make an entrance no one could forget ..." Lord Harris agreed seriously.

"You're starting to sound like Lord Fuks!" The viscount began to laugh more heartily, his son perched on his lap staring around the room calmly.

Sir Harris's palm slapped the table. "Well, we all know the man is a pillar of society we should all emulate. Very well, that settles it! I shall buy a hat with bells and wear it whenever I visit my beloved sister, Lady Marigold!"

At this, Annika and the queen couldn't even stop themselves.

The image of Lord Harris, the man who had taken away Lady Marigold's inheritance and overtaken her former house, showing up wearing a jester's hat, and her having to curtsy to him was too much to bear.

They all burst out howling, and no one could stop laughing for the better part of an hour.

It was a fine evening, indeed, filled with friends, and family, and of course, wonderful food.

EPILOGUE 2
CROWD CONTROL

Brendan Devark sat in the high-back chair that was far too large for him and peered out at the sea of Troivackian nobility that gazed up at him. Their faces were pale and grim …

Ever since news of their defeat in Daxaria and the death of the king, there had been great unrest amongst them.

"Do you, Prince Brendan Devark, swear to uphold Troivack's strength and discipline?" the official magistrate's sonorous voice echoed somberly through the throne room.

"I do," the seven-year-old child managed to reply without stammering.

"Do you swear to be a role model for your people, to rule firmly but fairly, with the true heart and courage befitting the King of Troivack?"

"I do."

The magistrate stepped forward and crossed the child's brow with frankincense oil.

"Do you swear to uphold the dignity and responsibility of your fore-bears from this day forward as Troivack's king?"

The prince was then handed the heavy iron scepter his father had wielded, its top melded with gold shaped as flames, as the golden crown, with a thin band of iron set in its center winding its way around the cir-cumference, was set upon his head.

"I do."

"By the power vested in me by the nobility of Troivack, and the Goddess herself, I declare you, Brendan Devark the First, King of Troivack!"

The room remained in a hush for a brief moment.

Brendan stared out into the faces of his people, and he pointedly avoided glancing at his mother, who was holding his younger brother, Henry, in her arms.

The faint echo of the back row of nobles stomping their feet in unison by the throne room doors fluttered through the bodies. Followed by the second row ... then the third ... then the fourth ... it carried on until the most powerful nobles that stood at his feet joined the steady beat.

Only when the sound of hundreds of pounding feet filled the entire room, thrumming heavily with Brendan's heartbeat, did they all raise their right hands to their hearts and press their left fists to the air.

The chant of the two hundred nobles began, "RA, RA, RA, RA, RA!" It rumbled as though it were one mighty voice, building in intensity until it was overwhelming.

Brendan eyes shifted to over their heads toward the great doors that stood open. Outside them was sunlight shining through the stained-glass window of the image of the Goddess, the Green Man, and their children.

It was then he realized the power he was given ... the power he was meant to manage and master as his father had ...

He also realized that during his journey, he would be alone.

Glancing at long last at his mother, Brendan felt his insides quake when she, the only woman allowed in the hall for the moment, curtsied to the ground behind her guards before her son.

Henry was the only one who met his gaze, yet all the three-year-old did at that moment was smile happily up at his brother.

Somehow, this made Brendan want to cry as every inch of him squirmed to stay in control ... To not let his inner trembling be seen. So instead, he turned back to the nobles and set his teeth.

The heavy luxurious mantel made out of the hide of a bear and white wolf was too large, and awkward. The scepter in his hand was beginning to make his arm ache, but that only made Brendan grip onto it harder.

When the shouts and stomps grew until it was absolutely deafening, the new king raised his free hand to silence them.

"My people," he began, shouting so that everyone, even those in the back of the room, could hear.

Father's voice could always be heard ... why is it so hard for me to be louder ... ? the anguished whisper in his head wondered for a moment before reciting the speech his advisers had helped him write.

"I have much to learn, and there is much I need to do to become what you deserve, but I will grow with Troivack. I will bring it back onto its feet until it stands taller than any great tree or mountain!"

The loud shouts and applause thundered in response.

"My father once told me ..."

Why does my throat feel so tight ... ?

"That ... it is our duty as men to help one another grow strong! Well, I need your help for now, but soon, I will be your strength!"

Once again the hall burst out into fierce cheers.

Then, with his arms shaking, Brendan reached to his side where his sword hung and drew it out so that its tip pointed to the skies. The scepter raised in the air with it as the earth shook from the yells and stomps from his people's show of support.

Brendan could feel their voracious need, strength, greed, love, fear, hatred, and ambition fill his blood and veins. The souls of his people consumed him whole, leaving him swirling about in their endless abyss without any sense of where to turn or how to move in the right direction.

His face lifted to the heavens, his arms feeling as though they were on fire; a lone tear escaped the corner of his eye that none of the souls that had already devoured him ever noticed.

"Lady Laurent ..."

"A slight inclination is required, Viscount. I am, after all, the wife of your political superior."

Fin let out an anguished sigh before pinching the bridge of his nose. "Lady Laurent, I understand you are to be my etiquette instructor; however ... what are *they* all doing here?" he asked while gesturing toward the rows and rows of chairs filled with a strange array of women from every class in the banquet hall.

"Well, as you know, the Coven of Wittica negotiated that a select few of their members would also be instructed as they will be setting up offices in our great cities."

The viscount nodded toward three of the women present that he knew to be coven members.

"Yes, but … there are at least … thirty women here in total," he observed dryly.

"Well, we are going to have you practice by greeting all of us to make sure you get it right," one woman Fin thought looked vaguely familiar blurted as she stood up a little too hastily and made her chair scrape loudly against the stone floor.

The other women surrounding her all were quick to agree, though there was a touch of blush on more than just a few faces.

"I see …"

Fin shifted uncomfortably in his seat in front of the audience, and he was starting to feel his ears begin to burn when the banquet room doors opened, and in stepped Mr. Howard.

"Lady Laurent, I received your missive and I—" The assistant stopped dead in his tracks as thirty heads swiveled to stare at him with a hungry glint in their eyes.

Freezing like an animal caught in the sights of a predator, the man took a moment to regard the number of noblewomen, maids, and witches present … and then his eyes rested on Finlay who sat with his arms crossed, his ankle over his knee, and an equally stricken expression on his face.

"Lady Laurent, you … sent for me?" Mr. Howard ventured carefully into the room, his gaze uneasily surveying the pointed attention he was receiving.

"Yes, I did. Thank you for joining us. I'm sure you are busy preparing to leave with His Majesty, so I won't keep you past the dining hour."

"The dining hour?! My lady, I have to—"

"—Help Lord Ashowan learn proper court decorum! Soon he will be left without your prestigious guidance, and many of us courtiers will be leaving with His Majesty and will not be able to help the viscount with his education!"

Mr. Howard looked to Fin, his face pale as the Lady Laurent descended upon him and tugged him forward in front of everyone.

"Now, if you could please take a seat next to Lord Ashowan and observe as he greets each of us. We would greatly appreciate your male perspective as he does so," the earl's wife explained primly, without a trace of guilt on her face.

Mr. Howard glanced at Fin as he seated himself and noticed the witch's eyes were closed as though he were trying to fall asleep to get out of the current situation.

"Why did you let them do this?" the assistant muttered while bobbing his head subserviently to the noblewoman.

"I had no idea *this* was going to happen. We'll simply have to suffer through the next three hours the best we can."

"*Three hours?!*" Mr. Howard began to launch himself out of his chair only to have Fin's hand snap out and stop him by pressing against his chest.

There was a collective gasp amongst the women, and both Fin and Mr. Howard grew rigid as they slowly turned their attention to their audience. There were several blushing faces, and smiles being hidden behind demure hands.

"Oh Gods … I will have to really kill you this time …" the assistant managed quietly while sounding as though he had been punched in the gut.

"Let's just get this over with. Be as professional as possible and we might get out of here alive," Fin communicated while barely moving his lips through his false polite smile toward Lady Laurent who had finally finished situating herself on the chair opposite them.

"Wonderful, now that we have an extra set of eyes to help us, Lord Ashowan, when you greet an earl, count, or marquess, you will lower yourself like so," The lady demonstrated a slight regal bow. "A duke like this …" Her bow deepened. "Of course you already know to greet the king, but just to be certain …" She bowed even more deeply.

"Ah, yes. What she is demonstrating is that you are only above barons, knights, and commoners. The dukes, earls, counts, and marquesses of the kingdom are higher ranking than yourself. Even though the original Viscount Jenoure was offered a higher position, he refused as he was offered the title while his first wife was ill. His Majesty made the same offer to you after the war; however—" Mr. Howard was beginning to turn his chastising tone onto Fin, who was rolling his eyes in response.

A series of excited whispers fluttered throughout the room, which had the two men stopping their interaction immediately.

"Oh, for the love of—" Mr. Howard was suddenly interrupted when the banquet hall doors once again opened.

"Pardon the intrusion, my lord, but— Oh!" Peter had stepped into the room, Tam cradled in his arms; the infant was whimpering with fat tears rolling down his olive-colored cheeks. However, when the aide gazed about the banquet hall and noticed the unexpected crowd, he immediately bowed before them.

"I did not realize there was a meeting, I will bother the viscount another time."

"Peter, it's fine. Do you need me to take Tam?" Fin stood, blatantly ignoring the starry gazes that followed him across the room, and took his son into his arms with practiced ease.

Smiling, the aide looked up at Fin who had already set to gently bouncing Tam in his arms. "Any time he gets bored and neither you or the viscountess are there, he immediately needs to go to a new room, but I'm in the middle of taking care of dinner. So I—"

"Not a problem; thank you for bringing him to me. Is Katarina still alright with Hannah?"

"Oh yes, the two seem to get along famously." Peter chuckled and Fin grinned back. He had to admit his daughter and the young blond aide seemed to be kindred spirits …

A strained cough from behind Fin had him turning around to notice Mr. Howard was the color of a beet with the women in a tizzy as they watched the exchange between himself and Peter and immediately began commenting and gossiping in slightly louder voices.

"What's wrong with them?" Peter whispered, a note of fear entering his voice.

The viscount let out an annoyed grunt. "Lady Laurent, would it perhaps be possible for us to postpone the lesson? I'd like to try and get Tam to go to sleep and—"

"He's already asleep!" a maid burst out excitedly, pointing giddily at the infant in Fin's arms, who was, indeed, napping contently in his father's arms.

Lady Laurent cast the maid a warning glance before turning back to the viscount. "I believe, Lord Ashowan, we will be perfectly fine to continue the lesson if we all remain quiet."

Fin looked around at the eager faces fixated on him. He glanced at Mr. Howard who appeared to be on the verge of tears, then next at Peter who seemed blissfully unaware but deeply confused.

Dropping his chin to his chest for a brief moment, Fin then addressed his many onlookers. "Alright, I think this has run its course. I am not gay. Nor have I ever been gay or been in love with Mr. Howard or Peter."

The aide at his side went rigid, and his cheeks pinkened.

Mr. Howard sat back in his chair and let out a long liberating breath of relief.

The women all sat frozen to their seats for a brief moment. There was no emotion on their faces, nor any movement.

For a moment, Fin worried they would become an angry bloodthirsty mob as the tension in the room swiftly rose to stifling levels ...

"Lord Ashowan, I ... am not sure why you are making such an announcement during our lesson, but rest assured we are all very aware of how much you love the viscountess," Lady Laurent interjected while looking innocently perplexed and awkward.

Reddening ever so slightly, Fin bowed to her. "My apologies if I've made things strange. I would like to find a place for Tam to finish his nap, however, so I will return after finding his mother. Pardon me."

With a final bow, Fin left the room with Peter trailing behind him unable to look at any of the women staring up at him.

Lady Laurent let out a long breath, her shoulders slumping forward ever so slightly the moment the banquet hall doors had firmly shut.

"Ah ... forgive Lord Ashowan, Lady Laurent. He means well, I think it just goes to show how much he requires your tutelage." Mr. Howard straightened in his seat and gave a dignified sniff.

Lady Laurent's eyes fluttered open, right as another wave of whispers echoed out amongst the women.

" ... apologizing for him!"

"So sweet ..."

" ... Unrequited!"

The earl's wife smoothed her skirts, as her confusion morphed into a new expression of deep understanding.

"I must apologize myself, Mr. Howard. That was insensitive of me. I'm sure you are equally upset by his thoughtless words."

Mr. Howard's jaw fell open. "N-No! Th-That isn't— Wait! H-He said ..." That was when the assistant realized that, while Fin had declared his own sexuality, he had expertly omitted his fellow victims' details. It also meant that if he tried to announce his own preferences after the witch, it wouldn't sound genuine ...

"That magnificent bastard," Mr. Howard growled under his breath.

Lady Laurent's hand flew to her chest as her eyes belied her shared pain. "Now, now, dear. Name calling won't make you feel better."

Looking to the skies as though waiting for divine beings to smite him, all the assistant could bring himself to say was ...

"Son of a mage."

THE END
(FIN)

ABOUT THE AUTHOR

Delemhach is the author of the House Witch series, which they started in order to share with readers some of the warmth, fun, and love of food they experienced while growing up. Born and raised in Canada, Delemhach discovered their love of fantasy and magic at a young age, and the affair has carried on well into their adulthood. Currently, they work multiple jobs, but the one they most enjoy, aside from writing, is privately teaching music to people of all ages.

Get whiskered away

with updates on your
favorite magical hijinks,
the coziest content, and all
things Delemhach!

Visit

laylo.com/delemhach

*to sign up for
Delemhach's newsletter!*

DISCOVER
STORIES UNBOUND

PodiumAudio.com

Printed in Great Britain
by Amazon

30554188R00212